D0967650

THE SIMEON CHAMBER

STEVEN PAUL MARTINI

TUDOR PUBLISHING COMPANY
NEW YORK CITY

A TUDOR BOOK

Published by special arrangement with Donald I. Fine, Inc.

October 1989

Tudor Books published by

Tudor Publishing Company
276 Fifth Avenue
New York, NY 10001

To the fathers, Ernie and Murray, in whose unqualified love I found the embers of inspiration.

Author's Note

This novel is a work of fiction, as noted on the copyright page. There is no "Simeon Chamber," no "Committee of Acquisition." While a naval blimb did crash on a street in Daly City near San Francisco in August 1942, and while its crew has never been found, Raymond Slade, James Spencer, George Johnson and Louis Davies are the offspring of the author's imagination and bear no relationship to members of the actual crew or their families. While William Randolph Hearst is known to have been a consumate collector of art, there is no evidence that he was ever defrauded or dealt knowingly or unknowingly in black market art. Francis Drake did sail the Pacific off of what is today San Francisco, and in the summer of 1579 he and his crew made camp for thirty-six days at a site the location of which is a matter of scientific and historic speculation. It is true that he called this place "Nova Albion." It is also known that Drake maintained a detailed journal of his voyage around the world. That journal has never been found and is presumed lost to history.

Acknowledgments

In writing this book I received the assistance and encouragement of many without whose support it would not have been possible. I am indebted to Murray Arnold, Keith Arnold and Dennis Higgins who supplied the cornerstone of all creative endeavors—honest criticism. To Dr. Robert Anthony, M.D., Ph.D., Forensic Pathologist with the Sacramento County Coroner's Office I owe thanks for collaboration in the commission of an accurate fictional homicide. I would like to thank Sally L. Scott, Regional Interpretive Specialist, and Rita Nunes, Special Assistant to the Regional Director, California Department of Parks and Recreation, Hearst Castle for their assistance in providing information and access to the Hearst San Simeon Historical Monument. I thank Victoria Blyth Hill, Senior Paper Conservator, Los Angeles County Museum of Art for information in the preservation and identification of documentary artifacts. To the staff of the California State Library at Sacramento I owe thanks for assistance in locating valuable research and resource materials.

To Donald I. Fine, George Wieser, and George Coleman I am indebted for their good grace, support and sponsorship of a first literary venture.

I thank my aunt Vivian Benedetti and my mother Rita Martini whose stories of the fated "Ghost Blimp" fixed firmly in my child's mind the lore of mystery and the seed of this story.

I owe unending gratitude to my wife Leah and my mother-in-law Betty for their tireless and selfless editing and encouragement.

And finally, but not least, I thank my 14-month-old daughter Meggie, whose sparkling eyes and infectious smile provided the ultimate discipline and resolve to finish this manuscript.

SPM
Auburn, California
March, 1988

Prologue

April 17, 1906
Marin County, California

A slight smile spread between hollow cheeks under haunted gray eyes as Earl Huber considered the fact that he owed his good fortune to a cockroach. He'd named her "Beauty," for she'd never been bested in the nightly races that Huber presided over for amusement in his solitary cell.

It was typical of his pitiless surroundings that even Huber's privacy had been purchased at the misfortune of another. For rumor had it that the convict Joaquin Sanchez had been beaten to death by two guards only days before Huber had been moved into the Mexican's single cell in the Old Spanish Block. Others might have cringed in superstition, but not Earl Huber. He accepted his newly found solitude as an omen of good fortune.

On that night two weeks earlier his ritual had not varied. Sealed for the night in his solitary cubicle, he lined up the box with the cockroaches directly at the edge of a granite block beneath his cot. He slapped the floor near the wooden container, and five of the antennaed beasts bolted like thoroughbreds from a starting gate and headed toward the wall, Beauty clearly in the lead.

Under his breath he kibitzed and whispered encouragement to the competitors, while in his mind he imagined bleachers fllled to overflowing with cheering wagerers.

Four feet from the starting point Beauty suddenly stopped, veered slightly to the left as if to cross over the partition between two of the large granite blocks and disappeared into a minute crack. Huber instantly lost interest in the race. He pushed the box under the cot and crawled on his hands and knees in search of his prized insect.

He sprinkled the area with stale bread crumbs to coax her out. He slapped the block with his hand, hoping the concussion would cause her to surface—all to no avail. Finally, in desperation he grabbed the metal spoon from his dinner plate and carefully worked the flat handle between the two blocks. After several minutes of fruitless probing, he tried to extract the spoon and discovered it was stuck fast in the granite crevice. Huber braced himself on both knees, gripped the oval spoon in one hand and wrapped it with the other palm. Pulling with all of his strength, he jerked on the spoon. With a grunt he tore it free and was thrown onto his back near the cot.

As Huber stood, examining the mangled handle of the spoon, he noticed that one stone had lifted from the uniform surface of the floor and now overlapped the edge of the adjoining block. Settling back to his knees and studying the three square feet of granite, Huber discovered that it was not a block at all, but a granite slab, no more than an inch thick. He slid the spoon handle under the flat piece of rock and pried it up enough to get his flngers underneath. He lifted the slab and propped it against the wall of the cell.

As he turned to examine the area left by the loose stone, his mind was instantly purged of any thoughts concerning the wayward cockroach. His gaze was met by the sight of an open shaft, three feet square, that descended from his cell beneath the missing stone. He dropped to his knees and discovered a smooth lip carefully tooled and etched in the surrounding granite blocks upon which the slab had rested.

Huber grabbed the coal-oil lamp from its hook on the wall and lowered it into the opening. The shaft dropped only four or five feet but appeared to widen after it passed beneath the cubical granite blocks that formed the floor of his cell. Pulling the light up and placing it on the floor, he lowered himself into the opening, picked up the lamp and carefully hunched down onto his knees.

He crawled about ten feet through the open cavern, becoming dizzy from the noxious vapors emitting from the coal-oil lamp. The stifling odor kindled panic in his mind, and he was about to retreat when he saw them: a small pile of half-used white candles, one set in a crude wooden holder. Quickly he lit a candle, blew into the glass chimney and abandoned the lamp.

Huber's eyes strained as his gaze wandered down the seemingly endless tunnel. The muted light of the candle flame was lost in shadows as the open shaft continued beyond his view. He became giddy with excitement, realizing for the first time that he had traveled beyond the limited confines of his cell walls. To his best guess he'd passed under the broad alleyway that separated the Old Spanish Block from the more modern cell blocks that adjoined it. He was amused by the thought that he now crawled with absolute impunity under the cells occupied by some other poor souls who rotted in the eight by ten feet of privacy allowed by the prison authorities.

Cautiously he inched his way along the earthen corridor, sucking in the sweet odor of dank soil. After years of breathing the dry dust of the jute mill, the scent of wet earth was itself a liberating experience.

For nearly twenty minutes he crawled in a straight line under the cell block and the open exercise yard. He'd lost all sense of distance, but he guessed that he was closing on the forty-foot-high perimeter wall, beyond which lay open ground and freedom.

Suddenly the flickering light of the candle flame reflected off a mound of broken and loose earth that marked the end of the tunnel. The earth was soft. Huber could see where some of it had broken free from the ceiling of the cavern.

For ten minutes he sat at the end of the tunnel and considered the project at hand. He would need some tools—a makeshift shovel, a short-handled pick, perhaps a pry bar. There were enough loose pieces of metal in the mill that would never be missed, especially now that he had a place to hide them. The logistics aside, his mind was troubled. Who had dug the tunnel—and left the candles? Had it been used for an earlier escape?

Huber quickly pushed the questions aside and considered his good fortune as he crawled back to his cell and replaced the slab over the opening. Within two days he'd gathered the short spans of metal needed for digging and transported them under his prison garb back to the cell. It took a bit longer to contrive the method of removing the newly dug earth from the tunnel. He fashioned two narrow tubes of jute cloth into crude sacks, which he wore inside the legs of his pants. Each night he would fill the tubes, and each morning at the mill he would pull the small pins from their ends and allow the previous night's diggings to drop unnoticed along the insides of his pant legs onto the dirt floor of the mill beneath the loom, where he spread it with his feet. A small portion of the dirt was removed in this way while the balance was merely spread along the floor of the tunnel itself, leaving ample room for Huber to crawl through.

He stitched rough clothing from jute cloth so as not to soil his prison stripes and draw attention to himself. For ten nights he dug, spreading and carrying dirt. The improvised shovel cut through the soft earth like a jackhammer through potting soil. While Huber was no novice with a pick and shovel, neither was he a mining engineer. He never questioned that the digging was effortless or wondered why the earth was not more compacted. If the dirt moved easily, so much the better. The work proceeded with more speed and the day of freedom was that much closer at hand.

He fashioned a length of metal that exactly matched his normal walking stride. Each evening, using this metal rod, he measured the length of the tunnel, and every noon, in the exercise yard, he casually paced a straight line from the cell block across the yard, stopping momentarily whenever other convicts crossed or blocked his path. Each day as he finished his journey the mountainous guard towers and granite block wall topped by strings of barbed wire loomed closer.

Then yesterday at noon Huber had marched across the yard, his hands casually in his pockets, his eyes downcast as he surveyed a straight line. He'd reached fifty-seven paces when his left foot came in contact with the base of the mammoth rampart. Huber nearly jumped in the air as he realized that the end of the tunnel was only two feet inside the wall. Calculating the thickness of its foundation and allowing for a slight increase in depth, he figured he would be on the outside in ten feet, an easy two-night dig.

He'd made more than five feet the previous night; and tonight, under the dark of a moonless sky, he would surface in the dry grass beyond the wall and disappear into the outside world.

His hands moistened with the sweat of anticipation as he passed the loom's shuttle between the threads of the warp, knowing that it would be the last time he would ever have to endure the mind-altering tedium. Never again would he be forced to surrender his spirit to the monotony of the jute mill or to submerge his consciousness in the din of the steam-powered looms and the vaporous dust that filled the cold gray shed. For seven long years he'd toiled under the prying eyes of gumshoed guards and endured their witless oppression. Now, by the auspicious hand of fate, he would cheat them of the eighteen years remaining on his term. As the yard whistle blew, announcing the end of the shift, Huber eased himself off the bench and took one last look at the drab gray walls of the jute mill and the endless yards of cloth yet to be cut and sewn into sacks. He filed into line and fifteen minutes later was seated on his cot waiting for the dinner pail to be passed through the small opening at the bottom of the cell door.

The pail came and he sat quietly on his bed and ate. Then he curled up on the cot and closed his eyes. Tonight would be an easy dig. He intended to meet the rigors of the outside world well rested and alert.

It was after one in the morning when he awoke. The cell block clatter of early evening had died down. Quickly and without any wasted motion Huber changed his prison stripes for the jute cloth and repeated the ritual with the spoon. He lit three of the candles from the lamp, then extinguished it. Rather than moving the granite slab to the wall he merely slid it partially off the open shaft, then lowered himself and the candles into the hole. From inside he carefully slid the slab back over the opening and allowed it to settle onto the lip carved in the surrounding granite blocks. To anyone entering the cell from that moment forward it would appear that the convict Earl Huber had simply vanished. It would be days, perhaps weeks, if ever, before they discovered the shaft and the tunnel. By then he could be thousands of miles away, with a different name and a new life.

As before, the digging was effortless. Only this time there was no need to spread the dirt far, he merely piled it in the tunnel behind him, taking care to leave enough room in case he should have to crawl back to the cell for any reason. He was a cautious man. Seven years behind bolted doors had bred patience if not tolerance. If his departure required another day, so be it.

He'd dug nearly a foot and a half when he struck the object with the point of his shovel. It wasn't solid, but emitted a dull thud as he stabbed the jerry-rigged spade back into the soft earth a second time. Using the shovel and his hands he uncovered it: a man's boot.

Suddenly it all made sense—the stockpile of candles, the soft earth, the unfinished tunnel. Each had been a grim clue to what lay ahead.

In his haste to flee Huber had not taken the time to read the signs. Now he was about to meet his predecessor, for whom the shaft had become a dark and horror-filled crypt—the convict Joaquin Sanchez. The rumors of his demise at the hands of guards had been planted by prison authorities to cover an apparent escape, to keep alive the myth that no one ever succeeded in breaching the foreboding walls. For now only the dead Mexican and Earl Huber knew the truth.

Huber studied the walls and the earthen ceiling overhead warily, then covered his mouth and nose with a portion of jute cloth. He was not a squeamish man, but with each shovelful of earth the stench of rotting flesh became more distinct in the confined chamber.

It took nearly an hour to uncover the body to its chest. He wrapped his hands around the ankles of the corpse and pulled. It didn't budge. He dug several more inches of earth from around the body and pulled again. This time it shifted, in one unified motion, with the rigidity of a board. He considered the revulsion of the task only for an instant. The cadaver had to be moved. It blocked his path—the way to freedom. Hunching over the dead man on his knees and turning his face away from the overpowering odor, he placed his hands beneath the chest cavity and lifted. He felt decayed flesh as it tore and came free in his hands. Huber squeezed his eyes tightly closed as he eased the body back in the tunnel, inch by inch, toward the mound of loose earth behind him. He did not open his eyes or turn his head until the task was completed. By then nausea and panic had nearly overwhelmed him. He crawled toward the end of the tunnel, taking only shallow breaths of the fouled air. He had to dig quickly. Freedom lay in this direction. And now the only other avenue of escape was retreat—over the rotting corpse.

He dug savagely for nearly twenty minutes. The ground was hard now and the digging slower, but the labor brought purpose to his endeavor and calm to his mind. His face was covered with a solution of grime and perspiration when he finally rested his shovel and steeled himself to look upon the face of his dead companion. He shifted the light of the candle and aimed the flame back up the passage toward the mound of discarded earth and the corpse. The head was caked with dirt, the features undistinguishable. The left arm was outstretched, the hand locked in a death grip around what appeared to be a small brick— perhaps used for hammering the point of a pick or shovel into the harder earth that now confronted Huber.

Hesitating, he reached toward the dead man's hand for the brick. The lifeless grip was like a vise and Huber had to move closer to the body and use both hands to pry the tool loose. With his fingers he scraped the caked earth from the edge of the brick for a better grasp. Suddenly he stopped. Under the grime-laden sweat Huber's face was ashen. Blood drained from his head as full recognition of the object reached his brain. There, locked in the rigored grip of the dead man, was a brick of pure gold bullion.

* * *

Overhead and a hundred feet to the east in the prison stable Huber could not see the restless shifting of the draft horses or hear their whinnied cries. In the still night air an inexplicable ripple spread across the water in their trough and lapped at the edges.

In his subterranean passage Huber moved the candle closer to the hand of his grim companion and the gold bar locked in its clutch. The light caught the glimmer of a shiny round object in the dirt just beyond the outstretched, stiff arm. It was a coin of irregular shape but unmistakable specie. His eyes ran in a line toward the cavity left by the excavated body. A trail of gold coins carpeted the floor, disappearing into the impression left in the dirt by the man's head and shoulders.

Huber moved toward the end of the tunnel and began to excavate the area. More coins appeared with every shovelful of earth, and with each stroke of the spade his excitement grew. He lost all track of time as he tore and ripped at the earth. The path of the tunnel veered sharply to the left, running laterally inside the prison wall, and took a sixty-degree plunge as he followed the course of the coins. Fatigue was overcome by frenzy. The mangled shovel and pry bar were abandoned in his wake, as hard dirt turned to mud and the odor of brine replaced the stench of rotting flesh. He continued to claw at the dirt with his hands and finally he uncovered the side of a wooden cask. Bashing at the staves of the barrel with the heel of his boot, he splintered the rotting wood. Instantly Huber found himself awash in an effluent of mud and gold coins.

The rumble began deep in the bowels of the earth, indistinct at first, then gaining momentum. Slowly the noise was transformed into motion, a slow gyration punctuated by more disturbing vibrations.

Five miles to the south, city streets buckled and brick chimneys collapsed through the roofs of houses, burying the occupants. Water mains ruptured like brittle straw, and the iron rails of the Southern Pacific twisted and writhed in a bizarre geologic dance. Unattended church bells clanged with an aimless and discordant din, and the ground wrenched as if in the grip of some horrific giant.

Huber never heard the first sounds or felt the initial movement. He was lost in a frenzy of discovery as he pulled the remains of the broken barrel from the dirt and unearthed a dark cavern at the end of the tunnel. He shifted the light of the candle toward the opening and stared in wonderment at the sight that met his eyes. It was an image to be fused in his mind for eternity, for an instant later the first shock wave struck. A thousand yards of cubic earth rained down from above—burying Earl Huber forever beneath a tortured and twisted landscape.

Chapter

1

San Francisco, 1975.

The ancients long ago learned that the essence of a lie is to be found in its deception, not its words. It was an axiom the subtleties of which Samuel J. Bogardus was soon to comprehend.

But at that moment he carried on an animated monologue in the private chambers of his brain, a conversation that periodically slipped past the confines of his lips in the form of half-mumbled epithets.

Bogardus was angry with himself or, perhaps more correctly, with his aging mother. Angie Bogardus was relentless. It was not that he was busy. He had settled a case only two days before and thus had avoided the anxiety and drudgery of an eight-day trial. It was more the irritation of dealing with Angie's referrals, as she called them—doddering friends from one or another of her social clubs or charities, all with special problems, none of which were ever susceptible to legal treatment or solution.

This time it came under the rubric of an adoption case, a field of law about which Sam knew little and cared less. To his repeated chagrin Bogardus had learned years before that his skills of advocacy, honed during more than a decade of active trial work, were to no avail when matched against the dogged persistence of his mother. It was a contest he had long ago conceded, for Angie wielded the double-edged sword of authority and guilt with the guile of a Samurai. Before Sam could hang up the phone he had committed himself to talking to his mother's friend. To Angie it was the same as taking the case.

The sun's rays found their way down through the canyons of the Financial District, warming the street against the light breezes off the Pacific. The balmy days of early fall blessed the city when the searing heat of California's Central Valley faded and favored San Francisco by leaving the fog out over the ocean. And while any longtime resident of the city could tell you that San Francisco weather was fickle, on this day at least, the place basked under crystal-clear skies in seventy-five-degree temperatures.

Bogardus walked the few blocks from his apartment on Bush Street to the cable car, rode part of the way to Broadway and then

thoughts had wandered increasingly from the partnership and the practice of law.

The brass wall plaque under the huge arched doorway leading to Pier Nine read:

Bogardus and Paterson
Attorneys and Counselors at Law

The "Counselors" was an affectation insisted upon by Susan Paterson, the more serious half of the partnership—and, all would agree, the better looking of the two lawyers. Susan Paterson, "Pat" to all who knew her, was a striking five-foot-eight-inch brunette with a feline form that excited youthful fantasies in old men. She possessed a tenacious singularity of mind and a first-rate legal intellect masked behind angelic blue eyes.

The partnership had begun as an amorous adventure in law school, where Bogardus had met Pat during his first year. He never stopped questioning his inexplicable good fortune in winning the statuesque beauty, who by her second year had rejected no fewer than three proposals of marriage from prominent attorneys and had shattered the boundless ego of a contracts professor intent on an extracurricular tryst.

Through three years of law school Sam and Pat shared a crowded single-bedroom flat in Berkeley in a tempestuous on-again-off-again romance. In the end, love had deteriorated into friendship, and while the stable base for a solid marriage had eluded them, a firm platform for a business and professional life together was not an unpleasant consolation.

Bogardus sauntered up the stairs and through the door to the office and was immediately confronted by a frizzy mop of brown hair hanging over a typewriter.

"Morning, Carol. How was your weekend?" Bogardus plucked his telephone messages from the tray on her desk and began to pick through them.

Carol Brompton was a plump girl in her early twenties with dark hair and a mouth overflowing with braces. She filled the inevitable role in a small law office, providing both clerical and paralegal services while attending law school in the evenings.

"Good morning, Mr. Bogardus." The genuine good nature of the girl beamed in her metallic smile. But her formality alerted Sam to the fact that a client was near. To Carol, Bogardus was always Sam unless a client was around. It was a practice no doubt drummed into her during one of the many staff meetings presided over by Pat and attended only by Carol, who left frequently to answer the phone. Sam refused to participate in office affairs, assuming that if he had anything to tell the other two souls in the office it could be done at any time.

The periodic office conferences said as much about the divergent personalities of the partners as anything else. Pat's guiding stars were organization and preparation, often to the point of compulsion. In contrast, Sam was impulsive, preferring to act on instinct, which had served him well over the years. He reveled in the unanticipated and cloaked himself in the unorthodox.

Bogardus moved past the secretary's desk toward his office. Turning his head slightly, he caught a glimpse of a woman seated to the left of the office entrance. She never looked up from her magazine.

Sam's office was a spacious room with a wall of high windows providing an oblique view of the bay and the tip of Yerba Buena Island under the Bay Bridge. Bobbing outside at the dock were two tugs and the pilot boat used for ferrying bar pilots out beyond the Golden Gate.

The office itself displayed a full wall photograph of early San Francisco, made of a mosaic of smaller pictures pieced together to form a panorama of the city in 1902.

The office furnishings, a mahogany desk and matching chair and credenza, were not expensive, but the pieces had been old when Sam had purchased them for his apartment during law school. They were slowly taking on the charm of antiques as the years passed. A brass floor lamp stood behind his desk to one side, along with a large black-cushioned executive swivel chair. The walls were cluttered with various license certificates, diplomas and two expensive framed lithographs that Sam had purchased on a binge after receiving a healthy personal injury settlement.

The office was devoid of any greenery. Sam had tried his luck with a Boston fern that he hung from the ceiling, but the beautiful plant began to wilt and die from lack of attention. Pat accused Bogardus of torturing the thing and removed it to her own office, where it thrived under the nurturing care of a woman's hand.

Sam just had time to settle into his chair and take stock of the phone messages when the intercom buzzed. He picked up the receiver.

"Ms. Davies is here for her nine o'clock appointment, Mr. Bogardus."

"Davis?" It wasn't a continuing matter. "What's the case?"

"The file's on your desk," said Carol.

"Just a minute."

Sam pushed the messages aside and scanned the assorted files spread out on the desk. He caught the name "Davies" on the tab of one of the folders and read upside down the description typed under the name: "Adoption."

"Damn it," Sam muttered under his breath. The least she could have done was to wait a couple of days. He sighed, opened the file and resigned himself to be done with it as quickly and painlessly as possible.

"Send her in." His tone was impatient.

A moment later the door to his office opened and through it walked the woman he had seen in the waiting room earlier. Framed in the doorway with the light behind her, her silhouette immediately captured Sam's complete attention. She was tall, slender and quite attractive. She moved gracefully from the door toward his desk. Almost absent-mindedly Sam rose and extended a hand in greeting.

"Good morning, Ms. Davis is it?"

"Davies," she corrected him. "Jennifer Davies."

"Can I offer you anything, coffee, tea?" Sam made a quick appraisal. The woman was well-dressed, well-mannered and well-heeled.

"Thank you, no. I had coffee in the outer office."

"Please take a seat."

Jennifer Davies slid gracefully into the plush-cushioned client chair and crossed one leg over the other. The silk dress clung to the contours of her body, the hem sliding partially up a well-shaped thigh. Sam made no effort to conceal his downward gaze. When he looked up her eyes had engaged his as she tugged the hem gently toward her knee, a slight smile evident on glistening raspberry lips. Her complexion was clear and tawny, her brunette hair short, cut just off the shoulders and swept back. Her jewelry, like the woman herself, had an air of elegance: a gold bracelet, a pearl necklace and matching earrings. Her face was gentle, with high cheekbones, thin lips and well-defined lines. Sam guessed her age to be mid-thirties. This was not the usual referral from his mother, and he began to recant his earlier remonstrations.

"Well, what can I do for you?" He studied the ring on her left hand. It was becoming impossible to tell, even for an experienced bachelor. She wore a simple gold ring on her third finger—not exactly a wedding band, but close.

"I'm not really sure where to begin. I'm trying to find my father."

Sam looked again at the file laying on the desk blotter. "I was led to believe that this was an adoption matter."

"It is. At least in part."

"Is your father missing?"

"Not exactly." The woman pursed her lips and in a matter-of-fact tone said, "He's dead—at least according to the United States Navy, my mother and my stepfather."

Sam shot her a quizzical look.

"Perhaps I'd better explain."

"It would help."

"I'm adopted, Mr. Bogardus—or at least I have an adoptive stepfather. My mother died last year. I'm interested in finding out who my natural father is. I believe the term they use today is birth parent."

"You say 'is.' A moment ago you said he was dead."

"I have reason to believe that he's alive." The woman shifted in her chair, uneasy with the conversation. "It's a rather long and involved story."

"Take your time." Sam was only half listening, for while her voice was not unpleasant it was no match for her other attractions, and his imagination had already begun to wander.

She took a deep breath. To those in the trade it might have been construed as the "gasp of guilt"—the last suck of honest air before the criminal client unburdens himself and tells his lawyer what really happened. It was common fare for the public defenders working the county jail, and Sam had been fed a steady diet during his time with that office. In the case of Jennifer Davies he attributed it to a slight case of nerves.

"For many years, through most of my childhood, I accepted the fact that my father was dead. My mother told me that he'd been killed during the war. I had no reason to question her. Well"—she paused, a pained expression in her eyes—"almost no reason." Davies took a slender gold cigarette case from her purse. "Do you mind?"

Sam shook his head.

"It happened when I was thirteen or fourteen. I overheard an argument between my mother and stepfather. She was shouting that it was unfair to me, insisting that they tell me who my father was. She said I had a right to know. But my stepfather said no, I was too young and that I wouldn't understand. I didn't hear enough of the conversation to know exactly what was going on, but I always assumed my father was in prison or shut away somewhere in an asylum, and that they—my mother and stepfather—wanted to shelter me from the shame and embarrassment." Davies lit the cigarette. Her hands trembled slightly. She dropped the lighter into her purse and took a shallow draw, immediately expelling the smoke.

"What makes you think I can help?"

"Well your mother was so nice. When she heard about my problem she was certain you could find the answer. In fact she was quite insistent."

"That's my mother." Sam rubbed his forehead and eyes with both hands. "How did you meet her?"

"Oh, I've never actually met her."

For a fleeting instant the thought flashed through his brain that the old lady had placed an ad—"Have lawyer—can help."

Jennifer Davies interrupted his waking nightmare. "I have an elderly aunt here in the city. She works at the hospital auxiliary and she's quite friendly with your mother. The two of them got to talking one afternoon . . ."

"I see." She was single all right. The equation suddenly made sense—the two old ladies, the beautiful niece and the eligible bachelor lawyer. His mother would never quit. Ever since he and Pat had split up Angie had spewed venom at the woman who jilted her son. She tried to fill the void with matches made over her dining room table, enlisting the aid of friends and family. Under other circumstances he might have been angry. But looking at Jennifer Davies, Bogardus found hostility to be one of his more remote emotions.

"Let's get back to your father."

"Yes, well, I've tried to get information from a number of public agencies—Social Welfare, the State Bureau of Vital Statistics. But I keep running into a stone wall. They all tell me the same thing, that adoption records are sealed and not public. I've been told there's no way I can find out who my father is unless he decides independently that he wants to see me."

Bogardus leaned back in his chair and coupled his hands behind his head. "Have you talked to your stepfather? Have you asked him for information?"

"Yes, repeatedly. But the story is always the same. He says my father died during the war. When I press him he becomes angry. He knows more than he's saying and I can tell that he's frightened." The woman's gaze dropped to the large handbag on her lap. "I think as long as my mother was alive, the two of them shared the secret. But now that she's gone, he's afraid of the responsibility, afraid he might hurt me by telling me the truth."

She paused for a moment. "He believes that he and my mother were my only real parents, and for me to search for my natural father now is somehow disloyal to her memory and our years together as a family." Her voice broke and trailed off. She shifted in her chair as she regained her composure. "But now I know he's not telling the truth."

"What makes you say that?"

The woman crushed her cigarette in the ashtray on Sam's desk and opened her purse, producing a large manila envelope bulging with papers. She handed it across the desk to Bogardus, who removed the papers and spread them out. They took several seconds to unfold. There were four large pieces of heavy paper. Sam placed the ashtray on the corner of one page and his desk lamp on the other to keep the papers from folding up like an accordion.

"About a year after my mother died I received a letter in the mail, unsigned and with no return address." She reached across the desk and pointed to a single piece of plain bond paper clipped to the larger pages.

Sam passed his eyes over the brief typed lines.

THESE PARCHMENTS TELL AN AN-CIENT TALE, A LEGACY FROM YOUR FATHER WHO LIVES AND PASSES THIS GIFT TO YOU AS A REMEMBRANCE.

Sam removed the paper clip and tried to read the larger stiff pages. He could make out individual words, but the context made no sense. The edges of the papers were tattered and some of the lettering was faded and worn. He had seen documents like these before, but always under glass cases in museums. They were old and, he assumed, of some value. He looked at the postmark on the envelope. It had been posted in San Francisco and addressed to a post office box in Saint Helena, Napa County, and the date was clearly legible. There was no return address.

"Is this your post office box number?"

"It actually belongs to my stepfather—for his business. Family mail sometimes comes there."

Sam turned the papers over on his desk and examined the back side. The texture of the paper was brittle and it had a translucent sheen. In the upper corner of one page Sam saw a faded ink stamp. He took a magnifying glass from the center drawer of his desk and turned the light of the lamp toward the mark. He ran the glass over the letters.

THE JADE HOUSE
OL0 CHINATOWN LANE
SAN FRANCISCO, CALIFORNIA

Under the stamped letters was a faint pencil scrawl:

Simeon C.

"What do you make of this?" Sam pointed to the stamp.

She shrugged her shoulders and shook her head.

He turned the pages over and examined the script again. On the last page his eyes caught a name, unmistakably a signature, written in a bold hand unlike the delicate text that preceded it. He didn't dwell on it but returned his eyes to the woman.

"Have you shown these to your stepfather?"

"No." Jennifer expelled a soft sigh. "It wouldn't do any good. It would only lead to another argument and I don't know if I can handle that right now."

"But maybe he can answer your questions."

"I think he probably can, but he won't."

Bogardus scanned each of the heavy pages with the magnifying glass but could not make out the script. It was composed of uniform letters, precisely drawn. From a distance they could pass for printing, but closer examination revealed minute wisps of ink where the writing instrument had been lifted between words.

"My stepfather has given me a good life, everything that I could ever ask for," said Jennifer. "When I first asked him questions about my father, after these papers came, all he would say was that the man died in the war. He told me he never met or knew my father and that my mother never talked about him."

"Your mother must have talked to you about your father, told you who he was."

"For whatever it's worth. She said his name was James Spencer. According to my mother he was a naval lieutenant stationed at Treasure Island."

Sam listened to her story. James Spencer had disappeared without a trace during the war. To longtime residents of San Francisco the unsolved mystery of the Ghost Blimp had become part of local mythology and the story was embellished with each telling. In August 1942 a naval blimp on routine antisubmarine patrol off the coast drifted back over the city, its engines silent. Following hours of aimless wafting on the updrafts of ocean breezes the craft turned the serenity of a quiet residential district into chaos as it settled onto Bellevue Avenue. The blimp was abandoned. The two-man crew who had boarded at Treasure Island only hours before were never found.

Jennifer finished her story and looked intently across the desk at Bogardus. There was a momentary silence. Sam wasn't sure he could really do anything for the woman. And yet the story of her father's disappearance and the seemingly ancient papers spread before him offered a curious diversion from the monotony of legal memoranda, depositions and interrogatories. And then there was Jennifer Davies herself. He had certainly wasted his time on less provocative enterprises in the past.

He rose from his desk, pushing both hands deep into his pockets, and walked slowly toward the window overlooking the bay. It wasn't really a legal matter. She could just as easily have consulted a private investigator; in fact, she probably should have. But Bogardus was intrigued by the papers and most of all by the signature on the last page.

He turned and looked at her. "I seriously doubt if there's anything I can do for you. From what you tell me this really isn't a legal matter." His tone was more in the nature of a disclaimer than a rejection. "What did you hope to discover from adoption records?"

"I'm not really sure. Maybe to find where my father was born. A place to begin looking. I'm not even sure that James Spencer was my father. It's only what my mother told me. With this . . ." She pointed toward the note on the lawyer's desk. "I think I am more confused than anything else. I thought that perhaps you could help."

"You're assuming a lot. First of all that these papers are in fact a link to your father. For that proposition all we have is an unsigned typed note. It could be a hoax. Do you know anyone who might do something like this as a joke?"

"Not that I can think of."

His gaze passed from the parchments spread on his desk to the woman seated across from it. He was hooked and he knew it. There was a considered pause, a show of sound professional judgment to remove the appearance of whimsy from his words. "Tell you what. If you'll leave the papers with me for a few days I'll make some inquiries and see what I can find out." He paused for an instant. "But I can't promise anything. I should be back to you within a week. Can we get together then?"

"Thank you. You don't know what a relief it

is just to be able to talk to someone about this. Yes, I can meet with you next week." She paused for a moment. "But there is one thing."

"Yes?"

"I don't want my stepfather to know that I've been to see you."

"Is there any reason why he should?"

"No." Her tone was abrupt and defensive.

"Well, then, this is a confidential matter, between attorney and client. It will remain that way unless you choose to change it." Bogardus smiled.

"You have to understand. I just don't want to hurt him."

"Fine." His tone conveyed assent without agreement, and Jennifer Davies was left to shoulder responsibility for the decision alone.

She took a pen from the marble stand on Sam's desk and scratched an address and phone number on the back of one of his cards. "This is my work number and office address. If you have to contact me please do so at this location, not the phone number in the file."

Sam shot her a quizzical glance.

"I live with my stepfather. And I'm afraid if you call . . . well I'd rather you didn't. Now, about your fee?" Jennifer reached for her purse.

"I normally charge eighty-five dollars an hour for my time and usually require a minimum retainer." Sam paused. "But given the nature of your problem and the fact that it doesn't appear to involve any real research or litigation, I'll waive the fee for now. If there are any expenses I'll send a bill."

"I couldn't let you do that," she protested.

"Tell you what, if I turn up anything we can discuss fees later. If it's a dead-end you can buy me dinner. A deal?"

"For the time being." She moistened her lips with her tongue. Bogardus couldn't be sure if it was a seductive signal or merely a nervous gesture. He hoped for the best.

She took his lead and rose from her chair.

"Thank you very much for your time and your interest. I know you will do what you can for me." Jennifer extended her hand and Sam took it. There was something strangely sensuous, almost intoxicating about the woman.

Jennifer Davies walked from the room, leaving only the lingering fragrance of her perfume in the air and the tattered parchments on Sam's desk.

He dropped back into his chair and returned his gaze to the strange pieces of paper and their unintelligible script.

"Very nice." His trance was broken by a sultry voice.

He looked up at Pat's thick brunette mane and curvaceous figure as she presented her back to him, leaning her hip against the frame of his half-open door to study the form of Jennifer Davies as she walked from the office.

"A new case—domestic, criminal?"

"More of a favor for a friend," said Sam.

"I see. And who is supplying the favor?" She looked at him from under dark arched eyebrows, a smirk on her lips.

"I'm supplying the favor," he said, "and my dear old mother has generously agreed to provide the friend."

"Generous indeed." She winked. While their relationship had long since become platonic, Pat could still mimic the jealous lover with sufficient panache to make even Sam sometimes wonder if there wasn't some lingering romantic remnant. Or was it just his own stirrings?

"Is there some problem?"

"Just looking out for my proprietary interests." She flashed a smile, exposing uniform, pearly white teeth, the envy of any cover girl. "After all, I wouldn't want one of us dipping the quill in the company ink without some benefit flowing to the firm."

"Well, I'll be certain to make a full accounting at the appropriate time."

Pat laughed and headed for her office.

As the door closed Sam reached for his telephone index. His eyes scanned the card labeled "J" until it found the name Jorgensen, Nick. He picked up the receiver and dialed a campus number at the University of California. It rang three times and was answered by a young man who was still laughing and talking to someone else as he spit out the words, "Western Civ Section."

"Is Nick Jorgensen there?"

"Professor Jorgensen? I don't know. Let me see."

Sam heard the suction of a hand being placed over the mouthpiece. "Has anybody seen Professor Jorgensen?" There was a faint reply from another more distant voice.

The student returned to the phone. "Yeah, I

think he's just down the hall talking to another faculty member. Can I ask who's calling?"

"Just tell him it's Sam Bogardus, that I want to take him to lunch. That should get his attention."

He waited while the message was relayed down the hall. A minute later Sam heard Nick's familiar voice over the line.

"Samuel! Haven't heard from you in almost a month. Where have you been?"

"Just the usual. Pollinating local hospitals with my business cards, lecturing the terminally ill on the need for a will. The usual acts of mercy as required."

Bogardus and Jorgensen went back nearly twenty years, to a time when Sam was an undergraduate and Nick a teaching assistant. After college the relationship had continued, and over the years the two had become fast friends who never let more than a few weeks go by without a telephone call or conversation over drinks.

"You got time for lunch today?" asked Sam.

"Well, that depends on who's paying."

"It's on me."

"Well you know me, I can always make time for my friends," said Nick.

"Yeah," Sam smiled. "Particularly when they have a wallet full of credit cards."

Nick laughed. "Well as they say, an appetite is a terrible thing to waste."

"Let's make it a late lunch; I'll have to pick up my car from the garage before I can make it to the bridge. Say I meet you at Jack London

Square at about twelve forty-five, near the old bar. There's something I want to show you."

"Good, see you then."

Sam hung up, gathered the Davies parchments from his desk and dropped them into his briefcase. He placed the card with Jennifer's office number and address in his wallet and made several notations in the file. Then he reached for a set of interrogatories in his In basket and began to scan the documents. But his mind was elsewhere—on the parchments sealed in his leather briefcase and the dark, imperious signature scrawled there.

There was a stiff breeze blowing off the ocean on the bluffs overlooking the Pacific at Fort Funston. The hang gliders were out en masse, floating above the beach on the updrafts rising off the faces of the sheer rock cliffs. They dipped their wings and plunged with their human cargos toward the rocky beach below, only to glide out over the water and climb again. The ruffle of fabric wings could be heard snapping as the delicate crafts soared fifty feet overhead.

Two men stood against the wooden railing, oblivious to the aerial acrobatics. They were dressed warmly against the stiff winds, one wearing an expensive camel hair coat, the other a sheepskin jacket with tufts of wool at the seams.

"I tell you she knows something. I followed her to the county hall of records this morning. She was looking for adoption records, and after that she went to a lawyer's office. She was in there for a long time. You know her as well as I do. She probably fed the shyster some cock-and-bull story. There's no telling what she might have said." The taller man was in his fifties, a bit stooped, with wisps of thin gray hair and dark brooding eyes. He leaned heavily on an ornate walking cane, and moved with a pronounced limp as he stepped away from the railing and toward some empty wooden benches erected over the aging concrete dome of an abandoned coastal gun emplacement.

The other man listened, running the fingers of one hand over the seams on the other arm of his expensive sheepskin coat as he leaned on the railing. You're an alarmist, he thought.

"I tell you we have to do something before it's too late. She can bury us both. I don't know about you, but I'm too old to go to prison." He studied the face of his colleague for some sign of agreement. There was only silence. Then, slowly, as if to emphasize the deliberation, the shorter man pursed his lips and removed his glasses, cleaning the lenses with a handkerchief from his coat pocket.

"There's nothing to discover." He held the frame of his glasses to the sky and studied them for smudges. "Adoption records can't tell her a thing. Besides, they were sealed years ago. Her old man is dead, at least as far as she's concerned. You worry too much, my friend. It's going to kill you someday."

"In case you've forgotten, there's no statute of limitations on murder." The man with the cane used his trump card.

"I had nothing to do with the Frenchman or his woman—that was all your doing."

"I think after thirty years of silence they're going to have some difficulty accepting the argument that you weren't an accessory. You have heard of misprision of felony." A brazen smile formed on the taller man's face.

"Sounds as if the girl is not the only one who's been talking to lawyers."

"Precisely." He raised the handle of the cane to his lips as if to smooth a nonexistent mustache. "Think about it." He'd made his point, then quickly turned the conversation toward a more conciliatory note. "Why would she have to see another lawyer? Tell me that."

"Maybe it was business. Maybe she needed some help on a case. I don't know. Don't worry about it. If there's a problem, I'll take care of it."

The taller man's eyes narrowed and engaged the face of his companion squarely. "I'm giving you fair warning. If you don't, I will."

The shorter man looked up, adjusted his glasses and fixed his companion with an icy stare. "No, you won't." His tone was calm but final.

The two glared at each other for several seconds. Then the man with the cane broke off and headed at a brisk pace toward the parking lot. The man in the sheepskin jacket leaned on the railing and watched as the taller man moved with an uneven gait along the wooden walkway. A long black stretch limousine pulled up to the curb to collect its passenger. A smartly dressed chauffeur exited from the driver's seat and opened the rear door. The man with the brooding eyes stopped, turned and raised the cane in his right hand in an ominous gesture of farewell. The sun glinted off the solid brass shaft of the cane as he disappeared into the sleek limousine and the door closed behind him. Seconds later the vehicle pulled away from the wooden platform toward the parking lot exit and the Great Highway.

It was nearly one o'clock in the afternoon when Sam finally found a parking space off the estuary in Oakland. He jogged along the waterfront toting a light leather briefcase. He could see the small log building at the end of the square in the distance. The log cabin was reputed to have been hauled from Alaska and reassembled stick by stick on the estuary, a faithful replica of the quarters shared by London near Dawson City during his escapade in the Yukon. It was overshadowed by upscale boutiques and glitzy restaurants.

He could see Nick's rotund form from a block away. As he drew closer his friend's warm and familiar smile was followed by a loud belly laugh. "My God, it's good to see you Sam. You did bring your credit card?" Nick slapped his thick arm around Sam's shoulder and chuckled, tugging him in the direction of the restaurants further down the estuary.

Nick Jorgensen was a classic example of the axiom that looks are deceptive. He wore a full beard cropped close to his face. Gentle brown eyes sparkled from under a broad forehead. But it was his portly build and exuberant personality that were his most endearing features. His thick brown hair had a natural wave that curled up at the back of his neck. Nick always looked like he needed a haircut. In tennis shoes and with his shirt pulled halfway out of his pants in the front, Jorgensen more closely resembled an amiable bear than a tenured university professor. But he was a brilliant scholar. His lectures on European history, often punctuated with ribald humor, captivated college jocks whose attention span was normally measured by the sweep hand of a stopwatch.

The two men passed the time in small talk as they walked toward the second story restaurant overlooking the estuary. The waterway was dotted with pleasure boats sailing down the narrow channel toward the open bay. A young blond in a short print skirt showed them to a table at the window.

"So what brings you over here in the middle of the week?" asked Nick.

"The delight of feasting my eyes on your chubby face." There was a genuine twinkle in Sam's eye, for he was only half joking. "After all, it's not every day that I have the chance to contribute to your gluttony."

"Come on, Bogardus, I get suspicious when you come all the way over here—but when you actually turn the combination dial on that rusty wallet of yours and offer to spring for lunch I know you want something."

"Well actually I could use your help." Sam fumbled with his briefcase, placing it on the table.

"Oh God, here it comes," said Nick, a grin spreading across his face. "Let me guess, you got nailed on a paternity rap and you want to borrow some of my blood for the test."

"No, not this time," said Sam. "Actually, the girl fingered you and I want to give you a chance to establish your impotency before the thing gets too serious." Nick let out a raucous laugh and heads in the crowded restaurant began to turn in their direction. Sam looked about sheepishly. Nick was not fazed by the attention. He had grown immune to the stares and disapproval that were the result of his loud laughter. Otherwise he would have died of embarrassment long before.

Sam removed the Davies papers from his briefcase and spread them across the table, using two ashtrays and the salt and pepper shakers to hold the corners of the parchment.

The pages immediately got Nick's full attention.

"These papers were delivered to me in my office less than two hours ago by a woman who says she received them in the mail with this unsigned note." Sam pointed to the paper clipped to the corner of the parchments.

He told Nick of Jennifer Davies, about the mystery of the Ghost Blimp and of the woman's search for her father. Nick looked at the typewritten note and turned the papers on the table so that he could see them upright on his side. He fingered the pages.

"Hmm. Real vellum. Not the cardboard stuff made to pass for parchment in curio shops and tourist traps."

He studied the writing, paying particular attention to notations in the outer margins.

"Does the woman have any idea where these came from?"

"She says she doesn't."

"It looks like a list of some kind." Nick turned the first page over and scanned the second. "I can't be sure, it would take some careful study. The script is clearly English. I would guess fifteenth, maybe sixteenth century."

Nick fingered the torn holes on the left-hand margins and turned over the second and third pages. "Looks like it was torn from some kind of binding—there are traces of glue and small thread holes here." Nick ran his fingers along the margin.

Then his eye was caught by some lettering at the bottom of the last page. It was a broad script, mostly in what appeared to be upper case letters set off by smaller print. He could discern the words "The Generalle" followed by what was clearly a signature. It was faded and part of the lettering had long since been rubbed from the page, but enough of the name remained for Nick to make it out:

FRANCIS DRAKE

"I'll be damned," said Nick. "Did you see this?"

Sam nodded. "I thought you'd be interested."

"If these parchments are authentic, I mean if they're the original of a document signed by Drake, they could be worth a small fortune to collectors."

"I had a stinking suspicion that they were something special," said Sam. "I don't want to dash your thrill of discovery, but I think they might be stolen."

Nick looked up. "What makes you say that?"

Sam shuffled the pages and found the one with the ink stamp on the back. "Unless I miss my guess, the Jade House on Old Chinatown Lane was not in business when Drake last visited the city."

"What do you make of it?"

"Beats the hell out of me. The woman who delivered them to me doesn't fit the profile of your common thief—too much class. Besides, if she took them what would she gain by delivering them to me—and why would she trust them to my safekeeping? No, if they're stolen I'd bet my ticket to practice that Jennifer Davies knows nothing about it."

"What would you like me to do?" asked Nick.

"Well, I thought maybe you could take the papers for now and see if you can decipher the writing. If you can't maybe some of your friends on the campus could provide some answers. If we knew what the documents were it might give some clue as to where they came from, and maybe some lead on Jennifer Davies's father. In the meantime I'll see if I can get some information on the adoption records and a lead on the Jade House."

The waitress approached the table to take their orders and Nick quickly scooped up the papers to make room for two water glasses. He held the parchments away from his body like some ancient tabloid as he continued to struggle with the script.

"This stuff is difficult to fathom, but it's more

the context and usage than the language itself. Many of the words are the same as the English used in any American newspaper today, but the order in which they appear makes Sanskrit of the whole thing," said Nick. "There's no sense in you and I struggling with it. There is a man I know, a Shakespearean scholar, who will have no difficulty with it at all. If he's not tied up he should be able to untangle the four pages in a couple of hours and give us a clear translation in writing." Nick took a deep breath. "God, to think I may be holding parchment that 'The General' himself set his scrawl to four hundred years ago!"

Jorgensen's eyes suddenly took on the gaze of a man whose thoughts were several centuries in the past. "You know, to most Catholics, even today, Drake was nothing but a common pirate. The Spaniards referred to him as 'El Draque.' He had a special flourish for sacking Catholic churches and parting the Pope from the riches of this world. Just the vision of the redbearded little runt put shivers up the backs of most of the captains sailing for Hispaniola. He ravaged Spanish ships off the Florida Keys and sacked a number of Spanish settlements in the late sixteenth century."

Sam studied his friend's face. Nick's eyes sparkled in the bright reflection of the sun off the waters of the estuary.

Nick fingered the pages and wrestled with the text. "To the uneducated, Drake was simply a pirate. Actually he was a privateer. His ship was chartered by the British Crown and financed by a group of investors, not unlike a joint venture or limited partnership of today. The only difference was that instead of dabbling in pork bellies or grain futures, Drake plundered foreign flag vessels, mostly Spanish, and returned a handsome profit to his investors from the booty he took."

The waitress returned with two beers. With obvious reluctance Nick handed the parchments back to Sam who placed them in the briefcase for safekeeping. Nick took a sip of beer.

"Drake's most famous exploit was his voyage around the world that started in the late fourteenth century. Unlike Magellan, who ended up on the business end of a Philippine spear, Drake actually finished the trip." He took another sip of beer and wiped some foam from his beard.

"When you talk about treasure galleons most people think of Cuba or the Gold Coast of Florida. It's true that most of the Spanish sea traffic of the day was concentrated there. What most people don't know is that Spain's Manila galleons, the largest sailing ships ever built, sailed from the Philippines to the area around Alaska and then south along the Pacific Coast of North America. For more than two hundred years they passed within sight of the Golden Gate, hauling gems, china, silk from the Orient— carting it all south to ports near Acapulco in Mexico."

"From there the cargo was carried overland by mules for transatlantic shipping. But many of those galleons never made it down the coast. They were swallowed up by storms, lost on the rocks in the fog—or just disappeared with no record."

"Are you telling me that treasure ships piled up on the rocks off the coast and nobody ever found a hint of treasure?" asked Sam.

"You have to remember this isn't the soft sand of the Caribbean. And the ships weren't carrying precious metals that would wash up on the beach in heavy storms." Nick raised his half-empty glass for another drink.

"It's a fact. While scholars and local historians continue to argue whether Drake ever landed at the bay that bears his name near Point Reyes, documents on file in the Archive of the Indies at Seville confirm conclusively that for more than two centuries the Manila galleons put in at that very spot to careen and provision their ships before heading south. In fact there have been plans in the works to dive on one of the wrecks for years—the *San Augustine*. Marine archaeologists believe it went down in less than fifty feet of water a quarter of a mile off Drake's Beach in 1595. The only thing stopping them is the capital for the venture."

Lunch arrived and Nick hovered over the large broiled hamburger on a sourdough roll. It was easily four inches thick but he had no difficulty crushing it down to mouth size.

Sam took delight in watching Nick eat. He couldn't help but envy anyone who could gain so much satisfaction and obvious pleasure from the single act of consuming food.

"This is good," said Nick. "I was getting pretty hungry."

"Is there ever a time when you aren't hungry?"

Nick winked and ignored him.

"As I was saying, those papers could be quite valuable. Assuming they're the authentic originals."

"If they are—authentic, I mean—what do you think they're worth?"

"I couldn't put a price on them. Only a cash buyer at an auction can do that. But I know Drake men, scholars who have spent the better part of their lives studying Drake's life, his exploits at court and his various voyages. These guys would kill for a five-minute glance at newly discovered parchments, especially if they shed any light on Drake's holdover in 'Nova Albion.'"

"You know," said Nick, "the blue bloods in Cape Cod have to live with the fact that they play second fiddle to the real 'New England,' which actually sits out there,"—Nick waved his arm out toward the bay—"probably in Marin County, according to all of the records that are available. That's the area that Drake called his 'Nova Albion'—'New England'—thirty years before Jamestown and forty years before the *Mayflower*."

"What possessed him to come up here?" asked Bogardus. "I thought all of the gold in the Americas, at least at that time, was in Mexico with the Aztecs or in Peru with the Incas."

"True, but Drake didn't know that. All he knew was that the Spaniards were pulling a king's ransom in silver from their mines in Peru. He'd heard stories about Inca and Aztec cities awash in gold. For all he knew the entire west coast of the Americas was sprinkled with the stuff like manna from heaven." Nick used his napkin to catch sandwich relish as it dripped down his beard. "But he had a more practical reason for coming north."

There was a blank look in Nick's eyes as his mind was transported to another age, and his cadence slowed.

"After he navigated his way through the Straits of Magellan, Drake had a field day sacking Spanish villages and plundering their sea traffic off Peru, Chile, and right up to the Isthmus of Panama. He caught a Manila galleon north of Panama in Mexican waters coming the other way and parted it from its cargo. The Spanish had no warships in the Pacific at that time—there was no need. No English ship had ever sailed that far west before. But Drake had a problem."

He paused and shot a sideways glance at Sam. "By the time he reached California the Spanish had assembled a veritable armada to track him down, and Drake needed to find an eastward passage through North America in the worst way. It would have been the fastest way back to England. The fabled search for a Northwest Passage was not the noble quest one reads about in most history books, at least not as far as Drake was concerned."

Nick picked up his fork and chased a French fry around his plate.

"Most scholars don't believe that Drake ever intended to sail around the world," said Nick. "What he really had was a little larceny in his heart and a quick getaway on his mind. We know from records that he went as far north as the Oregon coast, but the weather turned foul so he came back south. His ultimate trek across the Pacific was born of practical necessity. It was either that or decorate the end of a Spanish pike." Nick sipped his beer and gobbled the last bit of his sandwich.

Sam had only picked around the edges of his lunch and half of his sandwich remained on his plate.

"You gonna eat that?" asked Nick.

Sam smiled, "No, you go ahead." The vision of bloody heads hoisted on sharpened spears had curbed Bogardus's appetite.

Nick plucked the sandwich from the plate and went to work on it. He spoke with his mouth full. "From everything we know, Drake had about thirty tons of gold, silver, precious gems and other treasure on board the *Golden Hinde* when he finally landed at Nova Albion. He had to careen his ship—scrape the bottom and patch it—and gather provisions for the Pacific crossing. We don't know exactly what went on during the period that he stayed in California. We know he was here for more than a month, but the theories on where he landed and where he pitched his camp are as numerous as the scholars studying the question."

"I thought you guys at Berkeley had a plate of some kind left behind by Drake?"

"The brass plate," said Nick. "A fellow found it near Novato, twenty miles inland, in 1937, and for a while it looked like it might provide some answers, though no one could say why it wasn't found closer to the coast or the bay. After some debate and a lot of publicity in the papers, another man came forward and said he'd found the plate a couple of years earlier nearer the coast and that he'd carried it around in his car for a time before tossing it out on the highway thinking it was a piece of junk. There's a lot of conjecture about the plate, but metallurgical tests on the age of the brass indicate it's not old enough to be authentic. Besides, it doesn't answer the question of where Drake landed. Archaeologists have scoured the area near Novato where the plate was found and sampled the place near the coast where the second man said he first picked it up and they've come up with nothing."

He paused to take another bite. "There's probably only one thing that can ever settle the dispute as to where Drake landed," said Nick.

"What's that?"

"Drake's journal."

"Well, I would assume that he kept a ship's log."

"This was no ship's log. It was a detailed journal containing entries of the most minute details of his voyage. A personal diary, if you will, chronicling his innermost thoughts and fears, his private conversations with other officers, his dealings with indigenous peoples at each landing. There's just one hitch." Nick looked up at Bogardus. "Nobody knows where it is. We know the book existed because several crew members wrote and talked about it after the *Hinde* reached England. There are a number of theories on what happened to it. Some believe that Drake destroyed it himself in order to embellish upon the trip in later writings. Others think that it was confiscated by the king of France when Drake landed there on his return to England. The journal is reputed to have contained meticulous notes on all of the exploits of the trip, including drawings, in Drake's own hand, in the margins. It seems the captain fancied himself a real . . ." Nick's sentence trailed off and his gaze lifted to engage Sam's eyes directly. Sam's jaw sagged. " . . . artist," Nick finished the sentence.

Before Nick could say another word Sam had retrieved the brown leather briefcase. Nick pushed the plates to one side and mopped up the water condensation from under the glasses. Sam spread the parchments on the table and both men sat and stared in disbelief. There in the margins of each of the four pages were small, delicate ink drawings, one of a bird of prey perched on a stand, an object clutched in its talons, another showing human figures gathered behind tall grass and still another depicting a small boat or canoe. In all there were seven miniature ink drawings on the four pages.

Chapter

2

Threading his way through traffic onto the Bay Bridge, Bogardus wondered what connection could exist between a sixteenth-century manuscript and the disappearance of a naval officer three hundred years later. He was confident that the pages that he'd left with Nick would be deciphered by experts, but would they reveal anything?

As he approached the Treasure Island off-ramp from the bridge, Sam moved into the right lane and took the winding road down toward the naval base. He was stopped by a marine at the gate.

"Can I help you, sir?"

Sam looked up into the bright glare of the afternoon sun and shaded his eyes with his hand. "I'm here to look at some records of a naval board of inquiry convened back during

World War Two. Do you know where I can get some information?"

"Yes sir, you might try Fleet Operations Building, the public information counter. They can probably help you." The marine quickly gave directions, and five minutes later Sam was at the counter being assisted by a young sailor. He was ushered down a long corridor and asked to take a seat in a small reception area.

After several minutes a young officer approached Sam.

"Mr. Bogardus, I'm Lieutenant Keenan, attached to the Judge Advocate General's staff, Sixth Fleet. How can I help you?"

The officer was in his late twenties, impeccable in his attire, with straight dark hair parted neatly on the left—a preppie who had traded in his tweed jacket and argyle socks for a uniform.

"Hello, Lieutenant." Sam flashed a broad grin. "I'm here doing some investigation on a case." He pulled a business card from the breast pocket of his suit coat and passed it to the officer. "I'm looking for the official records of a naval board of inquiry that convened back in 1942. It involved the loss of a naval blimp that crashed in a residential part of San Francisco. I believe the crew was lost."

A slight smile began to form around the corners of the officer's mouth. "Why is everybody so excited about that blimp after all these years? You're the second person to ask about those records in the last week."

"Oh?" said Sam. "Who was the first?"

"A gentleman who was in here a few days

ago. We don't get requests for case files that old very often. The man seemed to know exactly what he was looking for. He had the whole nine yards on the case when he walked in, even the file number. Otherwise we'd still be looking."

"Do you have a name, anything?"

The officer looked quizzically at Sam.

"On the other man I mean, any name?"

"Oh, let me look."

The officer moved to the counter and looked at a large journal that lay open facing the other direction. He turned it around, flipped one page and ran his finger down the column. "Here it is, Mr. George Johnson, 1420 Olstead Street, San Francisco, California."

Sam opened his briefcase, took out a note pad and entered the name of George Johnson and the address from the book.

"Would you like to see the file?" asked the officer. "I think it's still in the reading room. We haven't had a chance to refile it in archives yet."

Sam followed the officer down a well-lit corridor and into a room with another counter and several library tables surrounded by chairs.

The officer went behind the counter and rummaged through a stack of files on a metal cart.

"Yes, here it is." The file was not voluminous, only one single manila folder, legal length and no more than an inch thick, a product of the period before commercial copying machines and word processors, when hearings and trials took days not months to complete.

"Here, if you'll sign this card I'll take your business card and have the clerk at the front counter enter the information in our log. You can take the file to a table and if you need any copying just ring the bell on the counter and a clerk will assist you. Is there anything else I can do for you, Mr. Bogardus?"

"No, I don't think so. It'll just take me a few minutes." Sam was actually surprised. Having heard the horror stories about the military he'd expected a raft of red tape and delays. Instead he had everything he could ask for, all wrapped up in an attitude of professional courtesy that was unheard of at the county courthouse, where he knew most of the clerks by their first names.

He sat at the table, opened the file and began flipping through the papers, There were a number of statements from eyewitnesses who had seen the blimp hit the beach by the Great Highway, and statements from others who had watched it drift aimlessly over the city before coming to rest on Bellevue Avenue. Sam scanned the statements quickly, looking for some key, some piece of information that might help him find a thread that could lead to Jennifer Davies's father. But there was nothing unusual.

The typed record of the formal hearings before the board of inquiry was fixed by a metal fastener to the back cover of the file folder. It took Sam twenty minutes to canvass the double spaced transcript. The document contained a bland account of the events leading up to the crash, from flight preparations early in the morning of August 16, 1942, to the mopping up of the destroyed airship several days later. In its findings the board concluded that the two crew members, Lieutenant James Spencer and

Chief Petty Officer Raymond Slade, were lost at sea during a routine antisubmarine patrol at an unknown location off the Pacific Coast near San Francisco, California. The cause of the accident—"Unknown." The board seemed particularly puzzled by the fact that the normal three-man flight crew had been pared to two members on the day of the accident. For some unexplained reason Slade had instructed the flight engineer to step out of the craft just seconds before it lifted off the runway. The engineer would no doubt spend the balance of his life wondering why he had been spared, thought Bogardus. Slade and Spencer knew something that day. But what?

The file contained a number of yellowed news clippings, the earliest dated August 17, 1942, the day following the crash. Several of the clippings showed faded pictures of the ill-fated craft drifting over the city. Other photos captured the gondola teetering on its single-wheel landing gear, the deflated gray envelope of the airship draped over it. Sam's eyes passed from the pictures to the news clippings with their bold headlines:

U.S. NAVY BLIMP FALLS IN
DALY CITY; CREW MISSING

Patrol Craft
Hits House in
Street Crash

A derelict navy blimp, its crew of two missing, drifted in from the ocean and crashed into the street in Daly City yesterday. Sagging in the middle like a broken cigar, with big rips visible in the bag and its motors idle, the blimp wandered crazily at treetop height over the Lake Merced area and drew a throng of hundreds pursuing it by automobile and afoot before it came gently to earth on a suburban street . . .

Several hours later, no trace had been found of the crew, although a continuing search was in progress at sea and in the area surrounding the crash scene. All of the parachutes and the rubber raft were found in the gondola. Two life belts were missing.

The news stories concerning the crash declined in intensity as the days passed, and they gradually slipped from the front page to the inside columns.

They told of a depth charge from the blimp found on the property of a local country club. The navy scrambled to come up with theories for the crash to explain the missing crew. But none of them fit the facts of a perfectly airworthy ship, its engines in working order with a full tank of fuel. Microscopic and chemical tests ruled out the possibility that the craft went down at sea before being blown back over the coast. There were no traces of saltwater anywhere on the blimp.

Sam continued to pick through the file. It contained a number of pieces of correspondence—telegrams and letters—to family members and next of kin. One letter was addressed to "Mrs. James Spencer," informing her that it was the conclusion of the board that her husband had been lost at sea while on patrol. Sam guessed that this was the letter that Jennifer Davies was shown by her mother as a child. There was another letter dated a week later. Sam read the half-page document:

Dear Mrs. Spencer:
I write to convey my deepest sympathies on the loss of your husband. All of us who knew Jim greatly admired him. I have been asked to go through his personal belongings at the base and return them to you. Enclosed you will find an inventory of these items, which will be delivered to you by courier in a few days. If there is anything that I can do please do not hesitate to call on me.

Captain Jack Caulford
U.S.N.

Sam turned the page and perused the attached inventory. Halfway down the list his eyes came to an abrupt stop. He peered at the words in disbelief.

Four page document stamped "The Jade House, Old Chinatown Lane, San Francisco, California."

Bogardus sat for a long time staring at the page. His eyes isolated the entry. Why would the parchments sent to Jennifer Davies's mother thirty years before suddenly be mailed to her daughter with a note that James Spencer was alive? More importantly, where had the parchments been all these years since the war?

He returned his attention to the file and found a list of exhibits and a large brown envelope clipped to the back page of the file folder itself. Sam opened the flap on the envelope and pulled out several yellowing photos. One was a picture of the blimp with its ground crew assembled in front of the huge airship. The figures were too small to discern any facial features. There were news photographs of the crash site and pictures of the blimp as it drifted over the city and finally a head and shoulder photograph of a man in a blue naval uniform and white service cap. Sam turned the photo over and on the back on a typed label was the name "Chief Petty Officer Raymond Slade." Sam turned the photo over and studied the face in the picture.

He looked in the envelope but there were no more photographs. He checked the list of documents and exhibits in the file. Item 37 read "Photograph of Lt. James Spencer." But the photograph wasn't in the file.

Sam took some paper clips from a container on the counter and clipped the deposition of the man on the beach, the picture of Slade and the two letters to Dorothy Spencer with the inventory identifying the parchments and then rang for the clerk.

A young enlisted man appeared at the counter. "I have some documents I'd like to have copied. Also, I can't seem to find one of the photographs identified on the exhibits list in the file."

The clerk took the file and looked at the list and then through the photos in the envelope. "I don't know what could have happened to it sir. I suppose it's possible someone could have removed it along the way." The clerk continued to rummage through the papers clipped in the folder. "Most of these files have been sitting in a warehouse for years, and there's no telling who may have looked at them or had possession of 'em over that time."

"Are there any other files on this case?"

"No, this is it, sir. I think the lieutenant probably told you, another gentleman asked for the same file last week. He was quite insistent that he see everything and we turned the place upside down to make sure that nothing else existed."

"Do you know if the other man asked to copy any of the documents?"

"No, I don't think he did. I would have done the copying if he had."

"I don't suppose that I could get a picture of James Spencer from any other navy files."

"Not likely. Most of the personnel records from the last war would have been carted off to central warehouses in the Midwest a good ten years ago. Those that weren't essential for military or veterans benefit programs would have been destroyed."

Sam continued to paw through the file while the enlisted man disappeared to make the copies. Three minutes later Bogardus collected his copies and headed for the parking lot.

Pausing at the car he casually turned to check the entrance to the administration building. The absence of any marine guards scurrying down the stairs behind him confirmed his theory. Someone had lifted the photograph of James Spencer and the navy had never missed it. Nor had they learned their lesson. Undoing two lower buttons on his dress shirt, Bogardus slipped the fingers of his right hand into the shirt and removed the navy file photograph of Raymond Slade. He studied it for several seconds, then placed it in the file folder with the copied materials. Xeroxed copies of black and white photos just didn't cut it.

A half hour later Sam was back in the city. It was nearly four in the afternoon when he arrived at the office. A note was taped to the back of his chair, an invitation from Pat to meet him for dinner. Sam had no illusions; he knew she wanted to discuss business.

There was also a telephone message from Angie. The note under the name told him to "Call before leaving the office."

He dialed his mother's number and after a single ring he heard the familiar high-pitched voice.

"Hello Mom."

"Oh Sam, I'm glad you called." He had to pull the phone away from his head to prevent damage to his eardrum. Angie possessed a piercing voice, particularly when she was excited or agitated, which as she grew older seemed to be nearly all the time. "I want you to come over to dinner tonight. I have a pot roast in the oven, potatoes, carrots—your favorite." She spoke in a rapid staccato. "I haven't had a chance to sit and talk with you in such a long time, I thought that perhaps we could . . ."

"Mom, I can't make it tonight."

" . . . just visit like we used to. Remember how it was before you went off to law school, before you met that girl? We had such wonderful times, just the two of us." The elevated pitch of her voice matched her euphoric spirits. As always when Angie asked for something, her mind had already eliminated the possibility of a negative reply.

"What time will you be here?"

"I can't come tonight, Mom."

"Well, sure you can."

"I can't. I have another commitment."

There was a brief pause before she spoke.

"You have to go out with her again, I suppose?"

Sam needed no clarification. Angie's use of the pronoun had become synonymous with Pat.

"I have a business meeting." There was no sense opening old wounds. Angie had vented her spleen on Pat since law school. He thought the hostility had ended when he moved out of Pat's apartment, but the bile had stopped flowing only for a brief period.

"I'd much rather be there," he lied. "But I'm afraid I have to sit and talk with some boring people about business over a table in a crowded restaurant."

"Tables, yes. You know I was wondering— that old table down in the basement. You know the one that sits by the furnace? I think that it could be finished and I could use it up here in the living room. What do you think?"

She wasn't going to get away with it, not this time. In recent months it had become her favorite ploy. Change the subject quickly and lure him into some other area. Before she was finished she would set a time for dinner and hang up.

"We were talking about dinner, Mom. Remember, I said I couldn't make it."

"Oh yes? Meals are such difficult times for me these days. You know it's very hard to cook for one person. I never realized that before."

"Yes Mom, I know. Maybe we can get together over the weekend. I'll give you a call. All right?"

"Well, what about the roast?"

"Freeze it. We'll make sandwiches. I'll give you a call later in the week. Bye, Mom."

Sam turned his attention to a stack of papers on his desk. He quickly proofed three letters typed earlier in the day by Carol and signed each, returned several calls and then dictated a letter on tape to Jennifer Davies, asking her to call the office for another appointment. He delivered verbal instructions to Carol on the tape, asking her to order a certified copy of Jennifer Davies's birth certificate and to inquire as to the procedure for obtaining any records of adoption.

Putting down the microcassette dictator Sam spun around in his chair to the credenza behind his desk and grabbed the San Francisco phone directory. He looked up the name George

Johnson. There were four listed. None showed an address on Olstead Street. Maybe he was unlisted. He reached for the Thomas Brothers map book for San Francisco and looked up Olstead Street. It didn't exist; nor, he assumed, did George Johnson.

It is an uncomfortable feeling for a lawyer when a client's story begins to unravel, when words don't conform to the documents in files or inconsistencies begin to creep in. Bogardus had experienced it many times during his years with the public defender, when his clients were an assortment of drug pushers, prostitutes and other habitual losers. Now it was all coming back. He could excuse the missing photograph of James Spencer in the navy files, she could know nothing about that, and George Johnson, the man who didn't exist. But the letter to Jennifer's mother and its cryptic reference to the parchments. It didn't wash. Why would parchments forwarded to the mother thirty years before suddenly be mailed to the daughter with a note that James Spencer was alive?

Sam straightened up a few papers on his desk, grabbed his coat and headed for the door. He walked slowly down the stairs and out under the arched doorway leading from the pier entrance, his thoughts mired in unanswered questions concerning the parchments and the identity of the man calling himself George Johnson. He didn't notice the black limousine across the Embarcadero in the parking lot beyond the abandoned railroad tracks. As he boarded the bus for the ride up Broadway, the large dark car pulled out of the parking lot and followed the bus up the street.

Nick Jorgensen wasted no time in tracking down Jasper Holmes on campus to show him the parchments from the Davies case. Holmes was an eccentric Englishman on a one-year sabbatical with the English literature department. After getting a glimpse of the documents, he insisted that Nick bring the parchments to his apartment that evening where the two of them could study them more thoroughly after dinner. Holmes was considered a foremost expert on Elizabethan prose, having published a two-volume translation of the official papers of Elizabeth Tudor.

Nick jumped at the invitation, and by seven that evening the two had the papers spread out across the large dining table and a smaller card table, examining every letter with magnifying glasses, Nick writing and making notes as Holmes deciphered the script. Jasper kept tripping over piles of books that he had taken from the table and laid on the floor to make room for the large pieces of parchment. His wife, Molly, worked in the kitchen cleaning up after dinner. She was a matronly woman who was used to her husband sticking his nose in some book till all hours of the night.

Holmes mumbled in a low monotone as he examined the parchments with an oversized magnifying glass under the bright glare of a desk lamp he had brought from the study.

"Gothic cursive script. I would say fifteenth, maybe sixteenth century," said Holmes. "The trick"—he paused in midsentence to focus the light of the desk lamp directly over the page—"is to know the common stumbling blocks, to train the eye to appreciate a range of visual distinctions with which we are unfamiliar today." Without looking up at Nick, Holmes pushed one of the parchments to the other side of the table and stretching across with a ruler pointed to a single word on the page. "See that?" he looked at Nick. "It's spelled three different ways just in the four pages we have here."

"What do you think?" asked Nick. "A sloppy forgery?"

"Not likely. An amateur forger would have at least taken care to conform all the spellings. If these are a fraud they were done by someone who knew what he was doing. The fact is that the writings of Elizabethan England bridged a period between the medieval and modern. There were virtually no common rules of punctuation, spelling or grammar. If it sounded right it was right," said Holmes. "No, the author either understood the grammatical chaos of the times and took pains to mimic it, or . . ."

Holmes took a considered pause and straightened up, arching his back.

"Or what?" asked Nick.

"Or the man who wrote these wore short baggy pants, tight stockings—and has been fertilizing the sea bed with his bones for the better part of four centuries."

"You mean they're authentic?"

"I can't say that with certainty. I'm no documents expert, but the style and prose sound like Drake. The man had what the Spaniards could only characterize as a morbid wit. He could never be satisfied with a simple entry in his log. His correspondence to the queen was usually filled with barbs about the Spanish, whom he genuinely hated. Here, look at this passage." Holmes pointed to a spot on one of the parchments. "The writer describes an eagle of gold with an emerald clutched in its talon, apparently part of the booty they took from a Spanish merchantman. He says 'we relieved the overwrought friar of his responsibility for the bird.' That is precisely how Sir Francis might tell the world that he and his band robbed some poor cleric. All I can say with certainty is that the tone of the writing is on the mark from my earlier readings."

Unsure how much he should reveal to Holmes and without thinking Nick asked, "Do you know anything about Drake's journal?"

Jasper Holmes looked up, arching an eyebrow. And as if a signal had suddenly been tripped, the Englishman's eyes narrowed and he stared motionless at Nick. "My God! Do you have any idea of the value of these pages if they're part of the journal?" There was an instantaneous pause, and then as if a light had suddenly flashed on in his head, Jasper said: "You have the rest of it don't you—the journal? You can tell me. Your secret would be safe with me." The words carried all the assurance of a thimblerigger at a county fair.

Nick wished he could recall the question, but the damage was done. Holmes knew more about Drake and his travels than Nick realized, and now he had planted the seed of curiosity. He would have to kill it before it could germinate.

Nick laughed. "Jasper, I don't have a damn thing other than what you see here on the table, and that was given to a friend who is naive in the extreme by a woman who purchased the pages at some tourist trap in Chinatown."

A look of incomprehension clouded the expression on the Englishman's face. Nick moved quickly to maintain the momentum and turned over the pages of parchment until he located the one bearing the stamp of the Jade House on Old Chinatown Lane. He pointed to the stamp on the back of the page and looked up apprehensively, uncertain whether Holmes had accepted the explanation. Sam would kill him if the Englishman leaked word of a new Drake find on the academic grapevine. It would be embarrassing if the documents were bogus, but worse—immeasurably worse—if they were authentic.

"I haven't been entirely truthful with you, Jasper, in part because I was embarrassed. You see, this woman is trying to sell these documents to my friend at an exorbitant price, on the assurance that they are part of the Drake journal." He paused and winked across the table at the Englishman. "Between you and me, I don't think the woman knows shit from shinola, or else she's just flat-ass trying to take my friend to the cleaners." The Englishman was still trying to unravel the idiom when Nick popped the question again.

"What do you know about it—the journal?"

"Well," he stammered, "there are a number of theories concerning the fate of the journal." Holmes adjusted his glasses. "I think the better reasoned view is that the book was seized by the French when Drake landed at Belle Isle near La Rochelle in France on his way back to England. According to some letters that were found in the archives in Seville, Drake is reputed to have stashed a quantity of gold and silver on the island, not sure that he would be welcomed back home by his monarch." Holmes raised his heavy gray eyebrows and looked over the top of his bifocals at Nick. "You see, he'd created quite an embarrassment for the British Crown by sacking Spanish ships and towns in the New World, supposedly without the knowledge or approval of his queen."

Nick breathed easier, sensing that Holmes's speech had returned to the cadence of a lecture, and his interest, at least for the moment, to the abstractions of history.

Suddenly Nick looked at his watch. "Damn! I have a seminar tomorrow morning and I have at least an hour of preparation to do to get ready."

Jasper, sensing that he was about to see the last of the parchments, leaned heavily on the edge of one of the pages. "Well you can leave these with me and I can have a translation for you in the morning."

"No, I'm afraid I just can't do that. My friend made me promise that I wouldn't let them out of my sight. If anything happened to them he'd have to pay the woman's asking price, and believe me, neither of us could raise the sum on our meager salaries, not unless you've got something going on the side." Nick gave a nervous laugh.

"Well if you want to stay it won't take long." Jasper's tone conveyed the confidence of a rug merchant who, having rejected a final offer of purchase, was relegated to begging.

"I wish I could, but not tonight. I really have to get my materials together for the seminar." Avoiding further entreaties, Nick managed to tug the final page of parchment from under Jasper's fingers and carefully placed them in his briefcase. "Perhaps we can finish it tomorrow night. I'll give you a call."

"Yes. Yes, please do."

Quickly Nick made his way to the door. He was halfway to his car before he realized that he had never thanked Molly for dinner. But he would live with the regret. He had no desire to get near Jasper again with the parchments.

It was three in the morning by the time Nick finished interpreting the last line of the script. Using the page already deciphered by Jasper, Nick had struggled to match up the letters and words of the translated text with the balance of the pages. There were a few rough spots, but he had scribbled the substance of Drake's message in a small notebook. He sat exhausted on the couch in the living room of his apartment and pieced the notes together. Like pieces of a jigsaw puzzle, the sentences began to take shape. The first three of the four pages were a laundry list of treasure seized by the crew of the *Peli-*

can, later christened the *Golden Hinde*, as it traveled a circuitous course from the Azores to the Caribbean and south along the coast of Patagonia, through the Straits of Magellan and up the Pacific coast of the Americas. Listed were a dazzling array of art works, precious gems and metals—four chains of solid gold, each three feet in length, a bag of pearls, two more bags of emeralds, fifteen barrels of silver bars, two large crates of gold bullion bars, twenty-two chests full of gold royals of plate and a crucifix of gold studded with emeralds. This special find Drake kept in his cabin in a locked cabinet along with an eagle of gold bearing a large emerald clutched in its talons. The bird he had plundered from a Spanish ship off the coast of Mexico. According to the manifest, Drake had taken many of the items listed from a Manila galleon as he sailed south from his exploration of the Oregon coast. It was a cruel irony for the Spanish and a stroke of good luck for Drake that two small ships adrift on a boundless ocean should come into contact off an unchartered coast. Drake captured the galleon, took her cargo and left the hapless Spaniards to sail south empty. The parchments confirmed the view of historians that Drake, contrary to the myth popularized in the movies and fiction, was merciful to his vanquished foes, never killing without cause or justification.

According to the brief narrative contained in the parchments, after taking the Manila galleon Drake's ship had sprung a leak and was in risk of foundering. The captain made haste to put in at the nearest safe harbor. It was this harbor that he christened his "Nova Albion." Nick scrawled the translation in his small notebook.

But it was the last entry of the four pages that raised the hair on the back of his neck. It was only five lines, and Nick read and reread it a dozen times. He stared at the words. The translation had to be wrong. He checked his notes and looked at the parchments again. There was no mistake.

Suddenly Nick comprehended the full impact of the message scratched on the pages. For the first time in four centuries human eyes had read the secret penned by the fiery English captain, and Nick knew that any search for Drake's journal would have more than merely academic significance.

"Listen Sam, we don't have time for this. I have two trials in the next seven weeks and you should be developing new business. I think in the last year that we've humored your mother enough to last her a lifetime." Pat's eyes shimmered under the candlelight of the restaurant, her hands clasped, her elbows resting on the table, flanking a half-empty wine glass.

"Nick's studying the documents now. I think they're worth money . . ."

"Where have I heard that before?"

It was a low blow. Pat had never allowed him to forget the episode in Alleghany. Almost five years had passed, but she continued to cultivate the incident, freshening the embarrassment whenever the need arose, which occurred with more frequency as boredom caused Sam to stray increasingly from his practice.

Jorgensen had appeared at the office one afternoon with a friend from college. It was a dead-bang, money-in-the-bank sure thing. The friend's family had ties in Alleghany dating to the 1850s. An old uncle knew the exact location of a strongbox filled with gold dust that had been stashed fifty years before by miners during a claim dispute. Without consulting Pat, Sam forked over fifteen hundred dollars of the firm's money and formed a limited partnership. They dug for a week with backhoes through a dozen old claims in the tiny foothill community. When the money ran out, all they had to show for their trouble were forty-three empty holes. The holes soon began to fill—with surrounding buildings. By fall, three abandoned shacks, undermined by the man-made craters and encouraged by heavy rains, collapsed. Bogardus learned to his dismay that in the back country of the Sierra Nevada the instincts for gold digging run deep. The termite-riddled hovels suddenly became "historic structures," their owners demanding damages in six figures.

Pat's irritation turned to ire when the first lawsuit arrived. As always, what was a crisis to Pat was a mere inconvenience to Sam. He tendered the suits to the firm's malpractice insurance carrier. The company's underwriter listened in stunned silence as Sam in near-reverent tones informed him of the loss. It seemed the law firm's work in forming the limited partnership constituted a professional service. Contrite to the end, Sam owned up to his error in failing to secure waivers of liability from the Alleghany property owners.

After burning the phone lines between its home office in Minnesota and its lawyers in Los Angeles, the carrier grudgingly settled the claims, paying a dime on the dollar. The property owners fueled their fireplaces with lumber from the abandoned shacks as they counted their blessings in cold, hard cash. Two days later the carrier canceled the firm's malpractice coverage, leaving Bogardus and Paterson "bare." In the end Sam merely shrugged. After all, insurance coverage only encourages lawsuits. It was not a theory he wished to restate as he gazed across the table into Pat's icy stare.

"In case you've forgotten, we're in the business of practicing law, not dealing in antiquities or half-baked treasure hunts. Give the papers back to the lady and tell her to find somebody else to listen to her story."

But it wasn't just Alleghany. Pat was jealous. Sam now knew that Angie had finally struck a responsive cord. The old lady had used Jennifer Davies to drive a wedge between him and Pat.

"What's the problem? Are you saying I'm not carrying my load in the office?"

"You know better than that." Her eyes narrowed. "There's an old saying—it takes more than an ampersand to make a partnership. If we don't get your mother out of the middle of our business now it will never end. She'll destroy the firm and you know it."

"I'll tell you what. If you're worried about losing money on the deal, I'll compensate the firm for the time I spend on the Davies matter. Hour for hour I'll pay the going rate. You won't lose a thing."

"It's not the money and you know it," she fumed.

"Then what is it?"

"It's you. Losing interest in the firm, your practice and . . ."

Sam waited for her to complete the sentence. But she didn't.

Three years earlier they would have fought until one of them walked away, driven by pride. Their pleasure would have come from later reconciliation. It was a measure of how far apart they had drifted that the argument merely blew itself out and in the end they found themselves still seated, staring across the small cocktail table.

"Let me play this one out. If the parchments turn out to be bogus, I'll run a routine check on adoption records for the lady and send her on her way."

Pat's eyes filled with skepticism. She shook her head and with an exasperated grin finally gave a reluctant nod. She knew that she could never deliver an ultimatum and make it stick, not without running the risk of dissolving the partnership, which was not something she was willing to do, not if there were other alternatives.

"Tell me, what's she like?"

"Who?"

"Let's not be sly. Your client. Jennifer what's-her-name."

"What's your interest?" Sam smiled.

"Purely proprietary."

"I'm not sure that answers my question."

"Don't flatter yourself." She picked up the glass of wine and licked the rim with her tongue in a seductive gesture. "I just want to know how much of a fool you're making out of yourself. After all it does reflect on the firm's good will and its reputation."

Given the doubts he was beginning to harbor about Davies and her story, Pat's question was more perceptive than she could have guessed. But Sam had no desire to fuel the fire of opposition.

"What's to say? She seems intelligent. Don't really know too much about her. She lives over in the wine country, Napa County I believe. Apparently she's adopted. Claims to be looking for her natural father who she thought was dead."

Pat toyed with the stem of her glass as her eyes wandered toward the ceiling above Sam's head.

"Why don't we make it easy on ourselves and turn it over to Jake? It'd be worth it. You could get back to work and he could run down the information at half of our hourly rate. We might even make some money on it."

"And I wouldn't have to see Ms. Davies again until I handed her the final report from the investigator."

"Exactly." Pat smiled.

He returned the grin.

"Let me think about it."

"Sure, I wouldn't want to pressure you." Sarcasm dripped from her words.

Sam felt the delicate touch of her high-heeled

instep as she rubbed her foot against his calf under the table and reached for the bottle of wine to refill his glass.

Louis Davies was a distinguished man in his early sixties. The lonely wisps of hair remaining on his head had long since turned white and presented an elegant contrast to the tan furrows of his forehead. Half-frame spectacles drooped near the end of his nose as he scanned the pages of the local newspaper. It was an evening ritual that hadn't changed in twenty years.

The swinging kitchen door pushed open. Marguerite, the family maid, entered the room carrying a steaming plate. She set it on the table in front of the old man as he carefully folded the paper and placed it on the table.

"Tomorrow's going to be busy," said Louis. "I'll be tied up most of the day doing some bottling down in the shed."

The old lady knew what went on in that shed. As Davies grew older he had developed a fondness for tasting the fruits of his harvest. He would sit for hours with Charlie, the old man who supervised the bottling operations. Together they would sample the wines and talk of the old days in the valley, before the roads had become littered with commercial tasting rooms and bed-and-breakfast inns, when the labels had been owned by old families; before the multinationals had moved in, before it was chic to make wine.

"I wonder if you could make me a bag lunch in the morning?"

"Certainly." The maid's voice carried a distinctive accent. Though she had lived in this country for more than thirty years and had taken pains to perfect her English, the Castilian trill could still be heard. Although she and Davies did not get along that well, Marguerite stayed on out of love and loyalty for Dorothy Davies.

"Where's Jennifer tonight?" He looked up at her.

"I'm sure I wouldn't know."

Davies didn't press the issue. He knew that since Jennifer had entered the household more than a year before he sensed friction between the two of them. It was natural that Marguerite would view the younger woman as a threat. Jennifer responded by spending increasing hours away from the house at her office in St. Helena.

"Marguerite, I've been meaning to ask if you could do me a favor." He looked intently at the old woman.

"If I can."

"There are some things belonging to Mrs. Davies upstairs in that old dresser in the closet. I just don't seem to be able to bring myself to go through it and clean it out. It really should be done."

Davies looked down at the table somberly. "I don't want to end up like one of those old farts who turns everything into a miniature museum and lives as if the pages on the calendar are stuck together. I know she's gone, and I can accept that, but I'm having trouble going through her personal belongings. It brings back too many memories. Maybe you could take a look and see what needs to be tossed out and take care of it if you get some time."

"Certainly." Her tone was stiff and formal. "I'll do it tomorrow, first thing."

Though Davies didn't know it; it was a task the old woman relished. That dresser stuffed away in the closet was a part of Dorothy's past, a part that Marguerite had often wondered about, back before Dorothy had become Mrs. Louis Davies. The maid remembered that years before, just after she'd come from Spain under a visa to work for the family, one afternoon she had attempted to return a shawl to the dresser only to be unceremoniously ushered out of the closet by Dorothy and instructed never to go near the old bureau again. In the years after that she had opened its drawers only once and then on express instructions from Dorothy, who lay on her death bed.

Bogardus had no difficulty getting to sleep. Two bottles of wine and relentless lobbying by Pat had given him more than a slight buzz. But after an hour between the sheets his head began to throb with an increasing intensity and he lay in an indecisive slumber, unable to muster the energy to make his way to the bathroom for aspirin. It was nearly two in the morning when his fitful sleep was disturbed by a slight squeaking, a plank of the old hardwood floor in his apartment moaning under the weight of a foot. Sam knew the sound instinctively. Someone was in the apartment with him, and his eyes opened wide in the darkness of his bedroom.

He lay motionless, listening. Again there was a soft squeak, barely discernible. Sam moved slowly under the sheets toward the edge of the bed, away from the bedroom door. His hand reached the top of the nightstand next to the bed. In the dark he felt with his hand down to the drawer and quietly slid it open. Like a blind man he pawed through the contents until his fingers brushed the checkered-wood handle of the .22-caliber Beretta. It took him several seconds to untangle the gun from the cluttered assortment of objects surrounding it.

With the pistol firmly in his hand under the sheets, Bogardus rolled to his right and faced the door. A dim shaft of light shone down the hallway from a street light through the living room window. Sam's eyes fixed on the light and watched. Several seconds passed with nothing. No sound. No movement. Suddenly the shaft of light was broken. Something or someone had moved in the other room. Sam gently threw back the sheet and swung his legs over the edge of the bed.

He stood slowly and tried to get his bearings in the dark room. He was dizzy from too much wine. A cold sweat peppered his forehead. He had never aimed the gun at any living thing before. He couldn't remember if he'd even loaded the pistol after the last cleaning. He felt for the clip in the handle. It was in place, but did it have any bullets in it?

Half naked, in bare feet on the hardwood floor, Bogardus considered his options. He could turn on the light and hold his visitor at pistol point, but with an empty pistol he could get himself killed. He could pull the trigger in the dark room. If it fired would the burglar run, or was he armed and would he return the fire? And what if the pistol reported only the deafening click of an empty chamber? Embarrassing as hell, thought Sam.

He felt for the small button on the side near the handle, the release for the clip. Without thinking to place his hand under the handle, he hit the button and the spring-loaded clip ejected from the handle and bounced on the hardwood floor. Sam was startled by the loud clatter of the metal clip hitting the wood. He moved his foot as if by reflex, kicking the clip out into the hallway.

The noise sent whoever was in the outer room scurrying for cover. Bogardus heard several heavy footsteps and then silence. His mind was racing. The element of surprise was lost. And he had resolved all doubt. The gun in his hand was now worthless. He got down onto his hands and knees and, reaching out, swept the floor as he crawled searching for the clip. He moved through the bedroom door and into the hallway. He covered six or seven feet out into the hall, across the shaft of light, and into the dark shadows beyond when his hand came in contact with a solid object. His heart raced—the clip. But the object didn't move when his hand hit it. It was fixed to the floor. Sam started to move his hand in an upward motion and instantly felt the fabric of a man's pant leg. Before he could move there was a flash of light behind his eyelids, a burning sensation across the top of his head, and a stabbing pain that sent a sharp jolt down his spinal column. He started to rise from his knees and everything went black.

Chapter

3

Nick Jorgensen had been calling Bogardus at his apartment every fifteen minutes since before six o'clock in the morning, but to no avail. Finally at eight he called the law office. Carol answered. She hadn't seen Sam and didn't expect him until later in the morning. Nick left a message and tried the apartment again. There was no answer.

Nick itched to tell Sam what he'd discovered the night before, to read to him from his notebook the scrawled transcription from the Davies parchments. He wondered, in the centuries since Drake's voyage, how many hands had felt the vellum of those pages, how many eyes had passed over the delicate letters formed there— yet failed to fathom the message inscribed.

Two hours later Nick finally abandoned his

efforts to reach Sam and headed for his ten-thirty lecture.

Across the bay in the apartment on Bush Street, Sam Bogardus rolled on the floor in agony. There was an incessant ringing in his ears. His head pulsed with stabbing explosions of pain. The warmth of the early morning sun reached him on the cold hardwood floor where he lay, slowly clearing the fog of unconsciousness. The ringing in his ears came to an abrupt stop. Only then did Sam realize it was the telephone in his living room that produced the ringing, and not the throbbing pain in his head.

He rolled listlessly onto his back and lay for a period propped at an angle against the wall, trying desperately to stop the spinning motion of the room, which appeared to him to be in total disarray, with chairs, tables and sofa floating by in upturned positions and cushions drifting separately in space.

Gradually his vision began to take hold, and the rotation of the room slowed and came to a stop. He lay still on the floor and noticed for the first time that the displacement of the furnishings in the room was no illusion. Chairs were turned over and broken. The sofa lay in the middle of the living room floor on its back, its fabric torn and its stuffed innards strewn in clumps around the room. Nothing remained upright. The stack of law books lay in a tangled pile of pages under the overturned bookcase.

As Sam struggled to his feet he saw the small kitchen through the open pass-through over the sink. Dishes lay broken on the floor, and the drawer of silverware had been pulled from its runner and thrown to the opposite side of the room. Even the carpet that covered the living room floor had not escaped damage. It was ripped and pulled from its tacking strips with a large butcher knife. The knife still lay embedded in the carpet padding.

Sam stumbled to his bedroom and found his bed turned upside down in the middle of the room. The mattress was torn and ripped in several places, its springs and padding protruding from the holes. The nightstand and dresser remained standing upright against the wall, but all of the drawers were pulled and the contents dumped in a pile on top of the upturned mattress.

Making his way to the bathroom Sam fell to his knees in front of the commode, lifted the seat and vomited into the toilet as waves of nausea racked his body. Blood dripped from his head and chin into the toilet. He steadied himself for several minutes over the bowl and then carefully rose to his feet, grasping at the wall for support. Half crawling to the living room Sam negotiated around broken furniture and finally found the wall-mounted telephone near the kitchen. He dialed the office number and Carol answered. Through a fog of slurred speech he tried to relate the events of the previous evening, but his thoughts were confused and his words tangled on his tongue. Finally he gave up and simply told her he was hurt in his apartment and needed help. With that he hung up the phone and slowly slid back onto several sofa cushions that lay behind him on the floor.

He lost all sense of time as he passed into a semiconscious state. He was engulfed by a black void broken only by occasional sounds of voices and glimpses of people—some familiar, some not. Now Pat was leaning over him, the feel of her soft hair on his face, and Carol was hovering, and strangers he could not identify floated over and around him. Sam's body levitated from the floor and was immersed in brilliant flashing lights—white, red and blue—and then nothing.

The office was decorated with an obviously feminine flair. The tapestry print upholstery on the two chairs across from the pedestal desk and the landscape lithographs all reflected the refined taste of Jennifer Davies. The small office jammed between two boutiques in the renovated Victorian building on the main street of St. Helena commanded a view in two directions from the large bay window on the second story.

Jennifer worked with a pen on a yellow pad scratching notes and updating her calendar, which in the last two weeks had become filled with appointments. She'd given up answering her own phone as business prospered and had turned instead to an answering service. What started as a part-time venture had mushroomed in seven months to the point where she seriously considered taking in an associate. She wasn't sure she enjoyed the work, but it did serve to keep her mind off of other things, at least for the moment.

Her concentration was broken by the abrupt ringing of the replica antique French phone on the credenza behind her. It was a private line she'd installed when she opened the office and then quickly bypassed in favor of a two-line business system as things had picked up. It hadn't rung in months.

"Hello."

"It's me." She listened in silence for several seconds.

"Read the letter to me." Jennifer doodled on the pad as she listened. The letters "USN" appeared on the page followed by the name "Jack Caulford" surrounded by curls of ink and ornate arrows.

"What? Read that last item from the list again." Rapidly she scrawled the words:

Four page document stamped The Jade House, Old Chinatown Lane, S.F.

"You're sure the letter was addressed to Dorothy?" There was a pause as she pressed her ear to the receiver and listened.

"No, don't discuss it with him. Put everything in an envelope. I'll call a messenger service and have them stop by and pick it up. I want to look at it today."

She dropped the phone into its cradle and stared out of the window for several minutes. There was a dazed look in her eyes as she picked up her briefcase and walked to the door. As she closed it behind her the taffeta shade on the antique door slapped against the glass panel from the inside, just above the gold-leaf letters reading:

LAW OFFICES

Slowly Bogardus emerged from a deep and restless sleep. His vision, while blurred, focused on the familiar faces that loomed over him. The room was bathed in stark white. A young nurse adjusted a bottle that hung from the side of his bed, and the faces of Pat, Angie, Carol and Nick all smiled down at him.

"Thank God! You're back in the land of the living." Carol's voice was soft and friendly.

"How do you feel?" asked Nick.

"Agh." Sam moved slightly in the bed. "Like a sack of wet shit."

"In most cases looks are deceptive, but in this instance I'd say you're right on." Pat winked at her partner as she spoke from the end of the bed.

Angie shot Paterson a cold stare that on a direct hit would have killed.

"The doc says it took eleven stitches to close that gash on your forehead," said Nick.

Sam reached up with his hand and felt the heavy padding of bandages over his left eye. Even with the thickness of gauze the slight pressure of his finger renewed the searing pain that penetrated to the core of his brain.

Angie Bogardus pushed between Carol and Nick to the side of the bed and took her son's hand. "I told you living alone was no good. Now maybe you'll listen to your mother and move back home with me." The ache in Sam's head became more intense.

"What happened?" asked Pat.

"What do you think happened? He was robbed! Mugged! That's obvious," said Angie. The old lady's open hostility toward Sam's partner was evident in the tone of her voice. "This city is becoming a jungle. People don't know where to turn anymore." Her piercing voice was penetrating Sam's head like an ice pick.

"Please, Mom, a little quieter."

Sam looked over at Pat. "I wish I knew what happened. The last thing I remember I was crawling around on my hands and knees on the floor of my apartment looking for the clip to my gun and then nothing."

"Your gun? Oh my God!" Angie's voice trailed off on an ascending note and her hands went to her mouth.

Sam looked over at Nick and rolled his eyes toward the ceiling. Nick moved to Angie's side. "Here, Mrs. Bogardus, let me help you." Half pulling the old lady, he led her to a chair several feet from the bed.

"Did you see who hit you?" asked Pat.

Sam tried to focus his mind on the events of the previous night—the dark apartment, his clumsy efforts with the pistol—but it was lost in a fog. "No. It was dark as pitch. But I heard him. Woke me out of a sound sleep. I got home last night, I guess it was close to midnight . . ."

"It wasn't last night," said Nick. "You've been out for the better part of two days now. We were beginning to think we'd have to take shifts sitting here, holding your hand."

"Two days? Did he take anything from my apartment?"

Nick shook his head. "By the time he finished with the place there was nothing worth taking."

Sam remembered his brief episode of consciousness, stumbling around in the chaos of his apartment. He had hoped that maybe it was just a bad dream.

"What do you think he was looking for?" Pat swept her hair over one shoulder and sat on the edge of the bed, crossing one leg over the other. Nick's eyes darted to the partially exposed thigh and back to Sam.

"I have no idea. I'll just have to go through everything when I get out of here and see what's missing."

Nick chuckled. "Good luck. That place wasn't exactly a bonded warehouse before it was trashed." He paused momentarily, a dry grin spreading across his face. "But it is a golden opportunity for a crafty lawyer to soak his friendly insurance company."

Angie cast a disapproving eye at Nick. "Sam would never think of such a thing."

"Of course not, Mrs. Bogardus. I should be stricken on the spot." There was a mocking tone of contrition in Nick's voice.

The old lady nodded as if to accept the apology. She picked up Sam's keys from the nightstand next to the bed. "I'll go over to the apartment and clean the place up tomorrow. I'll box everything up for you and call a moving company to take it home. And when you get out of here you can come home too. You should never have left in the first place. I told you that, didn't I?"

Sam knew she was on a roll. To Angie Bogardus redundancy was a virtue to be cultivated and developed. Once an idea had passed her lips it would be repeated in all of its myriad forms as if its echoes somehow lent certitude to the proposition.

He ignored the invitation in hopes that it would be forgotten quickly. But experience told him he was in for an encore just as soon as Angie could usher everybody out of the room. The thought only intensified the pain in his head. Trying to return the conversation to Nick's comment, Sam said: "Who the hell carries apartment insurance? Besides, you're gonna have to stop the lawyer bashing. Pat doesn't like it."

"Some people just have no sense of humor." Angie chimed in from the chair in the corner, seizing the opportunity to take a dig at Pat.

Pat looked at Sam with a pained expression. She rose from the edge of the bed and turned toward the wall. He couldn't catch most of the invective, but the word "bitch" came through distinctly.

A cold stare passed between the two women that did not go unobserved by Bogardus or Carol, who sensed that her services were needed. She whispered into Angie's ear. The older woman rose and followed Carol toward the door. "We'll be back in a couple of minutes," said Carol. "We are going to powder out collective noses."

"Take your time," said Pat. "Some noses are bigger than others." She winked at Carol as the secretary led the old lady from the room.

Nick quickly plopped himself into Angie's abandoned chair and started to tell Sam what he'd discovered two nights before.

With Sam and Pat listening intently, he read from his handwritten notes the interpretation of the four pages of parchment he'd worked out. He explained that from everything he could deduce the parchments were authentic and appeared to be part of Drake's missing journal. Nick carefully studied the two lawyers for expressions of disbelief. So far so good, he thought. It was the next part that strained credulity. He hesitated, uncertain if he should talk about the final five lines on the parchment with Pat present. He still bore the scars of her verbal lashing following the Alleghany fiasco.

"I think the documents could be significant for scholars in pinpointing the location of Nova Albion," said Nick.

Pat looked at him and lifted her eyebrows.

"Probably Marin County," Nick explained. "The place where Drake is reputed to have landed in the summer of 1579."

She nodded soberly, a slight smirk settling on her lips. The two of them were at it again, Jason and his Argonaut in search of the Fleece.

"There is one more thing," said Nick. He took a deep breath. "In translating the documents there is a brief passage near the end." Nick's voice trailed off. "It's really only a partial statement because it ends in mid-sentence.

The rest would be on another page that unfortunately we don't have."

"What is it?" asked Sam.

"I don't know if we should be talking about this here," Nick looked at the open door.

Without hesitation he walked over and looked out into the hall. He then stepped back into the room and closed the door. He paid no attention to the large man in the chauffeur's uniform who mingled with patients several feet away near the nurses' station.

The nurses had all stepped away, and the man peered over the counter at the large chart under the acetate cover on the other side. It showed a schematic of the rooms on the floor. The man's eyes focused on Room 417 and under it the name "Bogardus, S.J."

Pat sat upright on the edge of the bed, disbelief etched in her face. "What are you talking about?" She shot a quick glance at her partner. "You don't believe this nonsense? Some loosely wrapped woman from the limousine set up in the wine country shows up in your office with four pieces of paper containing a scrawl that some Shakespearean actor has to decipher, and you two are ready to throw over your careers and start renting backhoes again."

Sam ignored her. "What do you make of it, Nick?"

"I'll tell you one thing. If those parchments are the real thing they're worth a small fortune. The question is—where's the rest of the journal? If it still exists and we can find it, we'll have conclusive evidence of where Drake landed. From that we should be able to figure out the rest."

"Are you sure your translation is accurate?" asked Sam.

"It's not verbatim. But the message is clear."

"I don't believe this," said Pat in a mocking half-laugh. "Two grown men sitting here engaging in a fantasy. I guess I can understand Sam, he got kicked in the head the other night, but what's your excuse?" Pat's words carried the biting tone of ridicule as she looked Nick squarely in the eye.

"Listen, Sam, I don't need this," Nick bellowed. "If she can't deal with the situation maybe she should find something more profitable to do with her time. Maybe she should trot down to the emergency room and find a new client."

Pat rose from the edge of the bed with fire in her eyes just as a physician in a white smock blew through the door behind them. He was followed closely by a grim-lipped, intense nurse.

"What in the world is going on in here?" said the doctor. "We can hear you people all the way down the hall." He was young and arrogant. Sam guessed he was no more than an intern on his regular rounds, but he wallowed in authority and quickly took the chair on which Nick had been sitting and returned it to the other side of the room.

"This man has suffered a concussion and you people are making enough noise to raise the dead. You're going to have to leave."

Sam ignored the intern and turned to Nick.

"Are the parchments in a safe place?"

"It's taken care of. Don't worry," said Nick. "I have a friend sitting on them for the present, a forensics man who's checking the handwriting for authenticity. I'll know in a day or two if they're real. If so we'd better pool our wits and talk to your client to see if we can find the rest of the journal."

The intern, taking one look at the curvaceous Paterson, had turned his attention to her first and gingerly ushered her from the room, taking several seconds longer than necessary to talk to her in the hallway outside. He returned for Nick, who winked at Sam over his shoulder as he was led from the room.

"See you tomorrow," said Sam.

"We'll see about that," said the doctor.

Sam could only hope that the intern would be as efficient in barring Angie from the room. But somehow he knew it wasn't to be.

The young physician pushed Nick out the door, closing it behind him, and then returned to the bed. He began to probe Sam's bandage with his fingers, lifting the surgical tape that held the gauze to the forehead.

"Ahhh." The movement renewed the piercing pain in Sam's head.

"I'm afraid that you're going to have a scar when this heals, though most of it should be covered by the hairline." The intern spoke in a distracted monotone, a dialect no doubt copied from one of his professors. "We had to shave a small patch of hair for the stitches. It'll grow back in a few weeks. You were damn lucky. Whatever they hit you with actually chipped a small sliver of bone out of your skull. It was a glancing blow. If it'd hit straight on I'm afraid it would have punctured the skull. Suffice it to say you wouldn't be with us today."

The intern's fingers were rough, sending shock waves through Sam's head, intensifying the throbbing ache deep inside. The graphic description of his wound didn't make Sam feel any better, nor did the fact that he narrowly escaped death provide him with any answers as to the identity of his assailant. But he was beginning to understand the motive. Someone else wanted the Davies parchments. But who?

The intern moved away from the bed. "I'll have a nurse replace this bandage with a clean one, but for the moment keep your hands away from the stitches."

Sam had no intention of touching the burning wound. The doctor walked to the end of the bed and lifted the medical chart, making notations.

"How long am I going to be here?" asked Sam.

"That depends on what the neurologist has to say. But I would suspect two or three days minimum." The intern finished his notes and left the room.

Sam stared at the ceiling for several minutes, the throbbing in his head slowly subsiding as he slid off into a restful slumber.

It was nearly three in the afternoon when Jennifer returned to her office. A package in the familiar red, white and blue wrapper of the messenger service had been pushed through the mail slot in the door.

She dropped her briefcase by the desk and carefully opened the package. It was heavy, nearly an inch thick. As the wrapper peeled back the first pieces of paper came into view, a jumble of old magazine and news clippings. The yellowing newsprint on one of the articles carried a banner headline: "GHOST SHIP CRASHES IN DALY CITY." The three-column picture below told the whole story. The gondola of a blimp lay teetering on its engine mounts in the middle of a crowded street draped by the deflated air bag.

Jennifer passed her eyes over the lead paragraph of the story:

SAN FRANCISCO—An antisubmarine blimp from the U.S. Naval Command at Treasure Island crashed on the streets of Daly City yesterday afternoon, narrowly missing several houses and power lines. The blimp, which floated out of control over San Francisco for hours, was unmanned when it came to rest on Bellevue Avenue at 3:52 P.M. There is no word on the fate of the crew.

The story covered two columns, and clippings from another page were stapled to the first. Jennifer read the story carefully and paged through the other items in the stack of papers. A magazine article, dated two weeks after the newspaper clipping, provided more details of the crash. Jennifer's eyes were caught by the caption under the picture with the story:

To date there is no word on the fate of Lieutenant James Spencer and Chief Petty Officer Raymond Slade, the two crew members aboard the ill-fated blimp when it left Treasure Island. Both men were missing from the craft when it came to rest on a city street.

She lifted a pen from the set on her desk and circled the name "Raymond Slade," her eyes narrowing as she isolated it on the page.

She studied the magazine article and other clippings, reading and rereading each. In an outdated style they spawned endless speculation on the fate of the blimp crew. Unnamed sources conjectured that the crew had been captured by a Japanese submarine and carted off to Japan for interrogation in preparation for a major assault on the U.S. mainland.

Other theories included a freak gust of wind that rolled the gondola on its side in midair, throwing the men from the craft into the open sea below. Others hinted at possible foul play—a murder-suicide by one of the crew members. No solid evidence existed for any of the theories advanced in the articles.

Jennifer paged through the papers until she came to a large brown envelope with a navy insignia in the upper left-hand corner. She opened it and found a letter on official military stationery. It was signed by a Captain Jack Caulford and addressed to Dorothy Spencer. The terse sentences of condolence smacked of a routine form letter, the redundant protocol of wartime sympathies. She turned her attention to the list of personal belongings accompanying the letter and quickly found the entry she was looking for—the four pages of parchment with the Chinatown stamp. The pieces were beginning to fit into place.

There was only a fleeting awareness of recrimination as she considered the story she'd told Bogardus, for most of it was true. She had revealed all, except for the death of James Spencer and its sordid circumstances, which, after all, she had yet to confirm. Her eyes returned to the name Raymond Slade, circled on the page of newsprint. She knew that if the lawyer did his job, she would soon resolve the suspicions that had haunted her since childhood.

Chapter

4

Sam slept fitfully through the afternoon and following evening and woke to the sounds of early morning hospital clatter. During the night the needle feeding the I.V. solution into his left arm had been removed. His bladder reminded him that he was still human. Taking the initiative and wishing to avoid a bed pan, Bogardus pushed the covers to one side and slid his legs over the edge of the bed, feeling for the cold, hard linoleum. It was a long way to the floor, and when his feet finally found it Sam discovered that his legs were unsteady. The pain in his head had subsided, but he was dizzy and unsure of himself as he felt his way along the bed toward the bathroom between the two adjoining hospital rooms. By the time he reached the end of the bed Sam was able to walk without clinging to the furniture or the walls, though his body was stiff from nearly three days in bed. He entered the bathroom and felt for the light.

An instant after he threw the large plastic toggle switch the fluorescent tube over the sink flickered and came on. He squinted at the image in the mirror under the bright light. The attack in his apartment had taken its toll. The long narrow stitches in his head, still unbandaged from the intern's inspection of the previous afternoon, ran along his scalp on the left side of his forehead. A small patch of hair no more than half an inch in diameter had been shaved from his already receding hairline. There was a heavy growth of stubble on his face, which provided some color to the sallow complexion and baggy eyes that stared back at him from the mirror.

Sam finished in the bathroom, turned off the light and returned to his bed. He lay awake for several hours and considered the attack in his apartment, which was in ruins with no obvious articles of value taken. It was a second-floor room, not the usual target of an experienced burglar. Entry had to be made through the front door from a common hallway, increasing the risk of observation by others living in the apartment house.

No, Bogardus was certain that it was not a random burglary. The intruder was looking for something specific. There was only one thing it could be—the Davies parchments.

But why, after all of these years, had the documents surfaced, and how did his assailant know that he had them? His analysis kept returning to Jennifer Davies. He remembered the letter he'd dictated to her before leaving his office three days earlier. There was no need to wait now. The attack in his apartment excused the need for discretion. He would call Jennifer at her office, and if there was no answer he would call her at her stepfather's house. She could provide needed information. She could also be in danger.

Sam lay wide awake, his eyes fixed on the ceiling, his mind playing and replaying the events of the past week. Just before eight o'clock an orderly entered the room with a breakfast that could only be characterized as sterile. By eight-thirty he had devoured the shredded wheat, two pieces of buttered toast and juice and had gagged down a half cup of tepid coffee.

It was still early but Sam could not wait any longer. He reached for the telephone next to the bed and dialed the office. He was cut off by an operator who told him he would have to dial nine for an outside line. Sam redialed. He let it ring for several minutes. There was no answer. He hung up and dialed again, a "back-line" number that only he and Pat used. It rang three times and was finally answered. He recognized Pat's voice.

"Hi. Sam here."

"What are you doing calling at this hour? You're supposed to be taking it easy. That doctor read me the riot act yesterday afternoon."

"Yeah, and I'll bet it's an act that usually impresses the young ladies. Next time you see him tell him what you do for a living. The only thing they hate worse than disease is lawyers. Do I have any messages?"

"Nothing that can't wait. Carol and I can handle everything until you're up and around again."

"Fine. I don't think I had any scheduled court appearances until early next week. But I did have quite a bit of paperwork on the desk. Maybe you can take a look and see if anything is pressing."

"I've already taken care of it." There was a cool efficiency in her voice. "I filed the Armadeck articles of incorporation and reserved the corporate name with the Secretary of State in Sacramento. I've sent the articles under a cover letter to the client. I canceled two new client interviews and told them to call you back next week. Oh yes, I also obtained a continuance on the briefing schedule in the Buckster case. Talk about living on the edge. Your reply brief was due today, but I told the clerk you were in the hospital and the other side agreed to an open continuance."

"Carol didn't do any of my dictation, did she?" Sam cut in.

"I don't think so. I'm sure she would have run it by me if she had. She's not in yet, but I'll ask her when I see her this morning."

"There's no need," said Sam. "The only thing on the tape was a letter to Jennifer Davies, and I've decided to give her a call and schedule another meeting rather than write."

"Oh? I thought we were going to get an investigator to chase that one down."

"Yes, but you weren't pressuring, remember."

"Is that what I said?"

"Yeah, that's what you said. I wasn't that

drunk. Listen, do me a favor? Look on Carol's desk and see if you can find the file with Davies's telephone number. There should be one of my business cards inside. She wrote her office number on the other side. I'll also need the residence phone from the file jacket."

Pat whispered profanities under her breath as she left the phone. A few seconds later she returned.

"I have a residence phone, but no business card or office number."

Then Sam remembered. He'd placed the business card with her office number in his wallet. By now it would be locked in the hospital vault, common procedure on the admission of an unconscious patient. They had left only his keys and a small pocket comb, though Sam could see only the comb in the jumble of magazines and other gifts on the nightstand.

"That's okay, give me the home number."

She read as Sam jotted the number on a pad of paper from the nightstand.

"I should be talking to the doctor this morning," said Sam, "and I'm gonna shoot to get out of here tomorrow at the latest if he'll listen. I'd like to leave right now, but I doubt if he'd go for that."

"Take as long as you need. Everything's fine back here. Really."

"Pat, thanks. And say hello to Carol for me. Thank her for the mission of mercy with my mother yesterday. I never knew a ladies room could provide so much relief, particularly to the male of the species."

He hung up and dialed Jennifer Davies home

number. The phone rang several times and was finally answered by a man.

Sam hesitated for an instant, remembering Davies's admonition and her concern for her stepfather. It was too late now.

"Is Jennifer Davies in?"

"Yes, but I don't know if she's available right now. Can I ask who's calling?"

Before Sam could answer he heard a voice from a distance on the other end of the line then a muffled response from the man.

"Sure, I'll hang up down here."

A second later Sam heard Jennifer Davies come on the line.

"Hello, who is this?"

"Sam Bogardus, Ms. Davies."

"What in the world are you calling here for? I told you not to use this number." Sam's placid image of the vulnerable female was shattered. Her voice was aggressive and harsh. "Apparently the attorney-client privilege means absolutely nothing to you." Sam was taken aback by the hostility in her voice. But the events of the past two days had taken precedence over his concerns for confidentiality.

"I had no choice. I'm in the hospital in San Francisco." His tone was stern, not apologetic.

There was a brief silence on the other end of the line. Jennifer stuttered. "What's wrong? What happened?"

"I was attacked in my apartment a couple of nights ago by somebody looking for something." Sam hesitated. "I think they were looking for your parchments."

"The parchments—but why? Are you all right?"

"Except for a sizable knot on my head and a few stitches I'm fine."

"What makes you think anybody would be looking for the parchments?"

"I thought maybe you could tell me."

"What's that supposed to mean?"

"Only that my apartment is in ruins, nothing of any value is missing, it's on the second story, not an easy touch for your run-of-the-mill burglar. And they didn't run when they heard me." Sam thought for a moment. There was something more that he had not told anyone else. He'd only realized it himself at that moment. It was too foolish to put into words. But he'd had a strange feeling that someone followed him from the office that evening and that he was not alone when he'd left for lunch earlier in the day, after his meeting with Jennifer. Suddenly his mind was jarred.

"Oh my God—Nick. He has the parchments."

"What are you talking about?"

"Listen, I can't talk now. I have to see you. We have to talk. Can you meet me here later this morning during visiting hours, say at eleven?"

There was a brief hesitation. "Certainly. I'll be there." Her acceptance was grudging and Sam detected something else in her voice, something he'd not heard before—fear. She took down the directions and the hospital room number and hung up.

Sam immediately dialed Nick's office in Berkeley. The phone rang several times and was answered by a student. Nick hadn't arrived at the department yet and was not scheduled for a class until one that afternoon. Sam left an urgent message to have Nick call him at the hospital as soon as he arrived, then he hung up and dialed information for Nick's home number. Jorgensen used an alias rather than an unlisted number to avoid midnight calls from worried students before examinations. Sam got the number and dialed it, but there was no answer. He hung up the phone and waited for Nick's call, hoping that his worries were unfounded.

After talking to Sam on the phone, Pat had gone to Carol's desk and found the microcassette tape dictated three days earlier. She listened to the letter intended for Jennifer Davies. In it Sam told her of his discoveries at Treasure Island, about the letter from Jack Caulford and the attached list of personal items, including the four pages of parchments with the stamp from the Jade House on Old Chinatown Lane. Hearing the message in Sam's voice, its tone animated, conveying an energy that had been absent from his practice for more than a year, only served to heighten Pat's sense of defeat, the feeling that she was losing him. After their relationship had ended, they managed to save something of themselves in the partnership. But now that too seemed to be evaporating. Pat felt suddenly engulfed by a sense of helplessness, powerless to reverse the course of Sam's drift away from her. Soon there would be nothing left of the love they'd shared.

It was something she'd never confided to another soul, but Susan Paterson had come to regret the career choice she'd made. It wasn't that she didn't enjoy the practice of law; it satisfied her driving ambition and fed her ego. But she wanted it all, and something was missing. She had denied it through her twenties and early thirties. And while she hated the cliche she had to admit that the "biological clock" was catching up with her. In her own way she loved Sam Bogardus more than any other man she'd ever met, and if she didn't move quickly it would be too late for them.

Forty minutes later she stepped off the bus at the corner of Broadway and Old Chinatown Lane and began walking south into the heart of Chinatown. Under her arm she carried a light satchel briefcase and a small handbag.

Though it was not yet ten o'clock, the exotic odors from the multitude of small restaurants that lined the street had already begun to mingle with the fragrance of incense from the curio shops. The narrow streets were crowded with cars weaving their way around the parked trucks unloading their foodstuffs and merchandise at restaurants and small shops. A handful of early morning tourists wandered aimlessly along the sidewalks peering through shop windows. Local residents scurried in and out of stores, making the purchases needed for the day's cooking and housekeeping. Pat never noticed the two men who followed her a half block behind.

She had gone three blocks when she saw a large sign hanging out from a drab, two-story building over the sidewalk across the street that was more of a narrow alley:

THE JADE HOUSE

She wasn't surprised that the shop had remained in business during the thirty years since the war. Businesses in Chinatown were institutions handed down from one generation to the next. The Chinese were the one ethnic community that retained fee simple ownership of the land under their businesses. Developers who coveted the valuable square mile that was Chinatown met their match in the Asian shop owners who could not be enticed to sell for high-rise development. More importantly, their political power was sufficient to thwart urban renewal and other governmental schemes that had been used to dispossess others when their property became too valuable.

Pat crossed the street and entered the shop to the tinkle of the small bell over the door. Inside was a maze of oriental hand-carved furniture, porcelain vases and rows of glass display cases crammed with carved jade figurines and other items of onyx and polished hardwoods. The shabby exterior of the building was in stark contrast to the fine selection of merchandise and furnishings inside. This shop was not for the common tourist, but was one of those places reserved for antique dealers, interior designers and fine jewelers—those who catered to a professional clientele for whom price was no object when it came to that tax-deductible piece of art or antique for the office.

So overwhelmed was she by the quality of the merchandise that for a moment she became distracted from the principal purpose of her trip. She mused through the aisles of furniture, and stopped in front of an ornate cherrywood desk and matching chair, both inlaid with ivory. For a fleeting instant she visualized the pieces in her office. There were no prices listed on any of the items—an ominous sign to the wary shopper.

"May I help you?"

Pat turned to find an attractive Asian woman standing behind her. In her mid-thirties, the clear tan complexion of her face was framed by long, shimmering black hair that flowed over her shoulders. She was striking in a full-length silk dress that clung to the gentle curves of her body.

"I was just admiring the desk set. It's lovely."

"Yes, it is beautiful, isn't it?" The woman spoke flawless English, but then why shouldn't she? The girl was probably third- or fourth-generation San Franciscan.

Yet there was something strange about her. At first Pat couldn't isolate the feature that made the woman's appearance so unique. Then she realized it. Her eyes were not almond but round and gray-green in color. Their shape and hue contrasted sharply with the bronze complexion of the woman's face.

"That desk set was placed on consignment with the shop only last week," said the woman. "If you like I can check our books to see what the owner is asking. I know they are quite anxious to sell it."

"No, I'm sure it's well beyond my budget, at least at present."

The shopkeeper smiled graciously.

"Actually, I'm looking for information on an item sold by your shop sometime ago."

"What item is that?"

"Some pages of rare literature sold back during the war, in the early forties."

The woman smiled. "I'm sure I would know nothing about that. My father owned the shop back then and he has been dead for more than thirty years. What information do you want?"

It was an obvious question, but Pat had not really anticipated it. She wasn't precisely certain what she wanted, except to tell Sam that the parchments delivered by Jennifer Davies were worthless, a cheap fraud. Sam had to know that he was wasting his time, that he should return his attention to more important things—the practice of law and the woman who was his partner.

"Well," Pat stammered, "I wanted to know if perhaps your shop kept records on sales that far back, so that I might be able to trace the authenticity of these documents that have come into the possession of a friend of mine. You see, they bear the stamp of your shop."

The woman looked perplexed. If the records existed at all it would take days poring through dusty files in the basement to locate them. She had better things to do.

"I don't think I can help you." The Asian civility turned brusk.

Pat continued to discuss the matter, oblivious to the presence of a large man who had

entered the shop only seconds behind her. The
man strolled slowly up and down the aisles of
furnishings and studied the glass cases containing jade figurines and other hand-carved
items. He looked out of place in the shop. It
was his clothing as much as his build that
belied his interest as a shopper. The man wore
a uniform of sorts with a visored cap carried
under the crook of his arm.

"I am certain there are no records going back
that far. We would have no reason to keep
them. What exactly are these documents?"

Pat shrugged. She knew that the parchments
were valueless; she was merely humoring her
partner. There was little point in discretion.
But it was embarrassing. When it was all over
she would make Sam pay for putting her
through this.

"According to my friend, they are part of a
journal written by Sir Francis Drake." Pat
laughed. "I know it sounds ridiculous, but you
have to know my friend to understand. I think
he's being taken for a ride by another party
but he won't believe me. Let us just say that
you have an oportunity to save him from a
foolish mistake, that is if you'll take the time
to look. I'd be quite happy to help you"—Pat
hesitated for an instant—"and perhaps even
pay you for your time."

Pat could sense that the shopkeeper was beginning to soften. If she persisted there was a
chance that the woman would at least look for
the records.

The shopkeeper thought for a moment and
finally asked Pat to wait. She walked over to

the big man in the uniform and asked if she could help him. Without looking up the man replied in hushed tones. Pat couldn't hear his words, but a few seconds later the young woman returned.

"If you'll follow me please."

The shopkeeper led Pat through the maze of aisles to the rear of the shop and through a curtain hanging from an arched doorway that passed into a small, private work area. An assortment of hand tools littered a workbench. The wood frame of an antique chair rested on the bench, locked in the embrace of a large clamp.

The two women negotiated the narrow passage between the bench and the wall and arrived at the foot of a stairway. Pat followed the other woman up the steps and lost sight of her in the blanket of darkness that swallowed the two figures as they climbed. Sightlessly she followed the click of the woman's heels on the wooden stairs until, without explanation, they stopped. Suddenly a door at the top of the stairs opened and the stairwell was bathed in bright light. The woman beckoned Pat to follow and led her down a short hall into a living room furnished in oriental antiques. Pat was invited to take a seat and wait, as the other woman disappeared through a door at the opposite end of the room.

Pat sat on a velvet couch and fingered the intricate design of the wood filigree on the headrest. She took in the thick Persian carpet covering the floor in the center of the room and the delicate inlaid writing desk set against the opposite wall.

Like an applicant for employment with second thoughts before an interview, Pat fidgeted with the hem of her skirt and allowed her eyes to wander toward the coffered ceiling of the room.

Several moments later the woman returned, followed by an elderly man. He wore a goatee closely cropped to the chin, and wire-rimmed spectacles. His straight white hair lay like strings of alabaster sculptured by a recent combing. His face was not Asian but Caucasian. As they approached he stepped in front of the woman and extended his hand toward Pat who rose from the couch.

"Hello, I am Phillipe Lamonge, Jeannette's uncle and the owner of this shop. Perhaps I can help you."

He spoke with a strong and unmistakable French accent. Pat looked at the man and the woman standing next to him and saw a distinct family resemblance. The curiosity registered in her eyes and the Frenchman laughed.

"Yes, Jeannette is my niece. She is the daughter of my brother and his wife, who was Chinese, from Canton. Jeannette was born here in San Francisco." He looked at his niece. "You should go down and attend to the shop." She gave a gentle smile and nod to Pat, whose eyes followed the young woman as she disappeared down the hallway.

"Jeannette says you seek information. Perhaps I can help you."

"I hope so." Pat summoned her most sober tone, aware that in the business ethos of Chinatown women are not often accepted on anything approaching equal terms. "I am trying to save a very close friend from the embarrassment of dealing in what are obviously fraudulent documents."

In the reflex of his generation he searched her fingers for a ring and found none. "What makes you think they are fraudulent, Mademoiselle?"

The quick reply coupled with the Frenchman's icy stare left little doubt that he had been rapidly briefed on the Drake parchments by his niece.

"Well—the party offering them to my friend claims they're an original portion of a journal written by Francis Drake—the English pirate."

The Frenchman's face registered no expression. He stared in cold silence at Pat.

"Perhaps you don't understand. These documents bore the stamp of your shop. I assume at one time they belonged to the owner of this shop."

"Oh, I understand. But I cannot help you."

"Why not?"

"Mademoiselle, let me give you some advice. First, while it is true, as they say, that things are not always what they seem, after nearly seventy years I have quelled my cynicism sufficiently to learn that deception in life is the exception rather than the rule. And second"—the Frenchman paused as if to emphasize the point—"you should stop asking questions of strangers regarding these papers."

Pat was stunned by the rebuke. She was prepared for disinterest. She even anticipated the refusal of any assistance as a result of inconvenience or other proprietary concerns of the shop owner. But she was totally unprepared for this—the casual confirmation that the documents might be authentic.

"I don't understand. Why won't you help me?"

"Because I will not," said the Frenchman. "And do yourself a favor. Use some discretion in choosing with whom you speak concerning this matter."

Before Pat could respond she found herself ushered toward the hall and was staring down the flight of stairs as the Frenchman held the door open.

"Good day, Mademoiselle."

Pat descended the stairs and walked briskly through the work area and out through the shop, still trying to unravel the message conveyed in the old man's words. She was unused to such cavalier treatment by those of the opposite gender. His brusk manner had been a distraction, and she was angry with herself for not being more insistent.

As she swung the shop door closed behind her the man in the chauffeur's uniform suddenly lost interest in the bone china he'd been studying for several minutes and headed for the door.

Upstairs, the Frenchman walked back to his study, his movements slow as if in a trance. He opened the hand-carved doors on a large walnut hutch and from a drawer in the upper right-hand corner he removed an envelope yellowed and musty with age. He made no effort to open the envelope or remove its contents. He had long since committed the terse lines of the single-page document to memory. Instead he stood motionless, his cold gaze fixed on the printed lettering in the corner of the envelope— and the black swastika embossed above the words.

The pointed end of the pick reached the apex of its arc and started down toward the head. Each degree of movement was frozen in time like a frame of action illuminated by a strobe light. Alternating blackness one moment then stark white light glinting off the razor-sharp point, the pick inched toward his skull. Powerful hands and forearms roped by sinuous muscles propelled the piercing metal toward his head. Every effort at movement was thwarted. His body was locked in place by some invisible force. Straining to see past the bloody point of the pick, Sam searched the darkness for the face of his assailant. As he fought to focus, an unseen power rocked his body and a voice penetrated the silence of his assault.

"Mr. Bogardus. Wake up."

His body stirred and his eyes blinked open. He was staring into the face of Jennifer Davies. He fought to control the panic evident in his expression.

"I'm sorry. I must have been dreaming."

"More like a nightmare I'd say."

Sam felt beads of perspiration trickle down his face. The sheets of the hospital bed were soaked with the sweat of his turbulent slumber.

"I must have dozed off. Couldn't sleep much

last night." He struggled to pull one of the pillows toward the top of the bed and searched for the hand controls to raise the head. "Too many things to think about, I guess. Please have a seat." Sam gestured toward the chair next to the bed and Jennifer settled into it. He patted the perspiration from his face with a corner of the top sheet.

"What's this all about? On the phone you said whoever did this to you was looking for the parchments."

"I can't tell you everything right now. I don't have any hard evidence, but I believe the pages are authentic and could be quite valuable."

He studied her expression. It was stonelike. Her eyes drifted toward the unbandaged wound on his forehead and the naked stitches.

"What do you mean, authentic?"

"A friend of mine, who must for the moment remain nameless but who is expert in such matters, has managed to translate the text of the parchments. He believes they are part of a larger book or journal that is of significant historic interest." Sam hesitated for a moment, unsure whether to reveal the rest of Nick's translation. He opted on the side of caution. He wasn't entirely certain why he couldn't bring himself to disclose the information.

"I should know if the parchments are authentic within a day or so. For the moment they are in a safe place."

"That's very interesting," said Jennifer. Her voice was detached, her mind distracted. "But what have you discovered concerning my father?"

116

"I've asked my secretary to make a check for certain records that may give us a lead."

"I see. Can I make a couple of suggestions?"

"Certainly."

"According to everything I know there were two men on board that blimp the day it crashed. One was presumably my father, James Spencer. The other was a man by the name of Raymond Slade. I'd like to find out a little more about Mr. Slade. Before I came to see you I tried to do a little checking on my own with the D.M.V. Thought I might get lucky and turn up a set of latents or a picture on Slade. I struck out."

A pained expression came over Sam's face. "Why did you hire me, Ms. Davies?"

"What do you mean?"

"Well it sounds like you know precisely what you're looking for—and how to go about it."

She laughed nervously. "Not at all. You can see how much success I had."

It was a shallow attempt at feigned ignorance.

"I just wanted to find out a little about Slade in hopes that it might lead to my father."

"Like what?"

"Like where he came from. How long he'd served on the crew with my father. Perhaps you can find a picture of him?"

"I already have."

"What! Where is it?"

"Relax. I have it. It's locked away in your file back at the office." He wasn't about to tell her he'd jobbed it from the navy.

Sam had had Jake search microfilm records in the morgues of the two remaining newspapers for stories of the Ghost Blimp in hopes that he would turn up a picture of James Spencer. None had ever been published. All he had was the single picture of Slade.

"What did he look like?"

"Hell, I don't know. Average looking. I thought we were looking for your father. Why this sudden interest in Raymond Slade?"

"Like I said, maybe if we find out what happened to Slade we'll find out what happened to James Spencer."

"I've got a question for you."

She looked at him, her face a picture of innocence.

"How do you explain the fact that the parchments were sent to your mother under cover of a letter from the navy in 1942?"

"What?" Jennifer Davies might make a top-flight fashion model, but she would never make it in the movies. Her expression was as transparent as cheesecloth. She already knew about the letter, but Sam played it out.

"There's a letter in the navy files that itemizes the four pages of parchment as part of James Spencer's personal belongings after the crash."

"Then they did belong to my father."

"They belonged to James Spencer and they were sent to Dorothy Spencer. That was your mother's former name, wasn't it, before she met your stepfather?"

"I don't know. I mean yes. That's my mother. But I don't know how the parchments could have been sent to her and later to me. It doesn't make any sense."

"My thoughts exactly. Your mother never talked to you about the parchments?"

"Never."

"Who else knows about them?"

"Me, you, whoever you've spoken to concerning them."

"Your stepfather doesn't know about them?"

"No."

Sam sensed that with mention of her stepfather he had touched a raw nerve. Was it simply her concern for him, the loving interest of a child to protect a parent in their old age? Or was there something more?

"Tell me a little about your stepfather. What's he like?"

"There's not much to tell. He's old. His life's wrapped up mostly in the vineyard and his wines."

Jennifer was clearly uncomfortable as she discussed Louis Davies. Sam's mind wandered, paying little attention to her words. Instead he watched her easy gestures and listened to the melodic tone of her voice. There was something exotic about the woman—her dark hair framing the angular features of her face, her voice easy and soothing.

There was an obvious look of compassion in her eyes whenever her sight wandered to the wound on Sam's head.

Bogardus had dealt with enough con artists during his days with the public defender's office that he was not easily beguiled. And he knew that he was not getting the whole story, not yet. His daydream was broken by Jennifer's silent stare as she finished the brief description of her stepfather.

"You have no idea who might have sent the parchments to you?"

"None."

"Yes, well that will unfortunately remain a mystery for the time being," said Sam. "I think that you are probably safe, at least for the present. Whoever attacked me must have been fairly certain that I had the parchments. That should leave you in the clear . . ."

Jennifer broke in. "Listen I don't want anyone else to get hurt. It's not worth it. Perhaps we should go to the police with the parchments and let them take care of it."

"That would be a mistake," said Sam. "We don't know enough yet. The police aren't going to invest resources investigating a hunch. There's no solid evidence linking my assault with the parchments. No. Trust me. Let's wait a little while and get more information before we go to the cops."

Jennifer shrugged her shoulders. "If you think so . . ."

"I do. For the moment, don't take any chances. If anyone contacts you regarding the parchments, call me immediately. Do you understand?"

"Yes."

"And I don't want you doing any checking on your own. Wait until I get out of here and I'll take care of that."

She nodded.

Sam looked at the woman. She was vulnerable and appealing. A part of him wanted to help her, to answer all of her questions, to assure her that she was safe, that he would protect her, and most of all that he would find her father, if he lived. But there was a schism to Jennifer Davies, a hard businesslike facet to her personality. It had been present on the telephone that morning when he'd called her stepfather's house and again moments earlier when she'd suggested that he find more information on Raymond Slade. Bogardus could not be certain at any moment which of the two women he was dealing with—the hapless client who required his assistance or the stiff pursuer who seemed to follow some private agenda.

"I'll call you in the morning to see how you're feeling." And then she was gone.

Sam lay motionless for several moments, then reached for the telephone. He dialed the office and Carol answered.

"Hi. Sam here."

"How are you feeling?"

"Better today. Maybe by tmorrow I'll be out of this place and back to work."

"There's no rush."

"Yeah, Pat said the same thing. It's good to know that I'm so vital to the enterprise. Listen, there's something I want you to do. Do you still have that lawyer's directory there on your desk?"

"Yes."

"There's a name I want you to check."

"What county?"

Sam considered for a moment. "Let's start with Napa."

Pat had gone nearly four blocks after leaving the Jade House and was nearing an alley a half block from her bus stop when a distinguished man carrying an ornate walking cane approached in the opposite direction. The man asked Pat for directions to the Civic Center. Dressed in a knee-length camel hair coat and a felt homburg, the man appeared as an elegant anachronism, an image from a Movietone newsreel—the caricature of a diplomat in prewar Europe. It took her several seconds to get her bearings and point the man toward City Hall. He trudged off in that direction.

Consequently she was surprised twenty minutes later when she saw him again near the end of the block as she waited for her bus. But this time he was not alone. Standing with him near a long, dark stretch limousine was the chauffeur she had seen in the Jade House. She watched the two from the corner of her eye as she milled with the other commuters around the Muni signpost. The studied gaze of the two men never left her. A chill began to settle down Pat's spine.

As she boarded the bus she quickly handed her pass to the driver and headed for the rear bench seat. From the large rear window Pat saw the two men enter the limousine and pull out behind the Muni as it headed down Broadway. Her mind scrambled for an escape. But there was no reason to panic. She was surrounded by people on a crowded bus. At each stop more passengers boarded. By the time the bus crossed Columbus Avenue the only available space was standing room in the center aisle.

Casually Pat leaned over and whispered to

the old lady seated next to her. She was dressed in a frayed orange coat that covered her nearly to her feet and on her head was a print bandanna. The woman looked up at Pat as if the younger woman was demented. Pat leaned over and whispered a second time. This time the woman hesitated for a moment then shrugged and nodded in agreement.

Two stops later four passengers disembarked from the bus: two businessmen carrying briefcases, a jogger of dubious gender and an old woman, her head shrouded in a print scarf and her bulky frame bundled against the chill of the October afternoon by a long orange coat. The passengers scuttled off in opposite directions to the roar of diesel fumes as the bus pulled away from the curb, followed closely by a large dark limousine. The old lady stood motionless for several seconds as the vehicles moved out of sight, then straightened her posture and hailed a cab. Gingerly Pat disappeared into its back seat.

A smile spread across her lips. "Screw with Susan Paterson will you?"

She looked through the windshield at the bus caught in traffic near the Embarcadero and directed the cab driver to turn left at the next intersection. The limo and its passengers would plant themselves at the law office once they discovered they'd lost her. Pat would head for her apartment and call Carol from there. A quick visit to the limousine by Jake Carns and some of his friends would put an end to it. If the chauffeur and his fare were involved in Sam's assault, the cops could have what was left when Jake and his friends were finished. It wouldn't be much.

Pat pulled the briefcase and her purse from under the old lady's coat, lazily dangled one well-shaped thigh over the other and wallowed in smug indifference in the rear of the cab as it headed around the block and west on Broadway, through the tunnel toward the Sunset District and her apartment. Ten minutes later she stepped from the cab and crossed the street a half block from the shingle-sided, condo-converted apartment she called home. She was taking no chances, and dressed in the long coat and bandanna she shuffled along the sidewalk, the only telltale sign of youth the two-inch spike heels on her shoes. She ambled down the rear alley and into the building through the laundry room and went up the stairs. Pulling the scarf from her head and shedding the coat, she moved briskly down the corridor, inserted the key in the lock and entered her apartment. She leaned heavily against the inside of the door, closing it and fastening the security chain, and stood for several seconds breathing a deep sigh of relief as her hand felt for the switch plate and turned on the lights in the entry hall.

The searing pain prevented even the slightest gasp of sound from exiting her lips. Slowly, in quarter steps, she turned to face away from the sealed door, her eyes open, her vision already beginning to fade. For a fleeting instant she caught sight of her assailant's face, then her downward gaze fixed on the comic glimpse of a single yellow glove, its turned cuff mired in blood. She staggered backward against the door, impaling the object deeper into her vital organs, the mind-piercing agony causing the lids to drop over her eyes. She stood transfixed against the door. Warm blood trickled down onto her legs as her feet slid on the tiled entry, her buttocks coming to rest on the floor, her back propped against the door.

A single word passed her parted lips as the air was purged from her lungs . . . "Why?"

The word seemed surreal. The unendurable torment of the wound had already begun the process of separating mind from body. It was as if she was a dispassionate observer hovering somewhere over the scene, watching as the life-blood coursed from the body of another. The mind-altering agony began to subside. She made no effort to breathe, knowing it was futile, and she was slowly engulfed by a warm dark void as her mind danced in the playgrounds of her childhood. She saw herself cradled in the serene comfort of her mother's lap, and somewhere between visions of childhood bliss Susan Paterson slipped quietly from existence.

Chapter

5

Anthony Murray was perhaps the foremost archivist in the western United States. He was a man on constant call to some of the largest and most prestigious museums in the world. He was skilled not only in the preservation of ancient documents and books but was called upon regularly to authenticate them.

Murray worked in a small laboratory carved out of the Archeology Department on the Berkeley campus, in a maze of tables, test-tubes, Bunsen burners and various optical devices ranging from microscopes to a large round magnifying glass set into the center of a fluorescent lamp.

It was mid-afternoon. Murray and Nick Jorgensen had been at it all day, examining the Davies parchments.

Earlier in the day Murray had dispatched

Nick to the campus library for two books on Drake that contained clear reproductions of authenticated correspondence known to have been written in the explorer's hand. They worked in complete silence, Nick searching the texts for any mention of the journal and Murray inspecting the parchments and comparing the lettering with large-scale reproductions in books spread on the table.

Murray ran his right hand through strands of his thinning white hair. His features were fine and his complexion fair and soft from years of constant work in the dim recesses of museums and laboratories. He wore a white smock, and his fingers moved with the deftness of a surgeon as he returned them to the calipers to measure the dimensions of letters on the pages. He passed a magnifying glass from the library books to the words on the parchments, seeking points of similarity and difference.

It was ten minutes to three when Murray stood upright over the table, arched his back with a mild sigh and turned off the lamp that had illuminated the parchments. Nick, who by this time was snoring quietly in the corner with his shoes off and feet propped on top of the desk, sensed the movement in the room and woke with a start. He rubbed the sleep from his eyes and focused on Murray, who was in the shadows across the room.

"Well, what do you think?" asked Nick.

Murray unhooked a pair of wire-rimmed spectacles from behind his ears, lifted them from the bridge of his nose and walked slowly around the table toward Nick.

"They're either the best forgeries I've ever seen or they're authentic," said Murray. "If you were asking my professional opinion . . ."

"I am," said Nick.

"I think they're genuine." Murray wrinkled the skin on the bridge of his nose. "Listen, no two people form their letters or angle the script of their writing in precisely the same way. Moreover, an individual's hand changes little between early maturity and old age. No. The handwriting from Drake's known correspondence and the words on those parchments are peas from the same pod.

"And it's not easy stuff to forge," he added. "The script on those pages is very different from the writing we might scratch out today." His voice became high and resonant. Murray rubbed the bridge of his nose and replaced his glasses. "The handwriting of the cultured nobility of Europe before the use of typewritten words took on a uniformity of style that hasn't been seen for several centuries."

Murray stretched out his arms high over his head and arched his back to relieve the tension brought on by hours bending over the table. He reached for one of the library books, looked at the index and thumbed the pages, searching as he spoke. "Until the early 1500s a form of script known as 'secretary hand' was commonly used by men of learning in most of Europe. But in the late 1400s and early 1500s a variation on this form imported from Italy crept into the writing of most of Europe including England." Murray walked from the table to the desk where Nick was seated. He placed the open book on the desk and spun it around to face Nick, open to the page that Murray had found.

"Here's an excellent example of this so-called secretary-Italic hand." Murray pointed to an enlarged photographic reproduction of a portion of a letter in elegant uniform script. To Nick's eye the letters on the page appeared to have been printed. The only telltale signs of a human hand were minute wisps of ink around the tops of certain of the letters where the fibers of the quill pen left their traces.

"Elizabeth learned this style from her penmanship tutor, Roger Ascram, as a young girl," said Murray. "There was a great deal of peer pressure on the nobility to follow her lead. By the late 1500s virtually everyone who was anyone in England had mastered the Italic form and used it in any formal writings—including Drake."

"So?" Nick looked up at Murray.

"Well, it's not an easy form to mimic, as you can imagine. Hell, most of these people spent thousands of hours during their early childhood learning the form. It was ground into them. There probably aren't a half dozen people alive today who could copy the form without detection for a paragraph, let alone four pages the length of those parchments.

"And if that's not enough, come over here." Murray led Nick around to the other side of the table. He turned on an overhead lamp and pulled the book closer to the parchments that were spread on the table.

"Here, look at this." Murray pointed to a

large photograph of a handwritten letter reproduced in its entirety.

"This is a letter that Drake sent to the Earl of Essex several years before his voyage around the world. It's in the Italic form, but you can see that it was probably written quickly and without the usual pen lifts you'd see in a more scholarly writing. You'd expect the classic letters of the Italic form to be vertical and well-rounded in shape. But when written rapidly and without pen lifts between the words, it has a tendency to develop a slant and rounded arches in some of the letters. See the 'h' and the 'm'?" Murray pointed to the letters. "They developed points and more angular lines like these.

"This is the sign of more casual prose, a rapid business letter," continued Murray. Without turning from Nick he reached up and pulled a single page of the parchment to the edge of the table under the light. "Like these letters here." Murray pointed to several h's, m's and n's. The similarity between the letters in the book and those on the parchment was striking even to Nick's untrained eye.

"If you want my opinion," said Murray, "the two documents were written by the same man."

"Can you be absolutely certain?"

"Absolutely, without any doubt? No. But if a client were asking for my expert opinion regarding the provenance of these documents, I'd have to say they were written by Drake." He paused briefly. "There is a way to be certain, however."

"What's that?" asked Nick.

"A form of radiocarbon dating of the ink and paper."

"But that would require destruction of some of the parchment, wouldn't it?"

"Two years ago I'd have said yes. But there's a fellow up at U.C. Davis who's developed a new method of carbon dating using a cyclotron —a particle accelerator. As I understand it the process provides a reading of the molecular structure of the paper and ink and requires only microscopic scrapings from the article itself."

"Has it ever been used on ancient writings?"

"The project at Davis has been well-guarded, but news leaked out a few months back that they'd somehow gotten their hands on a Gutenberg Bible and were busy breaking down the structure of the ink. Modern manufacturers have never been able to replicate the ink used by Gutenberg. It contained some of the finest pigments ever put on paper, but the chemical formula was lost with the printer. It's believed that companies would pay a fortune for the original formula. Why not let me send some scrapings up to Davis and let them take a crack at it? Hell, they'll probably be able to tell you not only the age and composition, but whose greasy fingers have touched them during the past three hundred years."

Ten minutes later Murray had taken minute scrapings from each of the four parchments and deposited them in separate vials, labeling each. He carefully rolled the parchments and placed them in a long tube, capping the end with a plastic disk.

"You really shouldn't fold these," he said. "The parchment will take some abuse, but after a while it will begin to crack along the fold."

Nick took the tube from Murray. "For the time being I think we should keep this to ourselves." He remembered the look on the face of Jasper Holmes when the Englishman finally realized the parchments were part of the Drake journal, and he shuddered.

"Thanks, Tony. I think you've given us the confirmation we needed. I suppose I'll hear from you on the radiocarbon process?"

Murray nodded.

Nick turned and headed for the door.

Murray could sense some urgency in his friend's behavior.

He also knew from the state of the parchments that they had not come from any modern museum. They had been folded rather than kept flat and had not been treated with the usual preservatives employed by professional museum curators.

"Nick," Murray looked up from the table. "I haven't asked you where you got those parchments. I'm not sure I want to know. You realize how valuable they are?"

"Yeah, I think so," said Nick.

"Take care of them. And Nick, take care of yourself."

Nick nodded and headed out the door into the late afternoon sunshine.

The gnarled cypress trees, dwarfed and twisted by the eternal Pacific winds, offered an eerie backdrop to the small group gathered on the expansive lawn under a gray and dreary sky. An Episcopal minister, his shoulders draped by a canonical stole, spoke in hushed tones over the coffin that was layered in wilted carnations and long-stemmed roses.

"Grant, we beseech thee O Lord, that the soul of your departed servant, Susan Elizabeth Paterson, be committed to thy tender love and mercy, that she who has passed out of this life may by thine intercession and the intercession of all thy saints come into the fellowship of eternal bliss . . ."

Roses. They were always her favorite. A dozen, in a box a yard long, was her reparation of choice whenever they fought.

The patented eulogy droned on as Sam's mind replayed the events of the preceding two days, the late afternoon telephone call at the hospital from Carol, the uncontrolled sobbing and finally the resonant voice of Jake Carns on the line. When Carns's voice faltered and hesitated, Bogardus steeled himself for the worst. Instinctively he thought of his mother—Angie's gone. But when Jake finally told him, "It's Pat. She's been murdered," Sam's body went limp in the bed, his arm with the telephone receiver dropped onto the sheet and for more than a minute Jake's words spilled like milk from a pail into empty air.

An anonymous telephone call to the police—a woman had heard peculiar noises coming from the apartment. Moments later a tall man, his face lost in shadows, left by the front entrance. The woman, refusing to give her name, hung up, and the police rushed to the scene. In the chaos that erupted after the cops called the law office, Jake had gone to Pat's and identified the body. Sam pried the details from a reluctant Carns two hours later when they met at the hospital. Bogardus struggled with the grotesque mental image of Pat sitting with her legs sprawled on the floor, her upper torso pitched forward like a rag doll in the center of the entry hall. An arc of coagulated blood curved from the corpse to the door.

The minister closed his book and removed the vestment from his shoulders, moving toward an elderly woman with her face draped by a black veil. For all that they had nearly become related by marriage, Sam had only met Karen Paterson, Pat's mother, one time. It had not been an auspicious introduction. She was strait-laced, of conservative New England stock, and had worn her resentment on her sleeve when she discovered that her daughter and Sam shared living quarters.

Bogardus took one step toward the woman then stopped as her head and shoulders convulsed in a spasm of grief and the sounds of sobbing were heard over the hushed tones of the minister. He would convey his condolences later, perhaps in writing.

"The cops have any leads yet?" Jake Carns had wandered through the dispersing mourners and come up behind Sam who turned and shook his head in reply.

"Well, you can't expect miracles in two days. But you can be sure they'll push hard." Jake was right. A prominent attorney, an attractive woman killed in her own apartment—the story was still front-page news two days after the crime.

Carns was a burly man with gentle eyes and a large head that seemed to explode from powerful shoulders. His hands and fingers had the size and delicacy of softball gloves. They had made a lasting impression on Sam's chin the first time the two men had met nearly a decade earlier. An interest in competitive boxing, a holdover from Sam's days in college, had moved him in the direction of amateur bouts in his late twenties. Though Carns was ten inches taller and seventy-five pounds heavier, Bogardus had challenged him to a sparring match. Jake had wanted to decline, but the boisterous Bogardus left him no honorable avenue of retreat in the crowded gym. Carns decked him two rounds in, but later formed a quick affection for the young lawyer.

Since that first meeting the law firm had hired Jake on numerous occasions to serve process in divorce cases on husbands whose interests ran toward punching their wives. Pat once remarked that the appearance by Carns at counsel's table in court was worth more than any temporary restraining order a judge could issue. "It's magic, something macho that only men could understand," she'd said. "Court-ordered contempt or a ten-day jail term are concepts of unfathomable abstraction to the average wife-beater. But one icy stare from the intimidating Carns and they know they'll get the shit knocked out of 'em." It was vintage

Susan Paterson. No sugar-coating. God, how he would miss her.

After his father died Sam always took relief in the fact that life permitted one consolation. The faculty of human memory allowed him to replay the best moments of their lives together in the privacy of his own thoughts. While it carried some consolation for the loss, at times it also tortured him with images of lost opportunity, moments of love and affection unspoken and now gone forever. Mercifully there had been but few of these between father and son. But he could not say the same for his relationship with Pat. It had been littered with wasted possibilities, squandered moments of intimacy when his pride had prevented him from telling her how he really felt. Those moments now echoed like hoofbeats as they stampeded through the emptiness left by her death.

"How you holdin' up?" Sam felt the weight of one of Carns's meaty hands on his shoulder. A bulge appeared under the arm of Jake's oversized sport coat. Sarn knew it was not a wallet.

"Good." He lied quickly before his voice cracked.

"Is there anything I can do?"

"No." Sam smiled, a kind of signal that released Carns from any further obligation, and he wandered off in the direction of Nick Jorgensen. He'd already asked too much of Carns. With news of Pat's death he'd gotten Jake to deliver clothes to the hospital and together the two men had walked out without the formality of a physician's release. Sam would have to go back to the hospital and face the music in the afternoon, for the hospital safe still held the wallet, watch and keys that he hadn't seen since that first day when he came to in the hospital bed. Jake had provided nearly round-the-clock security for him and Nick, both of whom were camped in a basement apartment at Angie's house in the Colma section of Daly City. If there had been any question in his mind, Pat's murder had resolved it. Someone was after the Davies parchments, someone who was prepared to kill for them. Sam was taking no further chances. He'd shut down the law office, canceled all client interviews, sent Carol home and had all business phone calls forwarded to a friend's office. Two other lawyers, friends from law school, were handling the firm's workload.

In the two days since the murder Sam spent hours reconstructing the events leading up to Pat's death. Carol had confirmed that on the day of the murder Pat had left the office headed for Chinatown and the Jade House. Less than three hours later she was dead in her apartment.

The limousine carrying the immediate family pulled away from the curb and wound its way through the labyrinth of weed-cracked cemetery roads toward the highway, followed closely by several other cars.

Beyond the coffin Sam heard the sobbing of a woman and turned to see Angie, her head bobbing on Carol's shoulder as she cried. It was a shameless display of hypocrisy that passed within seconds. The old lady managed to summon complete composure by the time she and Carol reached the car twenty feet away.

Angie was wearing a sheer black gown that Sam was certain he'd seen her wear to bed on occasion. In her hair was a single silk flower, its petals frayed around the edges. In the last year his mother's attire had run the gamut from bag lady to the height of 1930s fashion. Looking at her Sam couldn't decide if she was ready to retire for the night or head for a cocktail soiree at the Cotton Club.

"I've got cold meats, French bread and hot coffee at the house. You are coming over?" Angie's inquiring expression passed from Carol to Jake and then to Nick. Sam couldn't help but think that Pat, if she were looking on from some exalted vantage point, would be amused by the fact that Angie would use her funeral as an occasion to entertain.

The invitation was accepted by a series of silent nods and shrugs as Sam and Nick headed for Sam's car parked several hundred feet down the road.

"Samuel Bogardus?" A thin man with a toothpick dangling from the corner of his mouth leaned his butt against the fender of Sam's Porsche.

Bogardus looked at him but didn't reply.

"Are you Sam Bogardus?"

"That depends who's asking."

The man reached into the inside pocket of his jacket and removed a small leather sheath. He flipped the cover to reveal a gold shield. "Sergeant Mayhew, S.F.P.D. We'd like to talk to you about your partner's murder."

Sam wondered what had taken them so long.

Then it struck him. Since his unannounced departure from the hospital he'd not been easy to find. It must have looked suspicious as hell, though hospital records would establish that he was flat on his back in the bed at the time of the murder. "Anything specific?"

"Just background questions—for the time being."

"I'm afraid I'm tied up right now."

"How about tomorrow?"

"I've got a meeting."

"Break it."

There was only the briefest hesitation on Sam's part. His experience with the public defender had taught him to force the state to commit early. Besides, if the focus of suspicion had already centered on him they'd have hauled him in without asking. "I can't. I'm afraid I'm not available until the day after."

Mayhew removed the toothpick from his mouth and seized the only initiative left. "Ten o'clock, sharp. Central Homicide Division, downtown."

Bogardus smiled as the detective turned and sauntered away in the direction of his visibly unmarked car. A patch of oil-laden road grime stained the right cheek of his tan slacks where they'd rested against Sam's fender.

"What was that all about?" Nick looked at the lawyer.

"That, my friend, was the ghost of bureaucratic bullshit, wearing clothes and walking upright. I'm sure you've seen him before."

"Ah yes," said Nick. "Distant cousin to the Dean of the Academic Senate."

*   *   *

The table was small, tucked in a back corner of the restaurant in an area of semidarkness pierced only by the occasional flicker of candlelight. The two men sat nursing drinks that the waitress had just delivered.

"They have the parchments." The tall, thin man looked intently across the table at his friend. "Maybe you can tell me how they got them?"

"How should I know?"

"She gave them to the lawyer."

"How do you know that?"

"Let's just say that I know."

"What have you done?" The shorter man's eyes burned with fire as he stared across the table. He knew something was wrong when he'd read about the murder in the paper.

"Well you weren't going to do anything. So I had to." The tall man spoke imperiously. "Let's just say I got a little information. And that's not all. They've traced the things back to the Jade House."

"What?"

"Ah," he paused. "So now I have your attention. How long do you think it will be before they find out about the committee?"

"Come on, they're not that resourceful. They're a pack of amateurs."

"So were we—when we started."

He couldn't deny it. It was true. One would not have thought it possible. In a fleeting instant he had made a decision that had changed him forever. It could not have been more life-altering if he'd consumed Jekyll's potion.

The conversation was interrupted by a slender waitress approaching with two salads. She placed the dishes in front of the men and leaned over the table with a foot-long pepper mill. The taller man dismissed her with an impatient wave of the back of his hand. The movement revealed the shiny brass handle of a walking cane resting on the arm of his chair. Fashioned in the form of an eagle's head, the sharply down-turned bill scratched into the oak armrest of the chair as the man lowered his hand. The waitress shot him a contemptuous look, turned and walked briskly from the table.

"Listen," said the shorter man. He played nervously with his fork. "There's no way they could find the members of the committee. The man took care of that years ago. I'm telling you there's nothing to worry about. Besides, even assuming they could find some of the committee, there's no way they could tie us in."

"You're sure of that? Well I'm not. Not sure enough to gamble a long prison sentence or worse."

The shorter man nibbled on bits of lettuce, avoiding any commitment as he listened.

"It's too late for half measures. We have to get those parchments and deal with whoever has seen them. We've got to talk to the girl and find out who knows about them."

"No!" The shorter man dropped his fork with the lettuce on it and looked across the table. "Listen to me. I don't know if you had anything to do with the murder of that lawyer or not. I don't want to know. But if you so much as contact Jennifer Davies the cops will be the least of your worries."

"What are you going to do—turn me in? You think they're going to let you walk away?" While the question was rhetorical, he would have been wise to press for an answer. What he did not know was that his companion no longer cared.

"Who was with you?" The shorter man answered the question with a question.

"When?"

"When you did the lawyer."

"You have too vivid an imagination. All I did was poke around a little trying to get the parchments back. Without those papers they have no hard evidence. You were a damn fool to leave them in that locker the day of the crash. If they hadn't been found and recorded by the navy we wouldn't be in this mess now."

"Have it your way. Who was with you when you went poking around, as you say?"

"My man, the big one."

"And you'll trust your life and liberty to the likes of that? How long do you think before he fingers you if they pick him up? He's not exactly inconspicuous. What if somebody saw him?"

"There was nothing to see." The denial lacked conviction. The taller man sat silently, his eyes staring off into the distance past his companion. The question had hit its mark. The tall, slender man laid down his fork and sat back, placing his hands on the armrests of his chair. He fingered the pick-like point of the brass beak on the handle of his cane and considered the loyalty quotient of his chauffeur.

Her mind was absorbed in the transcript of a deposition, a minor fender-bender that was headed for arbitration, when her office door opened. Jennifer swung around casually and lowered the bound transcript, peering over the top of the document.

Centered in the open doorway, an obscure smile on his face, stood Sam Bogardus.

"Hello, Counselor."

Jennifer was too stunned to reply. While her face remained unyielding, the surprise was evident in her eyes as Bogardus locked onto them like a polygrapher studying his instrument for telltale signs of deception.

"What are you doing here?" She finally managed to speak.

"I might ask you the same thing. You never bothered to mention the fact that you were a lawyer."

"You never asked."

"Guess I didn't, did I."

Something had caught in his subconscious the morning when he called her at her stepfather's house from the hospital. It wasn't just her sudden change of manner, the hostility in her voice, but something more, her mastery of legal jargon. What was it she'd said? "The attorney-client privilege means nothing ..." They were not the words of a layman. Clients might talk of confidentiality, or privacy, but not "the attorney-client privilege." And later that same day in the hospital when she'd goaded him to find a set of fingerprints for Raymond Slade, she'd slipped again—she'd asked him to find a set of "latents." He hadn't heard the term since leaving the public defender's office. It was only a hunch, but while he waited on the telephone for Carol to check Parker's Lawyers Directory he knew in his bones that she would find a listing in Napa County—that is, if Jennifer Davies was her real name. At least she hadn't lied about that.

"Now do you want to tell me what it's all about?"

"What do you mean?"

"I mean the hustle. The cock-and-bull story about wanting to search for adoption records."

Any lawyer who'd ever handled an adoption knew that under the circumstances of the Davies case adoption records would offer no information she didn't already have or that wasn't available from other, easier sources. James Spencer was presumed dead. Neither his identity nor his consent to the adoption were at issue. Sam had never bought the lame excuse that she was interested in finding his place of birth. That could have been obtained in a dozen ways—from Social Security, from records that her mother must surely have kept somewhere.

"This time I want the truth."

"I'm sorry you feel that way. Perhaps I should find someone else."

"Two days ago that would have been fine, but it seems I'm working for myself now."

"For yourself?"

"Yeah. I'm looking for somebody—somebody who killed a friend."

Except for the most calloused and hardened, news of death, particularly violent death, is mirrored in subtle degrees of shock and compassion in the eyes. In the case of Jennifer Davies the expression of alarm was almost instantly followed by an acceptance, as if the event somehow confirmed her most deep-seated fears.

"Oh, no."

"Yes. Her name was Susan Paterson. And now you're going to help me find out who killed her."

"Me? How can I help?"

"By telling me everything you know."

There was a deep sigh. "You're right, I didn't come to you for information concerning the adoption. I came to you because I thought you would be able to trace the parchments and because I thought you would take a real interest in my father and how he died. I didn't tell you the truth the day we talked in your office."

"The truth about what?"

"You asked me how I met your mother."

"I remember."

"I told you I hadn't, that my aunt knew her."

"Yes."

"That wasn't exactly true. I mean I do have an aunt and she does work with your mother at the hospital auxiliary. But I have met your mother. One time. It was in the hospital cafeteria over coffee. After my aunt told me about you, I wanted to check some things before I called your office. The following week I went to the hospital and talked with your mother."

"What did you want to know?"

"My aunt had mentioned that you were tired of your practice, she said your mother had told her about some of your outside interests, a treasure-hunting escapade somewhere in the mountains. She also said that you had a driving curiosity concerning local historic events in the city."

"What did that have to do with anything?"

"I wanted to be sure that you would take the case and that you would pursue it. Your mother confirmed that her family was familiar with the crash of the navy blimp. That they actually remembered seeing it back during the war."

Suddenly it all made sense. Angie had told her about Nick and their exploits in Alleghany. In a talkative mood she probably had mentioned that her son nearly quit law school to pursue an advanced degree in history. Jennifer knew that Sam would have available all of the technical resources to trace the parchments and a burning curiosity concerning the blimp and the fate of its crew.

An unquenchable rage began to settle over Bogardus. Without knowing it Angie had set in motion the events that would lead to Pat's murder. Her idle gossip had cost him the love of his life. But he saved the greatest portion of reproach for himself. Pat had asked him to hire an investigator for the Davies case. He had refused. He insisted on pursuing the leads himself over her repeated objections. If he'd only listened she would not have gone to Chinatown, she would still be with him. A rancorous virus flooded his mind and inflamed his being. The familiar yearning for revenge, so long absent, returned to invade his soul.

"The parchments and the note came in the mail just as I told you. You have to believe me. I have no idea who sent them or why."

"Why didn't you chase down the leads yourself?"

"I couldn't."

"Why not?"

"My stepfather. It would kill him if he thought I was searching for my father. As far as he's concerned he's the only father I ever had. Each time I raise the question of James Spencer it's like tearing one more thread in the fabric that bound us together as a family. I had to distance myself from the search, if only to protect him."

There was a brief pause, as if she'd stopped in mid-sentence.

"There is one other thing. Something I never told you, because I have no hard evidence."

Sam said nothing.

"I think that whoever wrote that note on the parchments was lying. I think my father is dead."

"Why do you say that?"

"It's just a feeling, call it intuition, call it what you like. But I think he was killed by the other man on that blimp—the man named Raymond Slade."

Ninety minutes later Sam was back in the apartment in Angie's basement.

"Looks like we'll be bunking together for a while, so we'd better make the best of it." Sam looked at Nick's mournful expression as the big man tested the lifeless mattress on the bottom bunk of what was obviously a child-sized bed. Finding it unsatisfactory, he moved to the cot that was in the other corner.

The basement was spacious and surprisingly warm given the damp overcast that shrouded the yard. A large gravity furnace fed the floor above with heat through a maze of ducts strapped to the exposed floor joists. To the left was a small kitchen, bath and shower. The three men stood in the room that had been Sam's playroom as a child and his bedroom during high school. Deeper into the basement beyond the furnace was an immense workroom with a bench that swept across the entire front of the house. It was covered with an array of old tools, most of which had long since become antiques, once belonging to Sam's grandfather, one of two blacksmiths in old Colma. A large window over the workbench looked out on the street in front of the house. To the left of the workbench through a grid of lattice was the garage—enough space for a single car sealed behind an overhead garage door that opened onto the street.

"You don't expect us to sleep here? I have classes to make. I can't stay away from my place forever." While he complained Nick's eyes were glued to Jake Carns. He'd seen his share of big men before, but none with the grace exhibited by Carns. Nick was mesmerized by Jake's combination of grace and raw power, with the facial profile that belonged on a Greek statue, crooked nose and all. There was nothing ponderous or awkward about the man. Jake moved with the poise and carriage one would expect from a professional dancer rather than a prizefighter. Realizing that he was staring, Nick diverted his eyes from Carns.

"All the comforts of home," he said, "and none of the worries." There was a mocking laugh. "Come on, Sam, how long do we stay?"

"As long as you can put up with my mother," said Sam, with a half smile.

"If I remember right I can deal with her cooking for some time." Nick remembered the sumptuous suppers put on by the old lady during Sam's college days, when he would be invited over for Sunday dinner. He looked at Jake. "Do you like to eat?" He laughed at his own superfluous question.

Jake cracked a grudging grin and nodded.

"Leave it to you to find the silver lining," said Sam. "Where are the parchments?"

"There on the table." Nick pointed to the cylindrical tube capped at each end that lay in the center of the small pine table.

"Murray says they're for real. He took some scrapings and sent them off to a lab for final analysis, but I think at this point the results will be anticlimactic."

"At least Pat didn't die for some fake." Sam's words dripped with sarcasm.

Nick made no comment. There was nothing he could say that would ease the pain Sam was feeling.

Bogardus picked up a book lying opened face down on the table next to the parchments: *The Marine Corps Manual of Hand-to-Hand Com-*

bat. A folded piece of tissue marked a page. He'd purchased the volume in the seventh grade after seeing a war movie featuring Audie Murphy. It had gathered dust ever since on a forgotten shelf in his room.

"Is there any coffee in this place? For two days now that damn hospital has kept me on decaf. My head's killing me. Must be going through withdrawal." He slapped the book shut and reshelved it.

Nick rummaged through the cabinets over the sink and came up with a jar of instant coffee and three mugs. He filled the small metal teapot on the stove and turned the gas on high under the burner.

Sam's mind was lost in the logistics of the next several days. "Tomorrow we pay a little visit to Chinatown and that shop Pat visited before she was killed. Then we'll split up and chase down some loose leads."

Sam looked at Jake Carns. "How would you like to go sleuthing?"

Jake said nothing but nodded. Sam knew that Carns was a man of few words, as Pat's killer would discover if Jake ever got his massive hands around the man's throat. For the time being Bogardus would try to keep things tactful and Carns under control.

"I'd like to get some information on a guy by the name of George Johnson." Jake had taken a small note pad and pencil from his coat pocket and was writing. "The guy shows an address on Olstead Street in San Francisco. Don't waste your time on it, the place doesn't exist. My guess is that D.M.V. might show a name and address on Olstead with a post office box for receipt of mail. It's just a hunch, but if he owns a car, he would have to be able to get vehicle registration mailed to an actual address. If you find it, stake out the box for a while and tail whoever shows up. And be careful. Unless I miss my bet this guy's connected with Pat's death. Don't do anything to him." Sam waited for some reply. Carns was noncommittal. "Jake." Finally, Carns nodded his assent.

"Nick, I've got something else for you. I have an old friend down in the D.A.'s office. We used to trade favors when I was with the P.D. He won't give us a copy of the police report in Pat's case, but he might feed us a few details out of the file. I'm going to call him and tell him that you'll be down to talk to him later today. Get whatever you can."

"Like what?"

"Use your imagination."

Bogardus sighed, knowing now it was his turn. "Guess I'm gonna have to go downtown and talk to the cops."

"What are you gonna tell 'em?" asked Nick.

"As little as possible, at least for the moment. We don't really know anything."

"Ain't that the truth."

"You're not gonna let 'em in on the parchments?"

"No. There's no hard evidence that the parchments have anything to do with Pat's murder or the assault in my apartment."

Nick arched an eyebrow.

"You've got to let me handle this my way."

"I didn't say anything." Nick raised his hands

as if to ward off the accusation. He knew it was useless to try to convince Sam to go to the police with the parchments. Besides, Nick had his own reasons for not wanting to go to the cops. He wasn't driven by revenge for Pat's death the way Sam was. Instead he'd become seduced by his own curiosity. It had infected him from the moment that Tony Murray had pronounced the parchments real. He was now convinced that the four soiled and worn pages sealed in the tube from Murray's lab contained the threads of a message that if fully revealed would unlock the legacy of Drake's voyage to the Americas.

Chapter

6

Jake Carns and Nick passed the time in a small coffee shop around the corner from the Jade House and took turns watching the street for Sam. Shortly before noon Nick saw the familiar blue Porsche pull up at the curb a half block away. He signaled to Jake and the two men walked briskly down the street toward Bogardus.

The color in Sam's face was slowly returning after his bout of the hospital, and some of the spring was back in his walk.

"Anything going on across the street?" Sam nodded in the direction of the Jade House.

"People keep going in and out, mostly shoppers from what I can see. Nothing unusual," said Jake.

Sam looked down the street for Nick's beat-up Ford but didn't see it. "Where are you parked?"

"I'm in a garage about two blocks down."

"Good." Sam reached into his pocket. "Here's the key to my car." The key was a spare in mint condition, as he'd not yet found his key ring. "I want you to stay in the car and watch the front of the shop. If we're not out in half an hour you call the cops and tell 'em to get over here on the double."

"Hey, wait a second. I want to know what's going on first." Nick had no intention of sitting quietly in the car and playing lookout until he had some answers.

"Your guess is as good as mine. All I know is that shop over there is connected to the parchments and it was the last place Pat visited before she was murdered. I figure that if push comes to shove Jake's gonna be more use to me in there than you."

Nick wasn't about to argue the point. "Okay, but we talk when you come out."

"If I come out." Sam winked at his bearded friend. "Don't worry. We'll be all right."

Nick headed for the car. Sam and Jake turned and walked across the street and down the narrow alley that was Chinatown Lane, disappearing through the front door of the Jade House.

There were several customers browsing in the well-lit shop. Sam and Jake didn't waste time but headed for the clerk's counter at the back of the store. A young woman with long, sleek black hair and a shapely figure stood at the cash register, bagging a purchase for an elderly man. Sam studied the woman as he waited in line behind the customer. She was attractive—Eurasian, he guessed.

She handed the bag to the customer and looked up at Sam. "May I help you?"

"I'm trying to get some information about a friend who was in your shop a few days ago. A young woman, well-dressed, very pretty, about your height, with long dark hair."

"Sir, we deal with many customers. I can't remember all of them."

"You would remember her. She was probably asking questions concerning some parchments bearing the stamp of your shop, papers that may have belonged to the owner or may have been held on consignment by him many years ago."

He could have stopped with the word "parchments." The recognition registered on her face as he uttered it.

"You talked to her?"

"Yes, I wait on all of the customers in the shop."

"What did she want?" asked Sam.

The woman hesitated. "As you say, she asked some questions about some papers. I couldn't help her, and she left."

"She didn't speak to anyone else while she was here?"

"No." The woman broke contact with Sam's gaze immediately, unable to keep the lie out of her eyes.

"That woman was my law partner. She's been murdered, and I'd like to know who she talked to when she came in here and what she talked about. Now you can either tell me or you can tell the police."

With the mention of murder the woman's expression of commercial complacency vanished. She hesitated for a moment and then spoke. "Please wait here."

She left the counter and disappeared behind a curtain into a work area behind the shop. She was gone for several minutes. When she reappeared she was followed by an elderly man. He was frail and stooped, with a distinct hunch to his shoulders, but he was dressed elegantly in a blue sport coat and open-collared shirt.

"These are the men I was telling you about." The woman gestured toward Sam. "I'm sorry, sir, I don't know your name."

"Bogardus—Sam Bogardus."

"Mr. Bogardus, this is my uncle, Phillipe Lamonge, the owner of the shop." The woman looked toward the older man. "I believe he can help you."

The face of the old man took on a perplexed and anxious look. He lifted his downcast eyes toward Sam and then to his niece, but said nothing.

"You've got to talk to someone," she said. "This has gone on too long, for too many years. If not these men, then the police."

"No, we can't go to the police," said the old man. The strength and vigor of his voice startled Sam. It was in stark contrast to the stooped posture and aged face. He spoke with a distinct French accent.

"Uncle, please." The woman looked at him. The plaintive tone of her voice matched the appeal in her eyes.

The old man looked up into Sam's face, hesitated for a moment and then said, "Monsieur, come with me."

Sam and Jake followed the old man through the curtain into the back of the shop and up the flight of stairs to the living quarters on the second floor. Jake kept his right hand jammed into his coat pocket, clutching the handle of a nine-millimeter Browning automatic pistol. He began to relax as the old man led them into an ornately furnished study and beckoned them to take a seat on a couch behind an intricately carved coffee table. Sam sat on the couch. Jake declined the invitation and instead took a seat on a large stuffed ottoman in the corner facing the door. He rested his back against the wall.

"I don't know where to begin," said the Frenchman. "Such a tangled web. So many mistakes. So many years of hiding the truth. I'm not sure what the truth is anymore."

Sam could sense a cathartic release in the man's voice, the kind of peace that comes only with the unburdening of some forbidden secret.

"What can you tell us about the parchments?" asked Sam.

The Frenchman moved aimlessly into the center of the room and looked down at Sam seated on the couch. "Those cursed pieces of paper. Monsieur, I tell you those pages have the blood of centuries on them. It would be better for you if you had never seen them." He paused thoughtfully. "Certainly better for your partner. You should burn them now before they bring more misery."

"Why? What do you know about them?"

"It's not what I know, Monsieur, but what

others know that you must fear if you have those pages."

Sam was tired of receiving riddles in reply to his questions.

He spoke sharply. "Did you talk to Susan Paterson when she came here the other day?"

"I didn't know her name. Yes, I spoke to her briefly."

"What did you tell her?"

"I warned her as I am warning you now."

Sam's impatience was beginning to show, but he restrained himself, afraid to upset the old man and lose perhaps his only clue to Pat's murder.

Lamonge wrung his hands and moved slowly to the chair behind the small writing table that was stacked high with loose papers and ledgers.

"What you see here in this shop is all that remains of a lifetime of work—all that remains of three lives. My brother and his wife are now dead because of those papers. I live in constant fear that their daughter, Jeannette, may be in jeopardy because of what I know. Are you sure you want to know, Monsieur?"

"Yes." Sam was insistent.

Resignation registered on the Frenchman's face. "Very well, my friend, then you shall know. The papers—or parchments as you call them— came into our possession in 1942, but to understand our position at the time you have to go back before that, to the fall of 1941. The country was just emerging from the deepest days of the Depression, though we didn't know it at the time. We had struggled for nearly five years, saving every penny to start this business, and we got it off the ground literally 'on a hope and a prayer,' as you say. Things were not easy and business was not good. Survival meant doing some things that we were not proud of—but they were necessary."

Lamonge shook his head slowly as if perplexed, his eyes cast down at the tangle of papers on the desk before him. "We were not always engaged in the ordinary retail business you see today. We would probably not have survived except that America entered the war in December of that year and rationing followed shortly after that. My brother used contacts that he had developed on the docks to obtain items that were scarce—sacks of sugar, flour, rice, automobile tires. People are funny." The Frenchman smiled. "They would kill for a set of automobile tires. There was a time when the storeroom of the shop and much of this second level were full to the ceiling with such things. As you can imagine, we had a brisk trade."

The man pushed several of the loose papers on the desk to one side and lit a small desk lamp to brighten the corner of the room where he sat. He looked at Jake, whose eyes followed every movement of his hands upon the desk.

"Our business brought us into contact with many different kinds of people—buyers and sellers. They were not always people that you wanted to deal with, but as I said it was necessary. One of these people was a military man, a member of your navy. He had access to depots and stores of military supplies, and for the right price anything was available to him.

"He called himself Jones. Of course, we all knew that wasn't his real name. He was stationed at Treasure Island and he routinely brought us sacks of sugar and sides of beef. We paid him well.

"He was a tall man, slender. I only dealt with him three times, when my brother was not in the shop. But I will never forget him. Even before my brother's death I thought there was something sinister about this sailor. If I'd only known then . . ."

The Frenchman reached behind him and uncorked a bottle of distilled water, pouring himself a small glass, then raising the bottle toward Sam and Jake.

Sam shook his head. "Please continue."

"Our dealings with this man went on for several months. After a time he approached my brother and said that he had other things that he wanted us to take on consignment, as he called it—objects of art that he would place with us to hold and to sell, but only to one particular buyer. He offered us a great deal of money for these transactions." The Frenchman shrugged his shoulders. "So we closed our eyes, asked no questions and entered the art business. It seemed harmless enough—vases, small statuary, and over a period of time the trade with this man Jones grew to include oil paintings, many of them never unwrapped, just delivered to the shop, held for a brief period of time and ultimately collected by this special buyer."

"Where did the items come from?"

"We weren't stupid, Monsieur. I think we

tried not to know, but we knew." He nodded his head slowly. "They were stolen. Oh, we had no hard evidence, but we knew it nonetheless." The Frenchman sipped from his glass and cleared his throat.

"All that this sailor ever demanded was that we prepare a sales slip for the purchase, so that it would appear legitimate. He told my brother that if anyone ever asked, all he had to say was that he purchased the items from a stranger whom he had never seen before."

"In any event the buying and selling of these art objects continued for several months. By that time we had been paid a great deal of money. The sailor referred to it as our commissions."

Jake had been listening quietly in the corner and finally relaxed, placing the automatic pistol in his pocket on safety and removing his hand from the coat to cross his arms.

"If I remember, it was June, or early July, that my brother told me he had received an envelope from this man Jones. My brother said that he had been instructed to give the sealed envelope to whoever delivered the next shipment of art."

"Then this Jones didn't deliver the art to the shop himself?" asked Sam.

"Oh, no. He took no risks himself. He never brought anything to the shop. He dignified his activities by calling himself a broker. No, the packages for his client were always delivered by another man, a large man dressed in crude working clothes. My brother recognized him from the docks. He was a sailor on a coastal freighter. This man always followed the same routine. He would appear at the shop with a package—sometimes large, sometimes small. He would say that it was 'a delivery for the committee.' "

"The committee?" asked Sam.

"Yes."

"What was the committee?"

"I will get to that."

Sam was in no position to make demands.

"Anyway, my brother had been given a sealed envelope to deliver. But for some reason, I don't know why, he became suspicious. Maybe it was something that the sailor, this Jones, had said or the way he said it—anyway, my brother steamed open the envelope. Inside was a single typed page—a schedule of merchant shipping then in port, the cargoes carried by some of the ships, projected departure times and their destinations. Both my brother and I knew that there could be only one purpose for such a list. Black market activities were one thing, espionage was another. We wanted no part of it.

"When the man from the freighter arrived my brother took possession of a large sealed envelope. He gave the man the agreed upon money. But he did not deliver the envelope containing the shipping schedule. My brother was scared. He'd had enough and he wanted, how do you say, to make an end of it."

"Your brother kept the package given to him by the courier?"

"Yes. And as you may have guessed by now, that packet contained the four pages, or parchments as you call them. But it also contained something more."

The old man rose from his chair and walked slowly to a large ornate chest against the wall behind his writing table. Jake followed his movements closely and placed his hand back into his coat pocket.

Lamonge opened a drawer and removed a worn leather folder and returned to his desk. Jake relaxed.

"I discovered this after my brother's death."

The old man pulled a single sheaf of letter-size paper from the folder. It was tattered on the edges and showed signs of wear along the folds.

"This letter was my brother's insurance policy, against the sailor and the committee," said the Frenchman. "Or so he thought." He slid the paper across the desk toward Sam, who held it under the light of the desk lamp. The single sheet carried the Nazi Swastika on its letterhead and words in German beneath the symbol, but the text was written in perfect English. It was dated April 30, 1942, and was simply addressed to "The Committee":

Gentlemen:

We have made a truly rare find as a result of our occupation of the Lowlands and France. Enclosed you will find sample pages of a manuscript written in the hand of the English explorer Francis Drake. It is part of a complete journal written by Drake and detailing the exploits of his voyage around the world (1577–79).

My principal has instructed me to make these pages of the Journal available to you so that you might satisfy yourselves as to the authenticity of the document. The entire journal is yours for the sum of one million dollars, American. Surely your benefactor will pay twice that for so rare a find. This offer will remain open for thirty days. Please make contact in the usual fashion.

Regards,

Reinhard Heydrich
Oberfurer S.D.

Sam wondered if the German who'd written the letter had bothered to translate the journal or the four pages of parchment. He guessed that he had not, or the price would surely have been much higher. Bogardus took a pen from the desk and made several notes on a pad that lay in front of him, tore off the slip of paper from the pad and placed it in his shirt pocket. He handed the letter back to the Frenchman, who replaced it carefully in the folder.

"The day after my brother received the parchments the courier returned to the shop. This time he came with the sailor Jones. They threatened my brother and made a shambles of the shop. They demanded the parchments and the shipping schedule that Jones had left with him. In fear for his life he surrendered both."

"What about the letter from the German? Didn't they ask for that?"

"No. Either they forgot about it or didn't notice that it was missing. Jones refused to return the deposit of five thousand dollars that we had advanced to the courier when he made the delivery. For two weeks my brother tried to locate him at Treasure Island to retrieve his money. Finally, about a week later, he saw the man Jones on the base and went to his superior. Of course he couldn't tell the officer about the black market activities, so he told him that this man—Slade was his real name—had stolen the parchments."

"What did you say his name was?"

"Raymond Slade," said the old man.

Sam leaned back in the chair and remembered the photo he had taken from the files of the naval board of inquiry—the photograph of Raymond Slade, the other missing crewman who had disappeared with James Spencer from the Ghost Blimp. He sat trancelike, listening to the old man describe how his brother and sister-in-law met their fate just days after their last encounter with Slade—the victims of a fiery single-car crash on a lonely stretch of highway in the delta. "Only the grace of God caused them to leave Jeannette with me that day," said the Frenchman.

"You never went to the police with any of this?"

"How could I? I had no evidence that this man Slade was responsible for their deaths. Besides, I couldn't implicate him without revealing my own black market activities. And I had the responsibility of raising my niece."

"Did you ever see this man Slade again?"

"No! I was too frightened. For weeks after my brother and Ming Lee were killed we stayed in the shop, afraid to go out."

"You don't have any idea what 'the Committee' is?"

There was a slight hesitation from the Frenchman. Sam was prepared to press the point when Lamonge turned and walked to the hutch again. He produced a small black book, a telephone directory, opened it and handed it to Sam. On the open page halfway down were the words "Committee of Acquisition," and next to them was a name—"Arthur Symington"—and what appeared to be a phone number, a two-letter prefix followed by only four digits. Sam knew the number would no longer be in use.

"Who's Arthur Symington?"

"He was the contact, the buyer for the committee. My brother identified him as the man who came to the shop to buy the art objects given to us by Slade."

"Do you know if he's still alive?"

"No," said Lamonge, "but I know that the number in that book used to ring at the offices of a newspaper here in San Francisco."

"A newspaper?"

"I called the number after I found the book and it rang at the switchboard of the newspaper."

"Which one?" asked Sam.

"I'm not sure after all of these years, but it was one of the big ones. It's still in business."

That narrowed the field to two.

"How much of this did you tell to my partner?"

The Frenchman looked down at the desk in front of him. "That is what is so tragic, Monsieur. I told her nothing. I merely warned her to be more discreet in her dealings concerning the parchments." He looked sheepishly at the lawyer. "And I asked her to leave. She seemed surprised, almost offended, when I confirmed that the documents might be genuine."

So Pat had been killed for nothing. Something deep within Bogardus began to boil. It was an alien sensation, something primordial, an urge the lawyer did not fully comprehend. Revenge was certainly not contrary to his nature, but in the past his vendettas had always been bridled by the rules of society. His mind had been conditioned to weigh precise legal principles, to balance human behavior against the black-letter precepts of the law. The sum of the equation was called "justice." This was something new. It found its roots in his very nature and flowed from instinct, not intellect. For now he knew that if given the opportunity, he would kill to avenge Pat's murder.

Lieutenant George Fletcher had the round red face of an aging cherub, resting over a fleshy double chin. He could no longer remember the last time he was able to fasten the collar on his assortment of button-down dress shirts. The knot on his narrow tie routinely rested on the ledge beneath his chest that was formed by a protruding stomach. What hair remained on his head was found in thin gray wisps that Fletcher preened with a pocket comb, more from habit than necessity. Two years from retirement, he was hopelessly out of shape and out of date, but his superiors knew that notwithstanding his appearance and lack of conditioning, George Fletcher was the best detective in the Central Homicide Division.

There was fog and a light drizzle outside his fifth-floor office window as Fletcher read the preliminary lab report and the field notes of the detectives who had responded to the scene. The murder had been planned and carefully executed. Not the work of a panic-stricken burglar caught in the act of rifling the woman's apartment. Nothing of value appeared to be missing. There were no signs of forced entry and no fingerprints other than the victim's. The only peculiarity were minute traces of sodium hydroxide (lye), and charred animal fat. It had been found on both the inside and outside knobs to the front door and the door to the victim's bedroom.

Fletcher ran through the obvious theories. A jealous lover. A client dissatisfied with the results of a criminal case. A disgruntled spouse in a domestic case. Perhaps the killer's way of lodging a consumer complaint. Or maybe Susan Paterson was a direct player in the booming cocaine market. There'd been enough drug-related executions in the city over the last five years to keep the medical examiners working in shifts trying to keep up.

The victim had no criminal record. A rap sheet from the Department of Justice in Sacramento turned up no arrests or convictions. A check with the F.B.I. netted similar results. There were no drugs found in her apartment.

And something else didn't fit. Why would a woman who was wearing a three-hundred-dollar silk Halston dress be carrying a frayed knee-length coat and scarf that looked like the discards from a rummage sale? Or did they belong to someone else, perhaps the killer?

Fletcher closed the legal-size manila folder containing the reports and pictures of the scene and pressed the button on his intercom.

"Jack, bring him in."

Fletcher leaned back and listened as the springs of his ancient oak swivel desk chair issued their familiar discordant groan under the weight of his body. The door to the office opened slowly, and in walked a gaunt man in his late thirties. A small bandage covered part of his forehead on the left side. His eyes had the haunted look of one who'd just lost a friend or loved one to violence. Fletcher had become all too familiar with that vacant, soulful expression during his years working the homicide beat.

Trailing along behind, Sergeant Jack Mayhew slipped inside the small office and closed the door. He played Jeff to Fletcher's Mutt. Tall and gangly, with a toothpick dangling from his lip, Mayhew dropped one cheek of his skinny behind onto the credenza in the corner and folded his arms, flashing alternate blank stares at the lawyer and the detective.

Fletcher didn't move from his chair. Instead he coldly studied the man's face. There was something familiar about the tall, lean lawyer. Fletcher had seen Sam Bogardus before, but couldn't place where.

"Mr. Bogardus, please take a seat. I'm Lieutenant Fletcher. I've been assigned to investigate the death of your partner Susan Paterson."

Sam settled onto the hard seat of the oak chair across the desk from the detective.

"She was a beautiful woman."

"In more ways than one," said Sam.

Fletcher looked hard at Bogardus and caught a brief hint of recognition in the lawyer's eyes. "Have we met before? You look familiar."

Sam hesitated. To lie or not—for an instant the option flashed through his brain. "You have a good memory, Lieutenant. It was the Henderson case—some years back—the indigent charged with assault with a deadly weapon down in the Tenderloin. I was with the public defender at the time and I believe you were assigned to the case after the booking."

"Ah yes," Fletcher's recognition of the lawyer was followed by instant regret. "I remember. Your man beat the rap."

"He didn't beat anything. The arresting officers should have been commended for their honesty to the court."

Fletcher wasn't sure if Sam was turning the sword in the wound or trying to offer him a sugar pill."

"Honesty, yes. That's what it must have been." Fletcher's voice was thick with sarcasm. He remembered all too well the courtroom scene. The two young officers at the preliminary hearing, each sequestered outside of the courtroom while the other was examined by Bogardus. The defendant was a two-time loser. A conviction for assault with a deadly weapon, given his priors, could carry a twelve-year term. There'd been no time for the D.A. to prep the two officers before the appearance.

Fletcher remembered clearly Bogardus's attack.

"Officer, can you tell me how long you talked to the defendant before you took his confession?"

"Oh. Three, four minutes."

"What did you talk about?"

"I don't remember."

"Was the defendant coherent?"

"Yes."

"Had he been drinking?"

"I doubt if there's been a time in the last twenty years when he hasn't been. But if you're asking me if he was drunk, the answer's no." The cop exuded the confidence of a veteran, having sealed off an obvious avenue of escape.

"Do you remember hearing the defendant make the confession?"

"Oh, absolutely. Took every word of it in my notebook."

Bogardus turned and picked up a file folder from the counsel table. "I notice from the arrest file there's no 637?"

"Sir?"

"Form 637. The department's Miranda sheet. It's customary for the arresting officer to complete one when he files his report."

The cold look of panic in the officer's eyes was undisguised. "I guess we forgot to fill one out."

"Who Mirandized the defendant, Officer?"

There was a brief hesitation. "I'm sure my pertner did." The cop waited for the obvious "Did you see your partner Mirandize him?" But the young officer would never know if he lacked the rectitude or possessed the boldness to lie under oath. The question was not asked. Instead the nail was driven into the coffin: "You did not personally Mirandize the defendant?"

"No." As the word left his lips the cop suddenly realized why his partner had not come out of the courtroom following his testimony. Bogardus had not wanted the two to talk, even for an instant. Their fate was sealed. Under oath each had taken the same avenue of escape. Both had eluded the responsibility by assuming the other had performed the ministerial act of reading the defendant his rights.

"That's all from this witness, Your Honor."

Less than a minute later came the motion to suppress from Bogardus. The defendant's confession, the only evidence linking him to the crime, was excluded and the case was dismissed.

Fletcher donned a sardonic smile. "The last time I looked those two were still juggling nightsticks down in the Tenderloin."

"You win some, you lose some, Lieutenant." Sam grinned back at him.

"Well, let's hope we have what the business types call a 'win-win' situation here." Fletcher tapped the file that rested on his desk. "What do you know about it?"

"Probably not as much as you do," said Sam.

"What was your partner doing at home in her apartment at three-thirty in the afternoon?"

"I have no idea. As I'm sure you already know, I was in the hospital when Pat was killed."

"Was that her nickname—Pat?"

Sam nodded.

"Yes, let's get to the hospital. I'm sure there's a doctor somewhere who'd like to know where the hell you are now. They're not used to patients just walking out of the place."

"What can I say? I was feeling better so I left."

"It couldn't have anything to do with your partner's murder, could it?"

"I found out about her death in the hospital. I wanted to get out to see if there was anything I could do."

"What time did you leave the hospital?"

"I guess it was a little before seven in the evening."

"Where did you go from there?"

"To the office." He lied. "Slept there on a couch that night." He had no intention of drawing the police to Angie's. They'd have a field day with the old lady and Sam wasn't sure how much she'd heard about the parchments and Jennifer Davies during her hospital visit and from conversations with Carol.

Mayhew's head ping-ponged back and forth between the two men with each exchange, his tongue sliding the toothpick from one corner of his mouth to the other.

"Did your partner have any family?"

"No husband or kids, if that's what you mean. Her mother lives on the East Coast and her father's dead."

"Yeah. We've already talked to Mrs. Paterson, the victim's mother."

From the look on Fletcher's face, Bogardus knew that Pat's mother had not given Sam her seal of approval. He should have spoken with her at the funeral. It might have dulled the edge of her suspicions.

"Don't suppose you have any idea who killed Susan Paterson?"

"No. Do you?"

Fletcher ignored him. "Know if anyone threatened Ms. Paterson's life recently or had any reason to kill her?"

"Not that I'm aware of."

"No cases with disgruntled clients—perhaps an angry husband in a divorce case, or a criminal client?"

"No. She did some criminal work and had a few domestic clients, but just the usual fare."

If it had been relevant he might have told them. It was true. She'd had her share of strange clients. The last was a man named Zack Barns. Barns was what was known in the trade as a "wand wagger"—one of those lonely men who stand in front of picture windows overlooking crowded streets and display their manliness to the world, or at least to as much of it as is willing to look. It was one of those things that most lawyers run across at least once in their career. Sam had had his fill of the molesters and the raincoat men while working misdemeanors with the P.D. Pat's turn in the tumbler came during private practice. She'd accepted the case, labeled "miscellaneous misdemeanor," on a referral from the criminal courts panel in January. Barns was a school bus driver who decided to display his wares to a twelve-year-old girl as he made the last stop of the day. When Pat advised him to cop a plea, Zack Barns became excited. Abstractions quickly turned to reality, and it fell to Sam to step into Pat's office and ask him to leave. Before doing so, however, Bogardus strongly advised him to resheath his tool. As he left the office Barns leveled obscenities at Pat—what a suspicious cop might view as a threat on her life, but what Sam recognized as the aroused sexual excitement of a sick man.

It was impossible to practice law in a large city and not deal with some of the human garbage that became its byproduct. But it was irrelevant to Pat's death and he had no intention of airing the episode for the cops' perverse enjoyment.

"Well, maybe you can tell me who put you in the hospital?"

"I'd be happy to if I could. Believe me, Lieutenant."

"So you have no idea who put that lump on your head or offed your partner?" A discernable note of sarcasm returned to Fletcher's voice.

"None," replied Sam. "What makes you think the two events are connected?"

"What makes you think they're not?" said Fletcher. "Just a damn coincidence, I suppose."

"This is getting us nowhere."

"I'll be the judge of that," said the detective. "For now just answer my questions."

"The attack in my apartment was a random burglary. I just had the misfortune to wake up when the thief was about to make off with my television or stereo."

"Well, if that's the case, why did the burglar leave without taking anything after he went to the trouble of beating your brains out?"

"So the theory's a little lame. Use your imagination. Maybe he got scared. Maybe he thought he killed me and panicked."

"Yeah, maybe," said Fletcher. "And maybe he was looking for something, something he couldn't find at your place so he went after your partner."

They were tilting at windmills, chasing distractions. Pat was not killed by some demented client. She was murdered by someone who mistakenly believed that she knew something about the Davies parchments. But Fletcher would never believe that and Bogardus had no inclination to tell him.

An uncomfortable silence settled as Fletcher homed in.

"What do you think, Lieutenant? You think we were running drugs?" Bogardus accepted the premise and tried to lead the detective away from the parchments.

"You tell me."

"I'm sure that by now you've had a chance to look at the police report on the burglary at my place. The only drugs your people found was a broken bottle of aspirin in the bathroom sink." Sam was adroitly cautious. Criminal clients never saw the inside of his apartment or his car—never had the chance to make a stash. The criminal defense bar, public and private, were prize targets for eager narcotics investigators and their paid informants. More than one had ended up taking the fall on evidence they swore was planted.

"I have no idea who assaulted me or who killed my partner. When you find out please let me know, because I'm very interested."

Fletcher studied Sam carefully and reached for the file on his desk. He leaned back in his chair and opened the folder.

"How long had you and the victim been associated?"

"You mean how long had we been in practice together?"

Fletcher smiled. "No, I mean how long had you known each other?"

"We went to law school together in the mid-sixties."

Fletcher waited for more. There was nothing.

"I'm told you two were an item?"

Pat's mother had unloaded on him. "We lived together for a while."

"And where was that?"

"In the Sunset District."

"The apartment where she was murdered?"

"Yes."

"When did you move out?"

"About two years ago now. It was a mutual understanding. We both wanted a little more room and some time to think."

"No hard feelings?"

"None."

"Are you seeing anybody else right now, Mr. Bogardus?"

"Nobody special."

"Did you still have occasion to date the victim?"

"Listen, Lieutenant, if the scope of your inquiry has centered on me, I think maybe I should have the benefit of counsel, that is unless you have a yearning to join your two young friends out in the Tenderloin."

"The scope of our inquiry hasn't centered on anybody, and if I need legal advice I'll confer with the district attorney's office. For the moment you can call this a friendly conversation. After all, you came in voluntarily and you're free to leave whenever you like."

Sam leaned toward the door as if preparing to go.

"But I assume you have an interest in helping us find your partner's killer?"

"If I could I would, but I don't know anything."

"Just a couple more questions."

"When was the last time you saw Ms. Paterson?"

Sam thought for a moment. "She visited me in the hospital."

"When was that?"

"Let's see. I guess it was the day before she was killed."

"What did you talk about?"

Fletcher was beginning to bear down. He was looking for a thread, for something specific.

"I don't remember. Hell, I was pretty groggy. She was concerned about my condition. We talked about the lump on my head and how it happened."

Fletcher leaned back in his chair, the springs punctuating the conversation with a low groan. "How did it happen, exactly?"

Sam related the events of the attack in his apartment in lurid detail in the hopes that it would pacify the detective. It didn't.

"Mr. Bogardus, what else did you talk about with Ms. Paterson at the hospital?"

Did Fletcher know something? Did he know about the parchments?

"Let me think." He paused for several seconds. "As I recall, that was it."

"That's all you talked about—the lump on your head and the attack in your apartment?"

Sam nodded.

"Who else was there?"

In for a penny in for a pound. "Nobody—that I can recall. You've got to remember I was half out of it, Lieutenant."

"I'm sure you were," said Fletcher, the disbelief in his eyes belying his words.

"And was that the last time you spoke with your partner?"

Sam paused for a moment. He remembered the telephone conversation the following morning—the call to get Jennifer Davies's phone number. They might have telephone records from his hospital phone.

"No, there was a brief telephone conversation the following morning—to discuss some business matters."

"What business matters?"

"Legal business matters," said Sam.

"I don't care if they involved divine inspiration, what did you talk about?"

"I'm sorry, but that's confidential. It's privileged, Lieutenant."

"You know if it relates to this case I can get a court order and force you to tell me." Fletcher stared at the lawyer across the desk.

Now who's blowing smoke, thought Sam. "No, Lieutenant, you can try."

There was a long pause as the two men locked eyes. Mayhew bit off the small end of his toothpick.

Sam saw that the detective was fingering something in the file, shuffling papers behind the cover of the folder that he held propped up against his protruding belly.

"Let me show you something, Mr. Bogardus."

Without warning, Fletcher flipped a large eight-by-ten glossy photograph onto the middle of the desk.

"Is that your partner?"

Sam felt a tight knot begin to form in his stomach, the same knot he had experienced when Jake called him in the hospital to tell him that Pat was dead. There on the desk in front of him was a picture of Pat, her legs askew, her upper torso tilted forward, her soft brunette hair dangling in the pool of matted blood, its red hue already turning a crimson shade of brown. The reality of the photograph lent horror to the mental image he had conjured in his mind following his first conversation with Jake Carns.

"You know who it is. Why ask me?"

"Yes I do, Mr. Bogardus, and the sooner you decide to cooperate with us the sooner we can catch the person or persons who did that to Ms. Paterson."

"I've told you all I know." Sam felt a nauseous bubble begin to rise in his throat and swallowed hard, driving it back down into his stomach. "Now, unless you want to hold me on some charge, I have business to take care of."

"No, we have no intention of holding you—at least not for the present. But keep yourself handy. It's likely that we'll need to talk again."

Sam rose to leave.

"Oh one more thing, Mr. Bogardus. Where can we reach you? We called at your office but could only get the answering service?"

Sam thought. "I'm staying with friends until my apartment gets put back together. For the time being you can reach me at my office or leave a message with the service and I'll get back to you."

There was a moment of hesitation from the detective. Sam's mind scrambled to come up with an address that he might give to Fletcher— any address but Angie's. Just as Sam was about to give Fletcher Nick's apartment address in Berkeley, the detective spoke.

"I would appreciate it if you'd return my call promptly if I have to get in touch with you again." The tone of his voice became solicitous.

"I will."

Mayhew began to stir from the credenza. "Lieutenant, don't you want to ask him ..."

Fletcher shot his subordinate a cold stare that nearly caused Mayhew to swallow what was left of the toothpick. "Ah yes. There is one more question. What hospital did they take you to following the attack in your apartment?"

"Saint Jerome's. Why do you ask?"

"And your room number?"

"I'm not sure. I think it was 417. You can probably find out with a phone call."

"I'm sure I can," said Fletcher.

"That's all, Mr. Bogardus—for now." He watched Sam as the lawyer walked out of the office and down the corridor toward the exit.

Mayhew looked over at his boss. "Why didn't you ask him ..."

"Jack—Jack. When are you gonna learn? You interrogate someone to get information, not to give it out." Fletcher flicked through the pages of a hand-scrawled police report lying under the Paterson file. It had been hastily prepared at three fifteen the preceding morning. A retired auto mechanic had been found dead in his hospital bed, a syringe tainted with mercury hanging from the I.V tube running into the man's arm. Paterson's murder and the assault on Bogardus were no coincidence. The detective's eyes ran to the hospital room number where the mechanic had been killed—Room 417.

Chapter

7

The polished oak table in the city's central library bore the idle scars of juvenile vandals. Initials carved with the sharp point of a pen marred the surface just above the books and magazines stacked in front of Nick Jorgensen.

He opened the hand-scrawled note penned by Bogardus in the Frenchman's parlor. Nick could have saved himself the trip. Reinhard Heydrich was a name familiar to anyone versed in the terror tactics of the Third Reich. An ambitious officer, Heydrich was the protégé and top lieutenant of Heinrich Himmler, chief of Hitler's dreaded S.S. His career was marked by a restless quest for power. He lived long enough to earn the name "Hangman Heydrich" for his relentless persecution of the Jews and methodical execution of political rivals during Hitler's purge of the S.A. in 1934.

Jorgensen paged through a thick volume, searching out indexed references to the Nazi officer. He found what he was looking for on page 1243. On May 29, 1942, on a rain-slick street in Prague, the icy-eyed Heydrich fell victim to an assassin's bomb. Nick looked at the date of Heydrich's letter that had been noted on Sam's slip of paper—April 30, 1942. According to Lamonge, his brother had not received the letter or the parchments until sometime in June of that year. Little wonder Slade did not demand the return of Heydrich's letter when he retrieved the parchments. The author was already dead. Nick stared vacantly at the entry in the book. By the whimsical hand of history, Slade and his principals had been freed to deal directly with the real purveyor of the Drake journal—Heinrich Himmler.

He pushed aside the massive text and picked up a large, glossy magazine. The cover displayed the provocative backside of an American actress; the edition was July 1972. Nick paged through the magazine until he found what he was looking for. The story was dominated by a full-page photograph of a massive blimp, its tailfin lifted skyward like the fluke of some majestic whale. The blimp was cast against an eerie, twilight blue background, the behemoth craft perched on a darkened runway, the horizon lost in shadows. The article was a feature piece typical of photo magazines of the period, and its angle was the curiosity of a bizarre unsolved mystery as seen through the perspective of history thirty years later.

Nick quickly scanned the story. It traced the

last flight of the Ghost Blimp from its departure on the morning of August 16, 1942, to its demise several hours later. Ever since Sam had told him about Jennifer Davies and the search for her father, something had gnawed at the edges of Nick's memory, something he'd read several years before. Not in a scholarly treatise or academic journal, but in a dental office waiting to have his teeth drilled. He studied the article. Near the end he found what he was looking for—a picture of the Ghost Blimp's gondola. It was not a drab wartime photograph, but in blazing color—the name "America" could be discerned stenciled under the windows, and on the looming gas bag over the passenger compartment in ten-foot letters was the word "GOODYEAR."

By the time Jennifer parked her car she was nearly twenty minutes late. The East India Tea Company was situated on a side street in the Financial District. When she entered the restaurant, Jennifer was surprised to see Sam seated at a table with another man. As she walked toward them she surveyed his companion. He wore a closely cropped beard, his eyes were jovial and his conversation animated. The two men talked over drinks.

Sam rose from his chair.

"Ms. Davies . . ."

She interrupted: "I thought we were beyond that. Please call me Jennifer."

Sam hadn't been confident of a warm reception following his abrupt appearance at her law office. But for whatever reason she had mellowed since their conversation. "Very well. Jennifer, I'd like you to meet my good friend Dr. Nick Jorgensen. Nick, Jennifer Davies."

Nick stood and extended his hand toward the woman, who took it in her own and responded with a smile.

"How do you do, Nick."

"Well I must admit I'm honored. I finally get to meet the mysterious lady of the parchments."

"It's mutual, I can assure you. You are of course the illustrious Nick Jorgensen of Alleghany fame."

Nick continued standing with a puzzled expression as Jennifer sat in the chair across from him.

"It seems that Ms. Davies—Jennifer—has been talking to my mother. I would venture to guess she knows everything about me, including the location of all birthmarks."

"That's something we might discuss at a later time." Jennifer smiled.

"Well perhaps sometime you can talk to my mother," said Nick. "Did I say that? You'll have to excuse me, sometimes my interests tend to run to the licentious."

She laughed. "What's this all about? Why all the secrecy—the clandestine meeting in an out-of-the-way restaurant?"

"Well, we have some news. It's not much, but it may be our first concrete lead in the direction of James Spencer."

"Really?"

"First let me get you a drink and then I'll tell you all I know up to this point." Sam called the cocktail waitress to the table. Jennifer ordered a glass of Chardonnay. Sam avoided the details of Pat's murder and his conversation with Fletcher at police headquarters that afternoon. He concentrated instead on his conversation with Phillipe Lamonge and watched Jennifer's demeanor closely as he mentioned the Committee of Acquisition and the name Arthur Symington. There was no hint of recognition. But Sam was convinced that she was still withholding something.

It was more than female intuition that led her to believe that Raymond Slade had killed James Spencer. Lamonge had met Slade. The sailor was intimately involved with the parchments, and Sam was convinced that his story was the linchpin in the chain of deceit leading to Pat's murder.

Perhaps it was naive, but Bogardus had decided that the time had come to tell Jennifer Davies about the significance of the parchments. He hoped that a show of trust would be met with reciprocity, that she would reveal the information she was withholding.

"There is something that I couldn't tell you when we met in the hospital," he said.

"What's that?"

"We've had the parchments analyzed and translated. They're authentic. We believe that they are part of a manifest of precious metals and gems that was on board a sailing vessel under the command of Francis Drake when he put in for provisions and repairs somewhere on the coast near San Francisco in the late 1500s." Sam paused and before he could speak again, Nick's enthusiasm propelled him into the conversation.

"The parchments indicate that Drake had nearly forty-two tons of gold and silver on board when he landed on the Pacific Coast at a place he called Nova Albion. By the time he provisioned the *Golden Hinde* and made repairs the ship was grossly overloaded. He had no idea what lay ahead. His Pacific charts, those he was able to plunder from a Spanish Manila galleon, provided only the roughest estimation of distance and currents."

While Jennifer seemed to comprehend everything that Nick was saying, the glazed look in her eyes revealed that its significance continued to elude her.

Nick related the events of earlier that morning. The telephone call had come from Madrid at 4:30 A.M. A colleague of Nick's on sabbatical in Spain had visited the Archives of the Indies. He had obtained the requested information.

The "Eagle of Cadiz" was reputed to be a masterpiece of Asian artwork. Crafted of solid gold extracted from Spain's mines in Peru, then cast and hammered into form by Chinese artisans in the Phillipines, the capstone of the piece was an emerald more than forty carats in weight clutched in the eagle's talons. The piece had last appeared in the literature in a Spanish bill of lading dated 14 March 1579. Consigned to a Manila galleon it had sailed east toward the Americas but was never to arrive at its final destination, the royal palace of Philip of Spain. All traces of it had disappeared.

That in itself was not unusual. In that day ships went down with tragic regularity, cargoes were routinely lost and records of transit were often poorly maintained, sometimes by design.

What was noteworthy was the fact that on June 29, 1579, before venturing out into the Pacific on his return to England, Francis Drake buried the "Eagle of Cadiz" along with a treasure trove of precious metals and gems on a lonely headland in what was now California. It was this message that Drake had committed to the four pages of parchment now belonging to Jennifer Davies.

Sam engaged Jennifer's eyes directly. Then he spoke. "The parchments reveal that Drake left approximately twelve tons of precious metal and gems somewhere here on the coast. The exact location is written in his journal."

Sam searched her face for some expression of comprehension. He didn't have to wait long. Her mind gravitated in the same direction as his the moment he learned of Pat's murder.

"The parchments and that book would provide a powerful incentive to kill, wouldn't they?"

Neither man responded. Sam wondered if James Spencer had known of the significance of the parchments. Jennifer, for some unstated reason, believed he was dead. Had he gone to his grave ignorant, or like Pat unbelieving?

"I'm afraid the fate of your father is inextricably bound to the four pages of parchment you received and the Drake journal," said Nick.

"We believe that Susan Paterson was murdered because someone mistakenly believed that she knew something about the parchments," said Sam.

"I don't want to change the subject," said

Jennifer, "but that reminds me. When we met in the hospital you indicated that you had obtained a file photograph of Raymond Slade from the navy. You didn't happen to bring it with you by any chance?"

"No."

"Oh well. You can get it for me later. It is strange though," she said, trying to shift gears back as smoothly as possible, "you would think that after all of these years someone would have found it—I mean twelve tons of precious metals."

Sam was left wondering why the photograph had come to her mind with the mention of Pat's murder.

"The area where Drake is believed to have landed is still largely undeveloped. It sits in the middle of thousands of acres of federally owned parkland," said Nick.

"And I suppose the two of you are going to find it?"

"We're going to try."

"And how do you propose to do that?"

"By locating Drake's journal."

"What makes you think you can find it?"

Nick chewed on an ice cube from his drink as the two of them sparred.

"Because I think it's here," said Sam. "There are only two possibilities. If the letter from the German that Lamonge showed me is accurate, the book was either purchased and delivered to the committee, or for some reason they refused or failed to buy it. The answer can probably be obtained by talking to Arthur Symington, if he's still alive and we can find him. If the journal is to be found he should know where. After all, he was the go-between, the designated buyer who went to the Jade House to gather all their goodies."

"I have a better idea. Why not just turn the parchments over to the police and let them handle it? That's what they're paid for."

Nick looked at her and nearly choked as he swallowed the sliver of ice. The thought of having the parchments locked up in some evidence locker, perhaps for years, while the cops chased down Pat's killer was anathema to him.

"And what do you think they'd do?" Before she could speak Sam answered his own question. "Exactly nothing. They would never buy the translation of the parchments. Hell, Pat didn't believe it herself. Why would somebody kill her for a secret that she herself thought was a joke? First question the cops would ask. You could stack experts from here to city hall vouching for the papers and the cops would throw us out the front door and laugh as we bounced down the steps."

"Besides, the parchments are priceless." Nick could no longer restrain himself. "You turn them over to the police and there's no telling what will happen to them or whether we'll ever see them again. As long as we have those pages we're in the catbird seat."

"You both forget one thing. Those parchments belong to me."

"True," said Sam. "But you might say that for the time being I hold them in trust. At least until I find out who killed my partner."

"I'm as interested in finding the answer to

that question as you are. I just don't want you to join her. That's why I'm instructing you to turn them over to the police and tell them whatever you know up to this point and then step away from the entire thing."

What did she know? Why all of a sudden had she lost interest in James Spencer? Jennifer Davies had never met Susan Paterson, and yet when Sam told her of Pat's murder that day in her law office a dark look of foreboding came over Jennifer's face. What was she concealing?

"Are you discharging me?"

"Yes, you're fired. Now you can return my property and I'll take it to the police."

"I'm afraid I'm not prepared to do that."

"Working for yourself?" She looked at him over her glass.

Sam nodded.

"That's what I was afraid of. So where does that leave us? I could sue you to recover the parchments."

"You could, but you won't. It would take too long. By the time you got to court I'd have the answers I'm looking for and you'd have the parchments back."

"Damn sure of yourself, aren't you? I could go to the police with what I know."

"In that case you can take their chuckles and the ride down the steps by yourself."

"Where are the parchments?" she asked.

"In a safe place," Sam replied.

"I want them back."

"When I'm finished."

"No, now."

Nick picked up his menu. "Well, shall we

order? I don't know about the rest of you but there's nothing like a good argument to whet my appetite."

Jennifer realized that she was getting nowhere.

"What are you going to do now?" she asked.

"Well, that depends on you." Sam engaged her eyes directly in the flickering light of the candle. "Will you help?"

"It doesn't look like I have a great deal of choice." Jennifer had been backed into a corner, and from the look in her eyes she didn't like it.

She summoned up every ounce of authority that her voice could muster. "On two conditions. The first is that you keep me informed of everything you discover."

"Agreed. And the second?" asked Sam.

"That I be permitted to accompany you at any time I choose whenever you are searching for information concerning my father or the parchments." She waited for a howl of protest, but Sam said nothing.

Bogardus was in a box. She might go to the police; and while it was probable that they would dismiss any story about Drake, if she kept it simple and told them merely that Sam had stolen the parchments from her, they would have to investigate the complaint. He didn't need any more complications. Besides, he had no intention of honoring her terms unconditionally—only until he found out what she knew about Raymond Slade.

"I suppose I can live with that." He spoke in a grudging tone.

"The first time I find out you haven't told

me everything, I will go straight to the police with what I know," said Jennifer.

"Hey listen, if we're gonna be partners we should start our relationship on a basis of trust." His face lit up with a smile that would have shamed the Cheshire Cat.

It was nearly ten o'clock by the time the trio finished eating. The conversation centered on Arthur Symington, the only apparent link to "the Committee." Symington was the key to the entire puzzle. It was a slim lead. After all these years Arthur Symington could be dead. People at the newspaper might not even remember him. It wasn't much to go on, but it was all they had.

The waitress appeared and removed the empty dishes from the table. Nick had just swallowed a last morsel of chutney and rice and tugged the linen napkin free from the top button of his shirt.

"Tomorrow morning I want you to call my office." Sam looked at Jennifer. "The answering service will put you through to me. I'll see if we can find this guy Symington. In the meantime, Nick, I want you to call Jake and tell him to take the parchments to a bank, a big one, and get a safe deposit box and stash them for the time being. If we get lucky we should have a lead on Symington by the end of the day."

He looked across at Jennifer. It was time for her contribution. "Is there anything of your mother's that might give us some additional information about the parchments? Maybe something she kept from your father's things that might give us a clue as to Raymond Slade, who he was?"

With the mention of Slade's name her look became dark, and without hesitation she said, "No."

"There must be something. Even if the man has been dead for thirty years, your mother was married to James Spencer. She must have kept something to remember him by."

"Not that I know of."

"It must have been one hell of a romance."

She bristled. He'd hit a raw nerve.

"I'll look—but I'm sure there's nothing."

If there was Sam was certain he'd never see it.

Nick sensed that he was intruding. He gulped down the last mouthful of coffee, placed his napkin on the table by the cup and pulled several bills from his wallet. "Well, if you two will excuse me I think I'll be hitting the road. Jennifer, it was nice meeting you."

She appeared relieved by the change of subject. "I'm sure we'll be seeing each other again."

"How are you getting back?" asked Sam.

Nick looked at his watch. "I had Jake drop me off and told him to pick me up at ten-fifteen. He should be out front by now."

Jennifer looked at Sam. "You don't happen to have a card with your office number on it, do you? I suppose I could get it from information."

Sam rummaged through his wallet. "I don't think I do."

Quickly Nick pulled a small stack of business cards from the lining of his wallet. Shuffling through them he found one without any notes on the back. He gave the card to Sam with a pen.

After jotting the number, Bogardus returned the pen to Nick. "I'll see you later."

"It was nice meeting you." Nick looked at Jennifer.

"Take care." She smiled.

Nick heard the light chatter of their conversation fade into the background, though it was still clearly audible. He was fumbling with his wallet, trying to replace the stack of business cards behind a fold of leather as he approached a table a few feet from his friends. Not looking, he hooked his foot into something draped from the back of a chair. He stumbled, dropping his wallet on the floor. Credit cards and cash spilled out.

A man seated at the table reached out to steady him.

"I'm so sorry. How stupid of me. I should have placed my cane on the other chair out of the way."

"No, it's just my innate clumsiness," said Nick.

The man knelt on one knee and began to retrieve the cards and Nick's wallet. Nick stooped to help.

The man handed the wallet to Nick. "Are you all right?"

"Oh, I'm fine." Nick picked up the walking cane that he had kicked loose from the chair. It was an elegant affair, heavier than Nick had expected, weighted by a solid brass handle in the form of a bird's head with a sharp bill. As if in a reflexive motion, Nick hooked the handle of the cane over the back of the chair, smiled at the man one last time and walked briskly from the restaurant.

The man seated himself at the table and after several seconds uncupped his hand to read the small business card that he had palmed from the floor. The embossed black ink read:

Dr. Nicholas Jorgensen, Ph.D.
University of California, Berkeley
Department of History

There was an office telephone number printed at the bottom of the card. He flipped it over. Written in faint pencil on the back side he read the name:

Jasper Holmes
515 Rose Street, Apt. 16
Berkeley

and below it a cryptic note, a single word— "Translation."

At 5:00 A.M. Sam awoke with a start. Mental images of Pat's lifeless body from the photograph dropped on the desk by Fletcher during their meeting made sleep impossible. To the sounds of Nick's snoring he slipped from Angie's basement apartment and dressed in pajamas with his briefcase under his arm walked past the furnace to the small kitchen. He put up a pot of coffee, then sat with his feet propped on another chair as he pulled from his case a three-page coroner's report.

He'd obtained the document from the police records section immediately after leaving Fletcher's interview. Under California law, copies of coroner's reports were public records available to anyone with the price of copying. Unfortunately, the police report from the scene could not be obtained until someone had been charged, and then usually only by subpoena or through formal discovery.

He started to read the report. It contained the usual boilerplate: "The victim is a well-nourished female in her mid- to late thirties, post mortem weight 124 pounds." The medical examiner estimated that Pat had lost approximately three pounds as a result of the trauma to her back and the migration of body fluids from the wound. It was his way of saying that she had bled to death.

Sam scanned the balance of the report. There was no evidence of contusions or abrasions to the body, no sign of any struggle. The only wound was a single oblique stab wound to the lower right quadrant of the back, and the actual incision was approximately one inch long, gaping to one and a half inches at the outer skin, with smooth edges. The ellipse of the wound was flat at one end and came to a point at the other. Examination of the point of entry led the medical examination to conclude that the weapon used was a single-edged blade of high-quality sharpened steel. The fact that the area around the entry wound showed no bruising on the surface caused him to opine that the murder weapon either contained no hilt or other protrusion at the handle or else the assailant had failed to drive the instrument deep enough to leave evidence of these structures.

Internal examination revealed that Pat had

virtually no chance of survival from the instant the weapon entered her back. Piercing in an upward thrust, the blade had severed the renal artery and entered the kidney. Death was nearly instantaneous. From the depth of the wound, the minimum length of the weapon was at least four and a half inches. With the apparent dimensions of the blade, the one-inch elliptical incision at the point of entry and wound depth only four and a half inches, it was the opinion of the medical examiner that the assailant had for whatever reason failed to drive the weapon all the way home.

Sam turned his attention to a typewritten heading at the bottom of the report: "Physical Evidence and Other Observations."

". . . Examination of the area immediately adjacent to the point of entry reveals microscopic evidence of sodium hydroxide (lye) and traces of monoglycerides and triglycerides of the type added to certain foodstuffs, such as cooking oils."

Nick had virtually struck out with the D.A.'s staff. Even with Sam running interference over the telephone, the only information he was able to get was the fact that the police lab had isolated the lye compound found near the wound and determined it to be of a type commonly used in a variety of oven cleaners.

Had the killer used a dirty butcher knife or paring knife from Pat's own kitchen? In the years since he'd met her he hadn't known Pat to cook more than three times. After tasting her food he knew why. She was also fastidious with her apartment. His dirty dishes in the sink had led to more arguments between the two of them than he cared to remember.

What troubled Bogardus was the fact that his contacts on the D.A.'s staff were being unusually closed-mouthed. They were intentionally withholding something. But what was it?

Sam struggled with the key to his office door—a tiny metal burr, he guessed. Carol had made a duplicate key for him since Sam hadn't found his own set. They weren't with his wallet or watch when he retrieved them from the hospital safe the day before.

The heat had been turned off for nearly a week and an icy chill pervaded the law office on the pier.

As he led Jennifer through the reception area, his gaze was repeatedly drawn to Pat's closed office door. Bogardus was able to cope with the tangible reality of her death, but he had difficulty accepting the more mundane fact that her office was now just another vacant room. In the hospital, when the phone call came, his mind allowed for the fact that she was dead. At the cemetery, standing beside the cold steel coffin—she was dead. But here in intimate surroundings his thoughts continually turned to merciful illusions. He felt he could open the door and she'd be there. As if by sheer force of will he could once again place her radiant face and soft brunette hair behind the desk in the familiar office.

"I would like to see that photograph of Raymond Slade." Jennifer's voice penetrated his melancholy.

"Why not?" She wanted to see the picture, and he wanted to know why it was so significant.

Sam walked to the cabinet of pending cases and looked under the letter "D." The Davies file was gone. He thought for a moment, then remembered the letter to Jennifer he'd dictated the afternoon of the attack in his apartment. He went to Carol's desk and rifled through the files awaiting typing. It wasn't there either. He took a deep breath and walked toward Pat's office. He opened the door and for several seconds he stared in stony silence. The room was illuminated only by a thin shaft of light passing through the aperture of the closed drapes. The bare walls had been denuded of the familiar plaques, license certificates and framed prints. The desk and credenza were swept clean of all papers and files. In the corner three boxes, one with Pat's desk blotter protruding from the top, awaited final packaging and shipping to her mother in Connecticut. The Boston fern that had thrived under Pat's nurturing care was yellow and limp in the darkened room. The office was in perfect symmetry with the morose aura that enveloped his spirit.

He flipped the light switch and a floor lamp behind the desk flickered on. He checked the drawers to the desk and the small cabinet in the credenza. They were empty.

Sam turned off the light, closed the door and returned to his office. It wasn't until he sank into the deep cushion of his desk chair that the enormity of it struck him.

"Where's the picture?"

"I'm afraid the file is out of the office right now."

"Where is it?"

"My secretary has some files that were scheduled for typing at her apartment. I had dictated a letter to you before I landed in the hospital. It must be there," he lied.

"Maybe we can go over and pick it up."

"It won't do any good."

"Why not?"

"She was going out today." He stopped the pursuit with one last lie.

The Davies file was gone. It had vanished, and with it the photograph of Raymond Slade. The thought sent a chill up Sam's spine as his eyes nervously scanned the darkened recesses of the abandoned law office.

The blue Porsche purred at seventy miles per hour along the Bayshore Freeway. Sam had expected to spend most of the day trying to pick up the trail of Arthur Symington. Phillipe Lamonge hadn't seen the man for more than thirty years. It was unlikely that anyone at the paper would remember him after all that time, much less know if he were alive and if so where he could be found.

"How did you find this guy Symington so quickly?" Jennifer asked.

Sam had been lucky. After Jennifer called, saying she would be late, he visited the first of the two newspapers in the city. He was armed with a thin cover story. Sam posed as Arthur Symington's distant nephew out on the coast for a quick business trip and interested in looking the old man up. But before he could even get into character, an aging security guard at the information desk said: "Oh, Art. Nope. He's not with the paper anymore. Hasn't been for years. Last I heard he was workin' under a special contract or something. Livin' down on the coast, some place called Cambria." Bogardus was almost embarrassed to take the note from the guard after the man confirmed the last known mailing address by phone with the personnel office upstairs. Sam thanked the guard profusely, turned and whispered as he walked away: "Quite a security system."

"Let's just hope the information is current." Sam gripped the steering wheel with both hands and looked over his left shoulder as he swung out into the fast lane.

"Where's Cambria?"

"About a hundred and fifty miles south, on the coast."

"Wait a second. I don't even have a change of clothes."

"You wanted to be in on everything. Don't complain, you're in."

"Will we be back tonight?"

"Not likely. Relax. You're gonna love it. A small village, very quaint."

Bogardus looked in the mirror and slid the Porsche back into the number two lane, around a slowly moving camper.

Jennifer settled into her seat for the long ride.

They sat in silence as the car purred down Highway 101 through the Silicon Valley and out into the countryside south of Salinas. The smooth whine of the rear engine droned in a monotone as the Porsche left the flat farm lands of the Salinas Valley and headed past King City. Sam wound up the engine another notch and Jennifer watched the speedometer go to eighty. Ninety minutes later he pulled off the highway in Paso Robles.

"Hungry?" Sam looked at her. It was nearly 2:00 P.M.

She was famished. "I can eat."

For the last hour her mind had been preoccupied with thoughts of Arthur Symington, a man whose name she had not known two days before. Did he know her father? Had he ever met him? More important, if the story Lamonge had told Sam was correct, Symington had met Raymond Slade and could identify him. All she would have to do is get him back to the city for a quick meeting and she would have the answer to the question that had gnawed at her for twenty years.

Sam pulled the Porsche into the parking lot of a large old Spanish Colonial building on the main street. The sign over the door read "Paso Robles Inn."

Three minutes later they were seated at a table near a window looking out over a rustic courtyard.

"Well, what do you think?" Sam looked across at her.

"What do you mean?"

"You must have some questions for Symington when we find him?"

He was fishing. What did she really want to know? Given the ray of hope represented by the note on the parchments, why did she insist that her father was dead, murdered by Raymond Slade? And why was Slade's picture so important?

"Symington's yours. I'm just along for the ride, remember."

"But you must have something that you'd like to ask him?"

"I'd like to know what the 'Committee of Acquisition' is, for starters. And what it had to do with my father, if anything." She paused for a second, then added, "I'd also like to know what he knows about Raymond Slade. When he saw the man last? If he can describe him?"

Like the flash of illumination from a bolt of lightning, Bogardus got the first glimpse of what it was that Jennifer Davies was not telling him. It was conveyed in the tense of her words, more than the content of her question. She believed that Raymond Slade was alive. Why else would his description be important? What did she know about Raymond Slade?

"You never told me why you were so interested in Slade's photograph."

"Just idle curiosity. It's a name that I've heard since childhood. I suppose I just wanted to put a face with it. Maybe in my mind there's a certain mystique about the man who was with my father on the day the blimp went down."

It was a plausible answer, but not the one Sam was searching for.

"You never told me why you're so certain that your father is dead."

"Did I say that?"

"Yes. Don't you remember? The day I dropped in at your law office."

"Oh. I probably said a lot of things that day.

I must admit I was more than a little embarrassed."

Sam was uncertain about many things in life, and the events of the past week had shaken his confidence in those few that he had come to accept. But of one thing he was sure—he had yet to get the entire truth from Jennifer Davies.

Jasper Holmes leaned on the desk, drumming his fingers on the wooden surface and staring into the face of the flustered undergraduate. The student's beet-red face matched his bright crimson sweater.

"My dear boy, I don't care what he told you. I want to know where I can find Professor Jorgensen, and I want to know now."

"He hasn't been in for two days," said the student.

"Tell me something I don't know. I've been camped at his office since Tuesday. Surely he must have checked with the department—collected his messages?" Holmes cast his eyes at the class schedule posted on the chart behind the student. Jorgensen had now missed two lectures, and arrangements had been made to have a teaching assistant fill in. Holmes knew that no tenured professor would miss his classes without making arrangements for a substitute.

The student looked around nervously. He was not in the habit of refusing information to faculty members. Still, Professor Jorgensen had been explicit in his instructions. No one except the faculty dean was to be given the telephone number or address in Daly City.

"I'm sorry. I can't give you that information." The student braced himself for the onslaught. Instead Holmes merely raised up and directed an imperious glare at the young man for several seconds.

"Well. We shall see about this." The Englishman turned on his heels and walked from the office, leaving the door open wide in his wake.

Holmes did not walk far. Twenty yards down the corridor he spied a young co-ed, a salacious blonde in a short skirt whom he recognized from his lower-division literature lecture. "Well, Ms. Eckert. Lovely to see you again." Jasper pumped up his best smile.

The girl was clearly surprised and a little embarrassed. The two students with whom she'd been talking wandered off, intimidated by the abrupt intrusion of the Englishman.

"I wonder if I might ask you to do me a favor, my dear?"

Sally Eckert stammered, and before she could reply, Jasper leaned over and whispered something in her ear.

Straightening up, he said: "I would be most grateful. I'm in a dreadful rush at the moment and I will need the car immediately after my next lecture."

The young girl pointed tentatively toward the faculty office of the history department where the door remained open.

"Yes, that's right. It's parked in space 36 in the faculty lot. And do me a favor. Don't tell him it's my car. It's rather embarrassing. Besides, I think he'll be more willing to assist if he thinks it belongs to you." Jasper winked and put his arm around the girl's shoulder, pushing her gently but firmly toward the office door.

Two minutes later he stood behind a group of undergraduates and watched Sally Eckert as she exited the faculty office. Following a half stride behind like an eager puppy dog, the young man in the crimson sweater struggled to keep pace, his eyes glued to the blonde. A wire coat hanger dangled from the boy's fingers. Holmes waited until the two dropped down the stairs out of sight and then walked quickly toward the office. He stepped inside, closed the door and locked it, then moved to the other side of the reception desk and rifled through the Roladex under the letter "J." It took him less than fifteen seconds to find what he wanted; a rough penciled notation on one of the index cards, "Prof. Jorgensen—127 Werner Avenue, Daly City." A telephone number followed.

Ten minutes later Jasper stood at the curb in front of the administration building. He leaned over and spoke through the half-open window into the passenger compartment of a black limousine.

"You know what to do now." The voice came from beyond the shadows inside the vehicle. "We have a deal, Professor. You deliver on your end and when I'm finished it's yours." The passenger tapped the glass partition separating him from the driver with the tip of a walking cane and the car pulled away from the curb. Holmes took a long stride into the street and instantly pivoted like a trooper in a drill team heading in the opposite direction. He stepped behind a large oleander bush and listened as the two figures passed unseen toward the administration building.

"Listen, I don't know anymore than you do. All I know is what he told me. That his keys were locked inside the car."

"Why did you tell me it was your car?"

"Because he told me to."

Jasper stepped away from the bush and admired the long slender legs and provocative wiggle of the young blonde as she scaled the stairs toward the building. The young man scurrying along behind swung the mangled and twisted remains of the wire coat hanger from his right hand. Holmes wondered whose car was parked in space 36 of the faculty lot—and whether its doors would respond to the owner's key at the end of the day.

Chapter

8

He thumped a small tambourine and skipped in an odd rhythmic gait through the door and down the aisle of the shop. His white muslin gown ended in the grizzled hair of his calf just below the knee. The cloth was splotched with stains and bore the dirt and wrinkles of restless nights on cold pavement. The man's shaven head was in stark contrast to the dark shadow of stubble that covered his face beneath glassy, vacant eyes.

"A flower, sister?" He reached down and held out a small plastic stem with a single red blossom, barely taking the time to remove the tag that had read "Disabled Veterans." His face beamed a disingenuous smile as he continued to dance in place, the odor of his body, a mixture of incense and sweat, slowly pervading the area around the cash register.

Jeannette Lamonge ignored him as she packaged the item for an old lady at the counter. The customer looked at the man's filthy feet and without a word grabbed her purchase and walked quickly from the shop.

Jeannette fixed the tall Hare Krishna with a cold stare. Gingerly he withdrew the extended hand with the flower and skipped toward the back of the shop, fingering a dozen small wooden carvings on the way. Jeannette kept one eye on him as she waited on the last customer. It was two minutes after five. If she'd only been a few seconds quicker she could have bolted the door and barred the last visitor. She stapled the receipt to the top of the bag and handed the package to the young girl who cast a wary eye at the patron in the rear of the shop.

"Thank you," said Jeannette, turning to deal with the Krishna.

"May I help you?" She stood several feet from the man and listened as the bell over the door rang with the departure of the girl.

"We need some incense," said the man. "Perhaps you could bless us with a modest gift."

"We have incense for sale, if that's what you want. We do not give merchandise away."

"You will be blessed manyfold in the next life for what you bestow on others in this world," said the man.

"I'm certain of it. Now if you wish to make a purchase, please do so. Otherwise I will have to ask you to leave as it's time to close the shop."

She noticed something strange about the

man's head. It was not exactly a lump, more of a slight bubble that protruded from the side of his skull just above the right ear.

The Krishna turned slowly and casually poked his head through the curtain separating the small workroom from the public part of the shop. When he turned to look at Jeannette again, the bubble over his ear had suddenly moved two inches to the back of his skull and his eyes had lost their glassy quality.

Suddenly, Jeannette felt a viselike grip on her arm as she was propelled down the aisle toward the front door to the shop.

"Lock it." The man spoke through clenched teeth. "Where's the old man? Is he upstairs?"

Wincing in pain from the pressure on her arm, Jeannette nodded.

Nick Jorgensen shook his head in desperation as he drew the tip of his red pen across the marred page of the blue book and scrawled a curt note in the margin—"Missed the point entirely." His eyes were beginning to blur as he gazed down at the examination booklets scattered on the floor at his feet. He had gotten a total of two hours sleep the night before. Angie had wakened him at three in the morning to ask him if the word "pernicious" had ten letters or only nine. She'd wandered into the downstairs apartment and flipped on the light. Wearing a brightly colored Mexican dress with a large Spanish comb in her hair, she had looked like an aging and wilted version of Carmen Miranda. She was carrying a crossword puzzle book. The old lady never seemed to sleep. Now he heard her calling again.

"Dr. Jorgensen, are you down there?"

"What is it now?" Nick spoke under his breath. "Yes, Mrs. Bogardus, what is it?" Nick dropped the pen and moved to the basement door.

"There's a telephone call, for Sam. The woman says she's willing to talk to you. You want to take it?"

Angie stood framed in the doorway at the head of the stairs, dressed in a fire-engine red evening gown and wearing an auburn wig that looked like it was molting.

Nick started up the stairs. "Do you know who it is?"

"Nope. What am I, a message machine. If Sam wants that he'll have to buy one . . ." Her voice trailed off as the balance of her complaints became lost in a mumbled monologue.

He followed her through the porch and into the old kitchen, where he found the receiver of the wall-mounted telephone dangling on the floor from the end of its cord.

"Hello. Who is this?"

There was no reply, though Nick could hear breathing and background noises from the other end.

Then a female voice came on the line. "Is this Mr. Bogardus?"

"No, I'm a friend of his. Sam's not here right now. Maybe I can help."

There was another pause. Nick could sense anxiety in the woman's voice. "Yes, perhaps you can."

"Who is this?" asked Nick.

"This is Jeannette Lamonge. Mr. Bogardus was in our shop the other day."

"The Jade House?" asked Nick.

"Yes."

"I'm working with Sam—Mr. Bogardus—I know about the parchments. Is something wrong?"

"No. Not at all." Her tone was insistent, almost defensive. "It's just that my uncle has remembered something that he forgot to tell Mr. Bogardus the other day."

"You can tell me and I'll relay it to Sam."

"No." The reply was sharp. Again there was a momentary pause, as if she had to compose herself before continuing. "I'm afraid it's too complicated for the telephone. My uncle would have to see the parchments to really explain it. It's very important. If perhaps you could bring the parchments to the shop I'm sure he could show you—and then perhaps you could tell Mr. Bogardus."

There was something wrong. Nick didn't need a voice-stress analysis to know it.

"Well, I don't think I can do that right now." He stalled.

"I'm sure Mr. Bogardus would want you to." Jeannette's voice came back a full octave higher.

Nick looked at his watch. "I don't think I can get away for at least an hour. And I'd have to pick up the parchments . . ." He lied, knowing that he had no chance of getting into the safe deposit vault at that hour. "I could probably be there by nine, perhaps nine-thirty."

"That would be fine, and . . ."

Suddenly Nick heard the phone go dead on the other end.

"Hello. Hello."

She'd hung up. Or someone else had done it for her.

The tall, slender man wore a heavy English tweed three-piece suit. His stride and bearing displayed a vitality belying his sixty-eight years as he passed the marble sarcophagus and ambled down the steps and across the open tiled piazza under the tarnished street lamps.

The sky erupted in an explosion of purple-pink hues as the sun sank below the horizon. The bleached ivory skull of the moon peeked from behind a layer of clouds to the east as it rose over the Santa Lucia Mountains. The man paid little attention to the panoramic view that spread in every direction from the mountaintop. Nor did he look back at the tiled roof or the intricate carved teak figures that adorned the facia of the Moorish mansion overlooking the Pacific. The environs of his job had long since passed into the commonplace in his mind. Millions came to marvel at the priceless art and its setting in the hilltop residence that at times bordered on the garish. But to Arthur Symington, Hearst's "Enchanted Hill" held a secret fascination. Longfellow and Disraeli had articulated the formula of his success. Symington had merely put their words to practical use. Everything does come to he who waits.

William Randolph Hearst had begun the construction of what the world would come to know as Hearst Castle in 1919. For nearly thirty years, until illness forced his departure in 1947, Hearst poured a fortune into the construction of the mansion and its three opulent guest houses and spent millions more in the acquisition of fine art with which to adorn the buildings. No one knew for certain how much the Chief had spent, but estimates ranged upward of fifty million, much of it in Depression-era dollars. When Hearst died in 1951, the main house stood incomplete, with ambitious plans and a poured foundation for yet another wing. But neither the Hearst Corporation nor the family possessed the fiscal extravagance of their patriarch, and all future work on the house was abandoned. It was boarded up and Symington nearly lost hope.

Within a decade, mounting taxes on the property and a desire to preserve and display its wealth of priceless art for public benefit caused the corporation to strike an accommodation with the state. Hearst Castle, its three guest residences and all of the personal property in them were deeded to the state to be operated as part of the California Park System in a perpetual memorial to the Chief. A decade and a half had proven the Hearst donation to be an incalculable act of public philanthropy. Hearst Castle and its surrounding environs were producing revenues from tourism that made it the envy of other museums, art galleries and most amusement parks. As it happened, the public dedication of the property was also a fortuitous turn of events for Arthur Symington.

The state searched for almost a year to find a consultant, someone familiar with the Hearst collection, to catalogue and identify the thousands of objects that it now owned. Symington was the natural choice. Anxiously, he took the position, waiting over the weeks and months that followed for the state to discover the scandal that had led to his earlier demise. But nothing happened. In time the old man became more confident, assured that his past was forgotten, that his dealings with the committee were known only to those who could no longer speak of them—for they were sealed in their graves.

As principal art consultant, his job was to identify and catalogue pieces from hundreds of unopened boxes that lay in storage sheds in the shadow of the great house. In the early months, immediately following his return, he laid plans to enter the chamber and to remove its contents—the items abandoned by the committee, of which he had taken rightful title as sole survivor. But as time passed Symington began to realize the permanence of his position and the advantages of the subterranean vault. Sequestered in its own enclave beneath the foundations, it provided him with a private conservatory, heated and cooled by the engines that operated the great house, its humidity controlled by sensitive equipment installed to protect the public treasures. Yet the room remained unseen by other eyes, its contents his and his alone.

In the years that followed he added to this private collection with regularity, small acquisitions that would not be missed by others on the staff—a few Grecian vases, of which Hearst had one of the largest collections in the world, Renaissance miniatures that he used to grace the walls and small statuary.

Symington feigned a tendency for insomnia and over time won the acceptance of security staff for his unorthodox hours of employment, often working through the night.

Then, as he did this night, after the crowds of tourists had left, after the guides returned to their homes for the evening and darkness enveloped the Enchanted Hill, Arthur Symington would steal down the steps beyond the Neptune Pool to the road and the rusting and forgotten gate to which he possessed the only key.

Most people pick up their mail in the morning. George Johnson was an exception. It was nearly two-fifteen in the afternoon when a nattily dressed man wearing a long coat, felt hat and sporting a walking cane appeared at the box to retrieve his mail. Carns stood at a high, glass-topped table in the center of the lobby twenty feet away, feigning notes in his open checkbook with the ballpoint of his pen still retracted. He watched as the man emptied the contents of the box and sorted it with gloved fingers, tossing the junk mail into a nearby trash receptacle.

It had taken a while to confirm, but Sam's hunch about George Johnson had been correct. Jake had contacted the Department of Motor Vehicles looking for information on the man, using the Olstead Street address to narrow the search. He hit a bureaucratic stone wall. The D.M.V. refused to provide any information unless the request was in writing. A reply could be expected in the mail two or three weeks following the written request. The clerk babbled something about privacy and disclosure, then hung up.

But the red tape was a mere inconvenience. Carns short-circuited the process with a telephone call to an old friend at a D.M.V. field office in San Jose. The man punched up the computer and in three minutes located the name and the bogus Olstead Street address. He also found what Jake was looking for, a post office box number at the San Francisco main branch.

Jake weathered the contemptuous glances of an old woman as he reached into the trash can and retrieved one of the discarded envelopes dropped into the barrel seconds before. It provided the final verification. The computerized label was addressed to George Johnson. Carns turned and followed the man from the building.

Jake had suppressed his better judgment in following the blind lead. It was a good way to get hurt, perhaps killed. Bogardus hadn't told him what Johnson had to do with Pat's murder, but somehow Carns suspected that the man in the camel hair coat with the elegant cane was closely linked to her death. Since their first meeting five years before, Carns and Pat had formed a close, almost filial, relationship. When Sam requested help Jake asked no questions. If he laid his hands on the man who killed Pat he would break his back.

He was surprised when his quarry entered a waiting cab at the sidewalk. Jake ran at full tilt to the parking lot and his car. He nearly drove through the lowered arm at the kiosk before paying the attendant as he sped to overtake the yellow cab with its well-dressed fare.

Carns followed the cab several blocks toward the Civic Center and Market Street before he realized its ultimate destination. By then it was nearly too late. If it hadn't been for the chance departure of another motorist from a curbside parking space a half block from the B.A.R.T tunnel Carns would have lost Johnson. As it was he had no time to prime the meter. Instead he ran to the stairs and down into the station. He came to an abrupt halt as he saw the man calling himself Johnson standing at a B.A.R.T. vending machine buying a ticket. Jake followed suit and entered the turnstile twenty feet behind the other man.

Johnson stood waiting with his back to one of the tiled pillars and the tracks as Jake descended the escalator and entered the platform near the train stop. Carns avoided all eye contact with the man and milled to the other side of the escalator ramp, where he was hidden from view. The station was nearly deserted. A dozen other commuters waited in the cathedral-like cavern, their attention periodically directed toward the open tube that disappeared into darkness under San Francisco.

Jake wandered to the other end of the concrete bulwark that formed the bottom of the escalator ramp and walked several feet out onto the platform, idly gazing toward the pillar and George Johnson. His heart skipped a beat. The man was gone. Jake moved back and looked up the rising escalator behind him. It was empty. Carns retraced his steps back onto the platform. There was no sign of the man. Dropping all pretense of disinterest Carns walked briskly down the platform. Pressure began to build in his ears as the train approached at high speed from the Daly City tube heading east. He was two feet from the pillar and walking at a good clip when Johnson suddenly stepped from behind the tiled concrete post directly into his path. Jake nearly bumped into him.

"Excuse me." Carns made the best of it, and with the impersonal apology continued his course toward a trash can ten feet away. He reached into his pocket and discarded a brand new handkerchief. Other than his checkbook and wallet it was the only prop he had.

The train pulled up to the platform and stopped. Its automated doors opened in near silence as the audio tape rattled off the train's East Bay destinations. Jake turned slowly and with peripheral vision saw Johnson still leaning against the pillar, this time facing the train. The last of a handful of commuters exited the cars and headed for the escalator. Five seconds passed, then ten. The doors to the train remained open.

With Johnson's first motion a sinking feeling came over Carns. Like the lackluster stride of a defensive back when instinct tells him he's been beaten in the end zone and the ball is in the air, Jake had been maneuvered out of position. Carns was nearly twenty feet from the B.A.R.T. car when Johnson took five quick strides and entered the train a half step ahead of the closing door.

Jake's eyes blazed, the image of the sinister grin fused in his mind, as George Johnson stood at the other side of the thick glass window and raised the brass handle of his cane to his fore-head in a mock salute as the train pulled away in a silent acceleration toward the tube and under the bay.

A large dark limousine was parked at the intersection of Old Chinatown Lane just four doors from the Jade House. It looked out of place against the trash cans and abandoned boxes in front of the drab shops. The tinted rear windows and the privacy screen separating the driver's compartment from the passenger area shrouded the rear of the limousine in darkness. The finned antenna of a mobile telephone protruding from the trunk punctuated the sleek lines of the vehicle. Nick walked casually behind the car and toward the alley a half block down.

As he reached the alley he removed the tire iron from under the inside of his coat. He'd taken it from the trunk of his car as a precaution.

The alley was pitch black and the pavement uneven. Nick had to feel his way down the long narrow corridor between the buildings, carefully hugging the brick wall. Skirting a large trash bin, he found his path illuminated by the mute light of a bent and battered lamp hanging over a scarred sign on the wall of the building. The faded letters read:

The Jade House

Before leaving Angie's he had tried to call Jake Carns, but there was no answer at his apartment. Nick wondered if the urgent message he'd left at the gym would be delivered when Jake arrived there. He considered the punch-drunk quality of the voice on the other end of the phone and had his doubts. Sam would kill him if he called the cops. Except for the nervous tone in the girl's voice and the abrupt end to her earlier telephone conversation there was no concrete information that anything was wrong. Maybe her uncle had remembered something. But Nick's skepticism was growing by the minute.

As he stood at the back door to the shop he checked his watch under the dim light overhead: 8:08 P.M. Jeannette and anyone else who was visiting her wouldn't be expecting him for at least another hour. If she and her uncle were alone Nick would suffer some mild embarrassment, entering unannounced through the rear of the shop, tire iron in hand. If his suspicions were correct he would at least have the element of surprise. He tried the handle of the door. It was locked. To the left was a window open several inches at the bottom, its exterior guarded by a light metal grating. Nick put his fingers through the expanded metal of the security screen and felt it give a little in the casement of the window as he pulled. Carefully he slid the tire iron under one edge of the steel latticework and held his breath for an instant, tensed his muscles and gave a sharp jerk. The grating came free from the wall and Nick trapped it with his chest against the bricks to keep it from clanging to the ground. A minute later he stood inside the rear workshop of the Jade House. He brushed dust from his clothing and closed the window behind him.

There were voices upstairs. Nick couldn't make out the words, only the resonamt sounds of loud talking. He looked toward the stairs that led to the second story and then moved quickly around the workbench and the half-assembled items of furniture stacked on it. Carefully he peered through the curtain separating the public part of the shop from the work area.

There was no movement in the shop. The only light came from street lamps outside at the front of the building. Nick's vision had adjusted to the darkness of the alley, and in the relative brightness from the lights that streamed through the windows of the shop he could see the rows of merchandise. The image of a bearded gnome peered from the headstand of an antique bed, its features carved in deep relief, taking on a nightmarish quality in the half-light. In a crouch Nick moved down the main aisle toward the front door. He worked his way around the edge of a large dining table that protruded out into the passageway.

Jorgensen generally flaunted his beer belly and rotund form. It had become an intimate part of his personality. On the theory that everyone loves a fat man, he made the most of what others might view as a disability. But inside the round form was another body, more athletic and, when required, deceptively agile.

He positioned himself behind a small rose-wood love seat in one of the large display windows at the front of the shop and peered out at the limousine parked just beyond the lights across the intersection where Chinatown Lane joined a main thoroughfare. The front chauffeur's compartment was empty. He placed one knee on the raised platform of the shop window for a better view but his eyes still couldn't penetrate the privacy windows of the limousine.

As he backed away from the window he felt something underfoot, something soft and alive —it oozed under the sole of his shoe like a small animal crushed and rolled by his weight. Nick froze, motionless, in front of the door at the entrance to the shop and looked down. In the fingers of light streaming through the window he saw a grotesque slice of pink-white flesh trapped under his shoe. Recoiling in horror, he stepped back several feet and stared wide-eyed like a frozen fish at the object on the floor. It had no form; an amorphous slab of putrid skin, marked only by the dust left by his shoe. For several seconds he studied it from a distance and then drew closer for a better look. As he did he observed that the object did have a form after all.

It had been more than twenty years since he'd seen one. It was amateur theater, but he remembered the uncanny effect—the transformation from mop-haired student to the imposing figure and Yul Brynner-like baldness of the King of Siam.

Nick reached down and carefully picked up the skull cap. Like the skin of a snake, the illusion of a slimy surface evaporated immediately on touch. The live rubber was dry, almost adhesive in its quality.

Clutching the tire iron, Nick moved quickly down the aisle toward the workshop at the back of the building.

Once behind the curtain he waited for several moments to allow his eyes to adjust to the darkness and concentrated on the sounds upstairs. He could distinguish several voices—a man and a woman and then another voice. He listened for several seconds but could not make out the words. Slowly he inched his way to the steps and began to climb toward the voices above.

Nick pressed his ear to the door and struggled to decipher words. The voices came from somewhere in another room deeper in the interior of the living quarters. With the tire iron in his left hand he grasped the handle of the doorknob with his right. Turning the knob with the respect one would normally reserve for the clock fuse of a bomb, Nick delicately twisted, half-expecting the door to be locked. It turned, and a slight crack in the door sent a shaft of brilliant light piercing down the stairway.

He was committed, there was no turning back now. He just wished that he had Jake standing behind him, or better yet in front of him.

The voices were now clearly audible. The two men were engaged in a heated argument. A woman pleaded with one of them to stop. Nick knew that the din of the voices would cover any noise he might make opening the door. He pushed it and walked into the well-lit room at the head of the stairs. It was a broad hallway with rooms at each end. The floor was covered with a Persian rug that served to muffle the sound of his footsteps. To the right the volume of the voices grew louder. Nick could see the shadows of figures through the half-open door at the end of the hall. He pressed himself against the wall directly across from the stairs and inched his way toward the open door.

"I know who your boss is. He killed my brother and his wife. You think that I am going to help you? You are wrong. Go ahead and kill me. You will get nothing from me." There was a strong French accent to the words.

"Please leave him alone. He's an old man. Can't you see that?"

Nick recognized the voice of the woman from his earlier telephone conversation. It was Jeannette Lamonge. He gripped the tire iron with both hands and moved closer to the door. He was now only inches from the opening to the room.

"I know that if he doesn't tell me what I want to know he's not gonna get any older. I'm only gonna ask you one more time. Then I'm gonna have some fun. What did you tell the lawyer?" The voice was raspy, the tone menacing. "The truth old man . . ."

"Or what?" asked the Frenchman.

There wasn't the slightest hesitation. "I was hoping you'd ask." There was a shrill cry from Jeannette as the shadows on the wall danced, and Nick heard the tearing of fabric.

"Leave her alone," said the Frenchman. "She knows nothing."

"That may be, but she's got a nice little set of jugs, don't you think? This is gonna be more fun than I thought. Let me ask you—does that thing really 'cross your heart' or is that just Madison Avenue hype? Do you want to take it off, or should I?"

"Let me go." From beginning to end Jeannette's voice rose a full octave in the three words.

"Ah. You want me to do it. How sweet."

There was a sharp snap of elastic, and Nick knew that Jeannette Lamonge no longer wore a bra. A muffled cry was followed by sobbing.

"That's better. Don't you think? My goodness, quite a mouthful there."

"Very well," the Frenchman broke. "I showed him the letter."

"Excuse me. What was that? Oh yes. I got so caught up in my work I almost forgot what we were talking about. Where were we? Let's see, we were talking about your conversation with the lawyer. You showed him a letter? What letter was that?"

Lamonge hesitated.

"Shall we try for the pants now, sweetheart?"

"The letter from the Germans," said the Frenchman.

"Don't say another word . . ." the woman's voice was choked off as her shadow again moved on the wall opposite the open door.

Nick knew he had to move quickly. He had no idea whether the man holding Jeannette would see him when he looked around the frame of the door—or whether he was armed. If Jorgensen barged into the room and the man had a gun Nick could get all three of them killed.

He turned and pressed the front of his body tightly to the wall, his head turned toward the frame of the door. His right eye cleared the door jam and he found himself looking at what, under any other circumstances, would have been a comical scene. A tall, burly man stood in the center of the room, his back to the door. He was clothed in a white dress that ended at mid-calf. Below the hemline one pant leg had unraveled over the man's bare feet. Nick remained pressed to the wall, his body motionless as his mind began to fit the pieces of the puzzle into place. He looked at the black strip on the unfolding gray pant leg and suddenly it all made sense. The limousine's chauffeur had paid a visit to Lamonge. The skull cap and the white dress were an incongruous disguise. Nick stared in stony silence at the back of the biggest Hare Krishna he'd ever seen.

The chauffeur stood ten feet away, hulking over Phillipe Lamonge, who was seated in a chair in front of him. He held Jeannette Lamonge, her neck in the crook of one of his massive arms. In the other hand was a four-inch blade sharpened on both edges and culminating in a needlelike point. The chauffeur toyed with the blade at the girl's naked waist and dallied with the weapon toward her midsection and the button on her pants.

An instant later Lamonge made eye contact with Nick and nearly rose from the chair. Nick quickly brought his finger to his lips in a gesture for silence and the Frenchman settled back, returning his gaze to the chauffeur.

There was a clear path to the back of the big man if only he didn't turn. If he moved or sensed Nick when he entered the room, it would be over for all of them. The large chauffeur would pulverize Nick, armed or not. The old man and Jeannette would be of little help. He guessed the man's height at over six and a half feet and his weight at close to 250 pounds. With luck Nick would get one shot at the back of the man's head with the tire iron. He would have to make it count.

"Where's the letter?"

Lamonge looked to Nick and quickly his eyes darted back to the assailant who held his niece. He said nothing.

The chauffeur slipped the blade into the waistband of the girl's pants. "Oh, good. I was hoping we would get to see more." In one violent motion he thrust the blade out, away from her body, jerking the girl's feet off the floor. A single button shot across the room like a bullet as the razor-sharp blade cut through the waist band. She struggled to free herself. The assailant quickly moved the blade to her midsection and slit the cloth holding the zipper. The pants fell loosely around the girl's naked thighs, the fabric torn to the crotch.

"Very nice. Very nice indeed." The chauffeur mimicked a good Cary Grant.

"The letter is in the desk drawer, there." Lamonge spoke quickly. His voice carried a tone of urgency.

"What letter? Oh that, yes. We'll have to take a look at that in a moment, won't we? After I'm finished here." His hand caressed a bare thigh, moving upward to the buttock and the sheer panties that separated Jeannette Lamonge from total humiliation.

Nick looked down for an instant at the cold, hard steel in his hand, two feet in length with a slight bend at one end. He reassured himself.

The tire iron could do the job. The only question now was whether he could.

With a single step he moved his body silently into the center of the doorway and gripped the iron with both hands. Each step was deliberate, in a direct line toward the man's back. Moving like a tightrope walker, Nick closed half the distance to his target. It was imperative that the man not turn or move his arms. If he did he would block the blow and turn the attack into a wrestling match with little question as to the outcome.

Another step. Nick was nearly within striking distance. He raised the tire iron over his right shoulder with both hands on the handle. The old man's eyes opened wide as they darted to Nick and back to the chauffeur who held Jeannette by the throat in the crook of his massive arm. In another second the Frenchman's expression would give him away.

"So round, so firm, so fully packed." The chauffeur spouted a litany of advertising cliches as his hips gyrated in a circular motion, his pelvis grinding against the girl's bare behind. He lifted her by the throat off her feet as she struggled with her legs to put distance between their midsections.

One more step. Each inch measured the difference between success and failure, life and death. He would get only one chance. It had to be a knockout blow. The chauffeur had to sense his presence. Why hadn't he moved? The wide-eyed stare of Phillipe Lamonge flashed like a neon sign from the chair. Nick reached back with both hands, and with his arms coiled like springs he inched closer to his target, his gaze riveted on the back of the man's head. Tensing the muscles in his stomach, Nick exploded, his arms bringing the tire iron over his shoulder in a high arc.

The tool was at the apex of his swing when the tip tangled in the cloth tassels of a Chinese lampshade that hung from the ceiling in the center of the room. The resistance of the material slowed his swing, and with the noise of the tearing tassels the big man instinctively flung Jeannette to the floor and in a single motion raised his right arm and shifted his body to one side.

There was a stifled cry of pain as the iron caught the man on the right shoulder, tearing through the thin fabric of the dress and culminating in a dull thud. The needle-sharp switchblade hit the floor and slid on polished hardwood under a sofa against the wall.

Stunned, the chauffeur withdrew several feet toward the corner of the room, a look of bewilderment in his eyes. Momentarily he stooped in pain and slowly lifted his head from his wounded shoulder to see the red stain of his own blood as it spread through the muslin of his gown. He raised his eyes and looked squarely at Nick, the muscles in his face tightening with rage.

Phillipe Lamonge had gone to his niece on the floor in the opposite corner of the room and helped her to her feet. She struggled and tripped on the tattered pants that fell around her ankles. Modesty compelled her to use one free hand to cover her bare breasts. The chauffeur feigned a lunge toward the girl and the old man. Nick cut him off, swinging the tire iron wildly to hold him at bay.

"The door," said Nick looking at Lamonge. "Get out of here. Now! Get help."

The Frenchman hesitated for a moment and looked at Nick, then at his niece. Then the old man and the girl scrambled toward the hall and the stairway to the shop. The big man picked up a chair and threw it at the door, just missing Lamonge as Nick lashed out again with the tire iron. He caught the back of the chauffeur's hand and the man grabbed his fingers, grimacing in pain.

For a moment the hulking figure on the other side of the room was still. He studied the red welt that began to rise across the knuckles of his hand and examined the fist, clenching and opening it as if to test some mechanical object after a mishap. For the first time Nick concentrated on the man's face. It was crimson with fury. The intensity gathered in his eyes as his rage boiled over, and in one maniacal charge the man lowered his shoulder and rushed at Nick, who swung the tire iron, catching his assailant with a glancing blow to the other arm. It did nothing to stop the man's momentum. Nick careened through the pedestal table under the telephone, his body reeling into a heavy armchair across the room. The chair overturned and the big man came down on top of Jorgensen.

There was a brief scuffle. Nick found himself ensnared in the coiled cord of the telephone, part of it wound around the handle of the tire iron. He grabbed the receiver and tried to untangle it, but the chauffeur already had his massive hands at opposite ends of the iron, his legs straddling Nick's chest. Nick held the center of the iron tightly with both hands, but the combined weight and leverage of the larger man made it a losing battle. He tried to lock his elbows but they bowed like green twigs about to snap. The muscles of his upper arms gave way as the tire iron settled across his throat and began to cut off his air. Vision became blurred and Nick lost the strength in his arms. In seconds the will to fight had completely left his body. His physical senses passed that point of ultimate pain that transforms life's consciousness to an ethereal indifference as the steady pressure on the cold hard steel began to crush his larynx.

The room of the old inn, while not luxurious, was quaint. A colorful quilt covered the double, high poster bed, and a delicate floral pattern papered the walls. The room was furnished with authentic antiques and looked out on a small, well-manicured courtyard.

By eight o'clock Sam and Jennifer had finished dinner and ordered coffee in Sam's room. Seated in a chair with his feet propped on the bed, Sam dumped the contents of a large brown paper bag on the table beside him and began poring through the items. Jennifer sat on the bed and watched in silence as he pawed through the handful of personal belongings from her mother's old dresser. The fact that she had produced any of it surprised him.

She watched his every move as she kicked off her shoes and leaned back against the headboard of the bed. "Why wait until morning?" she asked. "We have Symington's address. Why don't we simply drive over to his house and talk to him tonight?"

"I don't know about you, but I'm bushed. I think it would be wiser to talk to him tomorrow, when we're both fresh." Sam sensed that as the sun settled and darkness set in Jennifer grew increasingly pensive.

"Will your stepfather wonder where you are?"

"Not likely. I come and go as I choose."

"Maybe we should give him a call anyway. Just so that he doesn't worry." He gestured toward the phone on the nightstand.

"What's with you? Why this sudden interest in my stepfather?"

"No reason. Just thought it might be the kind thing to do." He guessed that the last thing Jennifer Davies wanted was to tell her stepfather she was in Cambria. The old man would certainly want to know why, and Bogardus believed that the colloquy that would follow, at least the half he might hear, could shed some light on Jennifer's real purpose.

"Forget it."

Sam examined each item from the bag and slowly passed it to Jennifer on the bed. He had transferred nearly all of the objects to the mattress when Jennifer spoke.

"There is something interesting about this." She held a photo album in her hand. "I have gone completely through it and there isn't a single picture of my father or Raymond Slade.

I mean there are pictures of everyone else, his ground crew and other sailors at the base, but not a single picture of either of them. And that's not all. Look at this." She moved over and postioned herself on the bed, with a pillow propped up behind her back, and picked up the photo album. She turned several pages and stopped. "Here it is." Jennifer turned the book so Sam could see.

There in the middle of the page was a perimeter of dried glue where a photograph had once been fastened.

The album pages of manila paper were yellowed and brittle with age. But the space where the picture had been pasted was as fresh as the day the book was purchased.

"What does the writing under there say?" asked Sam.

Jennifer read: " 'Spence, Ray Slade, Johnnie Peters—comrades in arms, March 1942.' " She rose from the bed and walked to the window, still holding the album.

Sam remembered the navy's file photograph of Slade. It too had now disappeared with the Davies file from his office. She was right. Someone was methodically removing all pictures of James Spencer and Raymond Slade, erasing their images as if neither man had ever existed. Why?

He picked up a cup of coffee from the tray on the table.

"Maybe your mother did it," he said.

There was no response. Instead her eyes narrowed and a dark frown came over her face. What was it that she wasn't telling him? For the first time in days Sam was beginning to believe that whatever it was, her motives were not sinister. Her actions appeared to be more the product of confusion, of some painful doubt, some crippling uncertainty. As she stared from the window at the courtyard below she had the look of a woman whose thoughts were lost in the past.

Jeannette Lamonge was hysterical by the time she reached the alley behind the shop. She was some distance ahead of her aging uncle, clutching what appeared to be an oil-soaked work rag to her upper body and screaming uncontrollably as she hobbled toward the street at the end of the alley. In her frenzied state she failed to notice the silhouette of the large man approaching from the street. Ten feet further on she ran headlong into him. He grabbed her forcefully, his fingers gripping the bare skin on her arms and back. He shook her in an effort to bring her out of her hysteria. "Where's Nick Jorgensen?" Jake's voice was firm and insistent.

Jeannette sobbed uncontrollably. "He's killing him." Tears from her eyes joined with saliva from her mouth and ran down her face. Her hands moved in a state of frenzy.

Her uncle, seeing a strange man pressing his niece against the brick wall of one of the buildings, approached cautiously. He was dazed and unable to speak. Then he recognized Jake Carns. Jake released his hold on Jeannette and she sank to the pavement, her back propped against the wall. He turned and ran off down the alley, past the old man and through the back entrance to the shop.

As he entered the back door to the shop Jake saw the open door to the second-story apartment and heard the sounds of scuffling upstairs. He scaled the steps two at a time and ran headlong in the direction of the commotion. As he entered the room he could see only a single figure, a large man with his broad back cloaked in white, on his knees behind a divan, his shoulders hunched, pressing with all his weight toward the floor. Carns moved quickly toward the man and with a single blow of his right fist he caught the side of the chauffeur's head and sent him sprawling, dazed, on the floor several feet away. Jake kicked the tire iron that lay propped across Nick Jorgensen's throat and it clattered across the floor. Nick's face was blue. Carns knelt on the floor beside him and pressed with both hands against Jorgensen's chest, alternately pressing and releasing. He tilted the head back, stuck a finger down Nick's throat, clearing the airway, and locked his mouth over Nick's. He had administered several heaving lungfuls of air when he noticed the man on the floor across the room sit up, shake his head and begin to rise on rubberlike legs. Jake continued to exhale fully into Nick's mouth, feeling the prostrate chest lift with each breath. With one eye he watched the figure in the white gown wobble to his feet, slowly surmounting the effects of the blow.

Carns looked at Nick, whose face had lost its cyanotic tinge. He glanced at Nick's chest and watched as it rose and fell, gradually resuming a normal pattern of breathing. Jorgensen's eyes were still closed, but his legs had begun to move in obvious distress.

Jake turned his attention to the large man standing only ten feet from him near the center of the room. The man's face and arms were bloodied. The chauffeur cast about, latching onto the first object within reach, a small chair, and flung it at Carns, who casually ducked as the chair crashed harmlessly into the wall behind him. Rage spilled from the chauffeur's eyes and spread across his face. He lowered his shoulder and charged. Jake moved to one side, grabbed the back of the man's gown with both hands and assisted him on a headlong plunge into the wood-paneled wall. The chauffeur's head hit the paneling, sending a shudder through the room as he crumpled in a heap to the floor. He lay motionless for several seconds, emitting slight moans, one hand twitching at his side.

Suddenly Nick began to cough, a violent spasm that brought blood to his mouth. He rolled his head from side to side on the floor and moved one hand to his throat, tenderly feeling the bruise left by the tire iron. Jake knelt and gently lifted Nick's back from the floor, dragging him a few feet to the divan where he propped him in a sitting position.

"Are you all right?" he asked.

Nick cleared his throat and tried several times to speak, searching for his voice, which appeared, at least for the moment, to have abandoned him.

Unable to warn him with words, Nick pushed Jake to the side with his last ounce of strength. Carns instinctively rolled on the floor as the flashing metal of the tire iron slashed by his face, missing his cheek by no more than an inch. The hulking form of the chauffeur was barely recognizable as human. A crimson red stain spread over the white material covering the shoulder where Nick had caught him with the tire iron. His face was a pulp, one eye completely closed. There was a massive bruise across the man's forehead that conformed in shape and size to a clear indentation in the oak wainscot on the wall. The chauffeur swung a second time with the iron and it whistled harmlessly a foot from Jake's head.

Jake moved into the center of the room with the large man in pursuit and swinging the tire iron wildly, lashing without precision at Jake's body. Jake kicked a chair into the corner of the room, clearing an area where he could move. He began to dance on his toes, backpedaling around the center of the room in a counter-clockwise direction, his forearms dangling limply at his sides, his fists clinched.

The chauffeur stepped toward him and swung with the tire iron. Carns eased his upper torso back several inches as the tip of the iron passed harmlessly in front of his face. The momentum of the heavy metal carried the man into a follow-through and before he could recover, Jake flashed his right fist into his opponent's good eye. Carns followed the first blow with a counter-punch to the man's left cheek that sent him staggering back several steps. Jake continued to move in a counterclockwise direction around the man who now twisted awkwardly in a circle in the center of the room. The chauffeur placed both hands on the tire iron and swung it like a baseball bat in Jake's direction but missed badly.

The chauffeur began to take lunging steps with the tire iron poised over his shoulder, both hands gripping the handle. On his third step Jake jabbed his left fist in the man's face, snapping his head back. He followed with a solid right blow to the forehead and another left to the man's chin. The last punch sent the man reeling backward toward the large bay window at the front of the study. Struggling to keep his legs under him, the man backpedaled in full stride. His back crushed the wooden muntin bars as his upper body smashed through the glass. For a brief instant he seemed perfectly poised, balanced with his buttocks on the windowpane and his upper torso beyond the wall of the building under the night sky like a trapeze artist on the bar. Then, his legs lifting as if in a backward somersault, the chauffeur pitched through the window to the street below.

Nick slowly rose to his feet, taking several seconds to steady himself, and walked to the window. Fingering the bruise on his throat he looked down through the gaping opening left by the shattered window. There, two stories below on the sidewalk, was a crumpled mass, the confusing stains and shadows of the grotesque gown only serving to further disguise the form of the broken body.

Chapter

9

Sam drove by the first time without seeing it and had to turn around several hundred feet down the country road. As he came back he saw the rural mailbox stuck on a post at the edge of a gravel drive. The letters in black paint on the side of the box read "Symington."

The blue Porsche wound its way up the narrow driveway overhung by branches of pine and redwood. On the right was a grove of well-pruned fruit trees. They drove past a barn and rolled to a stop in front of a single-story white wood-frame house. The building fit in well with its surroundings. One side was nearly lost in the grasp of a wild tangle of blackberry vines. A low picket fence and a bed of wildflowers punctuated with weeds separated the house from the driveway. Wisteria clung to the lathework that decorated the porch. The place had an air of abandonment.

Sam turned off the engine and looked at Jennifer. "How about if you stay here while I check to see if he's home?"

"I didn't come all this way to sit in the car." Jennifer reached for the door latch and was out of the Porsche before Sam could respond. "This really is lovely." She breathed deeply, sucking in the fresh marine air, stretching her arms over her head and rising up on her toes to stretch her legs.

Sam couldn't help but notice the gentle contours of her body. The tight-fitting wool slacks captured the curve of her buttocks and her long tapered legs. Her breasts pressed against the shimmering silk of her blouse as she arched her back. But any erotic urge was quickly dispelled. The feminine silhouette framed against the gray Pacific sky only served to invoke memories of Pat and to remind him of the reason for their journey.

"Are you going to get out or just sit there?"

He diverted his eyes from her, placed his dark glasses in the console near the gear shift and got out of the car.

Leaving Jennifer tracking in his wake, Sam walked up the path to the front door of the house and gave two raps with the heavy brass door knocker. But for that day's newspaper on the front porch Sam might have believed that the house was deserted. Several seconds passed. No one came and he knocked a second time. "Hello? Is anybody here?" There was no response.

Sam was about to check the rear of the house

when a woman peered over a fence twenty feet away. "Can I help you?"

Under the disheveled gray hair the woman's wrinkled face took on the character of an over-ripe sun-dried apple. She had been kneeling behind a low fence, pruning a vine.

"We're looking for Arthur Symington," said Sam. "Can you tell us where we might find him?"

"Mr. Symington keeps to himself mostly," said the woman. "But I would imagine he would be at work at this hour."

"Do you know where he works?"

"Where does anybody work around here? At the castle. Where else?"

"The castle?"

"Hearst Castle—up the road at San Simeon."

"Do you know what he does there?"

"I have no idea. If you have to see him today you might try the visitor's center up the road. They should be able to help you." She pointed with her finger in a casual northerly direction and disappeared behind the fence.

Five minutes later Sam and Jennifer were back on Highway 1, heading north.

"Arthur Symington appears to have more moves than a boa constrictor," said Sam. "If Lamonge is to be believed, Symington was up to his hips in the black market back during the war and now he turns up on the payroll at Hearst Castle."

Jennifer paid no attention. Her mind kept turning over something the old lady had said.

It had come to the fore again as they passed a road sign—"San Simeon: Population 653."

"What was the name written in pencil on the parchments?" she asked. "Simeon, wasn't it? Simeon C."

"Of course!" Sam took one hand from the steering wheel and slapped his forehead in a mock gesture of stupidity. "How could we have missed it?"

"It begins to fit, doesn't it?" Jennifer looked at him. "The foremost collector of antiquities in his day. One of the wealthiest men in the world. Which newspaper gave you Symington's address?"

"God, am I dense or what? Of course, it's still part of the Hearst chain."

"I don't know about you," said Jennifer, "but my interest in Mr. Symington is growing by the minute."

"Listen. Unless I get some answers, and get 'em now, you're headed for the bucket and you're gonna stay there until you tell me what's going on." Nick Jorgensen sat in the chair across from Fletcher's desk like a stone idol. As if Fletcher didn't have enough to deal with, now he had another body on his hands—an over-sized chauffeur with a rap sheet a yard long and a head that matched the contour of a Chinatown sidewalk. All he could get from Jorgensen was a request to see his lawyer. Fletcher had managed to get a little information out of the hysterical Jeannette Lamonge before she was sedated—enough to know that Bogardus was involved, and that the second death was somehow tied to the Paterson killing.

"Listen, Mr. Jorgensen. You're a bright man. According to the information in your wallet, you're on the faculty at Berkeley. Why don't you put some of that intelligence to practical use and tell me what this is all about?" He was trying a little sugar for a change. He knew he couldn't hold Jorgensen or Carns for long. Phillipe Lamonge had proved equally stubborn. All the old man would say was that he had been assaulted by the chauffeur in his own shop and that Jorgensen and Carns had come to his assistance. Given the story of the shop-keeper, that the chauffeur had used deadly force on Jorgensen before Carns had ended it, Fletcher knew that it was an open and shut case of justifiable homicide. But he was equally certain that the three of them knew more than they were saying.

"Despite what you might think, I'm not stupid, Mr. Jorgensen. I know damn well that this has something to do with the Paterson murder. Where is Sam Bogardus?"

"I wish I knew," said Nick. "He's my lawyer and it looks like I could use him right now, that is if you're charging me with anything." Nick arched an eyebrow and looked to Fletcher for some hint as to his intentions.

"What I want right now is a little information. What were you doing at the Jade House?"

"Would you believe shopping?"

"In the middle of the night? The place was closed."

"Sorry, but without a lawyer that's the best I can do," said Nick."

"No one would like to see your lawyer more than I," said Fletcher. "Do you know where he is? I'd be happy to call him for you. Call him— hell, I'll send a patrol car for him."

There was no response from Nick.

"Well this is getting us nowhere. I suppose I'll just have to wait and talk to the girl."

Both Fletcher and Nick knew that Jeannette Lamonge was the weak link. If Fletcher pressed she would crack like an egg. Nick wasn't sure how much she knew. But she knew about the parchments and for Nick that was enough. He wasn't enamored with the prospect of a night in jail, but he weighed the alternatives and took a deep breath. "I'm not saying a thing, Lieutenant."

"Very well." Fletcher picked up the phone and pressed the intercom. "Come in here." A moment later a uniformed officer opened the door. "Take Mr. Jorgensen back to the lock-up and bring in Carns."

Five minutes later Jake sat in the chair across from Fletcher.

"Well, your friend's hanging it all on you. He says you killed the chauffeur. What about it?" Fletcher looked Carns straight in the eye. If Jake was concerned, it didn't register on his face.

He looked at the detective. "I want to see my lawyer." Jake smiled.

"And let me guess who that might be—Sam Bogardus?"

Jake nodded.

Damn, thought Fletcher. He was getting nowhere. He was determined not to question Carns once the request for counsel had been made. He'd pushed it to the limit with Jorgensen. But Carns was streetwise. He had a minor record for assault and was not the least bit intimidated by his surroundings in the holding cell or Fletcher's office. If there was more to the chauffeur's killing than self-defense, a court might toss the evidence if there was any hint that Carns was denied counsel or coerced into a confession.

"Very well," said Fletcher. "Sergeant," he called in a loud voice. A moment later the officer opened the door. "Take Mr. Carns back to his cell."

Fletcher turned his attention to the rap sheet on his desk. The dead man had done time in two other states for strong-arm robbery and assault with a deadly weapon. No great loss to society, he mused. He pushed the rap sheet to one side and opened the plastic bag containing the man's personal belongings. There was a little change, a wallet with a driver's license and some other identification, a small tool that Fletcher was certain had been designed for picking locks, a pinkie ring and the switch-blade knife that officers had found under the sofa. Fletcher pressed the button on the side of the knife handle and a four-inch blade sprang from the handle. It was razor-sharp on both edges. He touched the needlelike point lightly with his index finger as Jack Mayhew entered the office.

"The boys are going through the limo right now, Lieutenant."

"Who's it registered to?"

"It's leased to an import-export company located here in the city."

"Any information on the company? Who owns it?"

"Nothing so far, but we're checking corporate records in Sacramento. We should have something by this afternoon. What are we gonna do with Jorgensen and Carns? We can't hold 'em much longer, not without bringing some charges." Mayhew leaned on Fletcher's desk.

The detective looked up, balancing the switchblade delicately in his fingers like a straight-edged razor. "This'd do a pretty good job on somebody, wouldn't you say?"

Mayhew plucked the perennial toothpick from his mouth.

Fletcher laid the knife on the desk. "Take it to forensics and see if it matches the wound in the girl's back. Also ask 'em if they checked the lock on the door of the apartment for any scratches inside—signs that it might have been picked. Hold Jorgensen 'til the wee hours, then release him and tail him. Take somebody with you. See where he goes. Maybe if he's tired enough and confused he'll lead us to Bogardus and we can get to the bottom of this thing. Hold Carns 'til noon tomorrow then release him."

Mayhew started toward the door and stopped. "Do you want me to put a tail on Carns as well?"

"No," Fletcher smiled. "He'd shake it in ten

minutes. But let me know the minute the girl, Lamonge, is well enough to be questioned."

Fletcher was beginning to question his original theory that Susan Paterson knew her killer and had opened the door for him. There were no signs of forced entry at the girl's apartment, which meant either that she let the killer in or that whoever committed the crime had a key —or had picked the lock cleanly.

It took Sam and Jennifer nearly forty minutes to find someone who could locate Arthur Symington. Sam spun a plausible tale for the benefit of a park ranger: He represented an art dealer in San Francisco who'd come into possession of some rare items believed to have once belonged to Hearst and to have been part of the San Simeon collection. He refused to discuss the particulars of the matter with anyone but Symington. After some telephone conversations between the guide center on the highway and the top of the hill, Sam and Jennifer were ushered to a state vehicle and driven up the steep road to the castle. They parked near a cluster of small trailers that served as offices for the guides. Sam went into one of the trailers briefly to sign a guest register and then he and Jennifer were led on foot to the main house. A tall, slender man wearing wire-rimmed spectacles and a tweed suit met them at a side entrance.

"You're the gentleman from San Francisco— the one they called about from below?" The man stood a shade under six feet tall, with fine, straight gray hair. His sunken cheeks ran like two furrows under deep-set, coal gray eyes that were transfused with suspicion.

Jennifer looked a little sheepish as she hung back. Sam merely shot a broad grin and extended a hand. "Yes, Sam Bogardus is the name." He'd already used his business card to establish credentials at the visitor's center. "I'm authorized to speak only with Mr. Symington."

"I'm Arthur Symington."

"Could we speak in private?"

"I don't think that's necessary," said Symington. "What is it that you have?" Symington fixed him with an icy gaze.

"Very well," said Sam, "we have some parchments that I believe were acquired by a group called the Committee of Acquisition sometime back during the war." Taking the tone of a salesman about to close a deal, Sam said, "I believe you may be familiar with the committee?"

Symington's face turned ashen and his eyes darted to the guide whose blank expression confirmed a lack of any comprehension, at least so far.

"Henry," Symington said to the guide, "perhaps I should speak with these people in private. This could take some time, and on reflection I think we would be more comfortable in my office."

In the brief span of ten seconds, the time it took Bogardus to utter the words "Committee of Acquisition," Symington's manner had gone from belligerent to solicitous. Sam leaned over and whispered into Jennifer's ear. "My goodness, but the man is mercurial."

The guide smiled broadly and courteously excused himself from the group.

"If you'll follow me." Symington led the way toward a small, inconspicuous door tucked in the shadows at the side of the main house.

The bus was only half full. The crowds of summer had departed. Weekday tours no longer taxed the guides to the point of exhaustion. The clustered herds of visitors were now smaller and the buses not always full.

"La Casa Grande is situated atop the Enchanted Hill at about sixteen hundred feet above sea level. During the years that it was used as a private residence, this road was bound by more than a mile of box hedges. A gardener's nightmare ... ."

The taped introduction used on the bus was coming to its conclusion as the vehicle lumbered up the steep road and entered an area of more formal gardens. They neared the top of the hill and passed through the chain-link gates that separated Hearst Corporation land from the relatively small parcel of state park property that embraced the castle and its three guest houses. The corporation still owned and continued to operate the vast majority of the 270,000 acres that had composed the Piedra Blanca Ranch purchased in the 1800s by George Hearst, an enterprising mining engineer and later a United States senator. Off to the left were the concrete columns of the now-abandoned pergola. Remnants of clinging vines hung from its overhead wooden trellis. Beneath the trail built into the slope of the hill were the rusted bars and moats of the animal enclosures, long abandoned and now overgrown with shrubbery.

The tape continued: "During its heyday the Hearst zoo was recognized as the world's largest privately owned aggregation of wild animals. In all, it contained close to a hundred species of domesticated and wild beasts. Long a favorite diversion of guests was a visit, at feeding time, to the quarters of the caged birds and animals, located a little distance down the hill from the castle. The Hearst menagerie included cheetahs, cockatoos, eagles, sacred monkeys from Japan and India, orangutans, leopards, panthers, chimpanzees and gorillas. That broken trelliswork above the animal enclosures shaded the two-mile bridle path. During its day some of the most famous personalities of Hollywood's Golden Age took their morning horseback ride under that trellis, using the horses from the stable at the rear of the castle. Clark Cable and Carole Lombard were frequent riders . . ."

The bus swayed visibly to the right as tourists on the other side leaned into the aisle for a better view.

A well-dressed man in the last row of seats paid no attention. His gaze was fixed straight ahead, oblivious to the sights around him. He was tall and gaunt, dressed in a blue pinstriped suit. The unseasonably warm fall weather had caused him to leave his overcoat and hat in his car in the parking lot. The man was out of place in the gaggle of casually clothed vacationers. His only common link with the other passengers was his advanced age. His gloved hands were draped over the brass handle of a cane that rested on the floor between his knees.

The bus came to a stop at one of the several broad stairways leading up to the piazza in front of the castle. Its load of passengers began to stream out of the two doors on the right side of the vehicle.

"Please step this way, ladies and gentlemen, so we can get started with the tour." A middle-aged woman dressed in a tan uniform skirt and blue blazer held up her hands and motioned the group toward the landing at the base of the stairs.

The man with the cane began to climb the stairs toward the house.

"Sir, where are you going?" The guide's tone was one of irritation.

"Oh, I'm Dr. George Johnson, Professor of Art from the Art Center in Los Angeles. I have an appointment to meet with Mr. Symington at ten o'clock."

"Well, you just can't go up to the house, sir. If you'll wait a moment I will get one of the other guides to take you up so that you can find Mr. Symington."

The woman turned and looked around. She spied three other people in matching blazers standing in the shadow of a large oak tree thirty feet away. "Ralph? Could you give us a little help?"

One of the guides broke away from the group and approached the woman.

"This gentleman has an appointment with Mr. Symington. Maybe you can help him."

"Yes sir," said the guide. The two of them moved away from the crowd of tourists.

"I'm afraid that all guests here on business must sign in at the office before entering the house," said the guide. "If you'll come this way we'll get you to sign our book and then we can find Mr. Symington." The two men walked off in the direction of a cluster of trailers near the chain-link fence and the crumbling trellis.

Arthur Symington led Jennifer and Sam through a door that opened onto an immense kitchen equipped with outdated restaurant-style appliances. Early-model refrigerators with wooden paneled doors lined one wall, and a double bank of gas ovens stood in the center of the room, flanked by large stainless steel tables. The appliances were obsolete and the fixtures were old and well-worn but immaculate. Sam and Jennifer followed Symington through the kitchen and down a narrow flight of stairs into a large open area illuminated by the glare of oversized floodlights dangling from the arched ceiling. At the end of the room was a heavy wooden table covered with assorted vases and cluttered with books and papers.

On the brief sojourn to his subterranean enclave, Symington had had time to collect his thoughts and gain some semblance of confidence.

Sam watched as the old man lit a long tapered brown cigarette mounted in an ivory holder, which he balanced delicately between effeminate fingers. Crossing his arms and striking a pose reminiscent of Jack Benny, Symington took a slight drag and blew vaporous smoke contemptuously at Sam.

"I'm sorry I can't offer you a seat, but this is where I work. I don't often entertain visitors." The belligerence was back in his voice. "Now, what is this all about?"

Sam came straight to the point. "Fine, let's cut through it. We know about the committee, and the journal. We have four pages of parchment from the book. We're also informed that you played a vital role in this sordid little mess. So you have a choice. You can either talk to us, or to the police."

"I don't know what you're talking about." The transparent insecurity in Symington's eyes belied the conviction of his words. He was well-dressed, immaculately manicured and highly educated. His every mannerism was polished to perfection—to be sure, he was a connoisseur of the finest wines and best foods. He was also a liar and a thief, and if Phillipe was to be believed, a man who played heavily in the black market during the war. So had Lamonge, but Bogardus could muster sympathy for the Frenchman since he had paid a heavy price for his mistake and lived with the knowledge that their collective greed had cost the lives of his brother and sister-in-law. But Arthur Symington had escaped unscathed and now planted himself imperiously beneath the house built by William Randolph Hearst and, from the cut of his clothes, was paid handsomely for his services by the state.

"Surely, Mr. Symington, you wouldn't want us to go to the police with what we know. I doubt if the state would be nearly as understanding as we are." Jennifer played on the same theme, following Sam's lead.

Symington looked at her and smiled. He moved closer to the table, aimlessly rearranging some of the papers and books. "Why should I care if you go to the police? I'm sure I have no idea what you're talking about." Hearing no further specifics from the two, Symington assumed he had heard the worst. They had suspicions, bits and pieces, but they had no idea how to assemble them. "Now if you'll excuse me I am a very busy man. I think you can find your way out."

Bogardus had no intention of being dismissed so easily. "We know that you acted as a go-between for black market art purchases between the committee and Slade."

With mention of the sailor's name Symington's eyes were energized by anxiety. They darted nervously first to Sam then to Jennifer. His desperate expression and the sweat on his brow dispelled any illusion that Symington actually expected them to leave.

"Listen, old man, a woman in San Francisco was murdered. She was my partner, and I'm beginning to suspect that maybe you had a hand in it."

"Murder?" Ash dropped from the end of Symington's cigarette onto papers spread on the desk as his hand trembled noticably. "I don't know anything about any murder."

His eyes bounced between Sam and Jennifer like two dark ping-pong balls. Any mask of indifference was now gone.

"Listen, you have to believe me, I know nothing of any murder."

"Then tell us what you do know," said Sam.

Symington hesitated.

"I'm waiting." Bogardus issued an icy stare.

"All right." There was a clear note of resignation in Symington's voice. "It's all ancient history at this point anyway." His tall, lean frame, which to this point had remained erect, began to droop. "Do you care if I sit?"

Sam nodded toward the chair behind the table.

Symington placed his hands on the armrests of the scarred Savonarola and slowly settled his body toward the seat. He looked up and took a deep breath. "Back in the late thirties and forties I worked for the Chief."

Sam shot him a questioning look.

"William Randolph Hearst. Technically I was employed by one of his newspapers as an art critic and sometime columnist. In actuality I served as one of his principal agents for the acquisition of new pieces for his collection—artworks, rare books, sculpture, virtually anything and everything I could lay my hands on. The man had a voracious appetite for collecting. And none of it was junk. He was a true connoisseur, not easy to please."

Jennifer spied a chair in the corner of the room that was covered with a stack of books. She removed them to the floor and pulled the chair toward the table, taking a seat across from Symington.

"Before the war I combed Europe, dismantling palace interiors and negotiating purchases of paintings, tapestries and anything else I thought would strike his fancy. I had a virtual field day in Spain during the Civil War." He gave an amused grin. "People there were so desperate for cash they would have sold us the topsoil if we could have carried it away. As it was we took everything that stood above it."

"What does this have to do with the committee?" asked Sam.

Symington issued a deep sigh. "I'm getting to that. The Chief's penchant for collecting was a disease. As surely as an alcoholic craves drink and a junkie needs his drugs, William Randolph Hearst was addicted to fine art. And it was no secret. The only thing that saved him from being taken to the cleaners by every rug merchant in Europe and Asia was his well-trained eye for the finer things of this world." Symington looked up and wrinkled his brow. "But that didn't stop some of his own people from deceiving him."

Sam sat on the edge of the massive oak table, turning on an angle to watch Symington.

"It was common knowledge in his companies that Hearst regularly raided the petty cash of many of his papers to finance his art habit. He would cruise into town for a quick inspection and clean out the office safe to make one more purchase. There were times when some of the papers had to get bank loans to make their payrolls, and these were profitable publications."

Symington let out a deep sigh and paused. "Well, some of the company brass figured that if he could do it they could too."

"I don't understand," said Jennifer.

"A number of the top executives from papers around the country got together in New York for a secret meeting in the late thirties. They formed a committee."

"The Committee of Acquisition?" asked Sam.

"The title wasn't creative but it served the purpose. In all there were eleven members. Together they controlled the most profitable publications under the Hearst umbrella and were answerable only to the Chief himself. You see, there was no corporation at that time and very few controls fiscal or otherwise over the Hearst empire. The committee decided that if Hearst wanted art they'd give it to him—in spades. The only hitch was that there would be a slight markup."

Sam furrowed his brow and shot a sideways glance at Jennifer, whose eyes were riveted on the old man.

"The committee had ready access to large amounts of operating capital from among their various publications. They siphoned some of this money to use in financing art purchases— pieces they knew the Chief would want."

"Let me guess who told them what he might want," said Sam. He detected a hint of shame, or what might pass for it, in the face of the arrogant old man.

"He brought it on himself." The belligerence was back in Symington's voice. "Besides, I was given no choice. I had my own problem—alcohol. I haven't taken a drink in over twenty-five years, but back then it was different. I couldn't stay away from the stuff. One of the members of the committee knew about it. He also knew that if Hearst found out I'd be fired in a minute. I managed to stay dry whenever I was up here on the hill. The Chief had his own problems in the form of Miss Davies."

Hearing her own name from the old man's mouth, Jennifer was momentarily startled.

"Marion Davies, the actress. Hearst's affair with her was a major embarrassment to the family, but she was the love of his life. And a real sweetheart." Symington issued a genuine smile. "We had one problem, she and I. We shared a common curse of drink. Hell, the Chief wouldn't even allow his guests, some of the biggest stars and politicians in the world, to bring booze up here. He was afraid she would go visiting at night looking for a bottle. Suffice it to say I either cooperated with the committee or lost my job. It would have meant separation from all of this." Symington waved his arm casually over the vases and other objects spread out on the table. "I was willing to do anything to avoid that."

"Tell us more about the committee," said Sam. "What did it have to do with Slade, and Drake's journal?"

Symington plucked the remains of the cigarette from its holder and crushed the butt in a small dish on the table. "As I was saying, the money that was siphoned off was in relatively small amounts, nothing that would catch anyone's attention from any single paper, but in the aggregate it was considerable, particularly when you adjust for Depression era dollars. I would make the purchase with the committee's money and transfer the item to some strawman who would pose as a new seller. Then I would tell the Chief that I had made a significant find. The strawman would add twenty, thirty, sometimes forty percent to the original price paid by the committee. The Chief would pay the inflated price, and after paying off the strawman the committee would pocket the difference. The operating capital would be returned to the respective companies and nobody was the wiser. You might call it an interest-free loan." Symington shook his head. "It was ingenious."

"I don't understand one thing," said Sam. "Why did the committee need to take company money? Why didn't it simply quote an inflated price to Hearst and use his purchase money to make the original buy?"

"You don't know much about the art market —and less about William Randolph Hearst." Symington smiled.

Sam shrugged. "Enlighten me."

"At those rarified prices, particularly back then, buyers and sellers were a very small, closely knit community. Word would have been out within a matter of days that the price paid by the Chief and the amount received by the seller didn't jive. Hearst didn't parlay one broken-down newspaper in San Francisco into a publishing empire on his good looks. No, the committee knew that it had to have a bogus middleman. A seller who would confirm to the world that the inflated price was what he received. There were a number of charlatans on the continent willing to play the part—for a price."

"And the journal?" said Sam.

Symington hesitated, as if he was about to divulge some family indiscretion. "The journal was the last in a long line of purchases that I negotiated on behalf of the committee. It was worked out through black market contacts I'd developed in Europe. During the Spanish Civil War I'd had the good fortune to meet a number of young, ambitious German Army officers, advisors to Franco and his military establishment. They dabbled in the art market themselves from time to time. While they had no real appreciation, they liked the money. Later when the Germans invaded Belgium, the Netherlands and France, these men knew there was a ready market in the West for any artworks their army plundered."

Symington leaned back in his chair and looked at the ceiling. "Hell, it made no difference to the committee where the stuff came from, as long as the Chief didn't know. It was easy pickins, particularly after this country entered the war in forty-one. The castle was boarded up and the Chief moved to apartments in San Francisco and New York. He came back only rarely."

"Why did he leave?" asked Jennifer.

"Some would call the rich eccentric. I prefer to say they are fickle," said Symington. "The authorities wouldn't allow him to use any lights up on his Enchanted Hill. Hell, he would have lit the place up like a beacon for Japanese subs and aircraft. To Hearst it wasn't worth having the place unless he could light it up like a Christmas tree. Anyway, it made it easy for us.

"I had the free run of the place. There was a skeleton staff in the house. They all knew me. None of them ever questioned my authority. We held meetings of the committee in the Chief's own library upstairs. As a group they had the collective balls of a brass monkey. We even carved out a special storage area up on top of the hill here—a place no one would ever look —to stash the purchases until they were formally delivered to the Chief. It was perfect."

There were footsteps at the other end of the cellar. Sam turned to see a slender woman in a sweater and long skirt approaching from out of the shadows.

"Mr. Symington?"

"Yes, Peggy."

"I just wanted to remind you about your ten o'clock appointment. He isn't here yet, but it's almost ten." The woman's voice was not unpleasant but cool in its efficiency.

"Fine let me know when he arrives. I'll talk to him upstairs."

"Fine." The woman turned and walked from the cellar.

"Never any visitors. Today I'm truly blessed." Symington bowed his head in Jennifer's direction, sarcasm dripping from the gesture. "An art instructor from Los Angeles. He wants to study some of the Italian Renaissance pieces. Where were we?"

"The Drake journal," said Sam.

"Ah yes. The final act of greed. In the summer of forty-two we received word that the

Germans had found the book in France. I found out later through independent sources that they discovered it in the library of a fourteenth-century abbey—I was never able to find out which one. But it appears that the king of France may have parted Drake from his journal on his stop there before his return to England on his round-the-world voyage. The Germans offered it to the committee for a million dollars. It was an extravagant price. By the same token the committee knew it was worth every penny. They believed they could get twice that from the Chief. It was a real find. Drake holds a special appeal for some people in California—the first Englishman to set foot in the state. And we knew that Hearst would make it the centerpiece of his library."

Symington tapped another cigarette from the package on the table and corked it into the holder. "We weren't sure the committee could siphon enough cash from the various newspapers to close the sale fast enough to avoid being discovered. Today I guess they'd call it a cash flow problem. The full committee met upstairs in the Gothic Study. They voted to make the purchase. I was to tell the Chief I'd found the journal through sources in England. We all knew he'd never touch the damn thing if he thought the Nazis had anything to do with it. I set up a strawman seller in London. The committee gathered the cash and we made arrangements for the purchase." Symington paused to light the cigarette and took several deep draws, expelling the smoke in perfectly formed rings.

He watched in silence as they drifted toward the vaulted brick ceiling of the cellar.

"What happened?" Jennifer shifted in her chair.

"It all collapsed," said Symington in a matter-of-fact tone. "The journal was carried by a German submarine to a coastal freighter off San Francisco. The committee found a noted scholar, a man who was intimately familiar with Drake's handwriting and the presumed contents of the journal, who could authenticate it. It shouldn't have been necessary. We were supposed to have obtained some sample pages from the book for authentication but there was some difficulty. They never arrived."

Jennifer's parchments, thought Sam.

"Anyway, our man was on board the freighter when the package arrived. He was in the process of examining the journal when it all unraveled. We were double-crossed by the man you mentioned earlier—Raymond Slade."

Symington rubbed his hands together and leaned his elbows on the table. "Slade was a man whose loyalty was only as good as the last dollar used to purchase it. We discovered later that in addition to his brisk black market trade he'd been selling information on ship movements both to the Germans and the Japanese. Not what you would call trustworthy, but he had all the right connections.

"Slade was second in command of an anti-submarine blimp that flew out of Treasure Island."

"We know," said Sam.

"What you probably don't know is that he

was supposed to keep military patrols out of the area of rendezvous until our man could authenticate the journal and transfer the money. Instead, the blimp flew in over the freighter and sent the German sub running for cover. Then he turned a machine gun on the freighter while his partner went down on a ladder, boarded the ship and at pistol point took the million dollars in cash and the journal."

"He had a partner?" said Jennifer. "Do you know who he was?"

Symington shook his head.

"And that's the last anybody ever saw of the two of them?" she asked.

"Not exactly," said Symington. "A week later I was contacted by telephone. It was Slade."

They heard a sound at the head of the stairs as the door opened. "Mr. Symington, your appointment is here."

"Fine Peggy. I'll be right up."

Symington stood behind the table. "Slade called because he wanted to sell the journal to the committee. He wasn't satisfied with the million he'd already stolen. He wanted another quarter of a million for the book."

Sam looked at Jennifer. An expression of calm resignation had come over her face, as if Symington's story had confirmed some deeply guarded secret. The announcement that Slade had survived the demise of the airship seemed to puncture some bubble of anxiety for Jennifer Davies.

"Could you describe Raymond Slade?" she asked.

"What's to say? He was an ordinary looking man."

"Is Raymond Slade alive?" Sam directed the question to Symington, but watched Jennifer Davies. She rose from her chair and walked away from the two men.

"I'm sure I would have no idea," said Symington.

"Do you think you could identify him if you saw him today?" she asked.

"If he's alive and if the years have not ravaged him too much, I suspect I could. I'll never forget the grin on the bastard's face the last time we met. It was a week after the blimp went down. We met to negotiate the terms for the purchase of the journal. He had the committee stretched over the barrel of a cannon, and he knew it. He'd taken a million dollars from us, but we couldn't go to the police. The committee was desperate to cover the money. One of the newspapers in the East missed a payroll. We all knew that Hearst would be onto us within days unless we could effect a quick sale of the journal and get him to pony up the cash. I don't know how they did it, but the committee scraped together another $250,000 and a rendezvous was set."

"What happened?" asked Sam.

"The Chief did us in. As rehearsed I laid it on thick. I told him we'd made a marvelous find in England, a treasure on a parallel with the Rosetta Stone—the journal of Sir Francis Drake's round-the-world voyage."

Symington began to laugh. "You know what he said? You're not going to believe this. He told me it would have to wait for a couple of months because he'd overextended his art budget. It seems he'd purchased several suits of armor from a dealer in New York and he was low on cash. Can you imagine?" Symington laughed. "The old man suddenly had an art budget. After thirty years of plundering every safe in his company for petty cash to feed an insatiable appetite for art, suddenly and without warning he'd gone on the wagon. He had a budget!" Symington's face was gripped in a mocking grin, his scornful laugh echoed off the walls of the chamber. "As I said earlier, Mr. Bogardus, beware of the rich, for they are fickle.

"Within a week he knew that money had been embezzled. And like a hound sniffing blood he cornered the members of the committee. One by one they talked, each implicating the other."

"What did Hearst do?"

"He fired them."

"That's all? You mean he didn't bring criminal charges?"

"No. Call it pride, ego—whatever. He wasn't about to permit a public bloodletting. He was very conscious of his reputation both as a businessman and a collector. He also knew that some of his competitors, other newspaper publishers, would have a field day at his expense. His reputation was worth more than money. To admit that he had been taken, not once, but many times over a long period—it was too much. Of course you have to remember that there were few men with a reach that could match his in those days. To earn the wrath of William Randolph Hearst was to be condemned to a life of obscurity, not only in publishing but in the world of politics and business generally.

"For me he reserved a special fate. I was unceremoniously hauled off the hill by private security and told I could never return. Hearst ordered me to a menial post at his paper in the city. I had little choice in the matter. My instinct told me that he wouldn't prosecute, but if I quit, if somehow I crawled out from under his heel, who knows what he would have done? For nine years I toiled in one insignificant position after another, never allowed to rise above the level of a minor functionary." A benign smile overtook his expression. "But even Hearst found it impossible to speak from the grave. I fared a little better after the old man's death, but by then this had all been locked behind boarded windows." He gestured to the house above. "It seemed that even in death circumstances conspired to carry out his will."

Symington started toward the door. "As pleasant as this has been, I'm afraid we'll just have to continue this conversation at another time." His tone was bathed in sarcasm.

"Mr. Symington, did you ever hear the name James Spencer?" Jennifer blocked his path around the desk.

He shook his head. "Am I supposed to know the man?"

"He was my father. He was on the blimp that day—the day it returned without its crew."

"Ah. I see." Symington arched an eyebrow. "Slade's confederate."

"We don't know that," said Sam. "It may

well be that this Slade killed Spencer before the blimp ever arrived at the ship."

"Well, as I said I don't know the man." He pushed his way past Jennifer and toward the stairs.

Sam took his arm. "Where's the journal?"

The old man turned, his eyes showering Bogardus with contempt as they settled on the hand clutching his arm. "Your guess is as good as mine. I never saw it."

"I don't buy it."

"Frankly, I don't care."

"Either we get the journal or we talk to the state," said Sam. "Your choice."

Suddenly Symington's expression turned pragmatic. "What assurance do I have that you'll stop with the book—that you won't bleed me dry?"

"We have no interest in anything but the journal. Whatever else you've done over the years is between you, your conscience and the state." Somehow Sam knew that the first two were of absolutely no consequence to Arthur Symington.

"All right." It was a small price to pay if it would silence them. "Wait here. I'll be back in less than an hour and we can talk further."

"We'll be here."

Chapter

10

The electrically charged particles were injected into the gun for their trip around the circular course of the small accelerator. Nearing the speed of light they would hurtle toward the point of impact. There the particles would be smashed, severing electrons from protons and revealing the molecular structure of the scrapings that Tony Murray had lifted from the parchments.

Edward Lefever was not a nuclear physicist, just a struggling graduate student in the history department. For extra cash to support his wife and two children he traveled once each week to Livermore, where he worked in a grants program pioneering the use of the cyclotron as a method for authenticating ancient artifacts.

Forty years earlier the particle accelerator

had produced the scientific breakthrough culminating in the development of the nuclear bomb. For the first time scientists were allowed to see inside the atom by smashing its component parts.

Now they were finding new and different ways to use the accelerator. The project on which Lefever worked was particularly exciting to historians and archaeologists. For decades they had been relegated to handwriting analysis or in some cases radiocarbon dating for the authentication of rare documents. The latter two methods were fraught with serious deficiencies. Analysis by so-called handwriting experts was subject to error and conflicting expert opinions. While scientific to a point, it ultimately relied on subjective judgments as to points of similarity and difference in pen strokes. Computer analysis and forensic examinations of paper and ink enhanced reliability, but the method was by no means conclusive.

Radiocarbon dating was developed in the late 1940s, but that method too was flawed. Keyed to a trace element, carbon-14, which bonded chemically with oxygen to form radioactive carbon dioxide, the process had severe limitations. To Lefever and his colleagues, the shortcomings of the process were many. The method was applicable only to organic matter, and dating of any object was possible only within broad time parameters. While it proved sufficient for geologists and archaeologists, it was often inadequate for historians interested in the relatively brief span of human civilization.

The grant project for which Lefever was employed used the cyclotron as a variation on the theme of carbon dating. Rather than measuring the rate of radioactive decay or the half-life of carbon-14, the particle accelerator was used to count the ions in the sample to be dated. It had the benefits of using a sample as small as a few milligrams of carbon, and it provided information beyond mere dating. The method permitted the inquirer to actually read the molecular structure of the item being examined, to compare it with a known object of the same period and in that way to conclusively determine its authenticity.

Lefever had delayed the test for nearly a week, waiting for a smll vial from Oxford University in England—scrapings from another document known to have been written by Francis Drake immediately following his return to England after his round-the-world voyage.

He performed some final calculations, adjusted his glasses and pressed the large red button on the control panel, initiating the process that would pulverize the microscopic scrapings into subatomic particles. There was a low whine from the accelerator followed rapidly by a muffled bang as if a cap pistol had been fired somewhere deep within the bowels of the circular-tracked accelerator.

He moved to the small video monitor and in quick succession punched a number of keys on the computer keyboard below the monitor. Instantly, several columns of characters appeared on the screen. Lefever consulted a small notebook on the desk next to the keyboard, flipped one page in the notebook and studied it for several minutes.

Then slowly he reached for the telephone receiver and punched an eight-digit number. On the third ring a voice answered. It was steeped in a thick English accent.

Lefever spoke quietly into the mouthpiece. "It's me. There's no question. It's authentic."

"You're certain?"

"Yes. The solution of carbon suspended in the ink is a match with the other writings. It has to have been part of a special order for Drake. The scrapings from Murray also show traces of a compound identical with that of sea salt. But the clincher are the traces of oil from the hands and fingers of the author. They appear on the samples from both documents, those from Murray and those from Oxford—the molecular structures of the two are identical. It's as conclusive as fingerprints."

"Good. How long can you sit on the results before you tell Murray?"

"I'm not sure. He's been talking directly with the professor. I can tell the prof that I just won't have time to get around to analyzing the results for a day or two."

"That should give us enough time. Bury it for two days, and by that time I'll have the journal and it won't matter."

"Okay." Lefever heard the click as the telephone receiver on the other end dropped into its cradle.

* * *

Nick pushed the compact rental car to its limit, passing vehicles in the slower lanes as he raced along 101 south toward Cambria. A small dark sedan kept pace a half mile back.

Jorgensen gazed vacantly at the road ahead and the passing countryside, then glanced at his watch. In twenty minutes he would be in San Luis Obispo. He was fighting to stay awake. Fletcher'd had him locked in a cell with two drunks all night. Nick had stolen perhaps an hour's sleep between the retching sessions of his two cellmates at the commode. The jailer had roused him at 4:00 A.M. and by the time he'd gotten out and back to Angie's, dodged her dozen questions and grabbed a shower and a change of clothes it was after 7:00. Angie had demanded to know where Sam was and whether his absence had anything to do with the parchments. Nick was surprised that the old lady knew about the documents. She must have been talking to Carol.

He could only hope that Sam and Jennifer hadn't already checked out of the inn. For the moment his principal concern was Jake, who was still in jail. There had been no arraignment, and so no bail had been set that Nick could post for his release. He knew that as soon as Sam found out, he would call friends in the city and Jake would be out in an hour. But Jorgensen had been unable to reach Bogardus by telephone. He'd tried a dozen pay phones at gas stations since leaving the city.

Sam would be mad as hell when he discovered that Nick had left the city, but he didn't care anymore. He was tired of sitting around waiting for telephone calls from Bogardus, calls that never came.

Nick felt the welt on his throat where the chauffeur had nearly crushed his windpipe the night before. There were scratches and abrasions on the skin but the swelling was beginning to go down. Until he shifted his body in the seat and felt the stiffness in his joints, his bout with the sadistic chauffeur seemed like a bad dream. The holding cell at City Hall had robbed him of all sense of time.

Nick rounded a horseshoe curve in the road and looked askance at the sprawling Madonna Inn. The pink facade and large sandstone boulders stood like a monument to money, the creation of a local tycoon whose fortune was anchored in highway construction. In a state where fast-food stands built in the image of hotdogs and geodesic oranges are considered to be historic structures, the complex had become a landmark, commonly accepted by motorists as the coastal halfway point between San Francisco in the north and Los Angeles in the south. He pushed on south along 101 toward the cutoff to the coast and Cambria on Highway 1.

Nick wondered why he hadn't received results of the final lab tests from Tony Murray. Murray had told him it would only take two days to establish the provenance of the pages of parchment. Nearly a week had now passed. He'd half-expected a message from Murray when he'd gotten back to Angie's after his night in jail, but there was nothing.

He passed through the outskirts of a small

town and slowed as he took the off-ramp toward Morro Bay and Highway 1.

The Westminster chimes repeated their melodic tone as the doorbell was rung a second time.

"I'm coming. I'm coming." Angie trudged down the long hallway. She slid the small wooden stool to the center of the front door and stepped up so she could reach the prism of the peephole with her eye. She was a woman careful to the point of paranoia. For forty years she had performed a daily ritual, checking each knob on the gas range, unplugging the television and tugging on the security chain at the front door before departing the house by the rear to walk to the grocery store a block away.

The man on the front porch was tall and to the far side of middle age, with a mass of well-groomed gray hair. He wore a tweed sport coat and bow tie. His eyes peered through tortoise-shell-framed glasses from under thick brows. His nose, a bit bulbous, was accentuated by the fish-eye lens of the peephole.

"What do you want?" Angie commanded in the tone of a drill sergeant.

"I'm looking for Professor Jorgensen. I'm a colleague from the campus." There was a strong English accent to the voice.

Angie paused for a moment to consider, then stepped off the stool, kicked it to the side of the hall and unlatched the chain. She opened the door and stood looking up at the well-dressed man, who cracked a broad smile.

"How do you do, madam? My name is Jason

Stone. I'm a close friend of Professor Jorgensen. He asked me to drop by to pick up some items for one of his classes."

Angie toyed with a few loose strands of hair in a self-conscious effort to tuck them back into the bun on the top of her head. She smiled, taken by the elegant looks and manners of the tall stranger.

"That's funny, he didn't say anything about it to me." Her voice took on an airy, genteel quality.

"Well, you know Nick. I suspect he would never trouble a lady with such trivial matters." Jasper Holmes bent slightly at the waist and issued his most disarming smile. "Why don't you call him to the door, and perhaps he can introduce us?" A blush settled into Angie's cheeks. It was a challenge Holmes knew she could not perform, since he'd spent the better part of the morning parked at the curb a half block from the house, waiting and watching until he saw Nick leave in a yellow taxi.

"I'm afraid he's not here right now."

"Oh, that is a shame, and I came all the way from Berkeley just for this purpose."

"I should have thought it was England." She laughed, trying to make small talk.

"Actually, Australia, madam. Sydney." Jasper drew out his a's, affecting a crude accent from down under.

"What is it you were supposed to pick up?" she asked.

"Some lecture notes for a class. Without them I'm afraid I'll be completely lost." He gave an impish laugh and shifted his leather briefcase to the other arm.

Angie stood in the doorway, her face a picture of indecision.

"I'm certain I would recognize the papers immediately if I saw them." Jasper tried to influence the verdict. "Professor Jorgensen will be quite upset if I'm compelled to cancel the class." The uncertainty in her eyes evaporated.

"I suppose it would be all right." Angie backed away from the door and allowed him in.

Three minutes later Jasper stood in the basement apartment and listened as Angie climbed the wooden stairs to the back porch. "Like putty in my hands," he snickered. Satisfied that he was alone he began to ransack the room, careful to return each item to its proper place. He was convinced there was no more than a fair chance the old woman would ever remember to mention his visit to Jorgensen when he returned, much less recall the bogus name he'd given her at the door. One more interested and charming smile, he thought, and she'd probably forget her own name.

He grinned inwardly as his ego floated to the ceiling. Unfortunately for Holmes, his eyes did not follow it, or he might have seen the small hole in the plaster directly overhead.

Australian my ass, thought Angie as she pressed her eye to the small hole drilled in the closet floor years before when Sam was a small boy and the basement room his play area. Proper supervision of children required sufficient interest and a little guile. Angie Bogardus possessed a healthy portion of both. She had taken on a renewed responsibility for her son's welfare now that the Paterson woman was out of his life.

She watched as Holmes grabbed a long cylindrical cardboard tube that rested against the wall in the corner and popped the plastic cap from the end to peer inside. He threw the empty tube against the bed in exasperation, and began poring through a stack of blue books on a corner table. Not finding what he was looking for, he rifled through the men's clothing hung on a rod against the far wall.

Suddenly he spied a briefcase on the floor propped against the leg of a chair. He opened it and dumped the contents on the bed. Brushing aside several small scraps of paper, the Englishman stopped motionless for a brief second and stared down at a single shiny object on the bed cover. Quickly he grasped the key and read the attached tag. It contained both the name of the bank and the account number for the safe deposit box. Finally he would have his chance to read the Drake parchments.

Holmes bolted from the basement and stopped only momentarily to check the back stairs before letting himself out of the yard by the side gate.

He cast an arrogant grin and touched the two fingers of his right hand to his forehead in a mock salute as he drove in front of Angie's house. "Next stop First United Bank," he whispered.

Behind the lace curtains in the large bay

window of the living room, Angie Bogardus squinted and rapidly penned onto a small pad the license number of the little foreign car as it disappeared down the hill.

"Mr. Symington, this is Dr. George Johnson from the Art Center in Los Angeles. He's here to examine some of the Italian Renaissance pieces in Casa del Mar."

As the man in the pinstripe suit swung around for the introduction, Arthur Symington stood paralyzed in the doorway to the kitchen, unable to speak. The awkwardness of the moment was evident in the air as seconds passed in silence. The secretary sensed the uneasiness of her boss. Finally Symington pried his eyes off of the visitor.

"Thank you, Peggy. You can go back to your office now. I'll call if I need further assistance."

The two men stood silent near the opening to the huge institutional pantry as the secretary left the house by the kitchen entrance.

Johnson spoke. "Are you surprised to see me after all these years?"

"Surprised is an understatement. What business can we possibly have after all this time?"

"Just one very quick matter and I'll be on my way, never to trouble you again."

Symington's expression was a blend of anxiety and contempt. He stood silent, unwilling to offer an opening that might extend the conversation.

"I want the journal."

"You what?" Symington couldn't believe the audacity.

"I want the journal. Where is it?"

Symington began to laugh. His voice filled the room and echoed out through the pantry to the morning room, where a tour was assembling. "You of all people—have no claim whatever to that book."

He would surely have been less cavalier had he been privy to the telephone call placed earlier that morning by the man who called himself George Johnson.

"Hello." The two syllables at the other end of the line had carried a distinctive English accent.

"Well, did you get them?"

"Like clockwork. The old lady never suspected a thing. They'd stashed them in a safe deposit box at a local bank. All I needed was the key and the box number. The teller at the bank asked me to sign the register, so I used Jorgensen's name. Remind me not to use that bank. As I suspected she never compared my scrawl with the signature card on file." The arrogance of his airy tone made Jasper Holmes sound like a man who had just seduced a vestal virgin.

"Have you had time to look at them?"

"I've done little else all night." Holmes paused for effect.

"And, my dear man, you won't believe what I found. It's little wonder Dr. Jorgensen was not anxious to have me reading over his shoulder at the apartment that evening. I'd venture to say that we're on the verge of the quintessential find of this century. Archaeologists will refer to it in the same breath with Tutankhamen's burial chamber."

"What are you talking about?" Thirty seconds later Johnson finally understood why Jennifer Davies and the other lawyer were so intent in their quest for the Drake journal. And now that he knew the secret he was equally determined to have it.

"I know it's not here in the castle. Hearst never received it, did he?" asked Johnson. "If he had it would have been reported in the papers. That means you have it, or you know who does."

"No. I don't have it."

"But you know where it is, don't you?"

Symington was trapped, caught like a board in a vise between the lawyer in the basement and now this. For an instant he wondered why after all the years the book had become so important that it should threaten his security twice in the same day.

Then, as if to satisfy the self-fulfilling prophecy of his interrogator, he answered, "Yes, I know who has it." It would at least buy him the time he needed to empty the chamber and disappear.

"Well?"

"A lawyer by the name of Samuel Bogardus. I delivered it to him earlier today."

With Symington's words Johnson deftly fingered the small button on the handle of his ornate cane.

The heavyset woman sauntered through the pantry door in pink slacks and a dark sweater. She moved with some grace for her size, hold-

284

ing a pair of dark glasses in one hand and clutching her purse in the other. The rooms were immense and institutional, more suited to a large hotel or restaurant than a private home. But Hearst liked to entertain and he did so in a grand style, as was evidenced by the mammoth kitchen that serviced La Casa Grande.

She moved around the stainless steel table toward the appliances on the opposite wall, her gaze caught by a single item. The antiquated Frigidaire refrigerator with its large wood-paneled door and top-mounted motor was identical to the one her mother had had when she was a child, only bigger. The shape of the door, the texture of the wood, the glossy enamel paint and antique handle each transported her to childhood memories, and for a moment she mused as if the icebox itself would contain her mother's pecan pie.

The illusion was broken when the woman saw the thin red stream running down the panel below the main door. It pooled in a small puddle on the floor in front of the refrigerator.

She reached out and tentatively tugged on the handle of the refrigerator door. To her surprise the old bolt slid smoothly from its casing in the lock. Then, without warning, as if she'd unleashed some grisly genie from behind the sealed door, it shot open, pushing her against the table in the center of the room. The body of a man bathed in blood tumbled from the refrigerator and sprawled onto the floor at her feet. His eyes were open, his legs thrashing. Terror filled every crease of the woman's face. Her heart pounded like a bass drum, her eyes wide with fright, her jaw hanging open and quivering as if afflicted by palsy. The woman stammered, trying to speak, then struggling to fill her lungs with air she emitted a mind-piercing scream.

Members of the tour party who'd begun to leave the pantry and enter the kitchen stood motionless, frozen in place by the hysteria of the woman who now backed slowly away from the refrigerator, both hands pressed tightly against her mouth and her gaze fixed on the floor. Cautiously, in halting steps, the other tourists moved toward the kitchen and around the array of appliances and tables to see what had happened.

With the first scream Sam and Jennifer rushed headlong toward the stairs that led up to the kitchen. Sam bolted up the steps two at a time and threw open the door. As he entered the kitchen he was confronted with the faces of a dozen dazed tourists, their eyes fixed on the floor.

Bogardus moved around the stainless steel table and suddenly stopped dead in his tracks. His breathing stopped for an instant as he stared down into the twisted face of Arthur Symington. Blood streamed from a wound in the old man's abdomen and pulsated onto the floor in spasmodic surges, while a trickle ran from the corner of his mouth. Bogardus quickly pulled off his jacket and moved next to the body, placing the coat over the abdominal wound and applying pressure.

The guide looked over. "Are you a doctor?" she asked.

"No."

"I'm gonna call for an ambulance. Can you stay with him?"

Sam nodded without looking at the woman.

"I won't be long." The guide ran from the kitchen.

Jennifer moved around the table and for the first time saw Symington lying in the pool of blood. She squelched a slight scream with both hands and turned away.

There was a buzz of voices from the gaggle of tourists who were now chattering among themselves. An older woman moved in to console the heavyset lady in the pink pants. Several of the women teamed up and led her from the kitchen back toward the pantry.

Sam knew that the ambulance was a futile gesture. Its intended cargo would be cold before it arrived. Arthur Symington was dying. His eyes were open wide, staring directly at Sam, and his lips quivered. The complexion of his face had begun to drain as the blood in his body coursed toward the wound in his abdomen. Between hisses of agony Symington tried to speak.

There was nothing he could do for the old man.

Sam leaned over the body and placed his lips against Symington's ear as if to calm him. "Where's the journal?" Sam spoke under his breath.

Symington's chest rose. "The chamber."

"What chamber? Where is it?" Bogardus carried on the conversation at close quarters, against the side of Symington's head.

"The Simeon chamber."

Sam pressed his head against the old man's ear again and whispered, then placed his own ear against Symington's lips. As the breath carrying his words was expelled, the prostrate body went limp. His legs ceased their aimless movement. Bogardus raised his head and looked down into the vacant trance of death fixed in the eyes of Arthur Symington. Sam slowly stood and looked at the small group of tourists. Their chatter had stopped, hushed by the obvious stillness of death that lay before them on the floor.

He rose and moved to Jennifer, who'd slowly backed out of the kitchen in an unconscious retreat from the lifeless form on the floor. She now stood near the doorway to the pantry. He gripped her shoulder to steady her and whispered into her ear. "Let's get the hell out of here before the police arrive."

The old lady peered through the rotting and bleached planks of the wooden fence. She had returned to the garden after putting two pies in the oven just in time to see the white sedan roll up the driveway and park in front of Arthur Symington's house. "Like a damn freeway today," she muttered under her breath. An elegantly dressed man wearing an expensive overcoat exited from the driver's side of the car. He was carrying a long metal object that seemed incongruous until he gripped it by the handle and dropped the tip to the ground. It was a walking cane. The man walked up the path to the front door of the house and paused. He did not knock on the door but instead pulled a pair of dark gloves from the pocket of his tapered suit coat. He made a casual turn, taking in the sights in all directions, and stood with his back to the door of the house as he tugged the tight-fitting gloves onto each hand. The old lady was about to rise and offer assistance when the man lifted the handle of the cane from his forearm where it hung and pressed something along the side of the handle. There was a sharp click and a slender metal blade sprung from the tip of the cane. It was long and stiletto-like, with a needle-sharp point.

The woman froze in place and pressed one eye closer to the crack in the fence. The man now had his back to her and was holding the cane near the tip with both hands, levering it back and forth in the jamb of the door. She could hear the splinter of wood. Suddenly the door opened. The man paused for a second and turned, looking over his shoulder as if to see if anyone was watching. The woman moved slowly to one side of the opening in the fence to en-sure her concealment. She waited several sec-onds. When she looked back the man was gone and the door was again closed.

The old lady moved in a half crouch away from the fence and toward the path leading to her house thirty yards away. She was puzzled. The man did not look like a burglar. He was too well dressed. But there was no doubt that he had broken into the house. It was a matter for the sheriff.

*   *   *

Inside Arthur Symington's house George Johnson moved quickly to a back room. It was cluttered with papers and books, the model of a scholar's warren. An ancient roll-top desk stood against one wall, the entire writing surface covered with open books, scraps of paper and clippings from magazines and newspapers. Many of the books were oversized, containing glossy lithographs of paintings and tapestries. Against the opposite wall the legs of a flimsy card table bent under the weight of more volumes and loose papers.

He sweat profusely under the long coat, but it was necessary to cover the blood that stained a portion of his suit jacket. It was a long shot. But he more than anyone knew that Arthur Symington had a reputation for deceit. It was something in the old man's eyes as the blade penetrated that told George Johnson that Symington's final words had been a lie.

He quickly rifled through the books, throwing them onto the floor as he finished examining each. He cleared the table, sweeping the last scrap of paper to the floor with his hand, and turned his attention to the desk. He pulled out the drawers one by one, dumping the contents of each into a pile on the table and quickly pawing through the items. In disgust he ran his arm through the last pile and sent most of the items on the table careening to the floor. There was no sign of the journal in Symington's study.

For an instant his eyes fixed on a large black and white framed photograph hanging askew on the wall over the desk. Much younger and with dark hair, Arthur Symington was dressed in a knaki shirt and pants, kneeling on the ground. He cradled a furry creature against his chest. It was an unusual outfit and an uncharacteristic pose for Hearst's pretentious art consultant.

Behind the figure in the picture was an ancient wheelbarrow with steel-rim wheels and a Ford Model-A flatbed truck loaded with kegs of nails and other construction materials. Off to the side were forms of freshly poured concrete with steel reinforcing bars protruding from the gray stew. The tail of the spider monkey nestled against Symington's chest wrapped serpent-like around the man's arm.

Johnson turned and surveyed the room one last time. Perhaps the lawyer had the journal after all, or if he didn't he knew where it was.

He had just turned off the dusty dirt road leading from Arthur Symington's and had gone about a quarter of a mile down the country road when George Johnson passed a sheriff's patrol car traveling at high speed in the opposite direction, with its overhead lightbar flashing amber, red and blue. The patrol car used no siren. The man watched cautiously in his rear view mirror as the sheriff's vehicle disappeared in the distance behind him.

By six in the evening Nick was able to relax at last. He had caught up with Sam and Jennifer at the inn and to his surprise Bogardus was not angry to see him. In fact the lawyer welcomed him with open arms, asking why he had not brought Carns along. It seemed Sam needed volunteers for some planned but as-yet-unstated venture, and Nick began to have second thoughts about his trip. Without pausing to ask questions he told Bogardus that Carns was in jail. A quick phone call to a friend at the city lock-up and Sam discovered that Jake Carns had been released on his own recognizance at noon that day.

They had dinner, Nick polishing off a healthy cut of prime rib. He nibbled on the last piece of French bread as Sam ate and Jennifer picked around the edges of her plate. She had no appetite after the events of the day. The twisted face of Arthur Symington, his bloodied body sprawled on the floor of the castle, was etched in her mind. It would be a long time, if ever, before she would forget it.

"I don't know, Sam. I'm beginning to think Jennifer's right. Maybe we should just turn the whole thing over to Fletcher and let the cops take care of it."

Nick waited for her echo of support, but it never came.

"The two of you will have to decide what to do." Her tone was glacial. It matched the ice in her eyes. Without explanation she had detached herself from the events of the last twenty-four hours. "Excuse me." She rose from the table and headed for the ladies room.

"What happened between the two of you?" Nick looked over at Sam.

"It's just a case of nerves, I think. She'll be all right in the morning."

"After seeing Symington get skewered like a roast on a spit, I guess I can understand it," said Nick. "But maybe she was right. Maybe this is a matter for the police."

Bogardus ignored the suggestion. Nick asked the waiter for a menu to review the dessert selection.

Sam couldn't help but notice how Nick's proposal for police intervention had suddenly lost its appeal for Jennifer. Two days before she had advocated the same thing. Why all of a sudden had she changed her mind? What was she up to? He shelved his concerns for the moment and took the opportunity to talk in private with Nick.

"There's something you two don't know," said Sam. "Before he died Symington told me where to find the journal."

A manufacturer of rubber masks could have patented the expression on Jorgensen's face. His fork was frozen in space halfway from the plate to his mouth. He dropped it back into the dish.

"From Jennifer's description I thought you were playing good samaritan down there on the floor, sacrificing your jacket to save the old man," said Nick.

"I'm afraid I was not entirely altruistic."

"Well, I'm waiting. Where is it—the journal?"

"It's going to require another trip to the castle."

"It's up there?"

"That's what the old man said before he died. And I'm going to need help to get it."

Chapter

11

Fletcher held the receiver pressed tightly to his ear. "Yes, I want you to stay with them and no, we can't pick 'em up. Bogardus is not a fugitive, at least not yet. There's nothing we could hold him on at this point, and he'd probably sue the hell out of the city if we tried. Do you have any idea who the woman is?"

Fletcher listened and wrote the name "Jennifer Davies" on a note pad on his desk.

"I'll check up on her and see what shows up, but Davies is a common name and they may have trouble getting a make. Jack, listen to me. Don't let 'em out of your sight. I don't care how many times they go up to the castle, stay with 'em."

He slammed the receiver into the cradle of the phone. "Damn it."

"What's wrong, Lieutenant?" The desk sergeant had just walked into the room with a file folder for Fletcher's In basket.

"Jorgensen led us right to Bogardus."

"I thought that's what you wanted."

"The problem is Bogardus is leading us in circles. So far the city's paid almost a hundred and fifty bucks for tickets to tour San Simeon for two of its finest."

"What?"

"Bogardus and his entourage have been up and down the hill at San Simeon like mountain goats. So far they've visited the main floor, the gardens, the two guest houses and most of the upper floors of the castle."

"A vacation?" The sergeant raised his eyebrows.

"Hardly," said Fletcher. "They're looking for something." Fletcher pieced together the bits of information he'd gotten from Jeannette Lamonge the day before at the hospital. He scanned the notes he'd taken during her interrogation. The girl finally calmed down enough to talk, but she hadn't been as helpful as he'd hoped. Her uncle had gotten to her and convinced her to tone down her story. Fletcher was sure of it.

Still, she did tell him that the chauffeur whose body they scraped off the sidewalk in front of the shop had been in the store on the day Paterson was murdered. She also revealed that Paterson had come into the shop asking about some parchments. Fletcher's knowledge of Francis Drake was vague at best. Beyond what little he could remember from high school history, he associated the name with one of the city's finer hotels.

Now Bogardus was busy exploring Hearst Castle, a veritable museum of priceless paintings and other treasures. No. It wasn't drugs that he was dealing with. Unless he missed his bet, Fletcher was now certain that Bogardus was hip deep in some art scam.

He looked up at the sergeant. "Listen, can you give me a hand?"

"Sure."

"I want you to run a C.I. and I. check on two people. Here's the first." He handed the sergeant the note paper with Jennifer's name on it. "I think it's a dead end without a set of her prints, but try anyway. The other name is Arthur Symington." He spelled the last name. "Give me everything you can on both of 'em."

"Who are they?"

"I have no idea who the girl is. As for the guy, Mayhew only got bits and pieces. According to the state police Symington was a private art consultant at the castle until yesterday when somebody stabbed him to death."

"Was Bogardus involved?"

"We don't know. But it is strange that wherever Bogardus and his pals go dead bodies seem to turn up." Fletcher wrinkled his forehead. "Then see if you can find a set of prints for Bogardus. Try Motor Vehicles. If they don't have a good set try the State Department, passports. He looks to me like the kind who has traveled abroad. If you find a set send them to the state police and see if they can get a match-up on anything relating to the Symington stabbing. We may nail him yet."

Fletcher fumbled with the papers on his desk. "Where's the address for that house in Daly City—the place Jorgensen was holed up in after we released him?"

The sergeant reached into the pile on the desk, retrieved a small slip of paper and handed it to Fletcher.

He looked at the address written on the slip and the name printed above it. "Angie Bogardus?" He looked questioningly at the sergeant.

"Yeah, the lawyer's old lady."

Fletcher wrinkled his eyebrows and folded the slip of paper into his shirt pocket. "Listen, if anybody calls I'll be out of the office for a few hours. If something hot breaks down the coast you can reach me on the radio."

Fletcher grabbed his coat and headed for the elevator.

The Medici might have considered the room magnificent. As far as Sam was concerned it was twentieth-century Hearst garish. A soft light filtered through the rose-colored windows of the Gothic Study. It was Hearst's private office, the nerve center of his publishing empire when he was in residence at San Simeon. Four large leaded glass chandeliers hung from the barrel-vaulted arches that supported the ceiling. The arches were covered with delicate murals of biblical and mythical scenes painted by one of the hundreds of artisans employed in the construction of the castle. The room was furnished with dark baroque pieces. A polished conference table with high relief carvings covering its serpentine legs stood in the center of the room. From a distance, the legs of the heavy table appeared as ropes of carved wood curving toward the floor. The table was surrounded by ten high-backed armchairs, each with tapestry-upholstered backs and seats. Parchment pages from monastic songbooks dating to the Middle Ages formed the lampshades for several floor lamps, and an immense ornate Flemish candlestick graced the drop-leaf table directly in front of them. Like most of the grand house, the ambience of the room was a mixture of Renaissance Europe and 1930s Americana. Hearst thought nothing of topping a fifteenth-century table with an Art Deco lamp and shade—a mixture of the elegant past and the practical present.

But Bogardus had no difficulty focusing his attention. His gaze was fixed on the heavy, dark wood book cabinets that lined the walls of the study below the windows. There, compressed between each of the massive curved arches, behind the metal filigree of the cabinet doors, were hundreds of volumes from Hearst's private collection. Sam's heart sank. What better place to hide the journal, he thought.

He raised his eyes and looked at the guide who'd paused for a moment in her monologue to allow the group to look about the room.

"How many books are there in this room?" asked Sam. His tone was that of an itinerant tourist.

The guide, a middle-aged woman, looked at him and smiled. "Approximately seventy-five hundred. We're not sure precisely because we've never had the opportunity to catalogue them. And there are no insurance records. Mr. Hearst never bothered to insure any of the books. They're all irreplaceable."

"Imagine that." Sam gazed about the room, the fatuous grin of a tourist plastered on his face.

"And the room downstairs, the main library. How many books are there?"

"We estimate another five thousand, mostly first editions, but again we haven't catalogued any of them."

Jennifer leaned toward him and whispered. "Do you think this is it, the Simeon chamber?"

"Beats the hell out of me. It was Hearst's playroom." This was the fourth trip up the hill for the three of them that day. After the first two trips Nick and Jennifer realized that Sam had no solid information as to the precise location of the journal; his only clue was the two words uttered by Arthur Symington before he died. The trio had managed to dodge the army of state and local police roaming over the grounds after Symington's death. Sam remembered with some anxiety the fact that he'd left his business card with the guide and used his real name in signing the registration book in the trailer that served as the guide center.

"So this is where the father of modern journalism held court. Bet that carpet's well stained with the droppings of editors summoned in here for a lesson in yellow journalism." Nick pushed his way between Jennifer and Sam. The guide shot him a scornful glance then turned on her heels, putting distance between herself and the bearded offender.

"This could be a slight problem," said Sam.

"Listen to him," Nick mumbled to himself. "Excuse me if I appear to be the potentate of pessimism, but I would call twelve thousand volumes locked behind filigreed cabinets in a house with a security system that would shame the Denver Mint more than *a slight problem*. Unless of course you think the three of us can do the job during the daytime—maybe between tours."

Bogardus suddenly knew he had raced up a blind alley, and like a tomcat after a female in heat he had driven Jennifer and Nick before him.

Collectively he was sure that they had walked at least twenty miles that day, most of it up and down spiraling concrete staircases from the twin bell towers of the main house to the esplanade and back up again. He'd pushed the three of them harder than a drill sergeant. And now it had all come down to this. Without Symington to lead them to the right shelf to put their fingers on the precise volume they would never be able to find Drake's journal.

He lingered as the tour party headed for the stairwell. Reluctantly, he took one last look at the great room and followed along behind, down the stairs.

The three of them sat in glum silence two seats behind the bus driver as the heavy motor began to drone in low gear down the steep road. A child sat with his father directly ahead of them, chattering incessantly as the bus moved past the chainlink gate and onto Hearst Corporation land for the ride to the public assembly area fifteen hundred feet below on the flat plain near the highway.

As they rounded a sharp horseshoe curve the child pointed from the window and asked, "What's that?" His father, who looked exhausted, ignored the latest in what had become a perpetual stream of questions. In a vacant trance Sam gazed from the window at the object of the boy's fascination. His eyes fixed on the rusted metal bars as Symington's dying message echoed in his mind. Without explanation the words took on the clarity of crystal, transformed by some mystical force in the synapse of the brain. There by the side of the road, embedded under the pergola of Orchard Hill, rested the concrete and metal enclosures of Hearst's private zoo.

Sam rummaged through the aisles of the souvenir shop at the bottom of the hill until he found what he wanted. Nick and Jennifer were swept along in his wake. Bogardus pulled a book from the shelf, donned his glasses and rapidly thumbed the pages. He found what he was looking for in less than a minute.

"Here it is. Webster's Dictionary defines the word as follows—'of, relating to, or resembling monkeys or apes.'"

"What are you talking about?" asked Jennifer.

"I'm talking about the 'Simian Chamber.' Don't you see? Whoever made that pencil scrawl on the parchments spelled worse than I do. He wrote 'Simeon C.' on the page and like fools we accepted it. But the word was 'simian'—with an i-a-n."

Nick looked at him with a gaze he normally reserved for the dimwitted.

Sam rushed down the aisle away from his two companions, overtaken by the frenetic search for another volume. In a few seconds he found what he was looking for, a rack of books dedicated to Hearst and his castle, placed for the benefit of tourists near the shop entrance. He pulled one large volume from the rack, turned several pages, paused and began to read:

" 'During its time the Hearst zoo was the largest privately owned collection of wild and rare animals assembled in a single location. In it were represented more than one hundred species of domestic and wild beasts. Included were members of the cat family, including cheetahs, lions, leopards, panthers and the California mountain lion. Particularly prized'—" Sam slowed his pace as if to emphasize the words—

" 'were Hearst's collection of primates, sacred monkeys from Japan and India, orangutans, chimpanzees and gorillas. When it was abandoned in the late 1930s, most of the inhabitants of the zoo were presented to various West Coast cities for their public zoos.' "

He looked up from the page. "That's it. The 'simian chamber' is a damned monkey cage— probably in the labyrinth of tunnels and service areas behind the zoo."

"Don't you think you're reaching just a little?" It was clever, but Nick was skeptical.

"Not at all. Think about it. The place was ideal. Nobody ever visited it except handpicked employees, all of whom were on the dole with the committee. No guest was going to want to walk down to look at an empty zoo. Without knowing it, by closing his zoo Hearst presented the committee with the perfect hiding place. And unless I miss my bet, that's where the journal is."

"What difference does it make?" Jennifer's voice was tinged with a tone of finality. "You can't go up there."

"Why not?"

"There's three reasons I can think of off the bat."

"Like what?"

"Trespass, burglary and grand theft—which one do you want?"

"What—to poke around in an abandoned zoo—to look for a book that Hearst didn't even know he had, that's been lost to history for nearly three hundred years? It's up there, I know it."

He looked at Jennifer and dropped his voice an octave. "I have no idea what it is that you haven't told me. But ask yourself one question. What have we got to lose, either of us? You may have lost a father. I have already lost a good friend."

By now Jennifer recognized the word for the euphemism it was. His partner had been much more than a friend to Bogardus. A fire burned deep in his soul, a blaze that found expression in his eyes whenever anyone mentioned the name of Susan Paterson. Before she could say anything Bogardus spoke her thoughts. "You're right, before I'm finished I have to deal with whoever killed her. And I suspect you're going to have to wrestle with your own demon, whatever it is. But that's going to happen whether we find the journal or not. So we may as well find it."

She wasn't sure if it was in the logic of his argument or the appeal in his eyes, but there was something persuasive in what he said. There was nothing either of them could do to change what had already happened. But at least for a brief time, temporarily, they could immerse their pain in a distracting balm, they could lose themselves in a search for the journal.

She stood silent for several seconds and then almost with an air of resignation said, "Why not?"

"Well I'm glad that's settled." Nick's tone conveyed an obtuse sense of relief and a total lack of comprehension. "I'm not going to bother to ask what it was about, since I'm sure neither of you would tell me anyway. But I do have a question. How are you going to get into the zoo?"

"Let me rephrase that," said Sam. "The question properly put is how are we going to get into the zoo?"

"That's what I was afraid of. I know you were busy counting the books on the shelves when we were up there, but did you happen to notice those high fences, the ones with the barbed wire across the top and the electronic alarms on the gates, not to mention the army of park rangers and hired security? And that's only what I could see. Now if that doesn't give you cause for concern, you might consider my limited credentials as a cat burglar."

"That's the beauty of it. We don't have to go anywhere near the house. You weren't listening to the tape on the bus. The zoo's on company land. It's not part of the state monument."

"But it's a stone's throw from the house."

"Yes, it's also outside the gates. If we leave at dusk, and move, we can be out before daybreak."

Nick realized that any opposition was futile in the face of his friend's blind enthusiasm. "What the hell, what's a few more nights in jail?"

"Fine," said Sam. "Then we go tonight. Nick and I will cross over the fence on the highway at dusk and make our way to the top of the hill across country, staying off the road as much as possible."

"How far do you think it is to the top?" asked Jennifer.

"According to the guide it was five miles on the road. I'm guessing that we can cut the distance in half by going straight up."

Nick tired of the conversation as he sat on a box of books, pulled off a shoe and began to rub one of his aching feet. The store clerk looked at him disapprovingly from behind the counter. Nick smiled and mumbled a profane greeting under his breath.

Sam turned his attention to logistics. "All right, first we get some supplies—flashlights, good shoes for hiking, a length of rope . . ."

"Why do we need rope?" Nick protested.

"Who knows? But if we get up there and we need it I don't want to run back to town—do you?"

"Just checking."

Jennifer had waited for an opening. This was as good as it was going to get. "You forgot one thing."

"What's that?"

"If you're going, so am I."

Sam had anticipated it. In fact he was surprised she hadn't pressed the issue earlier. "No, we're going to need somebody down here in case we get in trouble. If they pick us up we'll need somebody to call the city for help and get money to bail us out . . ."

"Then I guess you're staying. Because if anybody goes up that hill I intend to be along."

He paused briefly like a vendor entertaining the last offer of purchase.

"All right." He headed for the door of the shop and stepped out into the parklng lot with Jennifer a half step behind. "We'll drop you at the inn, then Nick and I will get the stuff. We'll be back to pick you up in an hour."

She was insulted by the transparency of his plan.

"Sam." Her voice froze him in mid-stride as he reached the passenger door of Nick's rental car. "If you're not back in an hour I'll call the cops and tell them everything I know—including where you've gone."

A frown spread over his face. "What size hiking shoes do you wear?"

"Six medium."

*   *   *

"Damn it. It'll turn over but it won't start."

"Can we use the radio?"

"What for?"

"To call the highway patrol or the county sheriff."

"Hell, we don't have any authority to be down here—we're two hundred miles outside our jurisdiction."

"If we lose those two and Fletcher finds out, we're gonna wish we were a thousand miles away."

Jack Mayhew was in a state of panic. He pushed his partner out of the driver's door, slid behind the wheel and turned the key in the ignition. He listened to the starter motor as it drained the life out of the battery. Mayhew watched as the sleek blue Porsche moved slowly down the main street of Cambria toward the highway.

"Don't worry about it. They're probably just going back to the room. We can catch up with them in five minutes once we get this thing started."

Trailing behind the Porsche in the distance a small white sedan moved past the unmarked police car with the two officers. The man at the wheel issued a sinister smile as he clutched the brass handle of the walking cane on the seat beside him. He watched the two detectives lift the hood and begin to work frantically on the engine. It was a child's prank, but effective.

Twenty minutes earlier the two cops had abandoned their car to follow Bogardus and his companion on foot. While they were gone the man had purchased a medium-sized potato from a small grocery store across from the parking lot, walked across to the unmarked police car and casually jammed the potato over the end of the car's exhaust pipe. The spud effectively sealed off the exhaust, preventing the car from starting. It would be the last place the two would think to look.

Sam and Nick had one final stop to make. Bogardus wanted a large-scale topographic map of the castle area. There was only one place in town where he could get it and the shop was closed. As he reached the highway he swung south.

"Where are you going? The inn's in the other direction."

"I know. But I'm gonna have to go down to Los Osos to get the map."

"Can't we do without it?"

"No." Sam shook his head. "Not at night. We're liable to walk off a cliff. It'll only take twenty minutes."

"You heard what Jennifer said. If we aren't back in an hour she'll call the cops."

"If we get late we'll give her a call and tell her what's holding us up."

As Sam headed south down the highway the white sedan turned right and drove north on Highway 1 toward the inn.

There was a slight rap on the door. Jennifer wasn't sure she heard it at first. The knock was so light she thought it might be someone in an adjoining room. She stopped and listened. There it was again.

"Just a second."

With the two men gone she'd taken the opportunity for a quick shower. Haphazardly toweling herself dry she quickly slipped into the paisley dress she'd worn on the trip down from the city. Her head was draped in a towel, her hair dripping from the shower as she groped for the door knob. Finding it she opened the door a crack and quickly turned, skipping for the bathroom.

She planted herself in front of the mirror over the sink and rubbed the towel through her hair. "I was beginning to think you guys weren't coming back. But then I guess you didn't have a lot of choice." She couldn't resist the dig. "Got my shoes?"

There was no sound from the other room. She stopped ruffling her hair with the towel and listened. "Sam? Did you get the stuff?"

There was no reply.

"Nick?"

Her pulse quickened. If they were playing some prank she would kill them both. She removed the towel from her head and looked into the mirror. She could see nothing in the outer room. Jennifer took two small steps toward the bathroom door. Her bare feet made no sound on the cold, hard tile. The door to the room was half open. But there was no one there. She stood framed in the bathroom door for several seconds, looking around the room. Everything appeared normal. The books on San Simeon lay open on the table where Sam and

Nick had left them. The jeans she'd purchased the day before hung from the hook of the hanger snared over the top of the closet door, which was slightly ajar from.

"Hello? Is anybody there?"

There was no reply. The image of Arthur Symington's bloody body writhing on the floor flashed in her mind. Her heart pounded.

"God, please let it be them." The words were half-spoken under her breath.

With halting steps she placed one foot in front of the other and made her way toward the partially open door to the room.

"If you two are out there so help me I'll tear your eyes out."

She took hold of the door with both hands and braced herself to close it quickly. There was no movement apparent in the outside hallway. She closed the door and quickly fastened the security chain. Then carefully bracing her foot against the bottom of the door, she opened it a crack and peered out into the hall. She could see clearly in one direction. The long narrow corridor was well-lit, disappearing down a flight of steps at the end. There was no one there.

She shut the door again, turned the dead bolt and for several seconds stood silently just inches inside the closed door, listening for sounds, footsteps, laughter, anything that might reveal the presence of another soul in the hallway outside of the room. There was nothing. Nearly a half minute passed with Jennifer standing motionless, her eyes cast down at the foot of the door, her ears straining for any noise.

The pulse that pounded in her neck and head slowed to a more normal pace. For a moment her thoughts returned to her wet hair dripping onto the carpet around her feet. She walked back to the bathroom and picked up the towel. Standing in the bathroom door she rubbed the towel gently through her hair, her eyes fixed on the door to the hall.

It was an impulse driven more by curiosity than caution. The knocking must have come from one of the other rooms down the hall. She walked to the door and slid the security chain off its runner. Then in a single movement Jennifer turned the bolt, threw the door open and stepped quickly out into the hall. It was empty. There was no one there. She listened for the sound of voices in the adjoining rooms, but there was nothing.

Jennifer took several steps down the hall, stopping frequently to listen. Nothing. With a sigh she turned and went back into the room, closing and bolting the door behind her, then fastening the chain. As she turned, her eyes traced a line from where she stood six or seven feet to the closet door. It was now closed, and her jeans with their hanger lay in a heap on the floor in front of it.

Mustard dripped onto his tie as Fletcher devoured the oversized hotdog and downed the lukewarm coffee from the styrofoam cup. It was becoming a routine, the third time in a week he'd had dinner behind the wheel of his car, chasing a lead on one of the burgeoning number of open files on his desk.

This time he sat on a well-lit boulevard in the Berkeley hills, staring at the upscale apartment house across the street. It was the kind of dwelling leased by faculty from the university. The average student could never afford the rent. He checked his notebook one more time, reassuring himself that the address supplied by the Department of Motor Vehicles was correct.

An hour earlier he'd stood in the living room of the Bogardus home in Daly City and listened as Angie described the visit of the Englishman who called himself an Australian. She recounted in lurid detail the man's search of the downstairs apartment and his theft of a small silver key. Fletcher jotted rapidly in his notebook as the old lady supplied a detailed physical description of her visitor. After questioning her briefly he was satisfied she knew nothing of what her son might be up to.

Fletcher pocketed his notebook and was about to head for the door when the old woman surprised him. She handed him a scrap of paper with the license number of the vehicle the Englishman was driving. He snatched it up. God, I should fire Mayhew and hire her, thought Fletcher.

He milled about the entrance of the apartment building. The door had an electronic security lock that could be opened by the residents from their apartments. Fletcher checked the directory of tenants, which showed a separate name listed next to each button under the speaker mounted in the wall, until he found the name "Holmes, J." A few moments later a young woman exited the front door behind a small dog on a leash. Fletcher pretended to study the listings on the directory. Before the door could close behind the woman he grabbed it and gracefully slipped inside the building. She looked at him questioningly for a moment from the other side of the glass, then shook the leash and walked off down the street.

Fletcher took the elevator to the second floor and walked down the long corridor to apartment 26. He knocked on the door and seconds later heard footsteps on the other side.

"Who is it?"

Fletcher had the right place. He could cut the accent with a knife.

"Mr. Holmes, I'm Lieutenant George Fletcher, San Francisco Homicide." He held up his badge to the prism peephole in the door. Several seconds passed. Finally Fletcher heard the security chain slide from its railing and the door opened.

There was a serious expression in the eyes of the proper-looking Englishman. "Yes? What can I do for you?"

"I'm investigating a murder." A ration of shock to cut through the veneer of British reserve.

"What murder?"

"May I come in?"

He had no apparent reason to bar the officer from his apartment. Still, the Englishman's eyes were filled with objections.

"I'm very busy right now, Lieutenant . . ." Jasper moved grudgingly from the door.

"Fletcher."

"Of course."

The detective stepped into the apartment and Holmes closed the door behind him.

"What is this all about?" Jasper stood in the tiny entry area as if his feet were glued to the floor.

"I'm investigating the murder of one Susan Paterson." Fletcher lifted the small notebook from the pocket of his sport coat and wandered casually toward the living room, leaving Holmes standing alone in the entry.

The front room was a jungle of disheveled textbooks and papers piled on every available flat surface including the floor. A small card table had been added like an annex to the dining table to handle the overflow of clutter.

"I don't think I know the woman," said Holmes, moving like a shadow in Fletcher's wake.

"She was a lawyer in San Francisco. Maybe you know her partner, Mr. Samuel Bogardus."

"No, I don't think I've ever heard that name either."

"Well maybe the name Nick Jorgensen will ring a bell?"

Fletcher fixed his gaze on the Englishman's eyes and watched the pupils dance with indecision— to lie or not. That the question coursed through Holmes's mind like a pulse of electricity was evidenced by a brief hesitation.

"I'm familiar with a member of the faculty

by that name. Surely he's not accused of murder?"

"No, Professor. Right now I'm just looking for a little information." Fletcher moved to the card table and absently fingered some of the papers spread on the surface.

Jasper moved nervously toward the table and began to roll up several large irregularly shaped pieces of heavy parchment. "Please, Lieutenant, it may look like a mess to you, but every scrap of paper is a small part in a large research puzzle. And right now I know where each is located." He slid the rolled parchments into a protective tube and leaned it against the wall beside the dining table.

Fletcher merely grunted in response.

"Please have a seat." Jasper gestured toward a large overstuffed armchair in the opposite corner of the room.

Fletcher declined the offer and instead reached for a straight-backed chair at the dining table, a foot from the cardboard tube. He sat down, his eyes wandering over the surface of the table. "It must be interesting work. What exactly do you teach?"

"English literature." Jasper bit off the syllables. "But I'm sure you didn't come all this way to examine my curriculum vitae."

Fletcher looked at him questioningly.

"My resume, Lieutenant."

The detective pursed his lips and nodded slowly as if in comprehension. "No. No, actually I came over here in response to a complaint."

"A complaint?"

"Yeah. It seems you visited a woman out in Daly City earlier today." Fletcher flipped open his notebook, more for effect than assistance. "Angie Bogardus."

Jasper turned his back to Fletcher as he moved toward the large armchair in the corner. The detective imagined the icy caress of panic that flowed through Holmes's brain with the realization that the old lady had seen through his alias. But as he turned and sat, any hint of apprehension was concealed behind a placid mask of British reserve. Jasper crossed one leg over the other knee and stared stonelike in silence at the officer.

Fletcher's eyes returned to his notebook. "She says you came to her home and tried to pass yourself off as a friend of Mr. Jorgensen's. She says you ransacked a downstairs apartment and took something."

A sedate smile spread across Jasper's face. "Surely she's joking. The woman has a fanciful imagination."

"No sir. She was dead serious."

"Listen, Lieutenant. I did visit the house. It so happens that Professor Jorgensen asked me to pick up some papers for a lecture at the campus as he was scheduled to be out of town. I stood on her front stoop and told the woman that. She was gracious enough to allow me into Professor Jorgensen's apartment. I found the necessary papers and left. I'm afraid that's the long and short of it."

"Why did you use an alias?"

"What alias?"

"Jason Stone. That's the name she gave me."

Jasper began to swallow saliva, the first crack in the otherwise impassive exterior. "I introduced myself as Jasper Holmes."

"That's not what she says."

"Well, she's wrong."

"I see."

"Then you didn't take a small key from the apartment?"

"Of course not."

Fletcher reached for the cardboard tube propped against the wall and drummed his fingers against the plastic cap on the top end. "And of course you don't know anything about the murder of Susan Paterson?"

"I've already told you, I never heard of the woman." Jasper's voice had gone up an octave from his last response.

"What do you know about the Drake parchments?" Fletcher concluded the question with a drum roll of his fingers on the plastic cap and watched as the Englishman's gaze riveted on the long cardboard cylinder. The lawyer's mother had rattled on incoherently about the parchments for several minutes before Fletcher could pry himself away, and she insisted that her son was in danger. The old lady was sure that whoever had killed his partner was now after Bogardus.

"Let's quit playing games," said Fletcher. "Make no mistake concerning the seriousness of your position. If you continue with this story you'll become an accessory after the fact of murder."

There was no response from the Englishman.

"Well," Fletcher slapped his knees and rose from the chair. "If you want it that way get your coat and we'll visit the bank. The custodian of the safe deposit vault gave me a dandy description—right down to your argyle socks."

Jasper's posture slumped in the chair. He let out a long sigh as his demeanor cracked like an egg. "You have to believe me, Lieutenant. I know nothing of any killing." His eyes searched the floor. "But I can enlighten you concerning the parchments. Though I doubt you'll believe much of it."

Sam fidgeted nervously in the booth as he allowed the phone to ring at least twenty times. There was no answer. He told himself she was in the shower and unable to hear it. That was one possibility. But he knew there was another. The trip to Los Osos took longer than he'd figured. Perhaps long enough for Jennifer to conclude that they'd gone up the hill without her. He weighed the possibility that she had carried through on her threat and gone to the police. He walked quickly to the car.

Back on the highway Sam pushed the accelerator to the floor and gunned the Porsche north. Nick dug his fingers into the upholstery of the passenger seat as the car slid through the curves and swung repeatedly into the opposing lane of traffic to pass slower-moving vehicles.

Jorgensen was a puddle of cold sweat by the time the Porsche pulled into the parking lot at the inn in Cambria. Sam was out of the car and halfway through the lobby headed for the stairs before Nick could get his seatbelt off and his door open.

Bogardus bolted up the stairs two at a time and ran to the room. As he knocked on the door it swung open.

"Jennifer?"

There was no answer.

The closet door was half open, caught on a pair of blue jeans that had fallen to the floor with their hanger and were now wedged under the mirrored door. Sam moved toward the bathroom and rapped on the door.

"Jennifer?"

He opened it and flipped on the light. The room was empty, the shower curtain drawn back to expose the combination shower-tub, beads of water still visible on the tile walls.

He pushed past the door and in a half-daze walked inside, staring in disbelief at the words printed in large block letters on the mirror. The crushed lipstick used for the message lay in the sink.

Nick finally caught up with him and stood in the bathroom door looking over his shoulder.

"What the hell's going on?" asked Nick.

Sam didn't reply, but turned and walked out of the bathroom.

Nick passed his eyes over the words on the mirror.

BRING THE JOURNAL TO THE SEVEN SISTERS BY FOUR TOMORROW AFTERNOON OR THE WOMAN DIES.

Sam stood motionless, looking into the mirror of the closet door as if to rebuke the figure staring back at him. The puzzle was coming apart again and this time Jennifer Davies's life hung in the balance.

"He's got her, Nick."

"Who's got her?"

"Slade."

"What?"

Sam turned and looked at his friend, a dark frown on his face. "Don't you understand? It's been Slade all along. He killed Jennifer's father on the blimp. He killed Lamonge's brother to keep him quiet. He murdered Pat because she was asking questions about the parchments, and he stabbed Symington because the man knew the answers. Now he has Jennifer, and all we have is a riddle."

Nick looked at him with a puzzled expression.

Sam nodded toward the message on the mirror. "The Seven Sisters."

For the first time since entering the room Nick smiled. "Let's hope that finding the journal will be so easy."

Sam shot him a questioning look.

"The Seven Sisters are a succession of white sandstone cliffs near Point Reyes on the Marin Coast. They reminded Drake of the white chalk cliffs of Dover. That's why he called the place his Nova Albion when he landed."

"Well at least we have a point of rendezvous. Now all we need is the journal."

"Why are you so certain it's Slade we're dealing with?"

Bogardus fixed him with a steady stare. "There's one thing I never told you or Jennifer. Up in the castle when Symington was dying on the floor I asked another question. I asked who stabbed him. He was only able to say two words before he died—'the sailor.' As a dying declaration it might not be good enough for a conviction with a jury, but its good enough for me."

The cold hard reality of the message smeared across the bathroom mirror suddenly hit home. Sam considered the consequences of failure. What would have been major disappointment if their search for the journal proved futile only a few hours before had now taken on the dimensions of hideous tragedy.

Nick walked slowly from the bathroom toward the bed. He stroked his beard with his left hand, his mind lost in thought.

"There may be more to it than that."

"What do you mean?"

"There's something I didn't tell you because until now I wasn't sure it was important," said Nick. "The other day before I left from Angie's to head down the coast I made a telephone call to Akron, Ohio."

Sam's expression was one of irritation. He was in no mood for one of Jorgensen's irrelevant tales.

"I talked with a man who flies blimps. In fact he flies the blimp that Jennifer's father disappeared from."

"What?" Sam was torn from his preoccupation with the message on the bathroom mirror.

"It seems that the air frame on the gondola

from that navy blimp is still in use. It's been refurbished and refitted. Sam, the gondola from the Ghost Blimp is part of the Goodyear airship *America*.

"And that's not all. I got some interesting information from the pilot. It seems he's had an abiding curiosity about the history of that old gondola for some time. He's done research, performed some calcultions, and he has an interesting theory.

"What is it?"

"Try this on for size. He thinks two men walked off that blimp back in 1942."

"Two?"

"Yep. He's studied photographs taken of the ship as it floated in at the beach near the cliff house. It appears that the blimp came in at sea level and touched down several times in the sand and again on a nearby golf course. Then for some unknown reason it took off like a rocket and climbed several thousand feet before it drifted over the city. It stayed up for hours before it came down. According to the pilot only one thing can account for a steep ascent of that kind—displacement of a lot of weight. They found one small depth charge on the golf course. But that wouldn't be enough, according to the pilot. He says that after accounting for the weight of the depth charge, the additional jettisoned weight would have had to be in the neighborhood of 300 to 350 pounds to account for the rate of ascent. When it came down in the city nothing else was missing from the ship."

"So he concluded . . . ," said Sam.

"That two men stepped off that blimp some-where on the golf course that day, and that both disappeared as if they walked into a time warp." Nick completed the sentence.

The cold hand of fear tickled Sam's spine. Two men had walked off that airship thirty years before. One of them was Raymond Slade. For the first time since his initial interview with Jennifer Davies more than two weeks before Sam considered the possibilities and set-tled the doubt in his mind. For something now told him that James Spencer was alive.

Chapter

12

A budding carpet of soft green grass was already beginning to take hold, growing up through brittle dead straw from the previous spring's pasture. The light of the setting sun was a brilliant hue of orange and purple as it streaked through a bank of fog resting on the horizon far out to sea.

Sam and Nick huddled in the shadows of one of the small log huts that served as hay barns for the dwindling herd of zebras that grazed on the hills below the castle. They were both winded and Nick's legs were beginning to cramp. He bent at the waist, placing his hands on his knees and taking deep breaths.

"It's times like this that your body sends a four-letter word to your brain." Nick dribbled thick saliva onto the straw at his feet. "S-T-O-P."

"We only have a short distance to go. Up

that gully and into that grove of oaks." Sam pointed off in the direction of the top of the hill. "We'll wait there until it's completely dark."

"Do you know where we are in relation to the animal enclosures?" Nick gasped between panting breaths.

Sam laid the heavy nylon rope on the ground at his feet and fumbled in the pocket of his jacket for the map. He knelt on one knee and opened the map on the loose dirt of the hut floor.

"The best I can figure is we're here." He pointed to an area on the map. "If I remember the road right the animal enclosures are here." He drew his fingers across the map less than an inch to another location.

It looked so close. But as Nick oriented himself on the map he saw that the line representing Highway 1 was only about three inches from their present location. It had taken them nearly two hours, and a quart of sweat, to cover the territory between the road and the hut.

"What are we going to do when we get there?" The question sounded stupid even as Nick asked it, but he had no idea what they were looking for.

"Your guess is as good as mine. From what Symington said it should be a pretty good sized room. Apparently they stashed a good quantity of sizable artworks there from time to time."

"You'd think something like that would be pretty obvious. I mean, don't you think grounds-keepers would stumble onto the place?"

Sam shrugged. "I don't know. When the zoo was active I doubt if anybody except the keepers would venture near the place. Symington and his committee probably had them on their payroll. After the zoo fell into disuse, from what I gather, the place was pretty much abandoned. The state gardeners had no reason to go near it since the enclosure was not on state lands, and the corporation had no interest in keeping it up."

"Well it's probably gonna be a dog to find, if it's . . ."

"Shhh." Sam held a single forefinger to his lips. Outside the hut were sounds of footsteps on the dry grass. Bogardus moved to the wall of the hut and, hunching low, peered around the peeling bark of the log wall. He emitted a deep sigh as he stared at the broad flank and brilliant stripes of an adult zebra grazing under a scrub oak a few feet away. The animal gazed back at him and with an air of nonchalance resumed its search for the green morsels of tender grass close to the ground.

Sam looked at Nick and shook his head. "I can do without any more of that." The veins in his neck were pounding and he could feel the surge of adrenalin race through his body.

He reached down and folded the map, pushing it back into his pocket. "Come on, let's go."

"Let's rest a couple more minutes."

Sam ignored the plea as he led the way out of the hut and up the steep hill toward the gully. They climbed for another forty minutes, stopping periodically to check the paved road each time before crossing. The road cut a series of switchbacks across their course of travel and presented bare spots in the otherwise lush foliage that protected them from the searching eyes of any security guards at the castle. The white twin towers of La Casa Grande loomed overhead and seemed to grow larger and more ominous each time they left the cover of the trees. Except for a few lights on the esplanade below the castle, the great house was dark, lit only by the shimmering light of a half-moon that was beginning to rise.

Sam plunged on, moving hand over foot in a near crawl, clawing his way breathlessly through a thicket of dense foliage on the side of the steep hill. After traversing ten or fifteen feet up the hill he suddenly found himself ensnared in a tangle of rose thorns. Carefully, he lifted the rose branches from the arm of his jacket and his pants, where the razor-sharp thorns clung, pricking and scratching his skin. He could hear Nick thrashing in the brush on the steep hill below him and a second later saw the bearded round red face of his friend poke through the underbrush.

"Damn it, Bogardus. If I'd known you wanted to use my body for a pin cushion I'd have brought thimbles." Nick reached judiciously with the forefinger and thumb of his right hand and plucked the thorns from the fabric of his shirt, letting the stems of the rosebush snap back into place.

"From the looks of that round body those thorns have no chance of reaching anything vital."

Nick ignored the comment, instead seizing the opportunity to catch his breath.

"Where the hell are we?"

Sam looked about, his eyes tracing the row of primeval columns that disappeared in the trees and brush on the rise beneath the castle.

"We're under the pergola." Sam pointed to a series of concrete columns winding a serpentine course around the hill toward the great house. The columns were spanned by beams of wood covered with aging vines of untended grapes. Like some long-abandoned temple to a Greek or Roman god, the pergola stood majestically against an orchard of forgotten fruit trees.

"This should be the area the guide called Orchard Hill. The cages should be just over the top of the hill on the other side." Sam plucked the last rose thorn from his pant leg and before Nick could get to his feet he was under the pergola and through the orchard that crowned the top of the hill.

Nick scurried along behind, content to be on the down-side of the hill for a change. His stride lengthened with each step, and as the steep decline of the hill increased Nick found his gait transformed from a fast walk to a jog. In less than ten strides the gentle slant of the hillside transformed itself to a precipice. Nick could no longer control his feet. He was headed down the steep incline in a full sprint. His arms waved frantically in circular motions as he careened down the hill, struggling to keep his legs under his body.

Sam heard the commotion behind him as Nick laid the flat bottoms of his feet to the hard ground, trying to bring himself to a stop.

In desperation, Jorgensen applied the only lesson of snow skiing he'd ever mastered—when in doubt, sit. He leaned back and planted his behind on the slope of the hill, sending up a low cloud of dust. He slid through a stout mulberry bush that slowed his progress and came to an abrupt stop with a thud against a solid wall of clear gray concrete.

Sam hustled down the hill behind him. "Are you all right?"

"Yeah. I think so," Nick goaned.

Sam slowly helped him to his feet. "Next time try to be a little more graceful. All we need to do is break a leg up here."

"If that happens you can leave me behind with a pistol and a single round." Sarcasm dripped from Nick's voice.

Sam smiled as he swatted the dust from the back of Nick's pants. He turned and looked up. "I think we've arrived."

There before them a solid ridge of concrete formed a continuous arc twenty feet high as it curved around and into the earth at the side of Orchard Hill. Like some immense bunker from a gun emplacement, the animal enclosure was constructed of steel-reinforced concrete, with walls two feet thick. The rear side of the enclosure was a semicircle of solid cement cut into the hillside.

Sam moved to the right along the curving structure and climbed the earthen backfill that rose nearly to the top of the wall on the high side of the hill.

He took the rope from his shoulder and tossed one end around a piece of rusting pipe that protruded from the top of the wall. After three attempts he managed to loop the rope around the pipe and catch the end as it came back. He fastened a quick slipknot and boosted himself the remaining seven feet to the top of the wall. Inside, the enclosure was bisected by cement partitions that formed separate chambers for different animals. Across the back was a picket line of iron bars, now rusted with age. A broad, deep pit with steep cement walls separated the front of the cages from the public area set aside for viewing.

A curving concrete catwalk spanned the enclosures over the top of the partitions. In the rear directly beneath him was a large open area separated from the cages by iron bars with a gate leading from the main enclosure to each of the smaller partitioned cages. The large area resembled an amphitheater. Sam guessed that it might have been used by Hearst and his entourage to view special shows from the bridge over the cages.

Nick made his way to the top of the enclosure and stood next to Sam.

"Where do you think we should start?"

"Down there." Sam gestured to the floor of the amphitheater. He pulled the rope up and dropped it into the enclosure and two seconds later slipped gracefully over the side and down to the bottom of the cages.

"Come on down." Sam's hushed voice echoed off the curved walls of concrete.

Nick hesitantly grabbed the rope and turned. Mimicking Sam's movements, he placed his feet against the concrete wall and step by step lowered himself into the pit, his thoughts already preoccupied with the return trip.

As Nick reached the bottom, Sam had already begun to examine the walls and floor of the amphitheater. They were solid concrete with no apparent openings or doors other than the barred gates leading to the cages at the front of the enclosure. Sam moved under the concrete catwalk that separated the cages from the amphitheater. It appeared to be a working area with high-pressure hose bibs for washing down the cages. The cement floor was stained with the rust of the aging iron bars. At the far end of the walkway under the bridge was a tunnel leading to a number of covered cages enclosed in a large room, a covered shelter to be used when the animals were not on display and during foul weather. A single exit led from the room out to the road traversing the front of the enclosure. Sam moved over and quickly examined the iron gate that sealed the exit. It was locked.

He walked back out into the amphitheater.

In the opposite direction under the catwalk Nick had discovered a small iron door. As Sam surveyed the enclosure he found only two breaks in the otherwise continuous span of concrete that surrounded them; the animal shelter with its single exit, and the small iron door being explored by Jorgensen.

Nick tried the metal latch handle. It wouldn't budge.

"Is it locked?"

"Either that or rusted," said Nick.

Sam found a discarded piece of metal pipe

six inches long. He slid the opening of the pipe over the latch handle of the door for leverage.

"I'd be careful if I were you." Jorgensen's words were prophetic, if not timely.

Gripping the handle with both hads, Sam pulled up on the pipe handle. The metal latch handle broke off, showering shavings of oxidized metal on the floor.

"Well, that was good. Any more ideas?" said Nick.

"Damn it."

"Let me see." Nick moved around him and examined the door. It was made of two solid plates of iron forming the top and bottom panels fixed on a welded steel frame that was bolted to the concrete by heavy metal hinges. Jorgensen reached into his pocket and came out with a Swiss Army knife that sported a dozen specialty blades.

"Those things are handy, but I don't think the can opener's gonna work on that door," said Sam.

Nick ignored him and opened one of the blades, a long, needlelike piece of stainless steel. He probed in the large keyhole beneath the broken latch handle. After several seconds Sam heard a distinct click inside the door. Nick reached up, gripping the broken nub of the latch handle. He turned it with a quick twist and the door sprung open an inch.

"Where did you learn to do that?"

"Let's just say that I've not spent my entire life locked in the pursuit of academic achievement." Nick smiled at him and winked.

Sam looked askance at Jorgensen, realizing

for the first time that there was a side to the man he had never before seen—a resourcefulness in the face of adversity that he had never expected. He wondered how much of the bumbling lack of grace was feigned, a part of Nick's body armor against a demanding society that cut little slack for the overweight.

It took the combined strength of both men to pull the door open far enough to enter. The rusted hinges groaned and buckled. It was pitch black inside. Nick pulled one of the small plastic flashlights from his coat pocket and snapped it on. The area inside the door was confined. Their light immediately bounced off the back wall of a cobweb-infested service closet. It contained metal pails and a cast-iron service sink. Wooden shelves covered the two side walls and were littered with assorted brushes, rags and other abandoned cleaning supplies. Sam squeezed his way into the opening behind Nick and moved his flashlight, looking around the tiny room.

The semantic puzzle he had solved so ingeniously at the book shop at Cambria was revealing itself to be nothing more than the self-delusion of an overactive imagination. With Jennifer abducted, the consequences of his folly were beginning to settle on him.

Nick was busy examining the wooden shelves on the two side walls.

Bogardus checked the floor. It was solid concrete, as were the walls behind the two shelves and the service sink. He directed the flashlight upward along the back wall. The beam was swallowed by a ceiling with no apparent limit, and shelves on one side continued up the wall well beyond reach for any practical purpose.

"Are you thinking what I am?" asked Nick.

Sam doused his flashlight, dropped it in his pocket and started to climb the shelves. "Try to give me some light up here." His voice echoed in the small room. Nick moved against the opposite wall and directed the beam of his flashlight just ahead of Sam's hands as he climbed. Bogardus could see that the shelves stopped about twelve feet up. The beam of the flashlight caught what appeared to be a line of large metal rivets just above the last shelf.

Sam clung to one of the two-by-sixes with one hand and pulled the flashlight from his coat pocket. As he flipped it on, the glare of the light illuminated a small iron door with panels fixed by large round rivets. There was no latch handle, only a large keyhole near the edge of the door halfway up.

"Look's like your turn," said Sam.

He scampered down the ladder and a minute later, Nick stood on the top rung repeating his magic with the little Swiss knife.

Sam stood a few rungs below him, holding a flashlight on the keyhole.

There was an audible clink inside the door as it swung open, clanging against the concrete on the side wall.

"Jesus! Hold it down." Sam jiggled the flashlight. The sound of metal against cement echoed in the small chamber and reverberated through the amphitheater outside the room. Nick stood motionless on the ladder, afraid to move for fear of hitting the door and knocking it against the wall a second time. Several seconds passed. Nick closed the knife and placed it in his jacket pocket, retrieving his flashlight. He snapped it on and directed the light into the open doorway high on the wall of the service closet. He saw only a dim reflection against a drab wall a good distance from the door. He moved the light around. On the wall just inside the open door was a light switch, an ancient twist-type that had not been seen in hardware stores since the Depression. Nick reached over with his hand and turned the switch. Instantly a soft yellow light bathed the open hatchway high on the wall where he stood and illuminated an immense room that spread out before him through the open door. A ladder led down from the opening into the room. Without a word Nick climbed through the door and down the ladder on the other side.

"What do you see?" Sam turned off his flashlight. The reflection of light from the open door above illuminated the service closet. Sam scaled the shelves toward the open door.

Nick stood at the bottom of the ladder facing out toward the cavernous room, the expression on his face fixed like a stone idol.

"My God!" Sam had reached the open door high on the wall and stood on the ladder with his upper body in the opening. There, spread before him, was a room the size of a small warehouse buried in the earth beneath Orchard Hill. The room was twenty-five to thirty feet in height from floor to ceiling. The walls were lined to a height of fifteen feet with long wooden shelves spanning the length and breadth of the cavern. The shelves were mostly bare or littered with old packing material and odd boxes with their lids scattered on the floor. A sarcophagus, seven feet long and weighing a ton or more, lay in the center of the room. Carved in deep relief from marble, the ancient coffin was complete with a lid that revealed an exquisite death mask. There were two small vases on the floor beside the sarcophagus. Against the far wall four wooden crates, three of which were open, lay scattered on the floor, lost in a sea of excelsior.

From his vantage at the top of the ladder Sam scanned the room, searching for anything that looked like a bound volume. But the clutter of the room was too much for a casual appraisal from a distance. He scampered down the ladder and joined Nick.

"This could take a while." Nick wiped perspiration from his forehead.

"It's incredible. Symington said that they used the chamber to stash things from time to time, but I wasn't prepared for this. You could play a football game in here." Sam kept turning in slow circles as he walked toward the center of the room. He gazed in utter disbelief at the rows of shelves lining the walls. He walked to one of them and picked up a small urn, one of the few items left from what appeared to be a final looting of the chamber by the committee. It was bronze and looked Greek in origin—and thousands of years old. He replaced the urn and swept a pile of raffia and excelsior from the shelf onto the floor.

"Now I know what a Pharaoh's tomb must look like after it's been plundered," said Sam.

"Look at this," Nick cried out in hushed tones from behind some crates in the center of the room.

"What is it?"

Sam made his way around the sarcophagus and looked over Nick's shoulder. On the back of one of the wooden boxes was the emblem of an eagle resting on a swastika. The lettering beneath was in German. The box was empty.

A sinking feeling came over the two men as they considered the possibility that the journal had once rested in the box at Nick's feet.

"They didn't leave much of value, did they?" said Nick.

"No."

"What's inside that crate?" Sam pointed to the only unopened box left on the floor.

Nick took out his pocketknife. Prying carefully to avoid snapping off the blade, he slowly lifted one edge of the lid enough to get his fingers under it. He tugged on the top of the box and the lid came free with a screech that echoed off the concrete walls. Nick threw the top aside and reached into the box to remove the shredded hemp used as packing material. He strained to lift the object from the wooden box. His eyes squinted to take in the intricate detail of a silver jewel casket encrusted with precious and semiprecious stones. Two large oval windows fashioned from shimmering polished stone crystals each several inches in diameter pierced the front of the casket.

"It's worth a fortune," said Nick, still on his

knees. "Italian Renaissance—fifteenth, maybe sixteenth century. It's a prize. Look at the engraving. It's magnificent."

Sam took the casket and placed it back in the box. "Come on, we've got to look for the journal and get the hell out of here." He started in one corner of the room, Nick in the other, searching the shelves for books and looking in crates that *might* contain Drake's journal. They looked for more than two hours, standing on boxes to reach the higher shelves.

As they moved around from opposite ends of the room toward each other, closing the distance of remaining area to be searched, Sam felt a sense of desperation. His eyes scanned the limited area between them and his hope began to sink. Nick had just finished going through the last box. They had not found a single bound volume.

"It's useless," said Sam, his voice tinged with bitterness. "It's not here. Either Symington lied or the committee was able to get to it before Hearst banished them all from the hill."

"I'm not so sure," said Nick.

Bogardus looked at him.

"What about that?" He pointed to the sarcophagus.

"Forget it, I already looked inside. It's empty," said Sam.

"No, that's not what I mean. I mean how did they get it in here?"

Sam looked at the mammoth block of carved marble. "Of course." The coffin was too large for the opening at the top of the ladder above the service closet.

"You're right. There has to be another opening in here."

Nick looked about at the shelves lining the walls. Each section was supported by long four-by-four posts and braced at the back by an open framework of crossed two-by-fours—except for one set of shelves. It had a solid wooden back made of notched tongue-and-groove planks. From a distance the shelf appeared to rest squarely against the concrete wall. Nick walked over to it and looked at the shelf. The back was set into the wall as if the concrete had been poured to fit it. Sam went to the other end and the two men alternately pulled and pushed, trying to move it. The shelf did not budge; it was somehow fixed to the wall. Sam moved his hand to gain a better grip and felt an edge of hard metal under one of the shelves. He knelt and looked underneath. A small handle was fastened to the underside, and a cable ran from the handle through the panel on the back. Bogardus gripped the handle and pulled. As he did, the entire section of shelf began to roll silently away from him, back into what had appeared to be the solid concrete wall but was in fact a door, large enough to admit a small truck. The section of shelving swung like an opening barn door in slow motion until it came to rest against the wall of a long tunnel carved from solid rock. On the floor of the tunnel was a narrow set of rusted rails.

"What is it?" asked Sam.

"A mine shaft." Nick stared down the dark passageway.

"What's it doing here?"

"My guess is it was here long before Hearst built the house. The committee must have used it to advantage when they designed the chamber. Unless I miss my bet they had George Hearst to thank—William Randolph's father. He bought the Piedra Blanca in the last century, believing there were valuable mineral rights. This is probably one of the early hard rock shafts he drilled looking for cinnabar or silver."

At the end of the long cavern Sam could see a faint hint of light.

"Just a second." Nick ran to the other side of the cavern and picked up the box with the jewel casket. "No sense leaving empty-handed." He joined Sam at the open door.

Sam led the way followed closely by Jorgensen. Guided by the narrow beams of their flashlights on the rusted rails the two men stepped around an abandoned ore cart and moved slowly down the tunnel. They had gone about three hundred feet when they came to a cross-shaft.

The place was turning into a maze. The thought flashed through Sam's mind—one wrong turn and they might never find their way out.

They walked on for several minutes, watching the ground for obstacles or down-shafts. As they rounded a slight curve in the tunnel Nick breathed a sigh of relief. There ahead of them were the bars of a large gate leading to the surface. He ran up to the iron bars and pushed. They were locked. He examined the lock.

"No sweat. It's a Swiss Army special." Nick

laughed, reaching for his knife. "I'll have it open in a second."

"Not yet. There's something we left back there."

"What's that?"

"The journal."

"It's not there, Sam. We looked."

"Yes it is. We just looked in the wrong place." Sam's voice carried the confidence of a man who was no longer guessing. "It's back there in the other shaft. The one that leads off in the direction of the house."

"What makes you so sure?"

"Symington's obsession with art."

"What are you talking about?"

Sam looked at his watch. It was nearly 2:00 A.M. "There's no time to explain. Come on."

Nick placed the box with the jeweled casket by the entrance to the shaft and ran to catch up with Sam. They moved more slowly through the other tunnel, careful to avoid down-shafts, and made their way underground toward the cluster of buildings on Hearst's Enchanted Hill. As they walked, the walls of the cross-shaft narrowed, forcing the two men to proceed single file. The passage was carved from solid gray granite. Sam could see occasional drill holes where ledges of rock had been pried or blasted away from the mountain.

Jorgensen's doubts were mounting with each step as the tunnel narrowed and closed in on them. He was now moving sideways with the walls to negotiate the opening in the rock. His ration of good humor had been consumed when Bogardus suddenly stopped.

"Let's get the hell out of here before I get claustrophobia." He reached over to grab Sam's shoulder just as Bogardus stepped out of the narrow corridor of rock into a broad cavern a dozen feet across. Framed by timbers, an arched wooden door with metal escutcheons was embedded in the rock wall directly across from the two men.

"It's incredible." Nick struggled in the dim illumination of his flashlight. "This door is Spanish Renaissance, fifteenth century." He traced the delicate painted panels with his finger. "Solid oak."

"What's it doing down here?"

"You want my guess? A relic from the Spanish Civil War."

Sam searched the door for a keyhole. There was none. He reached up and gripped the large iron ring mounted in the center of one of the panels. He twisted the ring and pulled. The door opened. Sam aimed the beam of his flashlight beyond the threshold and looked first at the floor. It was covered in large uneven tiles.

Sam took several steps toward the interior of the room when suddenly without warning the room was instantly bathed in bright light. Sam squinted and turned, startled. Nick leaned against the wall on the opposite side of the room, smiling, his hand on the switch, an ancient affair similar to the one in the storeroom near the animal enclosure.

The walls were covered in white plaster. Overhead the ceiling was constructed of wood with heavy beams supporting it. The room was small, no more than ten feet square. There were no furnishings. Two wall-mounted lamps made of wrought iron provided the light. In the far corner two steps led to a small landing partially hidden behind a wall. Nick walked up the stairs to the landing.

"This way. There's a flight of stairs going up here."

Sam followed. The stairs were steep and long, illuminated by a series of light fixtures in the curved plaster ceiling overhead. As they scaled the stairs, Sam looked back several times at the landing below that was receding into the distance.

"We're going to have to get out of here shortly if we're gonna have any chance to get down the mountain before daybreak," said Nick.

"Keep going."

The head of the stairs opened onto another small room. Nick found the light switch and turned it. The room was suddenly bathed in soft white light. Bogardus and Jorgensen stood speechless at the threshold near the top of the stairs. The plaster walls were cluttered with an array of oil paintings, each magnificently framed—austere faces staring from lightless backgrounds, broad landscapes and pastoral scenes. Nick moved in a near trance around the room, passing an area littered with scores of oval miniatures, each bearing the regal continence of European nobility, tiny faces from another age. They had found Arthur Symington's private chamber.

The high ceiling was formed of delicate wood panels painted in faded shades of green and gold, an obvious prize from some European castle. Surrounding the room halfway up the wall was a balustrade with a wrought iron railing that ringed the interior walls of the room. A ladder lead to the balcony.

"These are masterpieces. Holbein, Titian, Correggio." Nick traced an index finger over the signature of a large portrait high on the wall in the corner of the room. "My God—Fra Angelico. Do you have any idea what these are worth? We're looking at the plunder from major museums and galleries."

Sam ignored him and quickly climbed the ladder to the balustrade. High up, embedded in the plaster walls, were several bookshelves sealed behind leaded glass cabinet doors.

He reached the first cabinet, opened the doors and rifled the contents. Four shelves running from floor to ceiling were covered with bronze statuary. He ran around the balustrade to the next and peered through the glass. Several books appeared on the shelf along with a miniature oil painting. He opened the cabinet and grabbed the books one at a time. He pawed through their pages only briefly. Each was too small to match the parchments back in the safe deposit vault in the city, and the paper was of a different texture than the Davies parchments. He went to the next cabinet. There on a shelf lay a single parcel wrapped in oilcloth. He swung open the cabinet doors and lifted the package. It was heavy, more than four inches thick, eighteen inches on one side and a foot on the other, tied with a hemp cord. He turned it over, his pulse pounding with anticipation. Bogardus paused only momentarily as his eyes drank in the swastika and eagle of the Third Reich emblazoned on the cloth cover.

His breathing became erratic as he felt the hair on the back of his neck rise. Sam turned to look toward Nick, who was busy studying a Cellini bronze from the first cabinet.

"I think I've got it."

Nick scurried around the railing. He stopped just behind Sam and, seeing the hemp cord, pulled the small knife from his pocket. In a single motion he severed the cord. Carefully Sam unwrapped the oilcloth. Inside was a large book bound in heavy leather. There were no markings on the spine or either cover. Sam opened the front cover and felt the paper. It had a texture and color identical to the four pages of parchment sent to Jennifer. He turned the page and stared at the first visible letters, his eyes riveted on the bold scrawl across the center of the page. The large ornate script with wisps of ink trailing from the letters required no translation. He read the words aloud:

KNOW YE ALL MEN
THE JOURNAL OF FRANCIS DRAKE
GENERALLE AND COMMANDER OF HER
MAJESTIES SHIP "PELICAN"

"That's it," said Nick. "The *Pelican* was Drake's ship before she was rechristened the *Golden Hinde*."

Sam's heart raced and his temples pounded as he scanned several of the pages quickly. Each page followed the same form. In the far left margin were dates of departure and discovery followed by lengthy narrative, all in the same elegant hand—a bold elliptic script. The right margins were covered with numerous small ink drawings, some in colored inks of red, green and brown, many of the drawings so delicate in their design that they approached the quality of miniatures, while others showed signs of haste in their composition.

Nick looked over Sam's shoulder wide-eyed as he stared down at the massive book. His mind reeled. For three hundred years the truth of Drake's voyage had been relegated to conjecture and debate among scholars. Now for the first time the world would know with certainty where he landed in the New World and what he found when he arrived. Historians could scrutinize Drake's most intimate thoughts, fears and hopes, and share firsthand the excitement of his exploration and conquest.

They were both giddy with excitement. There before them on the shelf lay the narrative of England's first great oceanic explorer. A chronicle of adventure and death, of the biting cold and searing heat of the elements, of native peoples whose culture and society had long since passed into history. Sam pawed through the book, stopping to look at charts and drawings of land masses. He wondered if it would contain a map of Nova Albion—and maybe, just maybe, the location of Drake's cache of gold and silver? There was no time to look. He had it and now they had to get out before they were caught. If they were stopped by security on the hill it would take days to unravel the entire affair. And he didn't have days. He had a date with Raymond Slade at the Seven Sisters in less than twenty-four hours.

As they turned to leave suddenly there were the sounds of footsteps, an eerie echoing from the walls above the balustrade.

"The light," Nick whispered. There was panic in his eyes as he moved silently to the ladder and down to the switch on the wall. With a click the wall-mounted lamps went dark. The room took on an unearthly glow as four brilliant shafts of light streamed into the room from metal gratings above the book cabinets.

The footsteps grew louder—solid heels on hard marble.

Nick removed his shoes and scaled the ladder to join Sam, who hadn't moved from the shelf and the journal.

In silence Nick looked at him, a quizzical expression on his face. Sam shrugged his shoulders and shook his head in puzzlement, his eyes cast toward the ceiling. Then, motioning, Nick stooped low and coupled his hands together between his knees. Sam placed his right foot into the loop formed by Nick's hands and, steadying himself with one hand on Nick's shoulder, he stepped carefully with his other foot onto the bottom shelf of the book cabinet. Pressed against the wall above the cabinet and held firmly in place by Nick's outstretched hands in the small of his back Sam peered through the opening covered by the small metal grating.

There before him at floor level stood the immense Assembly Room of La Casa Grande, its opulent gilded columns framing the grand entrance to the room, its massive tapestries hanging from the vaulted majestic walls of marble and granite. Not more than five feet in front of Sam's face rested the glistening heel of a man's black boot, and draped over it the cuff of a pant leg. The toe of the boot flexed as the man took a step away from the wall and the grating. As the figure moved into the center of the room Sam could see the broad back of a uniformed security guard, a revolver strapped to his side. Sam drew shallow silent breaths for fear of being heard. The officer cupped his hands behind his back and walked toward one of the banks of hand-carved walnut choir seats lining the wall. Plopping his body down onto the chair, the guard leaned back and cupped his hands behind his head, closing his eyes for a quick nap.

Sam stood perched with his feet on one shelf of the cabinet and his body pressed against the upper shelves. With the weight of his companion off of his arms Nick relaxed, and suddenly it occurred to him—the meaning of Sam's words as they stood at the end of the tunnel and looked out at the night sky. He knew how Bogardus could be so certain that the journal was back in the tunnel. Documents and oil paintings were susceptible to dampness. Differences in humidity and temperature would take a toll on such items, even over short periods. They could not be stored for long in the dank surroundings of the storehouse near the animal enclosure. Symington knew that. He would never allow the committee to consign precious art or irreplaceable parchments to such a place. This room had been his sanctum sanctorum. It had escaped the plunder by the committee following their demise. Here, with the careful atmospheric controls of the great house and with dry heat supplied through the grates on the wall, the journal could last a millennium.

With his face pressed against the grating Sam peered through the metalwork at the guard who was sound asleep. His feet were sprawled on an Oriental carpet, his behind resting on the edge of the ornate choir chair, shoulders hunched against the high back of the chair.

Silently, Sam motioned with his hand and Nick guided his foot to the floor of the balustrade.

Sam picked up the oilcloth and rewrapped the journal. Taking off his belt he strapped it around the cloth-covered book and picked it up.

"Let's get the hell out of here while we have the chance."

Chapter

13

"What do you mean you lost them? God damn it!"* Notwithstanding his gruff demeanor it was out of character for Fletcher to swear. He reserved it for particular calamities and when they occurred the cops in his division gave him a wide berth.

Mayhew's only comfort derived from the fact that he was in a telephone booth two hundred miles away. His partner stood in the open door to the booth. Despite the night chill carried on the ocean breezes they were both sweating profusely, their white shirts splotched with motor oil and engine grime.

"We didn't come up totally empty, Lieutenant. After we got back to the inn we went up to the room. Bogardus and Jorgensen checked out twenty minutes before we got there. The strange thing is that the girl wasn't with them. According to the desk clerk she left about an hour before with another man. The desk clerk said he'd never seen the guy before.

"There's one more thing, Lieutenant." There was a pause on the line. Fletcher knew it had to be bad news.

"The cleaning lady at the inn said there was scribbling in lipstick all over the mirror in the bathroom when she went into the room to clean it. She was mad as hell."

Mayhew stopped as if to check his notes.

"Well? What did it say?"

"The maid thought it was a joke. The message said that if they wanted the woman back alive they should be someplace called the Seven Sisters by four o'clock tomorrow."

Fletcher said nothing for several seconds.

"What does it mean, Lieutenant?"

"It means you guys screwed up. Listen, I want the two of you back in the city and don't worry about the speed limit getting here. I want both of you in my office by nine A.M. tomorrow. Do you understand?"

"Yes sir." Before the words cleared his lips Mayhew heard the click of the telephone as Fletcher slammed the receiver down on the other end.

"Why do they keep sending me all the idiots?" Fletcher looked over at the desk sergeant who sat across from him.

The sergeant shook his head, "Have you ever heard of a place called the Seven Sisters?"

The sergeant wrinkled his eyebrows. "Maybe a bar?"

"Never mind. Listen, did you get anything on that car—the limousine that we picked up in Chinatown?"

"Yeah. The report's on your desk. Right there." The sergeant tapped a single piece of paper on the corner of the desk.

"Thanks." Fletcher passed his eyes over the brief report.

"Are you sure this is accurate? This is the owner of the car?"

"That's it," said the sergeant.

Fletcher looked down at the brief notation:

1974 Lincoln Mark V (modified "stretch" limousine)
VIN J387650928
Registered Owner: George Johnson

"What's the address?"

"It turned out to be a phony. Some address on Olstead Street in San Francisco. There is no Olstead Street in the city."

"Great. Put an all points bulletin out on Bogardus and Jorgensen. They're not dangerous. Just have 'em picked up. Make sure the highway patrol gets it. They're probably on the road somewhere between here and San Luis Obispo."

The sergeant turned for the door. "Oh, before I forget, you asked me to have that switchblade examined by forensics. It's negative. The medical examiner says that the dimensions on the blade are all wrong for the wound in the girl's back."

"Fine. Any more bad news?"

"Forensics is still checking for pick marks in

the lock at her apartment." The sergeant left the office and Fletcher picked up his notebook and scanned the entries of his interview with Jasper Holmes.

The Englishman exhibited the arrogance of a British lord, but his part in the unfolding drama appeared to be minor. Holmes's principal interest seemed to be academic. Possession of the four pages of parchment and the Drake journal were to be his ticket to educational glory.

The real player appeared to be the other man, the man Holmes said he talked to on the telephone and again in the limousine several days before at the campus. The fellow had promised Holmes that he would allow him access to the complete journal if the Englishman could provide him with an accurate translation of the four pages Fletcher had found at Holmes's Berkeley apartment. Unless Fletcher was wrong, the only tribute the Englishman would ever garner from his translation would come when he entered the collegiate equivalent of Valhalla. Angie Bogardus had probably saved his life.

Now it was time for Holmes to return the favor. He picked up the telephone and dialed Jasper's number in Berkeley. As the phone rang, Fletcher doodled on the scrap of paper, drawing curls and lines around his earlier note— "Four o'clock tomorrow." He underlined the three words "the Seven Sisters," as Holmes answered.

The whining of the engine lulled Sam into a shallow sleep as Nick guided the Porsche north up 101 toward San Francisco. A light drizzle peppered the windshield with a driven mist. The journal lay against Sam's chest, clutched in the deathlike embrace of his crossed arms. Even in slumber, Sam's mind danced with visions of the Spanish tiled chamber beneath the castle and the dark granite tunnels under the hill, of Jennifer's face and the grotesque image of Susan Paterson prostrate on the cold hard porcelain of the autopsy table.

The measured cadence of the windshield wipers mesmerized Nick into a state of drowsiness, his head repeatedly nodding toward his chest. The car drifted onto the shoulder and rumbled over potholes in the asphalt. The two of them woke with a start. Nick quickly guided the car back into the fast lane.

"Sorry."

Sam arched his back and stretched his arms as far as the low roof of the vehicle would allow. Sam was operating on less than an hour's sleep and Nick hardly any at all. As the countryside streaked by outside the windows both men knew what had to be done. They would take the journal to the Seven Sisters and somehow try to exchange it for Jennifer Davies—if she was still alive.

"I think we should call Jake when we get back," said Nick. "We're going to need him."

"You're probably right. You can take care of it when we get back to the city."

Nick nodded.

It was an idle errand. Sam had no intention of involving either of his friends further. He had no right. Because of his own stupidity Jennifer's life now hung in the balance. She had pleaded with him to go to the police, and like a fool he had refused. He would not make another mistake. He would not endanger anyone else. He was also abundantly familiar with the inert processes of justice. He had a more accelerated timetable in mind for Raymond Slade, and a more irrevocable disposition, a plan in which he refused to implicate his friends.

Pat's murder had rekindled Sam's primordial urge for revenge. The lawyer in him reasoned for due process and the cumbersome procedures of civilized society. But instincts more compelling drove him to meet Slade on his own terms, alone and unseen by any authority. Sam no longer wondered whether he was capable of killing. The only question was whether he would have the opportunity.

"I want to go to the office on our way through town so you can show me on a map where this place is—the Seven Sisters. Then I have to run a brief errand, something I have to do alone. You can call Jake from the office and I'll swing back through town and pick the two of you up before heading back up the coast."

Nick looked over at him and nodded in agreement.

The Porsche rolled under the ornate wrought iron sign arching over the gate.

MADRIGAL VINEYARDS
SONOMA, CALIFORNIA

Sam drove slowly down the long gravel drive toward the house. He was not looking forward to the meeting with Louis Davies, but it was something that he couldn't do by telephone —tell the old man that his stepdaughter had been abducted and was being held for ransom by a murderer.

He parked the car beside the steps leading to the front door and slowly walked up and pushed the doorbell. He waited several seconds. An old woman wearing a scarf over her hair and a simple print dress partially covered by an apron opened the door.

"Hello." She spoke with a distinct accent.

"I'm looking for Louis Davies. Is he in?"

"Not at the moment. But I'm expecting him shortly."

"I wonder if I might wait. It's very important."

"May I ask what it concerns?"

"It's a personal matter."

The old woman hesitated for a moment and then opened the door wide to admit him. She led him through a large entry hall and past a set of double doors into an elegantly furnished living room.

"Please take a seat. Can I offer you anything to drink?"

"No, I'm fine. Please don't let me disturb you."

Sam took a seat on the large couch facing the fireplace. The woman excused herself and left the room.

Sam pushed one hand into the deep pocket of his coat and felt the handle of the small snub-nosed revolver he had picked up at the office. He had removed the gun from a locked cabinet in his desk while Nick was busy on the phone in the other room, trying to reach Jake Carns. As his two friends planned a rendezvous at the office for two o'clock—a rendezvous that Sam would never keep—he'd opened the cylinder of the small handgun and had examined the five thirty-eight-special rounds seated in the chambers.

Now clutching the handle of the gun in his hand, Sam's head settled slowly back against the soft upholstery of the couch and he closed his eyes. Sleep had been an unwanted but relentless companion all the way from the city to the Davies vineyard. He could no longer resist its hypnotic lure. The sleep was sound, undisturbed, the slumber of one who had dismissed all doubt and dealt with all indecision. Bogardus now knew what he had to do.

He had no idea how long he had slept when suddenly something landed on his lap, waking him with a start.

He jerked his head from the back of the couch and looked down. There, rubbing its feline body against his chest, was a spotless white Persian cat, its coat puffed like a blowfish. It purred and pushed its face under Sam's chin, dragging its back in a serpentine movement across his chest. Self-consciously, Bogardus looked about the room to see if anyone had seen him sleeping. He was alone except for the cat. He gently pushed the animal from his lap onto the floor and stood in an effort to stave off sleep.

Sam walked from the couch toward the fireplace, examining an array of items on the mantel. His attention was captured by a gold watch sealed in a small glass case, a family heirloom. He tapped the glass.

"Ahem." The old woman cleared her throat. She had come into the room and stood in the door behind him, her face a picture of reproof.

"It's a beautiful watch," said Sam. "Looks like a Howard. My grandfather had one similar to it years ago."

She stood silently in the doorway.

Bogardus picked up a photograph from the mantel.

"Is this Mr. Davies—Jennifer's stepfather?"

"Yes."

He was in his mid-forties, austere, with a touch of gray at the temples. But Sam assumed that the picture had been taken some years before, for Bogardus had fixed the man's age from the earlier photograph, the one that he'd taken from Treasure Island. Staring back from the frame in his hand were the cold dark eyes of Raymond Slade.

Sam sat paralyzed behind the wheel of the Porsche on the bluff overlooking the blustery Pacific under a silver, cloud-laden sky. He was only a mile from the entrance to Drake's Beach, but his thoughts were lost in the tangle of Jennifer Davies's unspoken secret.

For days he had been tormented by the knowledge that she knew something about Raymond Slade, some perverse secret. Now he knew that those suspicions were not the product of idle speculation.

In Symington's vaulted warren under the castle Jennifer had pursued a single line of inquiry: "Do you think you would be able to

identify Raymond Slade if you saw him?" she'd
asked.

From that morning in the hospital when she
first came to visit him she had been obsessed
in her quest for the man's photograph, first
from the firm's file containing the Treasure
Island photo, and when that couldn't be found,
from her mother's old picture album.

But Slade was always one jump ahead. And
why not? Raymond Slade, alias Louis Davies,
had taken pains to remove any vestige of his
wartime image from the house where Jennifer
lived. Sam hadn't quite figured out how Slade
had gained access to the law office and taken
the office file, but he was certain that he had.

Bogardus had to have been blind not to see
it earlier.

But then Jennifer hadn't known for sure herself. That was why she needed the photograph.
After Pat's death Jennifer could no longer con-
fide in Bogardus. She lived with the growing
belief that her stepfather had committed murder. How could she disclose that gnawing suspicion to the man whose partner—whose lover—
Louis Davies had killed.

He guessed that she'd heard something that
day years before outside her parents' bedroom
when they had argued—something that she
couldn't bring herself to tell another living soul.
His mind turned the missing piece until, like a
child's puzzle, it fit the only vacant space. Jennifer Davies had lived with the thought that
her mother and Raymond Slade had had an
affair, a tryst that led the two of them to plan
the murder of her father, James Spencer, a

deed that Slade carried out on the blimp that fateful afternoon.

The Goodyear pilot was right. Two men came off the ship that day, but one of them was dead. How else could the disappearance of James Spencer be explained? If the man were alive he would never separate himself from his own child for a lifetime.

But could Slade really kill his own stepdaughter? Suddenly Sam realized that he knew nothing of Jennifer's relationship with Louis Davies. The man had killed her father. She had lived for years with the question that hung like an ominous cloud over her life, a dark shadow that appeared whenever she looked into his eyes. For a child seeking love it was a fate the equivalent of death. And now the suspicion that she harbored all of those years had been confirmed.

Sam's thoughts turned increasingly to Louis Davies, the man he'd never met and whose voice he had heard only once during that brief telephone conversation to Jennifer from the hospital. It was a bizarre sensation, the knowledge that he had spoken to Pat's killer only hours before she was murdered.

The afternoon light was already casting long shadows on the bleak span of beach that stretched north from the estuary. Sam parked the Porsche. A white sedan, the only vehicle in the otherwise deserted lot, was backed into a space three slots away. Directly in front of the Porsche was a sign leaning in the stiff ocean winds:

Drake's Beach

He sat motionless behind the wheel, his eyes fixed on the deserted beach and the bluffs surrounding it.

Off to the left fifty yards away stood a lone wooden structure, a combination nature display and small coffee shop.

Two women, one short and squat wearing a loud print dress and bandanna and the other tall in a long coat and hat, walked a small dog near the surf. The pup yapped at the waves crashing on the white sand as the shorter woman struggled in the stiff winds to keep her dress down over her plump legs. A young couple holding hands walked on some rocks several hundred yards up the beach, tiptoeing over the incoming tide, stopping periodically to check small pools for signs of sea life.

Sam walked toward the coffee shop and up the wooden ramp leading to the building. He paused at the end of the deck that was poised over the beach and surveyed the sweep of Drake's Bay. He could see several miles to the north as the headlands of Point Reyes curved sharply to the northwest, sheltering the otherwise open bay from the relentless swells of the North Pacific. The beach in front of the wooden deck was littered with small round stones washed down from a creek that ran along one side of the parking lot.

But there was no sign of the Seven Sisters— the undulating palisades that had reminded Drake so much of the Cliffs of Dover. To the south Sam's view was obscured by the rise of a hillock.

The door to the coffee shop behind Sam opened, releasing the sound of rock music from a radio that blared from the counter inside. Sam turned with a start and stared at a girl in her mid-twenties wearing a soiled canvas apron. She stood framed in the doorway.

"Are you Bogardus?" The expression on the girl's face was a mix of apathy and annoyance.

Sam studied her for an instant, concluded that the woman was too detached to be a threat and answered, "Yes."

"Your friend has gone on ahead. He said he'd wait for you near the marker at the estuary."

Sam looked at the woman wearily.

"My friend—was he alone or was there a woman with him?"

"I'm not Western Union, mister. I'm just delivering the man's message."

"How do I get to the estuary?"

She threw a lazy gesture with her arm in a general southerly direction, turned and walked back into the empty coffee shop.

Sam walked from the covered deck back to his car and opened the front luggage compartment. He picked up a pair of binoculars and hung them around his neck, then lifted the heavy package wrapped in oilcloth and tucked it under his arm.

He was just about to slam the hood of the Porsche when his gaze was seized by a small triangular swatch of cloth caught in the trunk latch of the other vehicle twenty feet away. Without removing his eyes from the car or the cloth Bogardus groped for the jack handle under the spare tire of the Porsche. As his hand felt the cold metal he stood motionless, looking at the silk paisley print of Jennifer Davies's dress trapped in the trunk lid of the small white sedan.

Bogardus had gone less than twenty paces from the wooden deck of the coffee shop when he turned with his back to the ocean, taking in the full sweep the headlands from Point Reyes south toward the Golden Gate. The undulating parapets of sandstone swept around the bay with Drake's Beach at the center. The hillside formed a geologic roller coaster spanning the arc of the bay. What had been screened from his view in the parking lot and on the deck of the coffee shop was readily apparent from the sea. There before his eyes were the Seven Sisters. The cliffs loomed overhead, pocked with small caverns and stained with rust from minute iron deposits.

Sam trudged through the deep sand and made his way to the edge of the water, where the moist, firm sand gave him a better footing. He was alone on the beach except for the two women and their small dog. He could see them in the distance through the mist, the dog barking at the waves, the two human figures keeping pace and moving south along the beach.

From his vantage point atop the cliff Raymond Slade placed the ornate walking cane in the tall marsh grass near his feet. He adjusted the scope of the high-powered rifle and zeroed in on Bogardus walking on the beach below, training the cross-hairs to a point just below the lawyer's chin. He then roamed with the eye of the powerful scope down his victim's body until the object of his interest came into focus. The package was carried securely under the crook of the arm. A smile curled from the corners of Slade's mouth. He rose from the bushes at the edge of the cliff and moved several yards further south. Below he had an unobstructed view of the massive wooden post—the Drake marker—and the brackish waters of the estuary. In the distance beyond the sand dunes two women walked with a small dog. A solitary fisherman drifted with the incoming tide in a small aluminum skiff on the estuary a hundred yards from the marker. He watched as the women on the beach wandered toward the far end of the sand spit two hundred yards away. The fisherman in his boat sat motionless, apparently baiting a hook. Satisfied that these other intruders presented no problem, he returned to the edge of the cliff and resumed his vigil over the lawyer.

Sam struggled through the tall marsh grass. The sharp tips of the bladelike leaves stung the back of his right hand as he clutched the oil-cloth package under his left arm. He reached into his pocket and felt the handle of the small revolver.

As Bogardus walked hip-deep through the spines of tall grass, the acrid thirst for vengeance parched his mouth. He considered the relative strengths and weaknesses of their respective positions. The discovery in the trunk of Slade's car radically altered the values he fed into the equation. Raymond Slade had nothing left with which to bargain. Only one of them would walk off the beach alive.

As the steep bluffs closed in from all sides sheltering the estuary from the Pacific, Sam found himself virtually alone on a high plateau of sand a quarter mile from the roaring surf.

A massive wooden piling, its girth three feet in diameter, rose fifteen feet above the beach at the edge of the estuary. Sam moved toward the post. Near the top a metal scroll affixed by the Navigator's Guild proclaimed the wind-swept dune to be the spot where Drake and his crew spent more than a month during that summer of 1579.

The area by the marker was deserted. Sam scanned the estuary, making a 360-degree sweep with the binoculars. His view of the sand spit at the end of the beach was completely obscured by the myriad dunes that surrounded him.

He dropped the field glasses to his chest and returned his right hand to the pocket of his coat and the handle of the revolver. As Bogardus turned toward the monument, he froze, his focus suddenly attracted by the movement of a man who stepped from behind the marker, a rifle poised in his hand, scope to his eye. Sam braced himself, his hand paralyzed on the grip of the pistol in his pocket. There, less than fifty feet away, stood instant death.

What seemed like an eternity passed in silence as the figure with the rifle stood motionless at the foot of the piling. Sam struggled for a view of the man's face shielded behind the scope of the rifle and gunman's raised forearm. For an instant Sam pried his eyes away from the specter of death to an object that offered the slim thread of hope. A brass walking cane stood propped against the post of the Drake marker, two feet to the right of the gunman. Perhaps Slade was disabled. Perhaps he would be a fraction of a second slow to react. Sam still could not make out the features of the man's face.

A centimeter at a time Bogardus lifted the point of the pistol still shielded from view in his pocket, raising the barrel toward the man by the marker.

"Move another inch and you're dead. Take your hand out of your pocket."

Sam hesitated.

"Now."

Slowly, grudgingly, Bogardus released his grip on the pistol. He raised both arms, lifting the package high in the air.

"Put the journal on the ground." The order was issued in a cold monotone.

Sam was tempted to dive into the tall grass and take his chances with the pistol. But the scoped rifle drew a bead on him like a laser beam. Bogardus weighed his options and decided to wait.

Sam took several steps toward the still black waters of the estuary, the book held high over his head. The gunman at the marker swiveled, maintaining a steady bead on his quarry.

"Put the rifle down," said Sam.

"Why should I?"

Bogardus said nothing but continued a seemingly vagrant movement toward the estuary. In two more strides the man would have his answer. Sam had reached a steep embankment, the finger of a small peninsula directly over a deep pool of stagnant water.

Moving one arm laterally he held the oilcloth package out over the water. "What do you think the journal will be worth after it's been saturated—that is, if you can find it again?"

"Drop the book and you'll never see the girl alive."

"That's rich." Sam's voice was tinged with sarcasm.

For an instant Sam watched the barrel of the rifle drift. The gunman was visibly shaken by Sam's cavalier attitude toward Jennifer's safety. For Raymond Slade the advantage of a high-powered rifle had not been enough. Sam was now certain that Slade had banked on the added protection offered by a hostage, a margin of safety that Sam had now rendered ineffectual by his attitude.

As Bogardus stood with his arm outstretched, the oilcloth package poised over the brackish waters of the estuary, a distant sound wafted on the ocean winds—the shrill pitch of a siren—the ambulance arriving in the parking lot in response to Sam's earlier telephone call.

Like the clanging of a fire bell in the night, the discordant tones of the siren changing pitches as it neared the beach unnerved the gunman at the marker. His eyes diverted to the beach in the direction of the approaching sound.

His stare suddenly turned cold as his finger cleared the safety on the rifle.

Swinging his outstretched arm like a windmill, Sam hurled the book at his assailant. The muzzle of the rifle lifted to catch the arc of the heavy package, the movement more an act of instinct than intent.

An instant later bits of paper sprayed the air like confetti at a ticker-tape parade as the brilliant flash and the ear-shattering explosion erupted with the synchronous reaction of lightning and thunder. The heavy package fell to the ground, its pages shredded by the exit of the high velocity round through its covers. The sound of the shot echoed off the steep bluffs surrounding the estuary, sending gulls screaming into the sky.

Sam dove into the tall grass at the edge of the estuary. He pulled the pistol from his pocket and looked up—straight into the tapered barrel of the rifle ten feet away. The gunman had closed on him with the first shot. Sam had overestimated the disability represented by the walking cane and now he lay prone on the ground, pistol at his side, staring death in the face.

Like a man before a firing squad Sam waited for the explosion of the shot. For a fleeting instant the inane question flashed in his mind— Is it true that a man never hears the shot that kills him? His body tensed for the impact of the bullet, his eyes fixed on the muzzle of the rifle.

But there was no recoil, no muzzle flash. Instead, the man's head behind the scope exploded in a ball of crimson mist, and his body was suspended in the air for an instant, a comic form with no distinguishable head; then it crumpled to the ground like a marionette without strings.

The man's body hit the ground like a sack of dirt as the sound of a distant shot rang out, reverberating off the bluffs above the marker.

A fusillade of gunfire erupted, the shots coming from the small beach surrounding the estuary.

Sam scurried on his knees toward a small dune and looked in the direction of the continuing gunfire.

The two women from the beach who had been walking with the dog lay prone on the sand, each holding a handgun and firing in rapid succession toward the estuary and the small aluminum fishing boat that had drifted within fifty yards of the marker. Bullets splashed in the water around the boat, some striking their mark and puncturing the thin metal of the boat with dull thuds. For the first time the small fat woman's face was turned toward Sam. It was covered with a full growth of beard.

Nick Jorgensen reached up and pulled the bandanna off of his head, still firing the large revolver in his other hand. Next to him on the sand Jake Carns emptied the clip of the forty-five automatic and quickly jammed another into the handle, pulling off five more shots before the small outboard on the boat pulled it beyond rang and into the cover of tall reeds deep in the estuary. Nick and Jake lay motionless on the sand for several seconds. Sam's eyes remained riveted on his two friends, his mind not fully comprehending what had just happened.

Sam and Jake stood looking down at the grotesque form of the body lying at their feet ten paces from the marker. What was left of the features of the man's face were unrecognizable, deformed by the crushing impact of the bullet fired from the small boat.

Nick stood speechless over the remains of the shredded package in the sand. He stooped, picked it up and looked at the neat round hole through the oilcloth in the topside of the package. Then he flipped it over. The cloth on the other side had disintegrated with the exit of the steel-jacketed round, as had the entire back cover and most of the book's contents. He watched as the winds carried the frayed pieces of paper over the dunes and into the water.

With his foot, Sam rolled the body in the sand onto its back. He reached into the dead man's inside coat pocket, finding a wallet, and removed a tattered driver's license. He stared at it for several seconds, his expression distant. Then he dropped the wallet and license in the sand.

Seeing the look of abject loss registered on the face of his friend, Sam plucked the book from Nick's hands, peeled the oilcloth from the front cover and turned it toward Jorgensen. Nick's eyes swelled with relief as they locked on the title: *Cases and Materials on the Law of Real Property.*

Sam dropped the book in the sand.

"Where's the journal?" asked Nick.

"Back in the trunk of my car."

George Fletcher scurried along in the wake of three uniformed officers who ran down the beach toward the sounds of the gunfire like bloodhounds hot on the scent of a fox.

Two hundred yards away Sam saw their approach.

"Listen Nick, I've got to get out of here." He looked down at the body in the sand. "When the cops get here tell them the coroner's toe tag should read Raymond Slade."

"Where are you going?"

"I have to talk to James Spencer."

Before Nick could say another word Sam was off at a dead run up the path to the top of the bluffs over the estuary.

As Sam drove under the wrought iron sign and down the long gravel drive he saw a blue BMW parked in front of the house, its driver's door open. He pulled up and parked next to the car. It's engine was running, and as he stepped out of the Porsche and moved around the other car Bogardus saw splotches of blood on the seat behind the wheel. He followed the drops from the car, up the stairs of the house and through the open front door.

He felt for the pistol in his pocket, but something told him that he wouldn't need it this time.

Sam walked through the entry hall and entered the great room that opened off of it.

On the couch in front of the fireplace lay an old man, his face flushed, his body propped against the far end of the plush white sofa. The maid who had let Sam into the house earlier in the afternoon was on her knees, cradling Louis Davies's head in her arms.

As she sensed Sam's presence the woman looked up with pleading eyes. "Senor, he won't let me call an ambulance."

"It's all right, Marguerite." The old man's voice was strained. Dark blood stained the lining of his jacket. His eyes shifted to Bogardus.

"Is Jennifer all right?"

"Yes. I called the hospital from a pay phone on the way over here. Slade used some pretty potent stuff to keep her quiet before he dumped her into the trunk of his car, but the doctor says she'll be fine in a day or two."

Sam knelt next to the sofa, opened Davies's coat and examined the wound. The shirt was saturated and dark blood pulsated from a wound in Davies's left side.

"We should call an ambulance."

"No, it's over. I want it this way. It'll be easier for her."

Davies looked at Sam with the benign smile of an aging grandfather. "When did you figure it out?"

"An hour ago," said Sam. "On the beach, when I looked at the driver's license and saw the name George Johnson. He'd used it once before—at Treasure Island. It took me a long time to figure out the pictures, why the photos of James Spencer were all missing. Then it hit me. Spencer's picture wasn't missing at all. Slade had merely switched the names on the photographs and removed his own picture from the file. Why did he do it?"

James Spencer, alias Louis Davies, looked at Bogardus and spoke: "Toward the end, just before she hired you, I began to sense the direction that Jennifer's suspicion was taking. She supposed that I was Raymond Slade and that her mother and I had become involved in a romantic cabal that resulted in the murder of her father years before. I made the mistake of telling Slade of her suspicions. He responded by manipulating the photographs. I guess it was his way of lending credence to her fears and submerging his own identity."

The old man shook his head. "I warned him that if he didn't leave Jennifer alone I'd kill him. I had him followed for a week by a private investigator. This afternoon the man called and told me about the message on the mirror at the hotel in Cambria. I knew he'd go to the estuary. The man had a positive flair for the dramatic. We'd met at that damn post a dozen times over the years. So I borrowed a friend's boat. The rest you know."

Sam lifted the bandanna from the maid's head and pressed it to the wound under Louis Davies's coat. The old man winced in pain and arched his back slowly, settling down onto the couch again.

"Why didn't you just tell her you were her father?" asked Sam.

"How do you tell the daughter you love that you're a deserter—a thief? All of this, the house, the vineyard, my business, found its seeds in the money that we took from the committee."

He coughed and spit up blood, then paused to catch his breath. "I knew about Slade's black market activities long before that day. I kept telling myself I needed more evidence, more information to go to the authorities. But I knew that wasn't it. In the end the plan to take the money was mine." The statement was almost boastful. "Raymond Slade never had any initiative. He was nothing but a poorly paid errand boy. I had to prop him up every step of the way. He stayed at the machine-gun on board the blimp while I went down and grabbed the book and a million dollars in cash. We dumped helium out of the ship as we steered her back to shore and then set her down on the golf course just long enough to jump out. When I got home to my wife and told her what we'd done she wanted me to give the money back and turn myself in." He smiled. "That's the kind of woman she was. But it was too late. We put our lives together as Mr. and Mrs. Louis Davies and proceeded to live a lie."

He paused for a second. "Funny thing is, it was easy—until Jennifer started asking questions about her father." Spencer coughed and grimaced with pain, a trickle of blood ran from the corner of his mouth.

Sam rose and walked toward the fireplace, his back to the couch.

"Who sent her the parchments?" he asked. As he turned, Sam looked into the death trance on the face of James Spencer, his eyes open, his stare fixed for eternity.

Slowly Marguerite Pallone released her arm from Davies's head and rose, stepping away from the couch. A single tear trickled down her right cheek.

"She never wanted this to happen," said the maid.

"What are you talking about?"

"Dorothy—Mrs. Davies. She had pleaded with him for years to tell Jennifer the truth. But he always refused. On her death bed she begged him. He would have none of it." She pulled a handkerchief from her sweater and brought it to her face, clearing the lone tear from her cheek. "The parchments . . . I sent them to Jennifer. It was Dorothy's last request of me before she died."

Sam stood looking at the maid who, having shed the only tear she could muster for Louis Davies, turned and walked from the room.

Finally he had it all. The lies, the deceptions of a lifetime. And as Sam stood looking down at the lifeless body of James Spencer his mind suddenly turned a phrase from his youth: "And after all, what is a lie? 'Tis but the truth in masquerade."

Chapter

14

A workman in bib overalls removed the brass plaque from under the arched doorway on Pier Nine. A new sign was raised into place. It bore the names "Bogardus and Davies." Underneath, in raised brass letters were the words "Attorneys and Counselors at Law." Sam couldn't bring himself to delete Pat's affectation—the designation "Counselors at Law" would remain a part of the firm's inscription. Perhaps it was his parting tribute to the woman he could never forget, a final gesture of affection.

Upstairs in Pat's old office Jennifer Davies sat at the desk filling in the blanks of a printed form to be retyped later by Carol. At the top of the page in bold type were the words "Petition for Conservatorship."

Jennifer couldn't understand it. Certainly at

times she was eccentric, but Sam was over-reacting. She ran the pen down the form past the words:

Conservatorship of the:
Person [ ]
Estate [ ]

and checked both boxes.

She returned to the top of the form and after the printed words "In re the Conservatorship of:" she wrote the name "Angela Kathleen Bogardus."

He had moved too quickly. Sam had put the old house in Colma up for sale. There was no talking to him. In two days it sold. Angie had been moved to a residence for senior citizens down the peninsula. It offered round-the-clock security and a level of care that was premature for a woman with Angie's mental faculties. Jennifer hoped that in time he would come to realize that he'd made a mistake and that he would undo the terrible injustice to the old woman.

But there was something peculiar. Angie didn't seem to object to the move. She blithely agreed to voice no opposition to the conservatorship when they appeared in court and took to her new surroundings at the home gleefully. On the few occasions when Jennifer visited with her, Angie didn't complain, and she continued to speak of her son in glowing terms. Sam never discussed the situation. It was as if mother and son had entered into some private compact, an agreement for which only they knew the mutual consideration.

Sam had not been blessed with a full night's sleep since the morning of his last visit to police headquarters and Fletcher's office. That was almost two weeks after the discovery of the journal and the confrontation on the beach. With the deaths of Raymond Slade and Louis Davies, Fletcher had closed the file on the Paterson murder and had lifted the ban of confidentiality on the evidence.

For some unknown reason Sam had humored a vexing sense of curiosity, and in a small room off of Fletcher's office he'd spent the better part of one morning reading the field notes of the officers who'd responded to the scene and examining the evidence that had not previously been released by the police.

He fiddled with the small audiotape cassette, snapped it into the portable recorder that Fletcher had loaned him and pushed the "Play" button. He picked up the police report and resumed his reading. The electronic beep signaled like a metronome every five seconds, alerting the caller that their words were being recorded.

"San Francisco Police Department."

Several seconds passed in silence, punctuated only by the repetitious beep.

"Hello, this is the San Francisco Police Department."

"Hello." The woman's voice was tentative. Sam laid the report on the desk and listened. "I'd like to report a crime."

"Yes." Again several seconds passed. "Is it a crime in progress?"

"I don't think so."

"You'll have to speak up, ma'am. I can barely hear you."

"It's the apartment down the hall." The voice was stronger now, clearly audible. "I think a woman may have been killed. I heard a loud crash and screaming. Then a tall man ran from the apartment. It was dark. I couldn't see his face. I'm afraid to go down there."

"The address ma'am?"

He listened as the caller gave Pat's apartment address.

"We're dispatching a patrol car immediately. You should stay in your apartment. Lock the door. Do you understand?"

"Yes."

"Can I have your name please?"

There was a click on the tape as the line went dead. Sam listened in stunned silence as Angie hung up the phone.

The blank end of the tape hissed its vacant tune into the recorder's speaker for several minutes before Bogardus reached over and turned it off.

It took him almost an hour before he could compose himself sufficiently to casually enter Fletcher's office and return the tape recorder and the file. For several minutes alone in the small room he toyed with the thought of erasing the conversation, but concluded it would only make the tape more obvious. Besides, it was sure to be preserved on a master tape at least for a while. No, it was better to allow them to send the entire file to some shelf in a storeroom to gather dust until the day came when in the natural course of bureaucracy the evidence in the murder case of Susan Paterson would be purged, consigned to some furnace or shredder.

For three days following his visit to Fletcher's office he turned the old house upside down until he found what he was looking for. It was shut away in an abandoned tool box once belonging to his grandfather, under the workbench in the basement. The yellow neoprene gloves spattered with lye, the residue of some commercial oven cleaner, were still stained with Pat's blood, and underneath in the box—the nicked wooden handle of the butcher knife that Angie had used to kill her. Rolled tightly in the section under the top tray of the box and stained by grease and motor oil was a legal-length manila folder. As he pulled it from the box the file flipped open and something fell from the folder to the concrete floor. Sam peered down at the glossy eight-by-ten photograph of Raymond Slade. He had found the Davies file. Susan Paterson, always prepared to the point of compulsion, unknown to either him or Carol had carried it to her death. Pat had taken it that day on her sojourn to the Jade House and it had been with her later at her apartment as Angie lurked in the shadows near the front door.

It was funny how the human mind worked. If anyone had accused Angie of the crime a week before he would have said they were crazy. But after hearing her voice on the tape the clues all flooded to the front of his consciousness—his missing key ring with the key to Pat's apartment that he'd not used since they broke up, the keys he remembered seeing in the hospital but could not find when he left. He finally found them—in the top drawer of Angie's bedroom dresser. The book that lay open marked with a piece of tissue on the pine table of the apartment in the basement, the book on hand-to-hand combat from his childhood collection—Sam pulled it from the shelf and opened it to the tissue. A bold subtitle halfway down the page read:

Knives—Silencing the Sentry

Beneath, in a text that mimicked a scholastic style, were reported the virtues of the "kidney thrust"—a blow so lethal that the victim died within seconds, unable to utter any sound as a result of shock and the excruciating pain.

It was almost as if she'd left a trail for him to follow—desperate signposts saying "See what I've done? See how much I love you?"

He remembered how after finding the tool box in the basement he'd gone outside into the back yard and dropped the gloves into the fifty-gallon drum and watched as the flames consumed them. Four days later he disposed of the knife in a pile of scrap metal in an auto wrecking yard.

In a way he could console himself with the thought that at least indirectly Slade had been responsible for Pat's death. Angie had clearly seen her opportunity in the havoc that was wreaked on Sam in his apartment. She had gleaned enough information from Carol to know that following that initial attack her son and those around him were in continuing danger as a result of the parchments. It was a perfect cover for her crime.

The presence of the Davies file at Pat's apartment that afternoon must have appeared as an act of serendipity to the old woman, since its disappearance would only serve to intensify the focus of suspicion elsewhere. When Slade butchered Symington with a blade at the castle, Angie must surely have believed that she had been born under a lucky star.

In the seeds of her insane act Sam finally came to terms with the restless pursuit of vengeance that had so clearly marked him. He knew now the terrible price to be exacted when retribution was allowed to dominate reason.

He stared vacantly at the physician across the desk and listened to what he already knew.

"In cases like this the prognosis is guarded at best. She's clearly experiencing manic episodes, having obvious delusions, some steeped heavily in religiosity. She continues to talk as if she's been commissioned by God to act as an avenging angel. How long has this been going on?"

"I'm not sure. I'm afraid I haven't been as close to her in the last few years as I should have been." Angie had engaged in periodic bouts of incoherent babble ever since he'd confronted her with the contents of the tool box. Then for hours she would be lucid, speaking as if nothing had happened, able to blank the episode completely from her consciousness. Sam knew that he was crippling the prospects for a complete recovery by withholding from the psychiatrist the facts surrounding Pat's death, but the physician could not be trusted with the secret that he alone shared with Angie.

Epilogue

The small group of scholars milled about on a bluff behind a private residence halfway up Mount Tamalpais waiting their turn to peer through the tiny port of the engineer's transom. Wind off the bay whipped up small clouds of dust. Tables had been set up and waiters poured champagne and wine into small plastic cups as groups of men and women carried on animated conversations. The Navigator's Guild was elated. At last the work of a generation of historians, sailors and scholars had been confirmed. There was no question. The map and the physical description in the journal were precise. History could now dispose of all doubt as to the location of Drake's encampment on the sweeping beach below the bluffs at the estuary. The fiery English captain had careened the *Golden Hinde* in the shallow waters of the sheltered estuary just as the Guild had theorized and written about in its monographs.

Sam Bogardus moved up toward the transom and leaned over to peer through the eyepiece. With a slight twist he adjusted the ring on the near side of the telescopic device and squinted.

Nick and a coterie of scholars from the university faculty had struggled with a transliteration of sections of the journal for nearly two weeks and had pieced together Drake's movements during his month-long stay at the point of land he had called "Portus Novae Albionis" —his Nova Albion. He had captured a small Spanish ship in Mexican waters on his sojourn north during the early part of May 1579. With the *Golden Hinde* careened in the shallow waters of the estuary for repairs, Drake had used this smaller ship and a handful of trusted seamen, presumbly on a scouting mission to reconnoiter the coastal area south of Drake's Bay. For five days this ship and its small crew disappeared in the fog-shrouded coast off the Golden Gate. When Drake and his retinue finally returned it was on foot, overland from the east. They had planted twelve tons of precious gems, gold and silver at a site charted with uncanny precision in the journal. It was a cache that Drake planned to retrieve on a later commission from his queen—a master stroke of brilliance, his insurance for yet another mission to the New World. Drake had scuttled the small Spanish ship in the waters of what he described as "a large inland sea." Without knowing it, Francis Drake had discovered San Francisco Bay.

At first a yellow blur, the image of the stucco-covered granite and brick walls of San Quentin Prison five miles away across the valley slowly came into focus. Sam twisted the eyepiece of the transom just slightly. The bleak monolith stretched along the peninsula to its tip at the water's edge, the high walls covered in rolls of razor-sharp concertina wire.

After discovery of the journal, using its precise directions geologists had attempted a number of test bores in the area beyond the prison walls. Except for several fragments of rotting jute cloth and a trace of wax from the remnants of a candle, they had come up empty. As with much of the area surrounding San Francisco Bay, San Quentin Point was geologically unstable, subject to the forces of liquefaction with the slightest shifting of the earth's crust. Heavy metals or stones caught in a churning stew of bay waters mixed with fill would be scattered and drawn downward perhaps hundreds of feet before the swirling mass solidified. History would never know for certain if the American legacy reputed to have been abandoned by Drake in his own journal really existed. But for Samuel Bogardus there would never be any doubt.

History's cruel irony, he thought. The point of land so prominent that an English seafarer could find it on a return voyage was too conspicuous for the state prison board to ignore two centuries later. Drake's original peninsula now lay blanketed by millions of cubic yards of earthen fill, its tip buried under the walls of the state's maximum security prison—and with it Drake's treasure, lost forever.